ALEXANDER'S
LEGACY
TO THE STRONGEST

Robert Fabbri read Drama and Theatre at London
University and worked in film and TV for twenty-
five years. He has a life-long passion for ancient
history, which inspired him to write the bestselling
Vespasian series and the Alexander's Legacy series.
He lives in London and Berlin.

ALEXANDER'S LEGACY
TO THE STRONGEST

ROBERT FABBRI

CORVUS

First published in Great Britain in 2020 by Corvus, an imprint
of Atlantic Books Ltd.

This paperback edition published in 2020.

10 9 8 7 6 5 4 3 2 1

A CIP catalogue record for this book is available from the British Library.

Printed and bound by CPI Group (UK) Ltd, Croydon, CR0 4YY

Paperback ISBN: 978 1 78649 798 7
E-book ISBN: 978 1 78649 799 4

Corvus
An imprint of Atlantic Books Ltd
Ormond House
26–27 Boswell Street
London
WC1N 3JZ

www.corvus-books.co.uk

To my agent, Ian Drury, with whom I share a passion for this period of history.

SELEUKOS
THE BULL-ELEPHANT

ROXANNA
THE WILD-CAT

PHILO
THE HOMELESS

ILLYRIA

THRACE

MACEDON
PELLA
PHILIPPI
EPIRUS
KARDIA
THESSALY
HELLESPONTINE
LAMIA
PHRYGIA
LYDIA
PHRYGIA
KAPPADOKIA
ARME
SARDIS
HALYS
ATHENS
EPHESUS
CELAENAE
CARIA
PISIDIA
CILICIA
TARSUS
MESOPOTAMIA
ISSUS
THAPSACUS
ASSYRIA

CYPRUS
SYRIA
CYRENE
BERYTOS
EUPHRATES
CYRENAICA
TYROS
DAMASCUS
BABYLON
NILE DELTA
HIEROSPHYMA
BABYL
ALEXANDRIA
PELUSIUM
MEMPHIS
ARABIA

EGYPT

NILE

W

PTOLEMY
THE BASTARD

KRATEROS
THE GENERAL

PE
THE

A list of characters can be found on page 404.

PROLOGUE

BABYLON, SUMMER 323 BC

'To the strongest.' The Great Ring of Macedon wavered in Alexander's dimming vision; his hand shook with the effort of raising it and then speaking. Emblazoned with the sixteen-pointed sun-blazon, the ring represented the power of life and death over the largest empire ever conquered in the known world; an empire that he must bequeath so early, too early, because he, Alexander, the third of that name to be King of Macedon, knew now that it was manifest: he was dying.

Rage surged within him at capricious gods who gave so much and yet exacted so high a toll. To die with his ambition half-sated was an injustice that soured his achievements, augmenting the bitter taste of death that rose in his gorge; for it was but the east that had fallen under his dominion; the west was yet to witness his glory. And yet, had he not been warned? Had not the god Amun cautioned him against hubris when he had consulted the deity's oracle in the oasis of Siwa, far out in the Egyptian desert, nigh on ten years ago? Was this then his chastisement for ignoring the god's words and reaching further than any mortal had previously dared? Had he had the energy, Alexander would have wept for himself and for the glory that was slipping through his fingers.

Without an obvious, natural heir, who would he allow to follow him? To whom would he give the chance to rise to such heights as he had already attained? The love of his life,

1

Hephaestion, the only person he had treated as an equal, both upon the field of battle and within the bed they shared, had been snatched from him less than a year previously; only Hephaestion, beautiful and proud Hephaestion, would have been worthy to expand what he, Alexander, had already created. But Hephaestion was no more.

Alexander held the ring towards the man standing to the right of his bed, closest to him, the most senior of his seven bodyguards surrounding him, all anxious to know his will in these final moments. All remained still, listening, in the vaulted chamber, decorated with glazed tiles of deep blue, crimson and gold, in the great palace of Nebuchadnezzar at the heart of Babylon; here in the gloom of a few weak oil-lamps, for little light seeped through the high windows from the early-evening, overcast sky, they waited to learn their fate.

Perdikkas, the commander of the Companion Cavalry, so far loyal to the Argead royal house of Macedon but ambitious in his own right and ruthless with it, took the symbol of ultimate authority from his king's forefinger; he asked his question a second time, his voice tense: 'To whom do you pass your ring, Alexander?' He glanced around his companions before looking back down at his dying king and adding: 'Is it to me?'

Alexander made no attempt to reply as he looked around the semi-circle of the men closest to him, all formidable military commanders capable of independent action and all with the human lust for power: Leonnatus, tall and vain, modelling his long blonde hair in the same style as his king, aping his looks, but whose devotion was such that he had used his own body to shield Alexander when he fell wounded in far-off India. Peucestas, next to him, already was showing signs of going native in his dress, having been the only bodyguard to have learnt Persian. Lysimachus, the most reckless of them all, was possessed of bravery that was often a hazard to his own comrades. Peithon, dour but steadfast; unquestioning in his execution of even the most cruel orders, when others might quail. And then there were the older two: Aristonous, who had been Alexander's father, Philip, the second of that

2

name's, bodyguard; the only survivor of the old regime, whose counsel was infused with the wisdom of one old in the ways of war. And finally, Ptolemy; what to make of Ptolemy whose looks hinted at him being a bastard brother? At once gentle and forgiving and yet capable of ruthless political adroitness should that part of his nature be abused; the least competent militarily but the most likely to succeed in the political long game.

Alexander looked past the seven, as Perdikkas repeated the question a third time, to the men beyond the bed; men who had followed him, sharing the dangers and the triumphs, on his ten-year journey of conquest, silent in the shadows as they strained to hear him answer. Passing along the dozen or so faces he knew so well, his weak gaze rested on Kassandros standing next to his younger half-brother, Iollas, and Alexander thought he detected triumph in his eyes; his sickness had started the day after Kassandros' arrival from Macedon as his father, Antipatros' messenger; had Antipatros, the man who had ruled as regent in the motherland for the past ten years, sent his eldest son with the woman's weapon of poison to murder him rather than obey the summons that Alexander had sent? Iollas was, after all, his cup-bearer and could easily have administered the dose. Alexander cursed Kassandros inwardly, having always hated the ginger-haired, pock-marked prig whose loathing had been returned in equal measure and augmented by his humiliation at having been left behind for all those years. His mind turned back to Antipatros, a thousand miles away in Pella, the capital of Macedon, and his constant feud with his, Alexander's, mother, Olympias, scheming and brooding back in her native Molossia, a part of the kingdom of Epirus; how would that resolve without him playing off one against the other? Who would kill whom?

But then, half obscured by a column at the far end of the dying-chamber, Alexander glimpsed a woman, a pregnant woman; his Bactrian wife, Roxanna, three months from full term. What chance would a half-caste child have? Not many shared his dream of uniting the peoples of east and west; there

3

would be few Macedonians of pure blood who would rally behind a half-breed infant born to an Eastern wildcat.

So it was with certainty, as he closed his eyes, that Alexander foresaw the struggles that would mark his passing, both in Macedon and here in Babylon and then throughout the subject Greek states, as well as among those of his satraps who had carved out fiefdoms of their own in the vast empire he had wrought; men such as Antigonos, The One-Eyed, satrap of Phrygia and Menander, satrap of Lydia, the last of Philip's generals.

Then there was Harpalus, his treasurer, whom he had already forgiven once for his dishonesty, who, rather than face Alexander's wrath a second time, had absconded with eight hundred talents of gold and silver, enough to raise a formidable army or live in luxury for the rest of his life; which would he choose?

And what would Krateros do? Krateros, the darling of the army, a general second to only Alexander himself, now somewhere between Babylon and Macedon, leading ten thousand veterans home; would he feel that he should have been named Alexander's successor? But Alexander, weakness creeping through him, had made his decision and, as Perdikkas once more put the question, he shook his head; why should he give away what he had won? Why should he give the chance to another to equal or surpass him? Why should not he, alone for ever, be known as 'The Great'? No, he would not do it; he was not going to name the Strongest; he was not going to give them any help.

Let them work it out for themselves.

Opening his eyes one last time, he looked up at the ceiling, his breathing fading.

All seven around the bed leant in, hoping to hear their name.

Alexander twitched one last smile. 'I foresee great struggles at my funeral games.' He gave a sigh; then the eyes, that had seen more wonders than any before in this world, closed.

And they saw no more.

4

Perdikkas,
The Half-Chosen

THE RING FELT heavy in his hand as Perdikkas' fingers closed about it; it was not for the gold of which it was wrought but for the power in which it was steeped. He looked down at the still face of Alexander, as beautiful in death as it had been in life, and felt his world teeter so that he had to steady himself with his other hand on the oaken bedhead, alive with ancient animalistic carvings.

He drew breath and then looked to his companions, the six other bodyguards sworn to the death to the king who was no more; on the countenance of each was evidence of the gravity of the moment: tears on the faces of Leonnatus and Peucestas, each heaving their chest with irregular sobs; Ptolemy, rigid, eyes closed as if deep in thought; Lysimachus clenched and unclenched the muscles of his jaw, his hands in white-knuckled fists; Aristonous struggled for breath and then, forgetting dignity, squatted down on the floor with one hand supporting him. Peithon stared at Alexander, his eyes wide, dead to emotion.

Perdikkas opened his hand and gazed at the ring. Now was his time – should he dare to claim it as his own; Alexander had chosen him to receive it after all. *And he chose well, for of all here in this room I am the most worthy; I am his true heir.* He picked it up and held it between thumb and forefinger, examining it: so small, so mighty. *Can I claim it? Would the others let me do so?* The answer came quick, as unwelcome as it was unsurprising.

In the second group, beyond the bed, his younger brother, Alketas, standing between Eumenes, the sly little Greek secretary, and the grizzled veteran, Meleagros, caught his eye and slowly shook his head; he had read Perdikkas' mind. In fact, all in the room had read his mind as all eyes were now upon him.

'He gave it to me,' Perdikkas affirmed, his voice imbued with the authority of the symbol he held before him. 'It was I whom he chose.'

Aristonous got to his feet, his voice weary. 'But he did not name you, Perdikkas, although I would that he had.'

'Nevertheless, I hold the ring.'

Ptolemy half-smiled, bemused, shrugging his shoulders. 'It's such a shame, but he half-chose you; and a half-chosen king is just half a king. Where's the other half?'

'Whether he chose anyone or not,' a voice, gravelled by the shouting of battlefield commands, boomed, 'it is for the army-assembly to decide who is Macedon's king; it has ever been thus.' Meleagros strode forward, his hand on his sword-hilt; his beard, full and grey, dominated his weathered face. 'It is for free Macedonians to decide who sits on the throne of Macedon; and it is the right of free Macedonians to see the body of the dead king.'

Two dark eyes stared at Perdikkas, daring him to defy ancient custom; eyes that were full of resentment, as he knew only too well, for Meleagros was almost twice his age and yet remained an infantry commander; Alexander had passed him over for promotion. However, it was not through ineptitude that he had failed to rise, it was because of his qualities as a leader of a phalanx. It took much skill to command the sixteen-man-wide-and-deep Macedonian phalanx unit; it took even more to command two score of these two-hundred-and-fifty-six-man *speira* in conjunction, and Meleagros was the best – *with the possible exception of Antigonos One-Eye*, Perdikkas allowed. To ensure the right pace as the unit manoeuvred over various terrains so that every man, wielding his sixteen-feet-long sarissa, pike, was able to keep formation could not be learnt in one campaigning season. The phalanx's strength was its ability to deliver five pikes for every one-man frontage; armies had broken on it since its introduction by Alexander's father, but only because of men like Meleagros knowing how to keep it ordered so that the front five ranks could bring their weapons to bear whilst the rear ranks used theirs to disrupt missiles raining down upon them. Meleagros kept his men safe and they loved him for it and they were many. Meleagros could not be dismissed.

Perdikkas knew that he was beaten, for the moment at least; to realise his ambition he needed the army, both infantry and cavalry, on his side and Meleagros spoke for the infantry. *Gods, how I hate the infantry and I hate this bastard for blocking my way – for now.* He smiled. 'You are, of course, right, Meleagros; we stand here debating amongst ourselves as to what we should do and we forget our duty to our men. We should muster the army and give them the news. Alexander's body should be removed to the throne-room so that the men can file past it and pay their respects. On that, at least, do we all agree?' He looked around the room and saw no dissent. 'Good. Meleagros, you call the infantry and I'll summon the cavalry; I'll also send out messengers to every satrapy with the news. And let's always remember we are brothers with Alexander.' He paused to let that sink it, nodded at them and then made for the door, wanting only some time to himself to reflect upon his position.

But it was not to be; as a dozen conversations broke out around the corpse of Alexander, echoing around the cavernous chamber, Perdikkas felt someone fall into step beside him.

'You need my help,' Eumenes said, without looking up at him, as they walked through the door and into the main central corridor of the palace.

Perdikkas looked down at the little Greek, a whole head shorter than him, and wondered what it had been that made Alexander give him the military command left vacant when he, Perdikkas, had replaced Hephaestion; there had been much disquiet when Alexander had rewarded Eumenes' years of service, firstly as Philip's secretary before transferring his allegiance to Alexander upon his assassination, by making him the first non-Macedonian commander of Companion Cavalry. 'What could *you* possibly do?'

'I was brought up to be polite to someone offering a service; in Kardia it is considered good manners. But, I grant you, we do differ in many ways from Macedon: for a start, we've always enjoyed *eating* our sheep.'

'And we've always enjoyed killing Greeks.'

'Not as much as the Greeks do themselves. But be that as it may, you do need my help.'

Perdikkas did not reply at first as they marched, now at speed, along the corridor, high and broad, musty with age, the geometrical paintwork fading and peeling in the humid atmosphere that afflicted Babylon. 'Alright; you've made me curious.'

'A noble condition, curiosity; it's only through curiosity that we can reach certainty as it causes us to explore a topic from all angles.'

'Yes, yes, very wise, I'm sure, but—'

'But you're just a blunt soldier and have no use for wisdom?'

'You know, Eumenes, one of the reasons that people dislike you so intensely is—'

'Because I keep on finishing their sentences for them?'

'Yes!'

'And there was me thinking that it was only because I'm an oily Greek. Oh well, I suppose one can't help but learn as one gets older, unless, of course, one is Peithon.' A sly glint came into his eye as he looked up at Perdikkas. 'Or Arrhidaeus.'

Perdikkas waved a dismissive hand. 'Arrhidaeus has never learnt a thing in his thirty years other than to try not to drool out of both sides of his mouth at the same time. He probably doesn't even know who his own father is.'

'He may not know he's Philip's son but we all do; as does the army.'

Perdikkas halted and turned to the Greek. 'What's that supposed to mean?'

'You see, I told you that you needed my help. You said it yourself, he's Philip's son which makes him Alexander's half-brother and, as such, his legitimate heir.'

'But he's a halfwit.'

'So? The only other two direct heirs are Heracles, Barsine's four-year-old bastard, or whatever is lurking in that eastern bitch Roxanna's belly. Now, Perdikkas, where will the army stand when presented with that choice?'

Perdikkas grunted and turned away. 'No one would choose a halfwit.'

'If you believe that then you're automatically ruling yourself out.'

'Piss off, you Greek runt, and leave me alone; you can make yourself useful by mustering your cavalry.'

But as Perdikkas walked away he was quite certain that he heard Eumenes mutter: 'You really do need my help and you will get it, like it or not.'

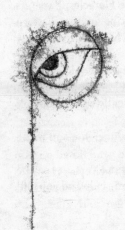

ANTIGONOS, THE ONE-EYED

GODS, HOW I *hate the cavalry.* Antigonos, the Macedonian governor of Phrygia, muttered a series of profanities under his breath as he watched the lance-armed, shieldless, heavy-cavalry on his left wing attempt to form up on rough ground, far further from the left flank of his phalanx than he had ordered. The error left too much space for his peltasts to cover once they had finished driving off the skirmishers from the scrubland protecting the enemy's opposite flank; it also pushed his javelin-armed, mercenary Thracian light-horse too far away for them to be able to respond with alacrity to any signal he might send. However, he hoped to finish the day's work with one mighty blow from his twelve-thousand-eight-hundred-strong phalanx. All his adult life Antigonos had been an infantry commander, leading his men from the front rank, looking no different to them, wielding a sarissa whilst shouting orders to the signaller six ranks behind; at fifty-nine he was still taking joy in the power of the war-machine that his old friend, King Philip, had introduced. And, as such, he knew the value of cavalry to protect the cumbersome flanks of the phalanx from enemy horse; but that was why he disliked them so much as they were constantly boasting that the infantry would be dead without them. Annoyingly, that was the truth.

'Go up there,' Antigonos bellowed at a young, mounted aide, 'and tell that idiot son of mine that when I say fifty paces I don't mean a hundred and fifty. I may only have one eye but it is not totally useless. And tell him to hurry up; there's no more than an hour of daylight left.' He scratched at his grey beard, grown full and long, and then took a bite from the onion that passed for his dinner. Despite his youth, his son, Demetrios, showed promise, Antigonos conceded, even if he did favour the cavalry as it far better suited his flamboyant behaviour; he just wished that he would take more heed of orders and reflect more upon the implications of doing as he pleased. A lesson in discipline was what the boy needed, Antigonos reflected, but he was constantly thwarted by his wife, Stratonice, who doted on him to the extent that he could do no wrong in her eyes; it was to drag Demetrios away from her skirts that he had brought his fifteen-year-old son on his first campaign and given him command of his companion cavalry.

Chewing, Antigonos examined the rest of his disposition from his command post on a knoll behind the centre of his army. He swallowed and then washed down the mouthful with strong, resonated wine; emitting a loud burp, he handed the wineskin to a waiting slave and took a deep breath of warm, late-afternoon air. He liked this country with its ragged hills and fast-flowing rivers; rock and scrub, hard land, land that reminded him of his home in the Macedonian uplands; land that chiselled a man rather than moulding him with gentle hands. But however good the land might be for the forming of a man's character, it was a liability to the conduct of smooth military operations. And it was with both those considerations in mind that he studied the Kappadokian satrap's army facing him, formed up with a river, a hundred paces wide, spanned by a three-arched stone bridge to its rear. He scanned the ranks of brightly robed clansmen, whose colours were enhanced by the sinking sun, clustered around a centre of a couple of thousand Persian regular infantry, in front of the bridge, stringing their bows behind their propped-up wicker pavises. In embroidered trousers and long bright-orange and deep-blue tunics and sporting dark-yellow tiaras, they were the original satrapy garrison that had helped Ariarathes, Darius' appointment, to hold out against

Macedonian conquest for the ten years since Alexander, after a brief foray as far as Gordion, bypassed central Anatolia, taking his army south by the coastal route.

But now Antigonos had cornered this warlord of the interior who had preyed upon his supply lines and left a trail of his men writhing on stakes throughout the country; or at least cornered his army for he had no doubt that whatever the result of the coming conflict, Ariarathes would escape. It was a shame after the effort of having force-marched from Ancyra along the King's Road, the mighty construction that linked the great cities of the Persian Empire with the Middle Sea. The speed of his move had caught Ariarathes' army as it attempted to cross the narrow bridge over the River Halys back into Kappadokia after their latest raid. Caught in a bottleneck, Ariarathes had no choice but to turn and fight as he tried to extract as many of his troops as possible from the precarious position; only the setting of the sun could save him. As he watched, Antigonos saw many scores of the rebels streaming over the bridge and he had no doubt in his mind that Ariarathes would have been the first across. *But I'll trim his wings today, whether he survives or not.* He looked behind towards the westering sun. *Provided I do it now and quickly.* A glance up to his left told him that Demetrios had finally formed up in the correct position; satisfied that all was in order, Antigonos stuffed the rest of the onion into his mouth, jogged down the knoll and then, rubbing his hands together and chuckling in anticipation of a good fight, made his way through the phalanx to his position in the front rank.

'Thank you, Philotas,' he said, taking his sarissa from a man of similar age. 'Time to drown as many of these rats as possible,' he added with a grin. Taking his round shield that had been slung over his shoulder, he threaded his left hand through the sling so that he could grip his pike with both hands and still rely on a degree of protection from the shield even though he could not wield it as a hoplite would his larger hoplon. Without looking behind, he shouted back to the horn-blower. 'Phalanx to advance, attack pace.'

Three long notes sounded and were repeated all along the half-mile frontage of the phalanx. As the last call rang out in the distance the first horn-blower took a deep breath and blew a long shrill note. Almost as one, the men of the front ranks stepped forward to be followed by the file behind them; with rank after rank rolling forward, giving a ripple effect like breakers surging to the shore, the army of Antigonos closed with the foe.

It was with the same pride that he always felt when advancing at the heart of a phalanx that Antigonos tramped forward, his great pike held upright so that he could keep his shield covering as much of his body as possible as they neared the enemy. *Gods, I could never tire of this.* He had fought in the phalanx ever since its inception, firstly in Philip's wars against the city state of Byzantion and the Thracian tribes to secure his eastern and northern borders; there the tribesmen had skewered themselves on the hedge of iron that protruded from the formation so that very few managed to close into the individualistic hand to hand combat they favoured. But it was in Greece that the new, deeper formation had really been tested; Philip gradually expanded his power south until it was to Macedon that the Greek cities deferred and the days when Macedonians were publicly derided as being no more than barely civilized provincials of question-able Hellenic blood were gone – those thoughts were now shared only in private. The heavier phalanx had crushed the hoplite formations and the lance-armed Macedonian cavalry swept their javelin-wielding opponents from the field. Antigonos had loved every moment, never happier than when he was in the heart of a battle.

However, he had been left behind by Alexander soon after he had crossed into Asia and defeated the first army that Darius had sent against him at Gaugamela; but it had not been a dishon-ourable dismissal: Alexander had chosen Antigonos to be his satrap in Phrygia precisely because of his joy of war. The young king had trusted him to conclude the siege of the Phrygia's capital, Celaenae, and then to complete the conquest of the inte-rior of Anatolia whilst he went south and east to steal an empire.

Ariarathes was the last Persian satrap to still resist in Anatolia and Antigonos thanked the gods for him for without him he would have nothing more to do other than collect taxes and hear appeals; in fact, sometimes he wondered to himself whether he had allowed Ariarathes to hold out on purpose just so that he would always have a good excuse to go campaigning. But now that news had reached him that Alexander had returned out of the east and had recently arrived in Babylon, Antigonos had decided that a very real attempt should be made to rid this part of the empire of the last rebel satrap; he did not want to face the young king, for the first time in almost ten years, without completing the task he had been entrusted with.

With the thunder of twelve thousand footsteps crunching down on hard ground in unison, the phalanx pressed on and Antigonos' heart was full. To his left he could make out the peltasts, named after their crescent, hide-covered-wicker *pelte* shields, drive the archers threatening that flank from the scrubland in which they had taken cover; blood had been spilt and life was good. With a final volley of javelins, aimed at the backs of the retreating skirmishers, the peltasts rallied and withdrew to their position between the phalanx and the covering cavalry that advanced, as ordered, at the same pace as the infantry. *Gods, I do so love this.* Antigonos' beard twitched as he smiled behind it; his one good eye gleamed with excitement and the puckered scar in his left socket, which gave him a fearsome countenance, wept bloody tears. *One hundred paces to go; gods this will be good.*

Looking out from behind their pavises, the Persian infantry aimed their bows high; a cloud of two thousand arrows rose into the sky and Antigonos' smile grew broader. 'Keep it steady, lads!' And down the arrows plunged, clattering through the swaying forest of upright pikes; their momentum broken, they did little harm; here and there a scream followed by a series of curses as the casualty's comrades stepped over the fallen man and struggled to avoid getting their feet caught on his discarded pike. Some gaps would open, Antigonos knew, but they would soon be filled as the file-closers pushed men forward; he did not need to look round to make sure that was happening.

Again, another shower of iron-tipped rain fell from the sky and again it was mostly soaked up by the canopy over the phalanx's heads, the missiles falling to the ground as if twigs broken off in a tempest. *Fifty paces, now.* 'Pikes!' Another signal blared out and was repeated along the line, but this time the manoeuvre did not need to be completed in unison; from the centre, spreading left and right, pikes came down as a wave, the front five ranks to horizontal and the rear ranks to an angle over the heads of the men in front, shielding them still from the continuing arrow-storm.

Hunching forwards, Antigonos counted his steady, even paces, impatient for each one, as the enemy neared; now the Persian aim was more direct and arrows began to slam into the front rank's shields that rocked with the impacts as they were not held secure with a fist gripping a handle but just slung loose over the arm. Now the casualties began to mount; unprotected faces and thighs became targets; screams of pain became commonplace as, with the wet thuds of a butcher's shop, iron-tipped missiles pierced flesh and came to a juddering halt on bone. Shaft after shaft hissed in and Antigonos smiled still; he had not been touched since one had taken his eye at Chaeronea when Philip had defeated the combined forces of Athens and Thebes. Since then he had been blessed of Ares, the god of war, and felt no fear walking into a blizzard of arrows. Now he could see the Persians' eyes as they aimed their shafts. An instinct made him duck his head; an arrow clanged off his bronze helmet, making his ears ring; he raised his face and laughed at the enemy, for they were going to die.

Taking up their pavises to use as more conventional shields, the Persians jammed their bows back into the cases on their hips, pulled long-thrusting spears from the ground and stood shoulder to shoulder, dark eyes staring at the oncoming phalanx, bristling with life-taking iron-points. Antigonos' laugh turned into a roar as he trudged the final few steps, the muscles in his arms aching with the strain of holding the pike level. His men roared with him, natural fear flowing from them to be replaced by the joy of combat.

And then he was there and now he could kill; with a power that filled him with joy, Antigonos thrust the pike forward at the hennaed-bearded face of the Persian before him, each man in the front rank judging the timing of the killing blow for himself; the Persian spun away from the pike-tip and grabbed the haft, attempting to yank it from Antigonos' grasp, but he pushed on, along with the rest of his men, forcing their way forward, so that within two paces the second rank sarissas were coming in under those in front of them at belly height. On they pushed, pace by pace, working their weapons, still well out of reach of the enemy who now struggled, as the third rank's points came into range, with the multitude of weapon-heads ranged against them.

A couple of Persians, braver than the rest, charged forward, their spears over their shoulders, twisting between the wooden hafts, making for Antigonos, whose pike point was now lost to view; but still he kept stabbing forward, blind, as the Persians approached to within range of their weapons. But Antigonos did not flinch for he knew the men behind him; out of the corner of his eye he saw a pike being raised as the fourth-ranker lifted his arms and thrust his weapon forward. With a scream, a Persian doubled over the wound in his groin, fists pulling at the pike embedded in it as another comrade behind Antigonos, with a sharp jab, dealt with the second man. And still they moved forward, the pressure mounting with every step, but the weight of the phalanx was what made it so difficult to stand against and all along the line the enemy floundered as their frontage buckled. It was the Kappadokian clansmen, to either side of the Persians, tough men from the mountainous interior, who turned first; unable to face the Macedonian war-machine with only javelins and swords they ran, in their thousands, towards the river for they knew that a Macedonian phalanx could not chase its quarry with any speed.

With pride Antigonos looked to his left and saw exactly what he had hoped to: his son, purple-edged white cloak billowing behind him, leading the charge, at the head of the wedge formation so favoured by the Macedonian Companion Cavalry, which would achieve what the phalanx could not. And it was with speed and fury that they swept into the broken Kappadokian ranks, the wedge increasing pressure the deeper it drove, crashing men aside and trampling many more beneath thrashing hoofs as lances stabbed at the backs of the routed, dealing out wounds of dishonour. It was then that the right flank cavalry hit, boxing the beaten army in; the Persians now knew they could not possibly hope to extricate themselves across the bridge to safety and they too turned in flight.

Antigonos raised a fist in the air; a horn rang out once more. The phalanx had done its work and would halt, resting, whilst it watched the glory-boys of the cavalry do the easy part of the action: murder the vulnerable.

All were driven before them as the heavy-cavalry swept through from both flanks. Further out, light-cavalry patrolled in swirling circles, picking off the few fortunate enough to escape; Antigonos had indicated before the action that he had no interest in prisoners unless it be Ariarathes himself as he had a particularly wide stake ready for the rebel to perch on. Only the enemy cavalry managed to escape with their mounts swimming to the far bank.

With the phalanx precluding any flight to the west, those who could not get on to the bridge, now heaving with a stampede of the desperate, had but one choice to make: certain death on the point of a cavalry lance or the river. And so the Halys churned with drowning men, each trying to survive at the expense of others as the current washed them away, sucking them under. Some, those with the luck of their gods on their side, managed to cling to one of the two great stone supports sunk into the riverbed, although many were hauled off by others grabbing at their ankles as they swept past. A few managed the climb up to the parapet but none made it over into the crush of humanity swarming across but were, rather, thrust back down into the river by men who saw that another person on the bridge would lessen their own chances of survival.

Antigonos laughed as he watched Demetrios and his comrades spear fleeing Persian infantrymen as they attempted to push their way onto the bridge. Their Boitian-style helmets, painted white with a golden wreath etched around them, glowed warm in the rays of the setting sun as, sitting well back on their mounts and gripping with their thighs, their feet hanging free, they controlled their beasts with a deftness born of a life in the saddle. Calf-length leather boots, a boiled-leather or bronze muscled-cuirass with fringed leather *pteruges* beneath it, protecting the groin, and tunics and cloaks of differing hues, red, white, dun or brown, they made for a fine sight Antigonos was forced to concede. And, as they slaughtered their way through to the crush attempting the bridge, few turned to oppose them for most had discarded their weapons as they fled.

Antigonos slapped Philotas on the shoulder as Demetrios' lance broke and he reversed it to use the butt-spike. 'The boy's enjoying himself; he seems to be getting a taste for Easterners' blood. And it's about time: Alexander was roughly the same age when he led troops in battle for the first time.'

Philotas grinned as Demetrios' flanker took a Persian's hand off as he attempted to drag the young lad from the saddle. 'Caunus is looking after him, so he shouldn't come to any harm. You'll just have to stress to him that it isn't always quite so easy.'

'He'll learn that soon enough.'

Demetrios' unit, an *ile* of one hundred and twenty-eight men, was now at the bridge, the leading six hacking and stabbing their way forward as the press of the vanquished thinned out and flight became swifter; and still they killed and still men fled before them. On they drove and the smile faded from Antigonos' face the further they went. *The little fool.* He turned to the signaller. 'Sound the recall!'

The horn blared rising notes that were repeated throughout the formation yet Demetrios led his men on until there were none left on the bridge to kill and he burst out onto the eastern bank and, in the last of the light, slew all he could find.

'If a Kappadokian doesn't kill him,' Antigonos muttered, 'then I will when he gets back.'

'No you won't, old friend; you'll cuff him round the ears and then give him a hug for being a fool, but a brave one.'

'My arse I will; it's foolish behaviour like that that gets people killed unnecessarily. He's either got to learn discipline or resign himself to a short life.'

'In my experience it's not always the foolish that suffer as a result of their actions.'

Antigonos' face darkened. 'If my son ever does that again, Philotas, I pray to Ares that you're right and he doesn't kill himself.'

ROXANNA, THE WILD-CAT

T HE CHILD KICKED within her. Roxanna put both hands to her belly; she sat, veiled, in the open window of her suite on the second floor of the palace in Babylon. Below her, in the immense central courtyard of the complex, now ablaze with torches as the sun sank from the overcast sky, the Macedonian army gathered for yet another meeting.

It was just one more strange thing that she had never been able to fathom about the way the Macedonian mind worked: why did they allow all their citizens to have a say? Before Alexander had defeated her father, Oxyartes – and then appointed him satrap of Paropamisadae – his will in her native Bactria was questioned on pain of impalement and yet, Alexander, a man who, she had to admit, had been far more powerful than her father could ever hope to be, actually listened to the opinions of the common soldiery. Indeed, it had been a near mutiny that had forced him to turn back from India. She shook her head at the lawlessness of a system whereby consensus ruled and swore that the boy-child she carried would not have such a handicap inflicted upon him when he came to the throne.

And that thought turned her mind back to her main preoccupation during Alexander's illness which had now become a burning issue since his death but two hours previously: how to ensure the boy would come to rule, for she knew that her life depended upon it.

Again the child gave a mighty kick and Roxanna cursed her late husband for abandoning her just at the time she needed him most. Just when she was going to triumph and produce an heir before his other two wives, the Persian bitches whom Alexander had married in the massed wedding at Susa when he had forced all his officers to take Persian spouses; just as she was on the point of becoming the most important person in Alexander's life now that her main rival, Hephaestion, was no more.

She turned and clicked her fingers at the three slave-girls waiting on their knees with their heads bowed, just as Roxanna liked it, in the far corner of the room. One girl got to her feet and padded, head still bowed, over the array of carpets of varying hues and designs of the type favoured in the east; she stopped close enough to her mistress so that Roxanna would not be forced to raise her voice, for that required energy and Roxanna believed that a queen should not be expected to expend her energy unnecessarily; it should be preserved for her king.

Roxanna ignored the girl, turning her attention back to the events unfolding below; horns were sounding and the fifteen-thousand-strong Macedonian citizens present in the army of Babylon, now formed up in their units, became silent as seven men mounted the podium in the centre of the courtyard.

'Which one?' Roxanna muttered to herself, under her breath, scrutinising Alexander's bodyguards. 'Who will it be?' She knew them all, some better than others, for she had vied with them all since her marriage three years ago, at the age of fifteen, as she had struggled to maintain her position in such a masculine society that was the army of Alexander.

It was Perdikkas, dressed in full uniform – helm, cuirass, leather apron, greaves and a cloak of deepest red – who stepped forward to address the assembly. Roxanna had thought it would be as she had seen him take the ring from Alexander but still cursed her luck: Leonnatus would have been far more malleable, his vanity made him so; Peucestas, the lover of pleasure and fine things, would have easily slipped into her bed or, indeed, Aristonous, to whom she could have appealed to his strong

21

sense of duty to the Argead royal dynasty of Macedon. But Perdikkas? How would she bend him to her will?

'Soldiers of Macedon,' Perdikkas declaimed, his voice high and carrying over the vast, shadowed host; the bronze of his helmet glistering in the torchlight as the light breeze fluttered its red horse-hair plume. 'I expect you have all heard of the tragedy that has befallen us for bad news is fleeter than good. Alexander, the third of his name, the Lion of Macedon, is dead. And we, his soldiers, will mourn him in the Macedonian manner. The campaign in Arabia is, therefore, postponed so that funeral games with rich prizes may be held over the next few days. But first we shall do what is right and proper: we shall, each and every one of us, pay our last respects to our king; his body has been moved to the throne-room. We will file past in our units. The cavalry shall go first. Once all have been witness to his death, then, and only then, will we have an assembly to appoint a new king, two days hence.'

As Perdikkas continued addressing the army, Roxanna snapped at her slave waiting behind her. 'Fetch Orestes, I have a letter to write.'

The secretary arrived within a few moments of the girl leaving the room, as if he had been awaiting her summons; perhaps he had been, Roxanna reflected, he had been most attentive since she had caused the little finger of his left hand clipped off for keeping her waiting too long after being called for. Alexander had chided her for inflicting such a punishment on a freeborn Greek and told her to make recompense but she had laughed at him and said that a queen should never be kept waiting and, besides, she had done it now and no amount of recompense would re-grow it. Alexander, fool that he was, had compensated the man from his own purse. 'To Perdikkas,' she said without turning around to see if the man was ready. 'From Queen Roxanna of Macedon, greetings.' She heard the stylus begin to scratch as she formulated the next line in her head, never once taking her eye off her quarry who was still addressing the troops below. 'I require your presence to discuss the regency and other topics of mutual benefit.'

'That is all, majesty?' Orestes asked as his stylus stilled.

'Of course it's all! Had there been more I would have said it! Now get out and write a fair copy and then bring it to me so I can have one of my maids deliver it.' Roxanna smiled to herself as she listened to Orestes hurriedly gather his things and scamper from the room. *Greeks, how I loathe them; especially those who can write. Who knows what secrets and spells they conceal?* Down in the courtyard Perdikkas had finished speaking and Ptolemy had taken the podium to declaim his grief. She wondered whether lots had been drawn but she rather thought not; what she was witnessing was the order of precedence that the bodyguards had sorted out amongst themselves.

By the time she had despatched her letter, Peucestas was the last to speak, following Lysimachus, Leonnatus and Aristonous – Peithon, being a man of few words, each preferably with few syllables, had not attempted to. As the assembly broke up and the great file-by had begun, Roxanna ordered a jug of sweet wine and commanded her maids to redo her hair and makeup as she awaited her guest.

Her coiffure could have been reworked thrice by the time Perdikkas was announced by her steward.

'You kept me waiting,' Roxanna said, her voice low, as the tall Macedonian strode into her chamber. She removed her veil and stared at him with almond eyes, giving a hint of a flutter of the eyelashes.

'You're lucky that I had the time to come at all; there have been messengers to send out and much to organise,' Perdikkas replied, sitting without asking leave or commenting on her naked face. 'Are you going to cut one of my fingers off as a warning against tardiness? Next time I suggest you come and find me.'

Roxanna's eyes flashed with anger; she waved her slaves out of the room. 'I'm your queen; I can summon you any time I wish.'

Perdikkas stared at her levelly, contemplating her with his sea-grey eyes; she did not relish it but held his gaze. Clean-shaven, like many close to Alexander, his face was lean with high cheekbones and a slender nose and close-clipped black hair; a pleasing face, she allowed, one that she would not mind being in close contact with, should the need arise. She glanced at his hands; he was not wearing the ring.

'You are not my queen, Roxanna,' Perdikkas said after a few moments, 'nor have you ever been. To me, and the rest of the army, you are nothing but a barbarian savage whom Alexander brought back from the east as a trophy. And you would do well to remember that in the coming days.'

'How dare you speak to me like that? I—'

'You are now no more than a vessel, Roxanna,' Perdikkas cut across her with force, pointing at her pregnancy, 'a useful vessel, granted, but a vessel nonetheless. What you carry within you has value, you do not. The only question is: how much value does it possess? Not much if it turns out to be female.'

Roxanna put a hand on her belly and clenched her jaw. 'He is a boy-child,' she hissed through her teeth, 'I know it.'

'How can you be certain?'

'A woman knows; he sits low within me and he kicks with all his strength.'

Perdikkas dismissed her assertion with a wave of his hand. 'Believe what you want; we will all know one way or the other in three months. Until then I would advise you to keep out of sight so the men aren't constantly reminded of the fact that Alexander's heir is a half-breed.'

'They love me.'

Perdikkas sighed and shook his head; the harshness came out of his voice. 'In the last year of his life, Alexander began training easterners in the Macedonian fashion, making phalangites out of them. When he sent Krateros home with ten thousand veterans he did not replace them with Macedonians but, rather, these new pseudo-Macedonians, and the men don't like it. If your child is a boy we will have a struggle to have him accepted by all Macedonians.'

'Which is why I summoned you.'

Perdikkas gave an exasperated look. 'Roxanna, I will not play games with you; I hold Alexander's ring, I am summoned by nobody. I came because I would rather talk to you here where there is a certain degree of privacy. Now, what did you want to say to me?'

Roxanna, realising that trying to assert her rightful position would just aggravate Perdikkas more, decided against forcing her claim to superiority. 'You need me, Perdikkas.' She was taken aback by his sudden outbreak of mirth. 'You laugh at me? Why?'

'You are the second person to have told me that this evening.'

'Who was the first?'

'You don't need to know that.'

I do, I do very much need to know who else is vying for his attention. 'I'm sure that he can't be nearly as useful as I can be.'

'I'm not sure that he could.'

Good, it's not a woman. 'You hold the ring, and your six colleagues in the Bodyguard have evidently deferred to you as it was you who addressed the army first this evening. Now, let us be practical: you would like to rule in Alexander's place but the others won't accept that, if they did you would be wearing that ring now, but you're not. I can offer you the regency of my son until he comes of age in fourteen years.'

'I could just take the regency; I have no need to receive it from your hand.'

Roxanna smiled; it was, she knew, her finest feature, which was why she bestowed it rarely, thereby adding to its effect. 'To be an effective regent you have to be ruling over a united realm and all your subjects must accept you as the regent. If I endorse you then that could well happen. But just imagine if I make that proposal to Leonnatus, for example; can there be two regents? I rather think not. And do you think that Leonnatus would turn down the chance of that power knowing what he thinks of himself? And who do you think Ptolemy would support if it were a choice between you and Leonnatus?'

'You wouldn't.'

The smile faded and her eyes hardened. 'I would, what's more, you know I could.'

Perdikkas considered the situation.

I think I have him.

'What do you want,' Perdikkas said eventually.

I do have him, now I just need to teach him some manners. 'Stability for my son; there can be only one true-born heir.'

'You want Heracles dead?'

'Heracles? No, that bastard is not a threat to me. Alexander never acknowledged Barsine so he has no precedence over my son. It's the two bitches in Susa.'

'Stateira and Parysatis? They can't threaten your position.'

'They're pregnant, both of them.'

'Impossible; Alexander hasn't seen them since Hephaestion's funeral cortège passed through Susa nine months ago. If he impregnated them then we would all know by now.'

'Even so, I want them dead and I want you to kill them for me.'

'Kill women? I don't do that; especially as the women concerned are Alexander's wives.'

'Send someone to do it then or I go to Leonnatus.'

'Do you really think Leonnatus would stoop to murdering women, knowing what he thinks of himself?' It was Perdikkas' turn to smile. 'Or any of the bodyguards, for that matter.'

Roxanna cursed the man inwardly and then tried a different tack. 'Shouldn't Alexander's wives all be in Babylon to mourn him? Surely Stateira and Parysatis would welcome the chance to weep by his body?'

Perdikkas gave a grim smile as he grasped the meaning of what Roxanna was saying. 'I will be responsible for their safety once they are here.'

'But not whilst they are on the road, how could you be?'

Again he looked at her long and hard and, from his eyes, Roxanna knew that she would triumph.

Perdikkas stood. 'Very well, Roxanna, I will summon Stateira and Parysatis to Babylon and you will endorse me as regent. If it becomes appropriate, I shall inform the senior officers of the army of your decision when we meet the day after tomorrow before the army assembly.'

'You may indeed do that,' Roxanna said with much grace whilst bestowing another rare smile. She watched him turn and leave the room, the smile fixed to her face. *So, Stateira and Parysatis, you will soon learn what happens to my rivals; just as did Hephaestion.*

PTOLEMY, THE BASTARD

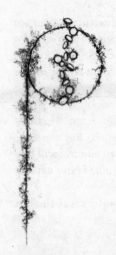

C LEVER, VERY CLEVER, Ptolemy
thought as he looked at the layout
of the throne-room in which he
and his colleagues were gathering, two
days after Alexander's death. He hated to
admit it, but, however much he disliked
the man, Perdikkas had been clever; but
Ptolemy had always found that enmity
did not need to preclude admiration.

At the far end of the hall the final few infantry units of the
army of Babylon continued to file past the body of their king,
lying dressed in his richest uniform: a purple cloak and tunic,
a gilded breastplate inlaid with gemstones and engraved with
gods, horses and the sixteen-point sun-blazon of Macedon and
knee-length boots of supple calfskin; his parade helmet rested
in the crook of his right arm. But it was not calling the meeting
in full view of the last part of the army paying its respects to
Alexander that impressed Ptolemy, it was what Perdikkas had
made of the other end of the room: the great carved-stone
throne of Nebuchadnezzar was draped with Alexander's robes,
his favoured hardened-leather battle-cuirass, inlaid with a
leaping horse on each pectoral, was placed, along with his
ceremonial sword, at its base; but the master-stroke in Ptolemy's
eyes was his diadem resting on the seat with The Great Ring
of Macedon laying within it.

*He's set up the meeting to be as if it is in the very presence of
Alexander,* Ptolemy thought, looking around the gathered
senior officers: the six other bodyguards plus Alketas,

Meleagros, Eumenes and the tall, burly Seleukos who was now the Taxiarch, the commander, of the Hypaspists, one of the two elite infantry units of the army; he had made his name, three years previously, commanding the newly formed elephant squadron. *How many of them will support Perdikkas?* Ptolemy mused as he studied each face. *Eumenes certainly because, as a Greek, he needs a Macedonian sponsor to stand any chance of reward.* His attention was drawn by an older man entering the room, weather-beaten with eyes like slits from years of squinting into the sun. *Nearchos, interesting; he has the same problem as Eumenes, but our formidable Cretan admiral will be a boon to whoever he chooses to support; it's a shame I have nothing to tempt him with.*

It was no surprise to Ptolemy that Kassandros was the last to arrive. *Now he will need watching; how such an arrogant piece of vixen vomit was sired by Antipatros, I'll never know. Still, I hear the old man's latest batch of daughters have matured nicely. Kassandros as a brother-in-law? Now there's a thought.* And indeed it was, for it set Ptolemy's mind working; no route to the life of wealth, leisure and power that he so craved after years of enduring the rigours of campaign should be left unexplored. And that was what Ptolemy was determined to reward himself with, seeing as no one else would; being reputedly the bastard son of King Philip, he had always been treated with subtle contempt. Only Alexander had accorded him respect, making him one of his bodyguards to the ill-concealed surprise of those better born. Having lived his life under the taint of bastardy, his happiness was his alone to grasp and he meant to have a firm grip on it over the coming months.

With the final arrival, Perdikkas called the meeting to order; all were dressed as if for battle to stress the urgency of the situation. *I'd best be on my guard as whatever is decided here will be with Alexander's blessing and I wouldn't wish another to get my prize.*

'Brothers,' Perdikkas began as they stood in the shadow of the ghost seated on the throne above them, 'I've called you here to decide upon a common proposal that we can put to the army assembly.'

A proposal that you hope will grant you full power whether as regent or king, Ptolemy mused whilst nodding his head with much solemnity as if Perdikkas' purpose was altruistic and for the common good rather than, as he suspected, self-serving. *I saw your eyes when Alexander gave you the ring.*

'As we all know, Alexander's first wife, Roxanna, is close to full term; if the child is a boy then we shall have a legitimate heir. I propose that we should wait to see the outcome of the birth.'

It was what was left unsaid that interested Ptolemy the most: who would rule until then? *Well, that's obvious.*

'Why wait when there is already a living heir?' The voice came from the fringe of the gathering. Nearchos, the Cretan admiral, stepped forward. 'Heracles is four years old, the regency would therefore be only ten years rather than fourteen.'

'Greek!' Peithon thundered. 'Macedon first!'

'You're speaking out of turn, my friend,' Eumenes said, wagging a finger at Nearchos. 'We must defer to our betters for our blood is but the thin Greek sort, not the strong, thick stuff that surges in Peithon's veins. But with patience I'm sure you'll get the chance to promote the interests of your bastard half-brother-in-law.'

Very good, Eumenes, Ptolemy thought as Nearchos was forced to step back to the fringes with the Macedonians shouting down his protests, *that's got rid of that.* As a mark of esteem, Alexander had given to Nearchos Barsine's eldest daughter, only twelve at the time, at the Susa weddings, making him Heracles' brother-in-law, and no doubt he fancied himself as his young relation's regent despite his Cretan blood.

'A bastard can never be king,' Perdikkas said, putting an end to the matter as the shouts died down.

'But a brother can,' Meleagros said, his voice rumbling through his beard. 'Listen to you talking about half-breeds sitting on the throne of Macedon. The children of the conquered. Roxanna!' He spat on the floor. 'She'll whelp a soft easterner no matter how much good Macedonian spunk Alexander pumped into her. And as for Barsine, being half Greek doesn't make up for the rest of her eastern blood; the Greeks have knelt in submission to us too, have they not?' He looked hard at the few Greeks in the meeting, challenging them to dispute the fact; none could. 'Let's stop all talk of mixed blood because, as with the eastern recruits coming into the ranks, the men don't like it; and why should they when we all know we have a pure-blooded mature male of the Argead dynasty ready to be crowned right here in Babylon.'

Now's my time. 'Arrhidaeus is a halfwit,' Ptolemy said.

'Give me a Macedonian halfwit any day,' Meleagros thundered, 'over a foreign half-breed.'

'Especially one with some Greek blood in him,' Eumenes said, his face a picture of innocence.

'Exactly!'

'But a halfwit cannot rule without a regent,' Ptolemy pointed out. 'Not even a Macedonian halfwit.'

Eumenes looked up at Peithon, standing next to him. 'And Macedonian halfwits are the best halfwits in the world, I believe; am I not right, Peithon?'

Peithon frowned as he considered the question but refrained from expressing his views on the prowess of Macedonian halfwits.

'So who will be the halfwit's regent?' Ptolemy asked. 'In fact, who will be the half-breed's regent, come to that? Because Alexander named none of us.' Ptolemy slowly turned his head towards Perdikkas with a countenance of deep regret. 'Did he, eh?'

Perdikkas' eyes narrowed. 'Are you putting yourself forward as king just because you might be Alexander's bastard half-brother?'

'My dear Perdikkas, whatever else I may be, I'm no fool. I like my luxuries and I know my limitations, militarily; the question is: does everyone else in this room? I would not be king for two reasons: firstly, my claim is a bastard's claim and, as you said, a bastard can never sit on the throne of Macedon.'

But that is not the only throne in the world. 'And, secondly, if we are going to carry on with Alexander's plans and go west I would be the wrong person to lead the army. And would you be the right person, Perdikkas?' Ptolemy pointed at Leonnatus. 'Or you, Leonnatus? Or perhaps you, Aristonous, or Lysimachus or Peucestas?' That Peithon lacked the qualities did not need to be questioned. 'There is only one person who would stand a chance of having the whole army behind him and he is three hundred leagues away: Krateros. Alexander himself almost named him, in that he sent him home to replace Antipatros as regent in Macedonia.'

'My father was not to be replaced!' Kassandros erupted. 'It was to be a temporary thing whilst he came east to give Alexander the benefit of his counsel. If anything it should be my father who rules, whether as king or as regent.'

It was Lysimachus' turn to spit. 'Do you think the army assembly will accept a man who has stayed at home for the last ten years and not shared one of its hardships?'

Kassandros turned on him, rage simmering within. 'A king can be made both in the army assembly or in Macedon at an assembly of the people.'

Lysimachus spat again. 'The people! I piss on the people and so would the army if they ever tried to inflict a king on them, especially one with such an ugly heir as you, Kassandros. Because that's what you want, isn't it? You and that ancient father of yours, who skulked in the west whilst better men won glory and died for it, think you could fill Alexander's place!'

Perdikkas pulled Kassandros back as he went for Lysimachus. 'Enough!'

Aristonous helped Perdikkas restrain him. 'Ptolemy's right, Krateros was named regent by Alexander and he also has the qualities of a general far greater than anyone here.'

'But he's leagues away.'

Ptolemy spread his hands. 'So how can he rule when it's immediate leadership that we need if we are to keep the army united and prevent the empire from fracturing?'

'Then if we want immediate leadership,' Aristonous said,

letting go of a simmering Kassandros, 'Perdikkas is the solution. He may not be an Argead, but he does have royal blood, nonetheless, which Krateros does not.'

'And he was given the ring,' Peucestas said.

So that's where you stand. 'But who would Alexander have given it to had Krateros been here?' Ptolemy quickly held a palm up. 'Don't answer that, it's immaterial. The fact is Krateros isn't here and none of us who are could rightly claim to take Alexander's place. And if you did claim the crown, Perdikkas, what do you think Krateros and his ten thousand veterans will do? Especially after you've done what you would have to do in order to secure your crown and prevent a civil war in the not-too-distant future: kill Roxanna and Alexander's child.'

Perdikkas shook his head. 'Which is why I would never accept the crown.'

You lying bastard. 'Ah, so you've thought about it, have you?'

'Of course I have; who here didn't as we stood round and watched Alexander die? Go on, be honest. We all did.'

I doubt Peithon did.

'So, what do you suggest, Ptolemy?'

It was the hitherto silent Leonnatus who had framed the question, Ptolemy noted, marking him down as a potential ally. 'A council comprising of four men, voted for by the army, who meet here, before the throne in the presence of the ghost of Alexander.'

Perdikkas looked at Ptolemy, incredulous. 'An army run by a committee? How would we ever manage to conquer the west?'

'We don't go west.'

'What? But Alexander—'

'Is dead,' Eumenes cut in. 'Ptolemy's right, we don't go west, if we do that then we'll lose all that we've already won.'

'So what would we do?' Perdikkas asked, looking at Ptolemy.

'We consolidate. We each take a satrapy and we rule in the name of Macedon with internal and external policy being decided by the committee of four.'

'That would never work.'

'Why not?' *Because you won't let it. But you now need me to help you out of the situation that I've put you in; and all it will cost you is Egypt.*

PERDIKKAS,
THE HALF-CHOSEN

'WHY NOT?' PTOLEMY asked in reply to Perdikkas' assertion.

That bastard of a bastard, Perdikkas thought, *he's shown a way whereby we don't need a king, nor, therefore, a regent. What does he want?* 'Because how would a committee of four be able to agree on anything, even assuming we could even decide who the four would be?'

'The army votes for them, as I said,' Ptolemy replied.

'You can't have the army voting for just anyone; we would have to put the candidates up for election.'

'Macedon must have a king, not a committee.' It was Peithon who had made the statement and when put so simply as that, it clarified the issue for Perdikkas and, indeed, for almost everyone else in the room, for all eyes turned to Peithon and most heads were nodding in agreement.

Perdikkas noticed a quick look shared between Ptolemy and Leonnatus and knew he had to act quickly. 'Peithon is absolutely right, we must have a king and that king must be of the Argead dynasty. Therefore I propose this: we wait until Roxanna gives birth and if it's a boy we then decide between him and Arrhidaeus. Either way, a regent will be needed, in the boy's case for fourteen years and in Arrhidaeus' case, for life.'

'And who will that regent be?' Ptolemy asked.

'Perdikkas,' Aristonous said.

'Perdikkas,' Peucestas agreed.

'I agree,' Lysimachus said.

'So do I,' Ptolemy followed, surprising Perdikkas. 'In conjunction with Leonnatus in Asia whilst Antipatros remains regent in Europe aided by Krateros when he arrives there.'

Perdikkas stared at Ptolemy, whose face remained neutral. *I'll wager that you're smirking behind that mask, you bastard. But I suppose the idea does have the merit of encouraging Krateros back to Europe and out of my way leaving me just Leonnatus to deal with. I would also get rid of Kassandros, he'll go back to his father, unless I give him something here so as I can keep an eye on him. Yes, it might work well for me.* 'So be it. Is there anyone who does not agree?'

It being such a fudged compromise, nobody could find any fault with it for it seemed that no one's position was directly threatened; even Meleagros showed no signs of dissent, Perdikkas noted with relief. 'Then I suggest we take an oath, here before Alexander, vowing to uphold this solution.' He glanced down to the other end of the hall where the infantry continued to pay their respects to Alexander. 'Furthermore, I suggest that we present the idea to the cavalry first as they have already completed their duty to Alexander.'

'Why not address the army as a whole?' Aristonous asked.

'If we have the support of the cavalry, the infantry might be more inclined to accept the compromise.'

'When did the infantry ever do anything because the cavalry did?' Eumenes questioned.

Meleagros grunted into his beard.

As Perdikkas administered the oath to all the senior officers, he prayed to Ares that the veteran infantry commander would have enough influence over his men to get them to back the decision without too much dissension.

'And what will we do if the infantry don't agree with the plan?' Eumenes asked Perdikkas as, the oath complete, they walked out into the courtyard; the cavalry had formed up and were being informed of the decision by their officers.

'They will.'

'You mean that you hope they will. Don't forget the infantry and cavalry nearly went to war with each other in India when the infantry wanted to turn back and the cavalry were for going on with Alexander. There is no love lost between them.' Eumenes looked at the three thousand or so cavalry troopers, on foot, discussing the proposal in their units. 'And which is the bigger arm?'

'But one can't survive without the other, not here, so far from home.'

'I know that and so do you,' Eumenes observed as the cavalry began to shout their approval, 'and so, in all likelihood, do they. But, tell me, do you really think that they do?' He pointed over his shoulder to the queue of infantry filing into the throne-room to pay their last respects to Alexander.

Perdikkas glanced back and did a double-take. 'Where are they? There were at least another few hundred of them to go when we came to a decision.'

Eumenes turned and looked to where the queue had once been. 'That doesn't bode well.' He gave Perdikkas a wry smile. 'I think you might just have engineered a situation whereby you either have their king or two kings. Not very satisfactory, I'd say. You see, you really do need my help; you're a soldier not a politician and with Alexander dead one really has to be a bit of both.' Eumenes shrugged and spread his hands. 'If you want to survive, that is; because, if that meeting taught us anything, there won't be many of us left by the time this is all over.'

'It'll never come to that; we've shared too much. We're comrades.' But Perdikkas heard a plaintive tone in his own voice and he feared that the little Greek may have the right of it as a roar rose above the cheering of the cavalry, coming from the direction of the infantry camp just beyond the palace walls. *They've rejected the proposal before we've even had a chance to put our case to them; they'll demand that we make the halfwit king.*

A knot developed in Perdikkas' belly as an infantry officer came striding through the gates into the courtyard and hurriedly made his way across its vast length to Meleagros.

'Well,' Perdikkas asked after the man had spoken with the old veteran. 'Have they rejected the proposal?'

Meleagros' eyes hardened and he gave a mirthless smile. 'They've done more than that. Eukleides here tells me that they've found Arrhidaeus, crowned him king and are calling him Philip, the third of that name.'

'They can't!'

Meleagros shrugged. 'Well, they have.'

Panic spread across Perdikkas' face. 'You have to stop them.'

'Why? It's what they want.'

'It's not what we decided and what we all swore to in front of Alexander's shade. Do you want to break that oath?'

Meleagros considered the issue before replying. 'Very well, I'll go to them.'

'Give them time to calm down and bring them to a full assembly of the army tomorrow morning.'

'That really wasn't clever,' Eumenes said as Meleagros and Eukleides walked away.

Perdikkas looked down at the Greek in surprise. 'Why not? It has to be stopped and he's the only man who the infantry will listen to.'

'I agree, he is the only man who the infantry will listen to; but the question is, what will he say to them?'

'He's sworn to our agreement.'

'If you had a choice between keeping an oath to a dead man or becoming regent to a halfwit with the support of the infantry, which would you choose?'

'I'd choose honour.' But Perdikkas' tone was again uncertain.

'You're right not to be sure, Perdikkas, because honour is the first thing that we will all lose when it comes to winning our share of the spoils; and that is what this will come down to, trust me. Now, if you want to win, you really do need my help, if only to stop you making mistakes like the one you've just made: re-uniting the mutinous infantry with their leader.'

The sly little Greek does have a point, Perdikkas conceded as he watched Meleagros disappear through the gate, *if he were referring to one of his kind, but Meleagros isn't Greek, he's a Macedonian with honour; he'll bring them to order. Gods, how I hate the infantry.*

ANTIGONOS,
THE ONE-EYED

'YOUR INFANTRY WERE just standing there doing nothing, Father!' Demetrios shouted, his voice cracking. 'I led my cavalry over the bridge to kill as many of the bastards as I could. They were running and we slew scores.'

Antigonos gripped the edge of his campaign table, restraining himself from taking a swipe at the young pup still splattered in blood from his two-day rampage; the lad's dark eyes were hard with defiance and the jaw-muscles on either side of his beardless face pulsed. 'And what if you had run into an ambush, eh? Had you thought about that before you went blundering around Kappadokia for two days, killing a few fugitives who were already well beaten?'

Demetrios dismissed the suggestion with a wave and slumped down on a three-legged stool; from outside the tent came the sound and smells of a victorious army breaking its fast: clinking pots and wood-smoke mixed with harsh laughter and freshly baked flat-bread. 'There was no organisation, Father; that was never going to happen.'

'But how could you be sure, Demetrios; you're fifteen and you're here to learn. When you're leading men into a dangerous situation you have to have certainty otherwise they die. You never advance somewhere that hasn't been scouted and that's exactly what you did.'

'If I had brought back Ariarathes we wouldn't be having this conversation.'

'My arse, we would; the only difference would be a rebel satrap with a pointed piece of wood up his arse decorating the front of my tent. So, you listen to me, whelp, I may be your father but I am also a general and, as such, I know that a general's first concern is for his men, even the cavalry! What I've witnessed you do was an act of foolish bravado that has absolutely no place in my army or any man's army, come to that. Now, as a general, I can't have my men put in that sort of unnecessary danger, so therefore, Demetrios, you have a choice. You can either promise me that you'll never advance onto unscouted ground again and that in future you will always obey my orders to the letter, or you can go home to your mother and learn how to sew.'

Demetrios' expression was one of outrage. 'You wouldn't dismiss me! I'm your son; I should naturally have a command.'

'No! Not naturally. If I think you're a hazard to yourself and my men then I would *naturally* relieve you of that command; if I did not, the men would lose confidence in you and you would wake up one morning dead with your throat cut and I'd be forced to execute some good lads for mutiny. Now go and get some rest and think on it because I'll say no more on the matter until I have your answer.'

Demetrios got to his feet; there was no sign of weariness in his eyes or in his movements. 'You can have my answer now, Father. I won't ever lead my men into the unknown again.'

'Good. And?'

'And I will obey your orders to the letter.'

'Good; now come here,' Antigonos said, rising. He walked towards his son and wrapped his heavily muscled arms about him. 'I was proud of you in the battle, Son; you killed well and you enjoyed it.'

'Thank you, Father; it was a good feeling the first time.'

'Yes; just make sure you don't enjoy it too much so that it clouds your judgement as it obviously did. Now be off with you and get some sleep. We're staying here for the day; make and mend whilst the scouts go out before we head on into Kappadokia.'

Demetrios managed a wan smile and rubbed a hand through the dark mane that was his hair. 'I will.' He turned to go.

'And get a slave to clean the blood off your uniform whilst you do; I like my officers to look the part and not like Kappadokian cutthroats.'

'Do you think that he'll take the lesson to heart?' Philotas asked, coming into the tent once Demetrios had left.

'I pray to Ares he has.' Antigonos poured himself some wine, picked up the water-pitcher but, thinking the better of it, downed his cup neat. 'The trouble is that Alexander and his generation have made every high-born youth believe that leading men in battle is a gods'-given ability to all Macedonian aristocracy and so therefore they have nothing to learn from the likes of you and me. And, let's face it, the experience lies with us and the luck lies with the younger generation; I could beat any one of those pups in the field, with the exception of Alexander himself.' He cocked his head. 'And, perhaps, Krateros; but he's more of our age.'

'Well, we'll never be able to test that assertion.'

'Thank the gods that's the truth of it.' Antigonos sat back down at his campaign desk and indicated for Philotas to take a place opposite him. 'My breakfast should be appearing soon; stay and join me.'

Philotas pulled up the three-legged stool vacated by Demetrios, smiling. 'Common soldiers' rations no doubt.'

'What's good enough for my men is good enough for me.' Antigonos poured them both more wine. 'Although I admit to making it far more palatable by substituting the muck the men get with a decent vintage from my estates.' He raised his cup and downed it in one. 'The resinated Cyclops is one of the kinder names I've heard the men call me.'

Philotas drained his wine and slammed the cup on the table with a satisfied burp. 'There are a lot worse than that, I can tell you, old friend; and I heard most of them on the forced-march in the last two days.'

Antigonos barked a laugh. 'They can call me what they will as long as they follow me at the speed I need to travel. I was pleased with them yesterday; had we arrived an hour later Ariarathes would have been across and could've held the bridge against us. I may not have got him, but at least I can tell Alexander that I destroyed his army and have him on the run. Tomorrow, now that Demetrios has finally returned, we'll go into Kappadokia and finish the job. Now that Alexander's back, with luck he'll allow me to go on into Armenia and we can have some fun there for a couple of seasons. What would you say to that, eh?'

Philotas helped himself to more wine. 'I would say that, before we go, let's do some research to find out whether the women there are worthwhile; I've had enough of the rough vixens they seem to use for breeding in these parts.'

'As you know, old friend, I never go anywhere unscouted.'

Philotas choked on his wine; a trickle came out of his nostrils. 'That hurt,' he said through his mirth, putting down his cup and wiping his face. 'And there was me thinking that you've sent scouts across the river into Kappadokia to make sure that Ariarathes hasn't got anything nasty waiting for us and all the time it was solely to check on the quality of his harem.'

'For my men, naturally, not for myself.'

'Naturally.'

'Stratonice would never allow it.'

Their laughter was curtailed by a couple of slaves bringing in a steaming pot of barley stew with herbs and some gristle attempting to pass for meat along with a round, flat loaf of bread. Antigonos indicated that they should put it down and leave.

'But seriously,' Antigonos said once they both had a full bowl before them, 'Do you really think Alexander will turn his eyes to the west now that he's back?'

Philotas considered the question, chewing on a hunk of bread soaked in gravy. 'His ambition is big enough; and I hear that Krateros was ordered to take the coastal road home to Macedon so that he could command the port cities to start amassing ships.'

43

'Yes, I heard that too.'

'But why go west before we're finished here?'

Antigonos dunked some bread into his stew. 'Why does Alexander do anything? For his own glory and no other reason. He doesn't think Armenia is worthy of him, which is why I'm hoping that he'll leave it to me. No, I really do believe that he's amassing a fleet to take him to the Greek cities of Southern Italia and Sicilia. Perhaps, even, he's got his eyes on Carthage.'

'Carthage? But that's leagues away; how would he maintain supply lines?'

'The same way he did it when he was out in the east—'

'Father!'

Antigonos looked up to see Demetrios coming into the tent. 'What is it? Have you changed your mind and decided to take sewing lessons from your mother?'

Demetrios' expression was one of shock. 'Alexander's dead, Father, three days ago. There's a messenger outside come by relay from Babylon.'

Antigonos shared a look of complete shock with Philotas. 'Dead? That can't be. You had better call the man in, Demetrios.'

'Of a fever,' the messenger said in response to Antigonos' first question; dusty from the road, he had gulped down the cup of well-watered wine he had been offered.

'And whom did he name as his heir?'

'There was a rumour going around that all he said was: "To the strongest". When Perdikkas sent us messengers out to all over the empire it seemed to me that all his companions were arguing about what Alexander had really meant.'

A wearied smile cracked on Antigonos' weathered face. 'I'm sure they were. Perdikkas sent you, you said?'

'Yes, it seemed to be him who had taken the lead; Alexander had given him his ring as he said "to the strongest".'

'But didn't name anyone.' *With three words the young bastard has just unleashed years of civil war and I'll wager he did it on purpose so that none will outshine him.* 'I'd best be making plans. 'Is that all you know?'

'Yes, sir; other than he really is dead, I saw the body with my

44

own eyes. Perdikkas allowed all of us going out to pay our respects first.'

'A very noble sentiment,' Antigonos said, getting to his feet, 'at least he's behaving as a Macedonian should.' He opened a chest on the floor next to his desk, took out a small purse and tossed it to the messenger. 'I'll have letters for you to take back, stay with my army until I call for you.'

'Thank you, sir, I will,' the man replied, turning to go whilst weighing the purse in his hand and liking the result.

'What does this mean, Father?' Demetrios asked.

'This means, my boy, that we're going to have to decide whose side we're on. Either we back whoever comes out on top in Babylon; that could be either Perdikkas, Ptolemy or Leonnatus, or, maybe, two of them scrapping for the empire. Or we support whoever rules in Macedon which, at the moment, is Antipatros but if Alexander's orders are obeyed, should be Krateros; but either way both of them will believe that as regent, named by Alexander, it should be them who take power and, never forget, there is still a formidable army in Macedon. And we also mustn't forget the dark plots of that witch, Olympias; she'll have spread pain and hatred before this has played out because she'll be wanting her blood on the throne.' He looked to Philotas. 'Perhaps my assertion will be tested after all.'

'It won't ever come to that; there'll be a bit of posturing and then an agreement will be reached as to who holds what. We won't risk the empire by turning on one another.'

Antigonos grunted. 'Let's hope you're right. What would you do in my situation in order to secure my position?'

'Me? Well, firstly I wouldn't go to Kappadokia tomorrow; I'd head back to Celaenae and start concentrating my troops ready to support the first man who makes it worth your while.'

'That is sage counsel, my friend; best not to waste time chasing rebels around the country when there may be profits to be made elsewhere.'

'Let me go to Kappadokia, Father,' Demetrios urged, but one look from Antigonos' eye made him think better of arguing.

'We go back west and wait to see what happens in the first month or so.' He gave a shrewd look to his son. 'Who knows, Demetrios, positioned where we are, right in the middle of things, we could come out of this very well; I can foresee a lot of people wanting us as their friends.'

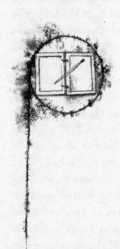

Eumenes, The Sly

A<small>ND HOW IS</small> *it that I'm not surprised and yet you are, Perdikkas, even though I warned you yesterday?* Eumenes was enjoying the look on Perdikkas' face as Meleagros paraded a limping fool, dressed in a purple tunic and cloak and wearing a kingly diadem upon his head. *Why do Macedonians find it so hard to believe anything that they find unpalatable until they see it with their own eyes?* 'What did I tell you?'

Perdikkas looked down at him from the rostra set at the centre of the courtyard, genuine shock in his eyes, which was far better, Eumenes allowed, than the supercilious expression he normally reserved for his Greek interlocutors. 'But he swore an oath; he was honour-bound to persuade the infantry to forget this madness of having an idiot for a king, not encourage them.'

'Whatever he was meant to do is irrelevant; the fact is that he's standing there in front of the whole army with Arrhidaeus and calling him King Philip, the third of that name. You have to react to the situation as you see it now and not as you would like it to be.'

The sun had risen over the immensity of the palace complex courtyard as the army had assembled in the hour after dawn. Both infantry and cavalry paraded together; the infantry in *speira* blocks of two hundred and fifty-six men taking up almost half the area and the cavalry lining the perimeter of the rest of the courtyard – but, taking no chances, Perdikkas had ordered them to be mounted. It was not until the sacrifices had been

47

made and Perdikkas, leading the other six bodyguards onto the rostra, had been about to address the assembly that Meleagros and Eukleides had pushed their way through the massed ranks of their men and hailed Arrhidaeus, garbed as Alexander, as King Philip. The king had drooled his appreciation of the honour and expressed the excitement he felt, as Meleagros placed the diadem on his head, by urinating down his leg and waving a carved wooden model of an elephant in the air.

Eumenes admired Meleagros' actions, even if he did not approve of them, for at least they supported the bloodline of King Philip, the second to be so called, the man who had raised him from obscurity; the man who had Eumenes' undying loyalty. And, as he regarded the indecision on Perdikkas' face, Eumenes toyed with the idea of walking over to Meleagros and offering his services that Perdikkas seemed so reluctant to accept; perhaps something could be made of the idiot king that would unite the army and keep the Argead royal house in place. But would Meleagros and his faction respect him and keep him safe, even if they did win through? *To be a Greek in a Macedonian world is no easy feat*, Eumenes reminded himself, *and to remain a live Greek as that world tears itself apart will be harder.* He glanced over his shoulder at Roxanna sitting, veiled, in an open window in her suite, two storeys above him, watching the proceedings with a hand on her belly. *Although to be an eastern wild-cat trying to stay alive with her whelp now a new king has been crowned will be harder still. But no one yet would want to take on the responsibility of killing Alexander's child, let alone me who owes his family everything. And that's the key to it: it's Alexander's and Philip's combined bloodline that must succeed and not just Philip's himself in the form of the idiot; and that is what lies in her womb.* He frowned as a thought came to him. *It's also in Kleopatra, Alexander's full-sister; there are perhaps more options than I first appreciated.* With that realisation, Eumenes decided to remain where he was even though the look of indecision on Perdikkas' face was intolerable. *Had I been born a Macedonian I would run rings around them all; so decisive in battle and yet the complete opposite in politics.* He glanced over at Ptolemy, whose amusement at the situation was palpable. *Except you, perhaps. You're enjoying this and I think I know why.*

As Meleagros called his men to order, Eumenes could bear it no more. 'The throne-room, Perdikkas,' he said, looking up. 'That's what you need to do; whoever has Alexander's body has his authority.'

The truth of the statement spurred Perdikkas into action. 'Leonnatus and Peucestas, stay here with the cavalry and be ready to move if it looks like turning violent; we must avoid spilling Macedonian blood at all costs otherwise there'll be no turning back. Lysimachus and Peithon, you go to the mercenary camp; I want to ensure that we can rely on them, especially the Greeks and the Thracians. Ptolemy and Aristonous, bring two hundred men and join me in the throne-room.' He turned and ran.

'Macedonians,' Meleagros bellowed, his voice echoing off the tiled walls of the palace, as Perdikkas hurried down the rostra's steps, 'today we have chosen a new king; a Macedonian king of pure Argead blood. Today we have chosen Philip, the third of that name, to lead us.'

No you haven't, Eumenes thought, *you've chosen Meleagros to lead you as a fool's regent; at least, that's what he hopes.*

'No more shall we tolerate the mixing of eastern blood with ours,' Meleagros continued, warming to his theme as Eumenes watched Ptolemy and Aristonous order the nearest two hundred men to dismount and follow Perdikkas to the throne-room. 'No more shall we see the Macedonian phalanx infiltrated by men who have never seen Macedon's hills and vales, tasted the water from her rivers, eaten her lamb and milled her grain...'

'I never had Meleagros down as a poet,' Eumenes commented, catching up with Ptolemy as the infantry officer continued his address. 'An excessive drinker with more grudges and prejudices than words in his vocabulary, certainly; but the fact that he seems to put those words together reasonably lyrically is quite the eye-opener.'

Ptolemy did not look at him. 'It's a shame for him, really, to discover such a talent in the last few days of his life.'

'I couldn't agree more. I did momentarily consider offering Meleagros my support but the idiot's blood doesn't have Alexander's mixed in it and that will be his downfall, that and the new king being a fool, of course.'

'Of course. But, tell me, why should you care about the Macedonian bloodline; you're a Greek.'

'I *am* a Greek, well spotted, Ptolemy. But I'm a strange Greek as I owe everything to two Macedonians. Without Philip's, and then Alexander's, patronage I would, more than likely, be dead by now at the hands of assassins sent by Hecataeus, the tyrant of my native Kardia.'

'He objected to your slipperiness and—'

'Tendency to always finishing other people's sentences for them? Yes, I suppose that didn't help but, mainly, he objected to my father trying to depose him; he was executed along with the rest of my family and so I fled to Macedonia.'

'I remember you arriving; we laughed at you for your inability to hold a boar-spear and at your learning.'

'My learning set me apart from you boar-spear holders which is why Philip made me his secretary; that and to annoy Hecataeus, of course. And because of that kindness I shall always be loyal to the only family I now have and, in the process, benefit considerably for it.'

'So you're not completely without selfish motive, then?'

'Who is entirely?'

'I think that there may well be advantage to be had in exploiting this confusion; and I can see you believe so too, as you seem to be enjoying this.'

Eumenes struggled to keep up with Ptolemy's long strides across the courtyard. 'Not as much as you are.'

'You might be right there; watching ineptitude is an enthralling pastime, especially when it's in a game that you intend to join.'

'A game that you intend to win?'

Ptolemy looked at Eumenes for the first time in the conversation as they entered the corridor that led down to the side entrance of the throne-room. 'Only a fool would try to win the game with the rules as they stand, as Meleagros will find out soon; and so will Perdikkas in the not-too-distant future if he continues on this path.'

'And which path is that?'

'Absolute power, his egotism won't allow for anything else. But if any of us have learnt anything in the last ten years it's that only Alexander could hold that commodity; and even he had to give in to the will of the infantry when they wanted to turn back.'

I think that we may be both on the same side – for the moment. 'I couldn't agree more; that's my analysis too.'

'Then why are you supporting Perdikkas?'

'Because he has the ring.'

'But—'

'He was not named, I know. But that possession alone gives him the authority to make the decision that we both know needs to be made.'

'Do we?'

'Yes, it was your suggestion, remember? You've managed to get Perdikkas to concede to having four regents, which I fully supported as it implies that the Argead dynasty will be preserved; but he still hasn't conceded the point of us each taking satrapies and I think I know which one you want.'

'Do you now? Are you offering to help me get it?'

'Put it this way; I would never be allowed it because it's far too rich a prize for a mere Greek; if I'm lucky and, despite my inferior blood, get anything out of this, and that is doubtful, then it will be a barren satrapy full of untamed savage tribesmen some-where out in the east. But at least it will be mine even if it isn't nearly as wealthy or as easy to defend as Egypt.'

Ptolemy smiled and stopped just outside the throne-room as the men filed in behind him. 'You are a clever little Greek. How did you know?'

'You enjoy your luxuries and women and would love to be fabulously wealthy without having to do too much for it. All that, and the occasional good battle, should someone try to disturb your pleasure, would, I'd wager, keep you very happy for the rest of your days.'

Ptolemy inclined his head a fraction. 'You have me exact, Eumenes: a normal man with normal desires; when I saw Egypt, when I accompanied Alexander to The Oracle of Amun in Siwa, I knew that it would suit me perfectly in my advanced years. And now that they approach, I do not wish them to be so strenuous that I cannot enjoy them to the full.'

'A sentiment that I agree with entirely.'

'So what do you want if you give me your support in this matter?'

Eumenes looked up at him. 'Nothing that you can't afford. Just your support for me not being left out of the division of the satrapies only because I'm a Greek.'

'Is that all?'

'That will be enough for the present.'

'For the present?'

'Let's just agree that you will be getting far more out of our mutual understanding than I will, so perhaps you could consider yourself in my debt?'

'You're a clever and a sly little Greek, aren't you?'

'Am I? Why, thank you, Ptolemy; and you're not so straightforward and open yourself.'

Ptolemy grinned despite himself. 'We have an agreement, but with one caveat—'

'That just because you agree to be in my debt does not mean that I can ask anything of you and you should be expected to honour it?'

'What I find most annoying about you is—'

'That I always finish people's sentences for them? Yes, I know; people often tell me that. It's a weakness of mine as a result of having a sharper intellect than most.' Eumenes turned and walked through the doors of the throne-room leaving Ptolemy smiling and shaking his head.

Now, for once I shall put my lack of Macedonian blood to good use, Eumenes told himself as he approached the bier upon which Alexander still rested. Despite it being the third day since his passing there was, intriguingly, no stench of decomposition and no outward sign of corruption; he looked exactly as he did at the moment of his death. Much to Eumenes' relief, the diadem was still around his head. *So the one they crowned Philip with is false; that should make things much easier. But how to get it? That will take a bit of work.* As Perdikkas put details of the newly arrived soldiers on every door to barricade them in, Eumenes lurked by the body but never felt securely enough that he was not noticed in order to try for the diadem. And it was almost a relief when Meleagros shouted from outside the main doors to the chamber: 'Open in the name of King Philip.'

'There is no King Philip,' Perdikkas called back.

'He was acclaimed by the army assembly and you were present, I saw you. Now, open up!'

Perdikkas made no reply and, having repeated the order a couple of times, Meleagros finally lost his patience; the doors vibrated under a barrage of heavy blows.

It was the work of a moment, as men rushed to add their weight to the doors; with his thumb and middle-finger, Eumenes plucked the diadem from Alexander's head and dropped it down the front of his tunic, feeling it lodge on his belt.

The pounding on the doors grew; an axe crashed through, and then another followed by two more, exploding splinters into the faces of the defenders as they leant their shoulders to the wood. But the flesh of a shoulder is no match for an axe blade and as the breaches became more frequent and the first men went down injured, the rest backed off for there was no hope.

Now this will be interesting, Eumenes considered, backing slowly away as Meleagros kicked the doors open and the infantry stormed in, javelins raised.

Perdikkas and Aristonous stood their ground but of Ptolemy there was no sign; Eumenes kept up a steady pace backwards as Meleagros approached Perdikkas with a triumphant sneer on his face. 'King Philip has come to claim the body of his brother for burial, Perdikkas; you have no right to deny him.'

'I am one of the regents, Meleagros; we all agreed to it and swore an oath in front of Alexander. Arrhidaeus is not king because he hasn't been proclaimed by the full army assembly; solely the infantry.'

'The infantry outnumber the cavalry so therefore their will must prevail.' Meleagros stepped closer to the corpse. 'Stand aside or die.'

Perdikkas' blood the first to be spilt? I think not. Eumenes continued his slow retreat, as the tension mounted.

Perdikkas faced Meleagros, motionless, for a few moments and then stepped back. 'Very well, you have control of the throne-room and the body.' He turned away and beckoned to Aristonous and his men. 'Come.'

That might well be the best decision Perdikkas has made so far, Eumenes reflected as he reached the door into the long corridor. Turning, he made his way with haste along its length, coming out into the courtyard to find Ptolemy waiting for him; the cavalry were nowhere to be seen.

'Leonnatus led them out when I told him that Perdikkas could not possibly hold the throne-room,' Ptolemy said, explaining their absence. 'He's taking them all the way out of the city.'

'A very sensible precaution.'

'And I think I shall be joining him until things settle down. I thought I might find Seleukos and go with him via the elephant camp in the gardens beyond the Ishtar Gate; his old command would be a handy addition if it should come to a fight and he still has their loyalty.'

'Oh, I don't think that there is any need for that; just when things are going so well and we're another step closer to achieving what we both want.'

'There's no need for it at the moment but whilst Meleagros remains alive there is always the possibility.'

'So let's hasten his demise by making use of the cavalry outside the walls and blocking off all food supplies to the city. It's so much easier to negotiate with the hungry.'

Ptolemy wagged a finger at Eumenes as Perdikkas and Aristonous led their men out of the corridor. 'You are a sly, scheming—'

'Little Greek, I know. How else do you think that I managed to become firstly Philip's secretary and then Alexander's; by being nice? Or was it really just my learning?'

'Are you coming?' Ptolemy asked as he turned to join Perdikkas.

'I don't think so; when Macedonians are arguing, the only person who can talk to both sides is a sly, scheming little Greek.'

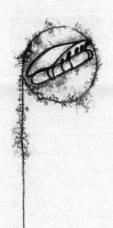

KRATEROS,
THE GENERAL

S MOKE BILLOWED, THICK and black, from each of the four dozen wooden huts in the cove. A line of women and children, chained together, sobbed and pleaded for mercy but there was to be none. Krateros had been specific on that point: the men were to be executed and the rest were headed for the slave-markets of Delos; that was the only way to deal with pirates.

Krateros jumped down from his bireme, newly beached on the cove's sand, to look at his men's handiwork; they had been thorough: a pile of freshly executed pirates was being raised, interspersed with plenty of driftwood, ready for burning as the slaves were corralled, waiting to be led off to a life of misery that, to Krateros' mind, was thoroughly deserved. However, it was not the fate of the inhabitants of this cove that interested Krateros, it was the tools of their trade he had come for: three *lembi*, swift little ships with single banks of fifteen oars a side, were beached at the centre of the cove and had been untouched by the raid, just as Krateros had ordered. He took off his *kausia*, the leather-topped, brimless woollen hat of a peasant, which he always wore rather than a helmet, and rubbed the sweat from his forehead as he examined his prizes. They were in excellent condition: ideal for the piratical work of attacking traders, they would also be a boost to the navy he was assembling; although too small to be of much use for troop transportation, they were perfect as supply vessels. And if

Alexander was really going to do what he envisaged, then there would be much need of supply vessels.

It was a bold vision Alexander had, to take the west and bring almost all the known world under his sway, but no bolder than his original dream of stealing an empire, and yet that was what he had done. Had it not been for the mutiny he would have stolen two, for Krateros had no doubt in his mind that all India would have fallen to him and they would have stood together on the shores of the farthest sea, looking towards the end of the world. But that was not to be and his infantry had forced Alexander to limit his dreams, something that he could never forgive them for and that was why Krateros was leading the worst-offending units home; and then he was to relieve Antipatros as governor of Macedon, a position he had not sought nor did he want. However, there was no rush to get there and he was putting the journey to good use. Already he had amassed almost four hundred ships of varying sizes and was gathering them at Tarsus, the capital of Cilicia set not far from the mouth of the Cydnus River.

Piracy had become a problem along Cilicia's coast since Alexander's conquest, as, by removing the Persian satrap and replacing him with a Macedonian, Alexander had unwittingly caused the conditions needed for successful piracy to be met. With no one to advise him against it, for the new satrap did not know the conditions of his province, Alexander took the Cilician navy with him to shadow him as he made his way east along the coast. Thus, free from naval patrols, the pirates flourished in coves protected by the high cliffs of the coastline.

Now Krateros was putting an end to that and at the same time creating the navy that would be needed for the next big adventure. The very thought of it made him smile with anticipation; at the age of forty-seven he knew that he still had some time left to him; having been denied a sight of the furthest sea to the east, the sight of the endless sea beyond the Pillars of Heracles would be equally as intoxicating – if Alexander allowed him to join the campaign and didn't force him to languish in the mire of Macedonian and Greek politics. He shivered at the thought and then banished it from his mind as he again admired his prizes and captives.

'That's a good evening's work, Antigenes,' Krateros said to the commander whom he had detailed to carry out the raid. 'Three ships, a pile of dead pirates and a nice long chain of slaves whose price will boost our war-chest.'

'I've kept a few of the prettier ones and a couple of the boys back for the lads to have a bounce on once they've burnt the dead.'

'Well done, they deserve a bit of fun after gaining three such good prizes; I might have a go with one myself once they've finished. It never hurts to be seen to be sharing the men's sport. Tell them they can keep anything they find amongst the ruins.' He looked out to sea, shading hazel eyes, to see two more biremes clearing the eastern point of the cove and nodded with approval at the timely arrival. 'Here's Kleitos with the replacement oarsmen.' He replaced his kausia and smiled at the thought of yet another job well done.

And that was how it had been since his arrival in Cilicia, three months previously, when he had resolved to wash two tunics in the same tub by destroying the pirate threat whilst building a fleet: sailing from Tarsus with three biremes, Krateros would land Antigenes and a unit of his Silver Shields a little distance from the target and then hold position just off the shore, preventing any escape by sea once the infantry set upon the village. Kleitos would follow in the other two biremes; one with replacement crews for any prizes captured and the other to put on a chase should a pirate vessel break out of the trap. It was a very successful system, Krateros allowed, and it was one which had the added bonus of keeping the Silver Shields busy. Veterans of Philip's wars, the men of the Silver Shields, so named after their silver-covered shields engraved with the sixteen-point sun-blazon of Macedon, were now all in their fifties and sixties; they had spent their lives on campaign and now were being pensioned off with plots of land back in Macedon, for it had been them who had been most vociferous in demanding that Alexander turn back. They said they wanted to return home but when Alexander had actually sent them home as they arrived in Babylon, as a punishment for curtailing his conquest, they had thought the better of it and had pleaded not to go. Still, Alexander had not relented and now, halfway through that journey, many wondered what a farm in Macedon would actually hold for them, old as they were.

Krateros had sympathy for them, for he too had been a soldier all his life and could not imagine being anything else. For their part, although they had ten to fifteen years more service than he, they loved him because they saw him as one of Philip's generals and, therefore, a man after their own minds: steeped in the traditions of Macedon before Alexander had watered them down with his embracement of the east. And it had been when this embracement had come to include the recruitment of foreigners, eastern foreigners at that, into the ranks of the Macedonian army he, Krateros, could remain silent no more. The words he had spoken to Alexander condemned him to exile from his presence in the form of leading the veterans home.

Although numbering now less than three thousand, they were still a formidable force; whether fighting in the phalanx with a pike or in looser order with a long-thrusting spear and a sword, as they did on these raids. They had spent their lives in the business of death and knew how to deal it out like few others. In short, of the ten thousand men Krateros was leading home, these were the most formidable and he needed them on his side as he had no idea what he might face when he got to Macedon to replace Antipatros. And that was one of the reasons why he tarried in Cilicia collecting ships: he foresaw conflict between himself and Antipatros, conflict that might only be solved by force of arms. The other reason was personal.

Smoke spiralled from the pyre and the cries of the captives selected for the amusement of the men rose with it. Circles formed around each of them as the Silver Shields cheered each other on as they took their turns at their pleasure. Krateros walked over to one of the groups; a grizzle-bearded file-leader was working a sweat up, tupping a howling youth of twelve or thirteen, held down by two of his comrades as the men around clapped hands to the rhythm. Krateros joined in the cheering, slapping a couple of men on their shoulders to move them aside so that he could join the circle. 'You fuck harder than you fight, Demeas,' he shouted over the noise.

Demeas, a hand grabbing each of the boy's hips, grunted as he thrust, unable to catch enough air to reply. With an increase in his rhythm, he came to a growling climax, cheered by his mates, and then, pulling out of the lad, he got to his feet and grinned at Krateros as another took up position and the clapping started again. 'I used to be able to fuck and make jokes whilst I was at it, sir; nowadays it's just one or the other.'

'Well, at least you can still do both. Enjoy your fun; you and your men did well today.'

'Thank you, general. Thank you for giving us this opportunity; we all appreciate it, as you know.'

Krateros raised a hand indicating that there was no reason to thank him and turned to inspect the newly arrived crews for the lembi who were boarding their new ships; nearby, the slaves were being hauled aboard Kleitos' two biremes, now beached next to his own. 'You keep your boys on the ship,' he called up to the triarchos, standing in the bow supervising the loading of the slaves. 'I don't want them getting in fights with Antigenes' lads over whose turn it is with the slaves.'

Kleitos, naked and with seaweed draped over his head and shoulders, waved his trident at him – he liked to play at being Poseidon when at sea, a foible that many thought blasphemous but it never seemed to do him any harm. 'Don't worry, general, most of my lads are happy with each other.' He grinned, before adding: 'By the way, there were another couple of ships following us half an hour behind, both of them ours. I don't know whether they're headed for here or going along the coast.'

But it was to the cove that the second ship was heading soon after the first, a trireme, painted jet-black, had passed with its oars dipping fast as if it were heading into battle. As the second ship neared the beach it was the wizened Polyperchon who Krateros saw standing in the bow; his second-in-command on the road back to Macedon.

Holding fast to the rail as the ship beached, Polyperchon belied his look of advanced years and leapt down onto the beach. 'General,' he said, striding over the sand with the ease of a far younger man, 'soon after you left Tarsus this morning an imperial messenger arrived.'

Krateros' heart jumped, perhaps Alexander had changed his mind and he would be spared the possible conflict with Antipatros. 'Well?'

Polyperchon rubbed his bald head and looked at him with rheumy eyes. 'Well, there's no other way to say this, general; but Alexander is dead these four days in Babylon.'

'Dead?'

'Dead.'

It was as if he were on a ship in a gale with the deck rocking beneath his feet; he looked at Polyperchon, trying to detect the hint of a tasteless joke in his lined and weathered face. There was none. The man spoke true.

Alexander was dead and the world had just changed for ever.

Krateros sank down, squatting on the sand, his left hand helping to keep his balance as his head reeled.

'Where does that leave us?' Polyperchon asked as another circle of men cheered a completed rape.

Krateros was silent for a few moments, blocking out all the sound. *Is that why I lingered here? Have the gods put Phila in my way to make me reluctant to go forward because they knew that I must soon turn back?* The vision of his new mistress lying naked on his bed in the palace at Tarsus distracted him for a few moments as he contemplated the swell of her breasts, her skin so pale and soft beneath his calloused-fingered touch; such love in her blue eyes as he caressed her sunset hair, almost the same hue as that of her half-brother, Kassandros; how two such different people could be sired by the same man mystified Krateros. And then Phila's face transformed into that of his Persian wife, Amastris, forced upon him at the Susa weddings; it was becoming easier to forsake her, Phila had seen to that. He shook his head to bring his thoughts back to the present and looked up at Polyperchon. 'What do we know about the situation in Babylon?'

'Only that it was to Perdikkas that Alexander gave the ring, but he did not name an heir; he said only: "to the strongest". But it was Perdikkas who sent the messengers out.'

'Perdikkas? He's no Alexander; he's not even a Hephaestion. He's where he is for his prowess on the field, not his ability in diplomacy or politics. Why Perdikkas? Surely Ptolemy would have been the better choice, or even Aristonous.'

Polyperchon scratched the back of his neck. 'I agree, but did you ever know Alexander to do anything without a reason?'

'Apart from burning down the palace at Persepolis when he was drunk, no. Even killing Kleitos The Black in a fit of rage had a purpose.'

'There, you have your answer, then.'

He's right, Alexander did this on purpose and it'll be us to suffer for it. Is that all the thanks we get after all these years? Krateros marked three points in a row in the sand and traced a line between the middle one and the one furthest away. 'If I go forward then the risk of conflict with Antipatros will be even greater because of Alexander's death; why would he possibly want to give up power now?' *And what would he say if he knew that I was bedding his daughter?* He then linked the middle point with the closest. 'But if I go back it would be seen as a declaration of war on whoever comes out on top in Babylon.'

'That's exactly how I saw it, general.'

Krateros smiled, it was wan. He rubbed out his sketch. 'Therefore we have no option but to wait here until we can decide who is the least threat: Perdikkas or Antipatros.' *But maybe Phila can help.*

ANTIPATROS,
THE REGENT

'EIGHT DAYS AGO? Are you sure?'
'Of course I am, Father,' Iollas
said. 'I saw the body myself.'
Antipatros slumped back down onto
his study chair and, resting his elbows on
the desk and rubbing his temples with his
fingers, stared up at his fifteen-year-old
son. 'How did he die?'

'Fever...Father.'

The slight hesitation in his son's voice caused Antipatros to
wonder whether that was the truth. *Would Kassandros really
have done something like that to protect me? No, but he would have
done it to protect himself as what would he be if I were regent no
longer?* He looked at Nicanor, his second son, in his late twenties,
the full brother to Kassandros and half-brother to Iollas. His
face, far more pleasing, open and full than his elder brother's,
showed genuine shock. *This comes as a complete surprise to him.*

'What sort of fever?' Nicanor asked, his voice quavering.

'They call it marsh fever or Babylon's bane; it affects the
lungs. Alexander had been wounded by an arrow which pierced
his lung in India and would have died there had Perdikkas not
have pulled it out.'

*That was more information than I asked for; Iollas is
unaccountably nervous. He was Alexander's cup-bearer, after all;
who better placed to poison the man? And who has more of a
motive than my eldest son? Is that why Kassandros insisted on travelling to Babylon to read my request for Alexander to clarify his*

orders to me when an ordinary messenger would have served? Antipatros got to his feet and walked to the open window; the sun was setting over Pella, the ancient capital of Macedon, laid out in a grid-plan around the central agora on a coastal plain. He stood, trying to take in the enormity of what had occurred, looking down from his study in the royal palace, perched on a small hill to the north of the square city. The sun, just clear of the mountains to the west, shafted down the east–west streets leaving the north–south thoroughfares in deep shadow. A chequerboard city; it was a sight he never tired of, he mused as he looked out to the port on the south side, where Iollas' jet-black trireme was berthed, connected to the sea five leagues away by a navigable inlet. *A sight Alexander will never see again; although, after the wonders he has seen, Pella would seem very dull, I'll wager. But to me this is everything, my whole life and should my sons have brought dishonour to me, then... Then what?* He took a deep breath of the evening air, laden with the scents of cooking and pine-resin, and turned to face the third of his five sons born thus far. 'So tell me, Iollas, what happened after Alexander's death from marsh fever?'

'And so I left immediately the compromise had been agreed,' Iollas said as he came to the end of his tale. 'Kassandros wanted you to know as quickly as possible, from a trusted tongue, that you had been named one of the council of four. I hardly slept for three days, using the imperial relay, until I boarded the fastest ship I could find, three days ago, in Tarsus.'

'Tarsus? Did you see your sister, Phila, whilst you were there?'

'Phila? I didn't know she was in Tarsus.'

'Yes, she's been there since her husband was killed completing the subjugation of the Pisidians.'

'If her husband is dead then why doesn't she come home?'

'I don't know; she's been coy about her reasons in the couple of letters she's written.'

'Well, I didn't have the time to see her, Father, as I had to get a ship; Kassandros had given me a warrant in your name and luckily I managed to get a swift vessel because there's a good choice there at the moment as Krateros is assembling a fleet.'

That news did not register well with Antipatros. 'For whom?'

'For Alexander...' Iollas' face showed gradual understanding. 'Oh, I see.'

'Do you? So this is where we are: there are four members of the council; two in Babylon, both good soldiers but one of whom, Leonnatus, is so puffed up in his vanity that failure to smile appreciatively at his sculptured good looks is enough for him to take permanent umbrage. The other, Perdikkas, is not made for the contest that Alexander has initiated, although he won't be aware of that and perhaps will continue unawares until he feels the blade slide between his ribs. Then there is Krateros, with the best troops in the army under his command, somewhere in Cilicia; and not only does he have the best troops but he also now has a fleet to transport them. And, finally, there's me here in Macedon with Krateros to the east with a mandate from Alexander to take over my position which, if I were to let him do that, would mean my death. To the south I have the restless Greek cities who will, no doubt, at Athens' behest, rebel once they hear the news and have time to get an army together; which will be early next year. And then to the east I have that Molossian bitch-queen, Olympias, lurking in Epirus, who will now do anything to destabilise me as soon as she learns of her son's death and she has no one to rein her in.' Antipatros thumped his fist on the desk. 'What is it with that woman that all she desires is power?'

'Doesn't everyone, Father?' Iollas asked, his voice forceful, taking Antipatros by surprise. 'Look at us: it's power that we're clinging to as a family. As you just said: you'll be dead if you give up your power to Krateros.'

Antipatros blinked, regarding his son with a new respect; he had grown in the two years that he had been away serving as one of Alexander's pages. He had evidently been listening and learning. 'You're right, Iollas, but Olympias is different from me in one major respect: I would preserve the kingdom and keep it safe and intact for the rightful heir to inherit. She, on the other hand, would ruin all that Philip and Alexander have built because, to her, power is the ability to behave as vindictively as you wish to your enemies and take whatever you want for yourself and your friends.' *Much like your older half-brother's view of power, unfortunately.*

Iollas' face showed that he was having difficulty in seeing his father's objection to his analysis of Olympias' motivations.

You too, Iollas? And yet you are Hyperia's boy and not whelped by my first wife like your two elder brothers. Zeus, why am I blessed with such short-sighted sons and yet have three daughters who understand that duty is to one's family before oneself. Antipatros looked with regret at his Iollas. 'Go on, leave me, both of you, I need to think. Iollas, go find your mother, she will be dying to see you after so long. But, mind, she's pregnant again.'

'Again, Father! But you're seventy-six.'

Nicanor grinned at his half-brother's prudish outrage.

Antipatros shrugged it off. 'And she's thirty-eight; what difference does it make? I'm still a man and she's a very attractive woman; in general, you'll find that pregnancy is the result of putting those two ingredients together in the same bed. Now go and tell her that I shall come to her rooms soon; I need to talk to her. And then don't forget to greet your sisters; Eurydike and Nicaea are both still here. *Yes, your sisters, Eurydike and Nicaea, as well as absent Phila. My beautiful girls; I'm going to have to spend each one of you well if I'm going to forge enough alliances to keep us all safe before I meet the Ferryman.* His sigh was long and deep. *Am I getting too old for this? If I am then it certainly is the counsel of the young that I need. Each day I thank the gods for Hyperia.*

'We need to deal with the threats in the order that they present themselves, Husband,' Hyperia said once Antipatros had acquainted her with his analysis of the situation, sitting in the shade of her veranda, looking north to the foothills swathed in pine forest. Her raven hair was ringletted and a single pearl hung on a fine chain at the base of her throat. 'And the first problem will be Greece. Demosthenes, for so long Athens' most anti-Macedon demagogue, remains in exile on Calauria and there he must stay. You should write to Aristotle and ask, in the name of the friendship that has passed between you since he was here as Alexander's tutor, to ensure that Demosthenes and Hyperides do not settle their differences; if they do they will most certainly carry the assembly towards exiling the leader of the pro-Macedon faction and then war will become inevitable seeing how much bitterness there is in Athens towards Alexander's Exile Charter.'

Antipatros groaned. 'Gods above and below, the Exile Charter! Why oh why did he force the Greek states to take back their exiles?'

'His reasons don't matter now, it's done. Since the decree was read out at the last Olympic Games every Greek knows about it. Athens hates the fact that it must give up its colony on Samos so that the original inhabitants, whom they expelled when they illegally annexed the island, can return. Unless you neutralise Hyperides and Demosthenes, they will use the Exile Charter as a rallying point for rebellion.'

Antipatros contemplated his wife's advice, resisting the temptation to carry on the conversation after a visit to the bedroom as he looked into her dark eyes and tried to ignore the pout of her lips. He took a sip of wine, closed his eyes and turned his face into the cool breeze blowing down from the hills to help his battle against desire. 'You're right, Hyperia; it's crucial to keep Demosthenes and Hyperides from reuniting and ousting Demades; if that were to happen then not even the pragmatism of Phocion would be able to stop the hotheads in Athens. I shall write to him as well, telling them what I fear; as Athens' oldest and most experienced military leader he must realise that war with Macedon is a foolish policy; he has but to point to the ruins of Thebes and remind the assembly that a quarter of the slaves in Pella, and other towns in Macedon, were once citizens of that proud but rash city.' Antipatros took another sip of wine and smiled at his wife. 'Yes, between them, Aristotle and Phocion should be able to keep the assembly tame and where Athens does not lead, the other cities cannot follow.'

'Precisely, but we must not take that for granted. We should mobilise once the harvest is in and send money to Thessaly and Boeotia to ensure their continuing loyalty; if you need to go south then it's vital that you have Boeotia to aim for and that you don't have a hostile Thessaly at your back.'

'Not to mention the fact that I need her cavalry. I'll be forced to leave a lot of my Macedonians here as I can't trust the Molossian witch not to persuade her cousin to take advantage of my absence; Aeacides would love to expand Epirus to the east.' Again he sighed long and deep. 'Why are we surrounded by enemies?'

Hyperia reached over and stroked her husband's knee. 'Everyone is surrounded by enemies, no matter how large or small the kingdom. The trick is to fight them one at a time or, preferably, get them to fight one another and do your work for you. That or, sometimes, just make them friends; which is what I suggest you do with one of your problems.'

Antipatros took his wife's hand and moved it to his thigh, pulling his chair closer to her to facilitate what he had in mind. 'Krateros?'

'Yes,' Hyperia said, keeping her hand firmly away from where she knew her husband wanted it to be. 'Have you noticed a rather interesting coincidence?'

'In what respect?'

'Tarsus.' She moved her hand a fraction higher.

'Tarsus? Phila's there. What of it?'

'And who else is there?'

Antipatros shrugged and looked down at the slowly advancing hand, feeling blood surging towards its objective. 'Krateros.'

'Well done, dear husband. And what do those two have in common?'

But Antipatros was finding it hard to concentrate.

Hyperia gave a look of mock exasperation, as if dealing with a gifted but obtuse child. 'Krateros has been there for far longer than he need; he could have had any one of his officers assemble a fleet and yet he chooses to stay.'

'Perhaps he's thinking of sailing his army to Macedon.'

'Now you're being really stupid.' She moved her hand further up his thigh. 'Do you happen to have your mind on something else? I've noticed with you, and I'm told it's the same with all men, you can have a very analytical mind and a very powerful erection but never both at the same time; apparently it's no coincidence. So I'll spell it out to you before I put you out of your misery. Krateros could have left in the spring but didn't; Phila became a widow in the spring and went to Tarsus, probably to take a ship back home to us, but didn't in the end. Now try to think with your head for a moment.'

With a mighty effort, Antipatros managed to tear his mind away from what those pouting lips promised. 'Ah, I see. You don't really think so, do you?'

'As the most important Macedonian in the city, Krateros would have been the obvious choice for her to go to for protection; she knows him, after all. Admittedly she was only a child when he went east, but still.'

'And she's…'

'Doing to Krateros what I'm just about to do to you.'

'The bastard!' Antipatros felt his ardour dying.

'Really? I'd say that he's playing right into our hands. He's coming back to Macedon with Amastris, the Persian wife whom he was forced to take at the Susa weddings. Don't you think he will be far more inclined to come home with a Macedonian wife?'

The decline in Antipatros' ardour reversed. 'Krateros as a son-in-law, not a rival? Now there's a thought.'

'Not only will Phila be marrying Macedon's greatest general – after you, of course, my sweet – but also she will be securing his fleet.'

'And if we go to war with Athens then we will be able to blockade the Hellespont and cut off her grain supply from her colonies around the Euxine.'

'And thrash her navy if she objects.'

'And I'll double the size of my army with the best troops Alexander had, who, until just now, I thought might be my foes. Brilliant! I shall write to the great general and make the offer.'

Hyperia wagged a finger at him. 'Impetuous man; don't write just yet. Let's see which way he moves, first, if he moves at all. Let's not give him what he wants until we know everything that we would like to gain from him.'

He took his wife's face in both hands. 'Hyperia, you are a genius.'

Coquettish was her look. 'Why thank you, kind sir. Do I get my reward now?' With a smile, Hyperia pulled away from his grasp and sank to her knees.

Antipatros closed his eyes and thanked the gods for wives and daughters, and always in that order.

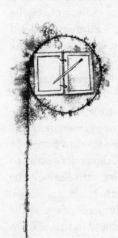

EUMENES, THE SLY

'You have no choice,' Eumenes pointed out for the third time.

Meleagros thumped his palm on the table, once again spilling his wine. 'I will not be talked into a corner by a Greek,' he growled, again for the third time.

And for the third time, Eumenes drew breath and tried to keep an even temper. *What is it with this brute that he fails to recognise the reality of the situation and instead thinks it's all some sort of Greek conspiracy?* He reflected on the observation for a moment. *Actually, I suppose he does have a point there, after all.* 'It's nothing to do with me,' he lied once more, for the third time. 'It was Perdikkas who ordered the city blockaded once he escaped the assassins you sent to kill him. And I can tell you, Meleagros, that had he not have faced them down and shamed them into slinking away, your situation could be a lot worse.'

'How could it be worse with Perdikkas dead?'

'Do you think every man in the infantry would applaud his death? The great Perdikkas himself, killed by Macedonians upon your order? Do you think even a half of them would approve, despite the current animosity between the infantry and the cavalry? Do you think that the Macedonians really want to start fighting each other after all their conquests?'

Meleagros was silent, frowning.

Eumenes looked across to Eukleides, seated next to Meleagros, silently beseeching him for help. All he received in turn was a puzzled stare. *Zeus, but it's hard work dealing with the Macedonian military mind.* 'A quarter of them, perhaps? No, they would have been appalled by the murder and you would quite probably be dead by now. Think! If even the men who volunteered to kill him couldn't do so out of shame and loyalty, what do you think the less extreme of the rank and file would feel?'

Meleagros clenched and unclenched his fists. 'Are you threatening me, Greek?'

'How many times must I say it? It's not me; I am but the intermediary. It's Perdikkas who is doing this; remember him? The man you drove out of the city when *you* tried to have him killed after he ceded the throne-room and Alexander's body to you. He's the one responsible. It's *his* cavalry patrolling all the gates on both sides of the river, along with Nearchos' ships, that's keeping the food out of the city.' Eumenes slapped his chest. 'It's not me, look, I'm here; I have no hand in this. All I'm trying to do is help the two sides reach a compromise before blood is spilt.'

As Meleagros contemplated this, Eukleides seemed finally to grasp the reality of the situation. 'Some of the lads are starting to complain about the growing scarcity of fresh food, sir,' he informed Meleagros.

'Who in particular?'
The ones paid by Perdikkas to do so.
'At the moment it seems to be mutterings in corners and that sort of thing.'

'What are they saying?'

'Well, they're blaming you for creating an impasse and are wondering whether you're qualified to lead them.'

That seems to be money well spent.

Meleagros scratched at his beard as if it were a badger that he was trying to remove from his chin. 'Root them out, Eukleides, I can't have my authority questioned.'

'And do what, sir? If you punish them then it will only cause more resentment and, with the cavalry tightening their grip around the city, it can only get worse because how can we take the phalanx out to face the cavalry on the plain without cavalry support on our flanks?'

Eumenes suppressed a smile. *And that's just the point; finally, you get there. Well done; I think you should both have a lie down after that.* 'If you agree to this proposition, Meleagros, then you'll be able to wheedle out the malcontents from your ranks once the deal is done and their support has faded away.'

'He may be Greek but he's right, sir,' Eukleides said with finality.

Meleagros had another go at his beard and then nodded his reluctant agreement to his colleague; he turned back to Eumenes, sitting opposite him. 'So the cavalry is prepared to accept Philip as king, if the infantry promise to accept the child of the eastern wildcat, Roxanna, as joint-king, should it be a boy; is that it?'

Progress at last. 'That's it.'

'And I am regent for Philip and become second-in-command of the entire army?'

'Yes.' *I think that's the part of the deal he really likes after years of just being a phalanx commander.*

'And Perdikkas stays as commander-in-chief and becomes regent of the half-breed if it's a boy.'

'Regent to Alexander's son, the Argead heir, yes.'

'And Antipatros and Krateros stay as regents in Europe?'

'Yes.'

'But what about Leonnatus? He's being left out now. Surely he won't appreciate losing his position to me as one of the council of four?'

'Sacrifices have to be made.' *And that particular one will encourage Perdikkas to accept the deal because it sidelines Leonnatus, who was foolish enough to show his support for Ptolemy.*

'And Perdikkas has agreed to this?'

One step forward and then another one back; how does the phalanx manage to advance so smoothly in battle? 'I don't know yet, do I? As I've said, for the last three days I've been going backwards and forwards between the two camps trying to work out a way by which one of you will recognise the other's king whilst foregoing your own. It is obvious to all by now,' *even to you, surely,* 'that it just won't happen; so the best idea that I can come up with is we have two kings out of necessity, as a compromise.' *Both as witless*

73

as each other, but never mind that small detail. 'Now, Meleagros, do you agree on behalf of the infantry that I can take these terms to Perdikkas?'

'Do you think he'll agree?'

Ah, so you want him to, do you? Excellent; you're as good as dead. 'I can but ask.'

'And why should I agree?' Perdikkas asked as Eumenes stood in his tent not long after; the sides had been lifted to allow a cooling breeze to flow through now that the sun was approaching the horizon. 'It may deprive Leonnatus of his position but I get an idiot as my second-in-command instead as well as a drooling fool as king. A king, what's more, over whom I have little control as Meleagros is his regent. And finally, if Roxanna does pop out a boy he becomes one of two kings or, perhaps, a half-king which would make me a half-regent.' He gritted his teeth and stamped his foot. 'Gods, how Ptolemy would love that, after accusing me of being half-chosen.'

Ptolemy did have a point; he's a clever lad. Eumenes put on his most sympathetic expression that had been well honed over years of dealing with the perceived slights suffered by these proud men. 'That's how it would appear on the surface but, consider this, Perdikkas: how would it be if the infantry agree to those terms – which they already seem to have done, having sent me to present them to you – but you end up regent to the fool and to the brat as well, should it be male, and with someone else as your second.'

'How would that happen?'

Enjoying the ambitious look on Perdikkas' face, Eumenes pointed to the pitcher of wine, it had been a long day.

Perdikkas poured them both a cup, offered one to the Greek and indicated that they should both sit down. 'I'm sorry; it was ill-mannered of me not to see that you were comfortable before we started talking.'

Eumenes was used to a lack of courtesy and, in fact, revelled in it as it meant he was being underestimated, understanding completely the value of being thus. 'Think nothing of it, my dear Perdikkas; these are difficult times for us all.' He made himself comfortable, took a sip of wine, *tolerable,* and sat back in his wicker-work chair. 'Tell me, Perdikkas, what is the first thing that a Macedonian general does once a dispute within the army, of some magnitude, has been settled?'

Perdikkas did not need to think. 'He purifies the army. Nothing else can happen until the Lustration ceremony has taken place.'

'Exactly. Now, assuming that you agree to these terms, what message would you send me back with?'

'I would say to Meleagros that it is agreed and we should have the Lustration tomorrow at the second hour after dawn.'

'And he won't even question that?'

'Of course not; he will expect it.'

Eumenes rolled his cup between the palms of his hands. *Now we shall see your aptitude for treachery, Perdikkas.* 'It so happens that the men you've been paying to sow discord in the infantry have been rather successful.'

Perdikkas took a sip and savoured the vintage whilst considering the statement. 'I'm pleased that I haven't wasted my money.'

'Meleagros wants to root them out from his ranks.'

'I'm sure he does.'

'I could suggest to him that the Lustration would be a suitable time to do it.'

Perdikkas frowned and leant forward in his chair. 'Do you think that I would be foolish enough in helping Meleagros rid himself of my agents?'

Eumenes raised a conciliatory hand. 'My dear Perdikkas; I did not for one moment imply that you should do that. I only said that I could suggest to him that the Lustration would be a suitable time to do it; however, I won't be saying to him that we *will* do it but neither will I say that we won't.'

'What do you mean?'

'Where would this Lustration ceremony take place?'

'The palace courtyard is big but not big enough for what we have to do so I suppose the best place would be out here on the plain.'

'And what would Meleagros say to that?'

Perdikkas shrugged. 'Well, he would agree; we have to purify the army, after all.'

'Especially as he thinks the ceremony will be used to get rid of all those who have been working against him and that you will help him do so as a part of the deal.'

Perdikkas' eyes narrowed.

I think he's starting to catch on. 'So, tomorrow you will cut a dog in half and take one piece to one side of the field and the other to the opposite side and then have the army pass between it whilst prayers and what-have-yous are said; all very pious. But, at the end, where will that leave the infantry?'

Perdikkas looked baffled by the question. 'On the plain, of course.'

'And the cavalry?'

The frown deepened. 'On the plain as well.'

'And the elephants?'

The notion was getting through to Perdikkas. 'On the plain with the cavalry.'

'And what happens to infantry caught, unsupported, out in the open, by cavalry?'

Perdikkas slowly smiled. 'Oh, Eumenes, you are a—'

'Sly little Greek?'

But it was not sly that best described how Eumenes felt the following morning as, sitting mounted next to Ptolemy in the front rank of the cavalry, he watched Perdikkas, with King Philip nominally assisting, sacrifice a substantial hunting hound in front of the army: it was apprehensive. Both infantry and cavalry were arrayed out on the plain, on the east side of the Euphrates, beyond the city's outer wall that enclosed the gardens which surrounded the entire eastern half of Babylon in a verdant swathe.

The sacrifice complete, the dog was cut in two, and then, to the accompaniment of the droning imprecations of the priests of Zeus and Ares, each half was dragged, smearing a bloody trail, to opposite sides of the field, north and south, a thousand paces apart.

With a blast of horns and a clash of swords on shields, the phalanx, without their pikes but drawn up in battle order, sixteen men deep, crashed forward with the thunder of twelve thousand feet marching to a steady beat. On they went, east, helms glowing brazen, with Meleagros and Eukleides leading them, as the priests kept up their prayers, cleansing the infantry in the eyes of the gods.

Eumenes turned to his neighbour. 'I forgot to ask you, Ptolemy, but how are the elephants this morning?'

Ptolemy continued looking straight ahead, shading his eyes against the morning sun. 'I believe they've had their breakfast and should be joining us at any moment.'

'How gratifying.'

'Yes, I thought so too.'

Eumenes glanced over to where Perdikkas now sat on his mount at the head of the cavalry formation with King Philip next to him, dressed again as Alexander and holding his elephant; his apprehension grew. *I hope the fool remembers what to do and I hope Perdikkas has the stomach to do this properly and then, perhaps, we can all get on with making ourselves fabulously rich whilst attempting to maintain Alexander's legacy in the most logical manner.*

The final rank of the phalanx passed between the divided carcass but the formation marched on further out onto the plain, three, four, five hundred paces, until, satisfied that there was enough room for the cavalry to pass between the sacrifice, Meleagros brought them to a halt; with much stamping of feet, the formation turned one hundred and eighty degrees to face their comrades. Meleagros and Eukleides then made their way through to the new front rank.

Raising his right fist, Perdikkas pumped it thrice. The calls of officers echoed along the line, five hundred men across and six ranks deep, and with the jangle of three thousand harnesses and clatter of twelve thousand hoofs, the cavalry moved forward at the trot.

Eumenes gripped his thighs tight to his horse's flanks, swaying his body to the rhythm of the beast, holding the reins in his left hand and with his right resting on his hip. The priests continued their dirge appealing to the gods to cleanse the cavalry in the same manner they had done the infantry. Through they went between the two halves of the carcass, horses snorting and whickering, bridles clinking and dust rising from thousands of hoofs; as the sixth rank cleared the sacred line, Perdikkas punched the air once more and again the cries of the officers rose from the formation but this time the order was much different, for it caused the formation to change. With the swiftness born of manoeuvring on many fields of battle, the cavalry formed wedges, eighteen in all, right across their line without breaking pace. Another air punch and another order shouted and the entire line broke into a canter; a communal moan rose from the phalanx as they realised their predicament.

With fifty paces separating the two arms of the army, Perdikkas brought his men to a halt.

Eumenes noted with amusement a smile flicker across Meleagros' face. *That will soon go.*

Meleagros turned and bellowed for order as disquiet grew within the infantry ranks.

'They don't look too happy, it has to be said,' Eumenes observed as he noted the concern on most of the men's faces.

'The same can't be said of Meleagros,' Ptolemy said, turning in his saddle. 'Ah, here come our guests. I'm always pleased to see the elephants; when they're on our side, naturally.'

'Naturally,' Eumenes agreed, craning his neck to see the two dozen surviving elephants remaining to the army of Babylon trundle onto the plain, trunks flicking and ears flapping; great bronze sheaths decorated their tusks and their mahouts sported gaily coloured tunics and turbans as they urged their beasts forward with gentle taps of their canes. At their centre, mounted in a howdah, stood the huge figure of Seleukos, whose command the elephant brigade had been before he had been given the Hypaspists as a reward for fine service. And now he was bringing his former charges out in support of Perdikkas. 'Although I must confess: being half the size of Seleukos it's hard not to find him as intimidating as a bull-elephant.'

Another moan rose from the phalanx and a thousand hushed conversations broke out.

At the sight of the elephants, Perdikkas kicked his horse forward and, accompanied by King Philip, rode to within twenty paces of the phalanx; the phalanx went quiet. 'Macedonians!' he roared, holding Alexander's ring aloft on his forefinger. His trailing white horsetail plume, decorating his helmet, fluttered in the breeze. 'For too long there has been bad blood between infantry and cavalry. On this day that blood is cleansed. But, as with the Lustration, which has cleansed the army as a whole, the bad blood between us needs a sacrifice. You will have noted your position, my friends. With one word from me the cavalry will be at your flanks, and then in amongst you; but that is not what any of us would want to happen. We cannot have Macedonian fight Macedonian; it must never come to that!' Perdikkas paused to let that sink in. 'We must put all this bad feeling behind us to ensure that such a challenge to the king's authority,' he shook the ring, 'and Alexander's authority, does not happen again. Here is your king.' He gestured to Philip, slouched on his horse next to him.

This will be interesting.

Startled by suddenly having to do something, Philip jerked upright in the saddle and looked around him in surprise.

Perdikkas hissed at him.

Philip nodded with slow understanding as the memory of his orders came back to him. He cleared his throat with a welter of drool and threw his head back; the words tumbled out in a rush: 'I command you to give up the three hundred foremost supporters of Meleagros for punishment.' The voice was surprisingly strong and, being naturally high, carried to all the members of the phalanx who gaped at the man they had chosen to rule them.

Perdikkas' relief at the king not forgetting his lines was apparent in his grim smile as he pointed to the elephants now just six hundred paces away. 'You do not have long to decide.'

Very nicely done, Perdikkas; that should concentrate their minds.

And concentrate their minds it did. Scuffles broke out within the massed ranks; some violent and bloody, others no more than an attempt to resist being manhandled to the front, as Meleagros and Eukleides, with the stark realisation that they had been double-crossed, slipped back into the depths of the formation

Perdikkas signalled behind him and a dozen troopers dismounted, bearing coils of rope. As the elephants arrived alongside the cavalry line, reinforcing it, the infantry produced their sacrifice; three hundred men, some resisting to the last, others accepting of their fate, were brought to the front by their own comrades.

'Bind their hands behind their backs and their ankles together,' Perdikkas ordered as the rope was distributed, 'and then leave them on the ground in front of you.'

'I do believe that our Perdikkas is rising to the occasion,' Eumenes commented with a satisfied countenance, his apprehension melting away. 'This is going to be far nastier than I had hoped.'

'Most gratifying,' Ptolemy agreed. 'A salutary lesson; one of the first rules of command. He's coming on a treat, our Perdikkas.'

And not asking them to give up Meleagros was a shrewd move; they might just have baulked at that. There will be plenty of time to deal with him later.

'Meleagros!' Perdikkas shouted, 'I know you're bravely hiding in there somewhere; never fear, I shall find you. However, in the meantime, order your command back one hundred paces; I don't want anyone killed accidentally.'

There was silence for a dozen heartbeats and then a horn rang out and the phalanx shuffled back, in a very unmilitary manner, the distance required of it leaving a line of bound prisoners on the ground before them.

It was not until the elephants took position, single-file, facing down the gap between the two formations that it became apparent as to what was to happen. Struggling against their bonds as they realised what lay in store for them, the condemned men shouted for mercy, prayed to their gods, pleaded with their comrades or just sobbed in misery that the last ten years should end thus.

But no entreaty could dissuade Perdikkas from his purpose, and that purpose was clear: to re-establish his authority; and none watching could deny that it was a fearsome way in which to do it as he signalled to Seleukos. With much trumpeting, the elephants rumbled forwards, slow at first but with a gradual increase in speed until the very earth trembled with their passing.

It was at full charge that the first heavy foot crushed the nearest head like a watermelon, spurting its juices wide in sudden explosion. And even the bravest of the three hundred screamed in terror at the sight; men, who had faced so many dangers and had risked their lives for Alexander on numerous occasions, soiled themselves at the sight of the towering beasts barrelling towards them, heads tossing, trunks waving and feet thundering. The pulping of the second prisoner's stomach and crushing of the third's legs sent the already writhing captives into heightened struggles to free themselves from their bonds. Some managed to get to their knees and a few even to their feet, hopping away from the oncoming menace in a ludicrous manner, bringing forth much mirth from the cavalry.

On the elephants came, each successive beast causing more damage to the stricken; pulverising them, grinding flesh and bone into a mash reeking of viscera. The kneeling men were bowled over by the first couple of beasts and then crushed by those following. Every life taken sent the marauding animals, trained to do just thus in war, into new frenzies as they dipped tusks and hurled broken carcasses into the air, spraying gore and vile juices over their wrinkled skin. One grim veteran, hopping for all he was worth, managed to clear the line of charge; cheered on by his comrades and laughed at by the cavalry, he pumped his bound legs back and forth, his hands tied behind his back, as an elephant veered aside to chase him. It was through his wrists that the tip of the tusk pierced him first, to then smash through his lower spine; his legs ceased to function but his weight was supported by the bronze-encased ivory that sheered up through him to burst out of his sternum in a spray of blood. With horror in his eyes he stared down at the gore-smeared protrusion for an instant before, screaming, he was hurled aloft, useless legs flapping free, to land in a crumpled tangle of limbs on unforgiving ground. Round his tormentor came, as its fellow beasts carried on down the shrieking line of prisoners – half now no more than so much jelly – to pummel its victim into the earth; back and forth it trampled, grinding what had once been a proud, Macedonian phalangite into a thick soup of cracked bone, gristle and gore.

'I don't think there'll be much stomach for defending Meleagros after this,' Eumenes said as another screaming veteran was tossed high and then caught, impaled, on a crimson tusk. 'They have their king, fool though he may be; although they all seem to have conveniently forgotten that he is half Thessalian and therefore just as much a half-breed as whatever Roxanna whelps.' He turned to give Ptolemy a pleasant smile. 'Half-breeds on the Macedonian throne, what next? Bastards?'

Ptolemy's return smile was equally as congenial. 'Sly little Greeks, perhaps?'

'There you go too far, my dear Ptolemy. Although I will gladly take a satrapy. I imagine that Perdikkas is fast coming to the conclusion that it would be folly to carry on with Alexander's plans to go west with the army so fractured.'

'Thus leaving it for me.'

Eumenes looked at Ptolemy in surprise. 'You're not serious, are you?'

'Not completely, but when I do get Egypt it would be foolish not to take Cyrenaica and then…well then we shall see.'

'I'm sure we will.' *Ptolemy in Egypt but looking west not east? Now that would be a most useful development; perhaps I'll keep my word to him after all and not come between him and his prize.* It was as the last man died, his chest crushed beneath a bloodied foot, that Seleukos signalled to his mahouts to restrain their beasts and rally them to the west of the cavalry. As the trumpeting died down, the army was left in stunned silence staring at the three hundred smudges of men as the horror of what had just been witnessed was processed.

Perdikkas let them dwell on the punishment for a few score racing heartbeats before he once again kicked his horse forward, with Philip at his side, to address the whole army.

Now he has their attention; now we can get down to business.

Perdikkas,
The Half-Chosen

PERDIKKAS LOOKED DOWN with distaste at the mush that had once been a soldier of Alexander, trampled into the ground. *No doubt I spoke to him at some point in the last ten years; perhaps even shared a joke or a skin of wine with him.* He looked along the long line of similar bloody blemishes spread along the frontage of the phalanx. *With each one of them I shouldn't be surprised. But it's their own fault; they pay the price for obstructing me.* It was with a tinge of regret that he reviewed his actions now that the executions were over, but he could not fault what he had done. *I had no choice; I hold the ring and my authority shouldn't be questioned.*

He raised his eyes to the solid block of the phalanx, whose ranks he had just purged, to see a mixture of fear and respect in the men's eyes as if they had understood the necessity of his act. *Now to give them what they want and then I can concentrate fully on keeping the empire together. Curse that Ptolemy for being right, we must consolidate and that can't be done by following Alexander's last plans. And curse that little Greek for making it impossible to reject this drooling idiot next to me as king.* He glanced sidelong at the figure of Philip, riding next to him, and was, as ever, reminded of the man's father and namesake, such was the similarity between them: strong chin and forehead with bulging brows, dark eyes and a thin mouth. Outwardly it would be hard to notice that there was anything amiss with him, other than his insistence on taking his toy elephant everywhere, shambolic hair, an almost constant inane grin that resulted in drool dribbling from the corner of his mouth and a tendency to wet himself when overexcited. In most other respects he seemed perfectly normal; he had a powerful physique and could – so Perdikkas had been informed – rut like a rabbit, being the possessor of a prodigious penis; however, he did have a propensity for overdoing things and more than a few of his partners – all of them slaves, naturally – had suffered grievously from his attentions, one had even bled to death.

It was within him that the problem lay; although he could reason, it was only to the ability of an eight-year-old child and it was as an eight-year-old child that Perdikkas would deal with the king.

'Are you ready to call the men to order, Philip? Remember, you are king and are allowed to talk to all the men at once.'

Philip looked at him, excitement in his eyes and a cheery grin on his face. 'Can I? Oh can I, please?'

'Yes you can. Tell them that you want them to listen to what I have to say.'

'Yes, yes; I'll do that. Shall I say something to them too?'

'No, just what I've told you to say.'

'What about that nice Meleagros who made me king? Should I ask them to listen to what he has to say as well?'

Perdikkas reached over and put his hand on Philip's arm, squeezing it, reassuring him. 'Don't you remember? Meleagros is a very bad man and nobody should listen to what he has to say at all, ever again. We're going to send him to meet the Ferryman.'

At the mention of the Ferryman, Philip became nervous, looking around in jerky movements as if Charon himself were stalking him. 'I don't like the Ferryman.'

'Yes, well now just do as I've said and don't worry about the Ferryman,' Perdikkas said, trying to keep the impatience out of his voice.

'Yes, yes, of course, Perdikkas.' The inane grin returned and a trail of drool fell from the corner of Philip's mouth. He took a deep breath. 'Macedonians!' The shout was shrill but, coming from within such a large frame, effective; gradually quiet became manifest over the field. 'Macedonians!' Philip shouted once more, warming to his task. 'I want you to listen to what Perdikkas has to say.'

Before Philip could have the chance to go off-script, Perdikkas urged his mount forward. 'Men of the army of Babylon,' he shouted, wheeling his horse around so that he addressed both the infantry and the cavalry. 'Through the blood shed today we have purged ourselves; we are now one again!' He paused and was rewarded with a cheer; giving him heart for what he was about to say. 'In the eight days since Alexander's death we have been at odds with each other but now we are united behind King Philip and the as yet unborn King Alexander.' This was greeted with more cheering. *Gods, if he turns out to be a girl then life will be so much easier.* 'When Alexander died he still had great plans; as you all know, we were due to campaign in Arabia to bring the peninsular within our empire. This was not to be just an idle conquest, it had a strategic purpose: it meant that there would be no hostile people to our backs when Alexander took us west.' This time his pause was met by silence and, judging by the look on the faces nearest to him, it was of the stunned variety. 'Yes, west. And it was to be with his new army of Asians as well as us, his loyal Macedonians.'

It never hurts to get them all fired up over Alexander's perceived favouring of the conquered, Perdikkas mused as mutterings rose from both infantry and cavalry alike. *At least they're united in their hatred of foreigners.*

'He was forming a fleet and was to lead us to the Greek cities in far-off Italia and Sicilia, as well as overland across Africa and on to Carthage, a place that few of you will ever have heard of. Then he was going to lead us to the Endless sea; another journey of ten years, perhaps more for, who knows, he might have been tempted by the legend of Hyperborea, the realm beyond the north wind.' The idea of such a desolate place caused uproar throughout the army and Perdikkas smiled to himself. He could now get them to do his bidding; he could now get them to do what he could not unilaterally do without fear of accusations of cowardice aimed at him in time: he could get the army to expunge Alexander's vision. 'Is that how you would spend the coming years, men of Macedon? Shall we bring Alexander's plans to fruition and set off on another journey of conquest? Shall we ride to bring fear into the hearts of the Hyperboreans?'

A resounding negative thundered from all present on the field; so loud, even, that it took Perdikkas by surprise and made his horse skitter. 'What was that you said, Macedonians? Shall we go?'

Again the answer was negative and again it was unanimous.

Perdikkas held his arms up for quiet and the roar rumbled down into a hiss of muted mutterings. 'Are you asking your king to cancel Alexander's plans, men of Macedon?'

And they pleaded with him now, pleaded not to go west; pleaded to stay in Babylon or return home, anything but go west.

'Very well.' Perdikkas turned to Philip, who seemed to be thoroughly enjoying himself by the size of the grin on his face. 'Tell them you're calling the army assembly and they can vote on the matter.'

'Oh, can I? That'll be fun; the army assembly, that's what made me king, wasn't it? I like the army assembly.'

'Good, I'm very pleased. Well, invoke it.'

Confusion caused Philip to frown as he tried to repeat the word. 'Imboke? Imvote?'

'Call the army assembly, summon it, whatever. Just put your arms up and when there is silence say that you are calling the army assembly to vote on Alexander's last plans.'

That seemed to satisfy Philip and he did as asked with a degree of fluency, Perdikkas was pleased to note. *Perhaps I can train him up so that he will be a decent mouthpiece for me; he may have his uses after all.* 'And what does the infantry say?' Perdikkas shouted once the question had been put to them.

'Cancel!'

'And what does the cavalry say?'

And the answer was the same; the army had rid itself of Alexander's vision and Perdikkas was free to do as he wished. *And now I can concentrate on preserving Alexander's legacy; bugger*

Ptolemy. Still, he was right: we consolidate and each take a satrapy to rule in Philip's name with me as his regent here in Babylon and with positions of honour for Antipatros and Krateros to prevent any bad feeling. As for Ptolemy, I suppose I'll have to give him what he wants, but I'll hobble him somehow; I'll contemplate it overnight. And Eumenes, that odious little Greek, if he thinks that he's going to get anything worthwhile he can think again; I know exactly what to give him.

'Kappadokia.'

'Kappadokia?'

'Yes, Kappadokia.' Perdikkas could barely keep a straight face as he regarded the outrage on the little Greek's face the following morning when the senior officers met before the empty throne; at the far end of the room, embalmers had finally begun their work on Alexander's curiously uncorrupted corpse.

'But it isn't even subdued yet; Ariarathes, the Persian satrap is still in place,' Eumenes protested.

'And you're just the man to go root him out.'

'And how am I supposed to do that without an army?'

'I shall write to Antigonos, commanding him to help you seeing as he has failed in his duty to Alexander by not already subduing it.' *Now this is the part that I shall really enjoy.* Perdikkas turned to Leonnatus. 'Hellespontine Phrygia?'

Leonnatus held his head high and looked down his nose at Perdikkas whilst flicking from his right eye a few errant hairs escaped from his Alexanderesque coiffure. 'What about it?'

'It's yours, which means that you and Lysimachus, over on the other side of the Hellespont in Thracia, will have control of all shipping going to and from the Euxine; very lucrative, I should say.' *Is that a big enough incentive for him?* By the look in Leonnatus' eyes, Perdikkas could tell that it was a tempting proposition, even though he knew that his pride was still wounded from his relegation from the regency.

'How have you come up with these appointments, Perdikkas?' Leonnatus asked after a few moments' contemplation; mutterings from the dozen other men around the table indicated that it was a question they all wanted answering.

Perdikkas cursed the man inwardly for forcing him to justify himself but realised that he had no option but to do so. 'There is no reason to remove Antipatros from Macedon, Menander from Lydia, Assander from Caria or Antigonos from Phrygia, so they stay. Krateros will share Europe with Antipatros, being his second-in-command. Lysimachus actually asked for Thracia as he's keen to have an unruly province to tame and to secure our northern borders against the Getae. Peucestas has learnt Persian and has taken to wearing trousers so is the obvious choice for Persis. Eudamus is welcome to India and the eastern satrapies are best ruled by the local men that Darius had appointed as they know their own people. Nearchos is having Syria and will take over the fleet that Krateros is collecting and base it in Tyre.'

'Oh, so you think Krateros will give that up, do you?' Eumenes asked, shaking his head in disbelief.

'Of course he will; I shall write and order him to do so.'

'Oh, good; how reassuring.'

Perdikkas glared at the Greek for a few moments before continuing. 'I'm staying here in Babylon to oversee Asia, with Archon as nominal satrap. Attalus, who marries my sister Atalanta this month, is in command of the river fleet and Seleukos will serve as my second-in-command of the army now that Meleagros is under sentence of death when we find him; Kassandros takes over from Seleukos as commander of the Hypaspists. Alketas is taking Assyria.' His brother gave a satisfied smirk. 'So unless you want Media, which I was going to allot to Peithon, or somewhere even further east, I could order Roxanna's father, Oxyartes, to give up his satrapy of Paropamisadae and see how he likes it; Hellespontine Phrygia seems like a convenient and rich choice. Or you could do as Aristonous has done and opt for nothing.'

'And what about Egypt?'

PTOLEMY, THE BASTARD

YES, AND WHAT about Egypt? Ptolemy had listened throughout the meeting, hoping to hear his name associated with that satrapy and was, by now, fairly confident that he should receive his prize as all the others had been allocated. It had been Perdikkas' manner during the meeting that had annoyed him most, and, judging by the mutterings from around the assembled, many of the others too. By having got control of King Philip, sitting, grinning inanely, next to Perdikkas, to the extent that the simpleton did everything his new master required of him, Perdikkas had manoeuvred himself into a position of absolute power. *Absolute power at least in Asia, as Europe is a different matter; as I intend Africa to be.*

'Egypt already has a satrap, Cleomenes, appointed by Alexander,' Perdikkas said.

'But he's a Greek from Naucratis,' Leonnatus protested.

Yes, and a very nasty one at that and probably more avaricious than me.

'Who has proved to be an effective administrator; whatever happens, he will stay in Egypt.'

That is not what I wanted to hear.

But Perdikkas was not finished. 'Which is why he will remain as second-in-command in the satrapy to advise Ptolemy when he takes up his post there.'

Now that is what I wanted to hear. But if Perdikkas thinks that he can keep Cleomenes there to be his spy, he can think again.

'Very well, Perdikkas,' Leonnatus said, after a brief look at Ptolemy, 'I'll take it.'

'Good,' Perdikkas said, in a tone that implied that he was enjoying himself considerably. 'I was hoping that you would as I'm sure that between you and Antigonos you will be able to help Eumenes pacify his satrapy, which will also include Paphlagonia.'

'But that is traditionally part of Hellespontine Phrygia.'

'Not any more.'

Leonnatus glanced at the little Greek and said nothing; his expression was eloquent enough. It was equally eloquent in his regarding of Perdikkas.

Ptolemy's expression remained neutral. *Perdikkas, Perdikkas, you really are a blunderer; if you think that arrogant narcissist is going to lift a finger to help out our Greek friend then you are sadly deluded. And as for the Resinated Cyclops, it's hard to tell who he hates the most, Greeks or little Greeks, either way, well... or perhaps you are aware of that and this is your clumsy attempt to give Eumenes nothing whilst being seen to be giving him a lot.*

'You're quiet, Ptolemy,' Perdikkas said, breaking off eye contact with Leonnatus.

'Are you expecting me to thank you, Perdikkas?' Ptolemy asked in a surprised tone. 'In fact, are you expecting anyone here to thank you for giving them only what they had earnt over the last ten years?' He looked meaningfully at Leonnatus and then Eumenes. 'Egypt is no more than I deserve; some here didn't even get what they deserved. No, Perdikkas, you may have Alexander's ring and you may have control of the king but you know that you are nothing without the rest of us. Only like this can we hold the empire together and so, therefore, in taking up our satrapies we are only doing our duty to Macedon and to Alexander's memory, as were you in making the distribution. I don't expect thanks for doing my duty and nor should you.'

'But I gave you Egypt, that was what you wanted, wasn't it?'

'Yes, it was. And you're staying here in Babylon to *oversee* Asia which, I would guess, is what you wanted – whatever it means. Everyone has got what they want, even Aristonous who asked for nothing; everyone except for Leonnatus and Eumenes. But

I'm sure they will deal with it, somehow, as will you have to deal with the consequences.'

Perdikkas stared at him in confusion.

You really can't see what you've done, can you? You've just pushed Leonnatus into the arms of Antipatros and, no doubt, Antigonos too, when he refuses your order for him to help Eumenes; and if you want any friends in that part of the empire then you'll be forced to help the little Greek win his satrapy yourself. But if you can't see that then I'm certainly not going to tell you; it would ruin the fun of hearing of your reaction when you do finally get there. 'Never mind, Perdikkas,' Ptolemy said with a warm smile, 'perhaps I'm just being gloomy in my assessment of your diplomatic skills.' He looked around the assembled officers of Alexander's army; men he had shared so much with; faces he knew so well and yet now felt that they were all receding from him, becoming strangers, as the bond that had held them together gradually dissolved. 'Well, gentlemen, I shall take my leave of you. I don't suppose that we shall ever all be together in the same room again so I would like to say one thing for the time that we have all shared; a time that I know, whatever happens in the future, we shall all of us always hold dear…'

The commotion at the other end of the chamber was sudden and violent, cutting Ptolemy off, causing all to turn towards where Alexander lay; the embalmers halted their work of emptying the corpse of its internal organs.

'I had claimed sanctuary!' a voice shouted from the middle of a scrum of men. 'Sanctuary, you godless scum!'

Well, well, our old friend Meleagros does have a very antiquated way of going about things; sanctuary? Really? How did he think that would help when the only option for anyone in this room is to see him dead?

'Where did you find him, Neoptolemus?' Perdikkas demanded of the officer in charge as Meleagros, bleeding from his nose and mouth, and with his tunic torn, was forced to his knees under the empty throne. 'Was it in a sanctuary?'

'You told me to seize him wherever he was,' Neoptolemus replied in his thick Molossian accent; the three men with him struggled to hold their captive down.

'Molossians have never troubled themselves too much with decency,' Eumenes observed, much to Ptolemy's inner amusement.

'Piss off, you undeserving Greek runt,' Neoptolemus spat, venom in his voice and hatred in his eyes.

No love lost there ever since Alexander promoted Eumenes to a cavalry command over our Molossian friend; that might be useful for me some day.

'I was claiming sanctuary in the Temple of Baal,' Meleagros insisted, refusing to give up struggling. 'They killed Eukleides on the altar steps.'

Neoptolemus shrugged. 'He's no god of mine or yours so why should you expect him to protect you?'

Why indeed, you foolish old man? And why, after all these years of brave service, did you take the coward's choice of sanctuary? Had I had any sympathy for you, I would have just lost it.

Perdikkas looked down at Meleagros; Ptolemy could tell that the same thought was going through his head. *That might be the first time that he and I have agreed.* 'The king has signed your death warrant for treason, Meleagros,' Perdikkas said, 'do you have anything to say before sentence is carried out?'

'I made you king!' Meleagros spat.

And now he makes you dead.

Philip's grin widened as he looked to Perdikkas for reassurance and held his elephant close to his breast. 'He did make me king, didn't he?'

'No, majesty, the army made you king; this man wanted to take advantage of that and use your power for himself.'

And you don't? Oh, Perdikkas, your blatant hypocrisy is something that we can all admire.

'Take him outside,' Perdikkas ordered, 'and make it dignified.'

With a couple of powerful wrenches, Meleagros broke free and jumped to his feet, spinning and crashing a fist into Neoptolemus' face, arcing him back with blood flying from a crushed nose. With a speed that surprised all for one so advanced in years, Meleagros chopped the side of his hand into the throat of one of his captors as he shoulder-barged another from his way to make a break down the throne-room.

'Get him!' Neoptolemus shouted at the uninjured guard, whilst trying to stem the flow of blood from his nostrils. 'Kill him.'

The guard pelted after the fugitive, whipping his sword from his scabbard as he pumped his legs with all the vigour of a young man.

Looking back over his shoulder, Meleagros saw that he was outmatched for pace and pushed himself harder, straight onto the outstretched foot of one of the embalmers. Over he went, crunching down on his chin, to slide along the polished marble floor. The guard was on him in an instant, knee in the small of his back and left hand pulling his grazed chin up; with no pause to verify his orders, the tip of his sword plunged into Meleagros' back. With bulging-muscle strength he forced his blade up into Meleagros who stiffened and then spasmed as honed iron cut the life from him.

That's the first one of us gone; ironic that it should be at the foot of Alexander's corpse, Ptolemy noted with a grim shake of his head; he looked around his fellow officers, all of whom were taking obvious satisfaction in the death of the man who had come so close to splitting the army. *I wonder how many of them I'll ever see again as I'm sure Meleagros won't be the last.* With a final, disbelieving look at the grinning king he turned to go. 'Goodbye, gentlemen; it's been great but that time is no more. I hope to see some of you again.' *Either on the dining couch or across the battlefield, depending on whether you help me or hinder me as I make myself Egypt's king.*

OLYMPIAS, THE MOTHER

SHRILL AND FELL was the scream that echoed through the corridors and chambers of the palace of Passeron, the capital of Epirus. On it went as a woman, of striking late-twenties beauty, ran, skirts lifted, with undignified haste towards its source. Pushing a frightened slave-girl aside, she crashed open a tall oaken door to barge into a high-ceilinged room, adorned with many images of women, and some men, copulating with snakes of all sizes.

At its centre lay a crumpled woman, in her fifties, emitting a wail that would quail the cold hearts of the Harpies. Her prostrate body shuddered with each new grief-stricken howl.

'Mother! Mother! What is it?' the younger woman shouted above the noise, shaking a heaving shoulder. 'Mother! Mother! Get a hold of yourself. What is it?'

With red-rimmed eyes, Olympias looked up at her daughter, brandishing a scrunched scroll in her fist. 'Ten days ago, Kleopatra! Ten!'

'What ten days ago?'

'Dead! Dead! Murdered by that toad, Antipatros, I shouldn't wonder, or that bastard son of his. Dead!'

'Who's dead, Mother?'

Olympias looked at her daughter as if she were the biggest fool in Epirus. 'Alexander, that's who. My son, your brother, Alexander. What will become of me now?' Ripping up the scroll, she threw the pieces in her daughter's face, howled and then began to tear at her hair, pulling it out in chunks so that the white, undyed roots were exposed.

With a shout to summon the help of the dozen slaves now hovering in the doorway, Kleopatra grabbed at the flailing wrists, restraining her mother as hanks of hair flew from her fingers. 'Hold her legs!' she screamed over Olympias' wails at a shaven-headed youth. 'Bring wine!' she ordered to no one in particular, sending at least four girls scurrying off in search of the beverage. 'Here, take an arm each,' she barked to two older slaves. 'Try to keep her still.' Kleopatra waited until the two men had firm grips on her mother before she clamped her hands onto Olympias' kohl-smeared, tear-stained cheeks and strained to halt the violent shaking of her head. 'Mother! Mother! Control yourself. Mother!'

Thrashing her limbs as the slaves attempted to hold her down, Olympias howled and wailed, oblivious to her daughter shouting at her with her face just a hand's breadth away from her own.

It was the suddenness of the first slap and the speed of the second that brought some degree of focus back to the mourning queen. Her eyes cleared and she stared in shock at her daughter. 'You hit me!'

'Yes, Mother, twice.'

'You *hit* me?'

'Yes, Mother, I did; and I'll do so again if you lose your dignity like that once more.'

Olympias turned her head left and right, eyeing the slaves holding her arms with a malevolence that forced them to quickly release their grip and back off; the youth struggling with the ankles dropped them and, with eyes lowered, retreated towards the door. 'I'll have you all whipped until I can see the white of your ribs,' Olympias hissed, her voice serpentine.

'No, Mother, you will not,' Kleopatra said, shooing the three slaves from the room with the back of her hand as a girl came through the door with a jug of wine and two cups. 'I ordered them to put hands on you for your own good; now drink.' She poured a cup of wine, handed it to her mother and dismissed the remaining slaves in the room.

Once the door was closed, Olympias pulled herself up and sat cross-legged on the floor, her hair awry and her make-up running; she took a long draft, swallowed and then steadied herself with a deep breath, exhaling long and slow. 'What's to become of me?'

'Mother!'

The sharpness of Kleopatra's tone startled Olympias; wine slopped over her dress.

'It's not just you, Mother, it's me as well. Now is not the time for histrionics; we must think the situation through logically.'

Olympias closed her eyes and took a deep breath. *She's right; thanks to Dionysus that I birthed a daughter not totally a prey to her emotions.* 'Very well, Kleopatra; I'll control myself and grieve for my son later.'

Kleopatra took a restorative gulp of wine and then refreshed both their cups. 'Now, calm as you can, tell me whom the letter was from and what it said exactly.'

Olympias thought for a few moments, sipping steadily. 'It was from Perdikkas and all it said was that Alexander had died of fever in Babylon leaving no named successor and his wife Roxanna pregnant. It's Perdikkas' plan to build a catafalque to transport the mummified body back to Macedon for internment in the royal crypt.'

'Perdikkas is organising this?'

'Yes.'

'So, he must have assumed Alexander's authority despite him not naming an heir?'

'Yes, I suppose he must have; that's interesting. You would have thought that it would have been Krateros as the most senior general.'

Kleopatra shook her head. 'He's on the way home; according to our spies he's in Cilicia enjoying Phila, Antipatros' eldest daughter by Hyperia.'

At the name of the regent of Macedon, Olympias hissed, 'I hope he splits her in two.'

Kleopatra ignored her mother's venom. 'So, already we have conflict as Krateros may feel that it ought to be he and not

Perdikkas who should take over Alexander's mantle. Therefore, the questions are: which way will he turn? East or west? When will he make his move? And which direction would it be best for us for him to choose?'

Olympias contemplated her daughter's thoughts; she downed the rest of her wine and then nodded, holding her cup out for refilling. 'You're right, Kleopatra: Krateros is the key. If he decides to go back then he won't replace that toad, Antipatros, as regent and I will still be excluded from influence in the governing of Macedon. So we must make sure he carries on west and ousts the toad by force if necessary.'

Kleopatra poured the remaining wine into each of their cups. 'I agree. But if you were Krateros, how would you make your decision, bearing in mind that he only has a little over ten thousand troops under his command and both Perdikkas and Antipatros have far more?'

Olympias thought for a few moments and then smiled. *I've taught this one well; she has the subtlety that I sometimes lack through impetuousness.* 'I would wait to see who makes the first offer of friendship to me, Perdikkas or Antipatros,' she paused and hissed as if the very presence of the name on her tongue was an abhorrence, 'knowing that my troops give me the ability to change the balance of power between the two of them.'

'Precisely; so we want Antipatros to approach Krateros with an alliance, not Perdikkas. In fact, Perdikkas must be seen as a threat to Krateros, one who needs to be countered.'

'But Krateros is meant to be replacing Antipatros.'

'When Alexander was alive, yes; but now that he's dead?' Kleopatra shrugged, raising her hands. 'Anything can happen.'

'So what will make Antipatros,' again she hissed as the name issued from her mouth, 'hold out the hand of friendship to the man who, by rights, should be taking his power?'

'War, Mother, war. In the morning we need to have an audience with the king – however much you resent him for ignoring you since he came of age last year and your regency ended. Put that behind you as we must convince him that he should make a few promises to the Greek states, Athens in particular. Nothing too overt: offers of friendship or mutual support in the difficult times ahead, vague hints about the injustice of the Exile Charter, that sort of thing; just enough to whet their appetites for freedom.'

'How will Aeacides be persuaded to do anything for me? He's refused to speak to me since he threw me out of the council chamber when I tried to claim my seat at the table.'

'Are you surprised after you hissed at him like a nest of snakes and tried to scratch his eyes out? I'm not. But now you have something he would want.'

'What?'

'Alexander's wife is pregnant with your grandchild. Aeacides' daughter, Deidamia, is two years old. What if the child is a boy?'

'What if it's not?'

'Will Aeacides want to risk losing the chance for his daughter to bear the heirs of Alexander? I think you can bend him to your will. And, what's more, you don't have to keep your promise to sanction the betrothal.'

Olympias studied her daughter, proud of her devious mind. *I forget that she was the queen of this country until her husband died and my nephew came to the Eperiot throne. Aeacides owes me for his ingratitude, banishing me from his council and giving me no influence after serving as his regent for six years. Yes, he owes me at least this and it could well work; if Antipatros is threatened from the south by the Greek states and we threaten him from the west then who can he turn to, at the moment, other than Krateros and his ten thousand just across the sea?* 'Yes, I see. And if we get Krateros to Macedon we can then play him off against Antipatros and that will just leave us finding a way of gaining influence over Perdikkas and then I'll be right back in the centre of power for the first time since Aeacides' coming of age.'

Kleopatra took her mother's hand. 'Don't you worry about Perdikkas; we'll deal with him when the time comes. First you must see my cousin, the king.'

'I don't trust you,' Aeacides said, his eyes narrowed as he looked down from his throne to his aunt standing, posed with jaw jutting and fist on hip; four armed and shielded guards separated them.

'Roxanna *is* pregnant,' Olympias insisted, her voice echoing around the stone walls of the colonnaded audience chamber.

'I've no doubt of that, dearest aunt; I too had a letter from Perdikkas.'

'You!'

'Of course, I'm the king of Epirus and am deservedly treated with respect. No, I don't trust that you will keep your word to marry the boy to Deidamia.'

'Deidamia is my great-niece, who better from my point of view to marry my grandson?'

'Who isn't even born yet.'

'Who will be born soon.'

'And if *he* is born a *she* then do you promise to marry her to my son who is also as yet to be born – or, to be precise, is yet to be conceived?'

Olympias frowned. *What does he get from that? A son of his can have no claim to the throne of Macedon even if he were to marry the daughter of Alexander; the noble families would never tolerate it.*

Kleopatra stepped from the shadow of a column half-way down the room. 'It's his price, Mother,' she said as if reading Olympias' mind. 'He gains nothing by it but prevents you from marrying a grand-daughter off elsewhere to better advantage.'

She's right; the odious creature exacts a high toll for a few letters.

'Who allowed you in here?' Aeacides demanded of Kleopatra, petulance playing on his boyish face.

'You must remember, Cousin, my husband sat on that throne before he was killed in the wars in Italia. I come and go as I please.'

'I should have had you killed.'

'And my brother would have returned the favour, which is why you didn't.'

'But he's dead now so what's to prevent me from indulging my wish?'

'Fear, Cousin, fear. Fear of killing anyone related to the man who so far surpasses you. You know you would be hunted down, and hiding behind your little throne won't save you. So enough of empty threats; are you going to do as my mother asks on such generous terms or are we going to be obliged to force you?'

'Force me? How?'

'If I told you that then the threat would disappear.'

Olympias stared hard at her nephew, disliking his pudgy lips and soft, rounded jaw; her daughter's husband, King Alexandros of Epirius, had been a real man, so opposite to this womanish boy. *Kleopatra should have succeeded her husband, not this proud but weak man. But those are the laws of succession and such is a woman's place in the world and she only gave her husband daughters: we can only rule through our men.*

Aeacides laughed, it was forced and hollow. 'Of course I'm going to do as you asked; in fact, there was no need to ask it of me as it was exactly what I planned to do when I heard of Alexander's death. It is to my advantage should the Greek states rise up against Macedonian rule; Epirus always benefits from a weakened Macedon looking another way.'

Olympias choked down her nose in disgust. 'A very shrewd observation, dear Nephew. I suggest you start with Hyperides in Athens and Demosthenes currently in exile on Calauria.'

'They were at the very top of my list, dearest Aunt.'

'The odious little shit,' Olympias hissed as she and Kleopatra walked from the audience chamber. 'Pretending that he had already thought of the idea in order to save face.'

Kleopatra waved a dismissive hand. 'I don't care how he couched it; the important thing is that he's doing as you asked.'

'Without you having to force him.'

'Exactly.'

Olympias was curious. 'Tell me, just how would you have forced him?'

Kleopatra turned to her mother and smiled. 'That's just the point, I couldn't. It was an empty threat but Aeacides is frightened enough of me to believe me capable of anything.'

Olympias put her hand to her mouth to stifle a laugh. *If only you had been born a man, Kleopatra, then we would not be in the state we now find ourselves; we would have the most suitable heir to*

Alexander. A frown slowly developed on her brow as her scheming mind churned. *Wait, perhaps there might be a way; a way which would have the advantage of me getting back to the centre of power without having to wait for the eastern bitch's whelp, if it is a boy.* Again, Olympias played through the scenario in her head. *Yes, that could work and it could also spell the end of Antipatros. It'll need good timing and I must keep it from Kleopatra as she won't like it, not one bit.*

PHILO, THE HOMELESS

WITH THEIR SECOND volley, the mounted archers perfected the range; arrows thumped with staccato reports into the round hoplon shields hastily erected into a protective wall and roof for the two-hundred-and-forty-strong unit of Greek mercenaries.

'Hold fast, lads! Hold fast!' The shout was muffled by the press of bodies, the front rank kneeling as the second, third and fourth crouched behind, all heaving ragged breaths of hot, dry air infused with sweat and garlic.

Another succession of juddering impacts hit the shields; a solitary scream rose and faded into a gurgle.

'Keep tight and close that gap!'

'We are keeping tight!'

'Save it for the horse-fuckers, Demeas!'

'We never get a chance to have a go at them before the cunts run, Philo!'

Philo did not bother to answer Demeas, crouching next to him in the front rank of the defensive formation, for he knew he could not argue with the man's assessment of fact. He would, however, be disciplining him for answering back as soon as they returned to Alexandria Oxiana, the mud-brick town on the Oxus river that it had been their misfortune to garrison for the past five years since Alexander had doomed them to spend the rest of their days so far out in the wilderness. *Curse the arrogant young pup for leaving us here.* He braced himself as three arrows from the next volley thudded into his shield and then risked a peek through a narrow gap. Fifty paces away, swarming about on small, hardy mountain ponies, the Bactrian tribesmen released another ragged volley, as much aimed at the hoplites as at the caravan sheltering at their rear. Behind their double-humped Bactrian camels, loaded with goods, cowered the twenty merchants Philo and his men had been escorting along the Persian Royal Road, since it had crossed into Bactria from the satrapy of Sogdiana. *Not that borders make any difference out here in these wild fringes of empire,* Philo reflected, resealing the gap as a black speck suddenly grew into a shaft hurtling towards him. His shield bucked as the arrow cracked into its rim where his eye had been a heartbeat before. *Such is the randomness of life and death.*

'They'll soon tire of this, lads; they always do,' Philo shouted, to boost his men's morale as well as his own. But it was true: the tribesmen always did tire of peppering the caravan escorts with arrows and withdrew into the arid, treeless fastness whence they had appeared; it was the way of things as they would never dare to charge close formation hoplites with their long thrusting-spears, even though they were caught out in the open. Nor did they have the patience nor the ammunition to gradually whittle them down; and so they would make one or two more false charges and rallies, releasing arrows forwards and backwards, whilst some of their number would salvage anything they could from the few camels that they may have brought down in their initial attack, provided they were far enough away, which, today, they were not. Three camels, one still writhing and screeching with pain, lay just twenty paces from the hoplites, their loads strewn about them. *The bastards will let us go soon enough so that they can get at that haul,* Philo reflected with relief.

And thus was life on the eastern frontier of Alexander's so-called empire. Philo always failed to suppress a smile when the concept of empire crossed his mind, for, to him, an empire was a united entity and what he was witnessing most certainly was not; here there was no central government, no sense of identity, nothing but barbarism and despotism. He and his men were the only link to what any Greek would consider as being civilized and, despite his profession, Philo considered himself to be civilized in a most refined way.

Educated to the highest degree on his native Samos, he and his family had suffered from Athens' annexation of the island, forty years previously, and exiled. Homeless, rather than seek the charity of others, at sixteen, Philo had left his wandering kin to sell the one thing of value that remained to him: his strength of arm. Selling the last of the possessions that they had managed to escape with, he and his family had raised just enough to purchase the hoplite panoply of helmet, hardened-linen cuirass, hoplon, sword and greaves and with that he had gone to serve in the army of Darius, the third of that name, the Great King of Persia. Life had been good and pay regular for thirty years, thirty years in which he had managed, with his earnings, to see his family settled in a fine house in Ephesus, just across the water from their stolen island. Thirty years in which he had risen to be a chiliarch of hoplites in the pay of the Persian empire and had become accustomed to the finer things in life that service to the Great King could bring. But then the arrogant pup had come to turn his world upside down for a second time, brushing aside the Persian army at the River Granicus and then again three years later at Issus where he, Philo, had been captured.

'Get ready to make a move, lads,' Philo shouted as he felt the incoming missile-hail lessen; he risked another quick look through a gap and, sure enough, the tribesmen were beginning to draw back as their quivers emptied. 'How many casualties, Lysander?'

'One dead, sir,' Philo's squat second-in-command on this mission shouted from the back of the formation, 'and four injured, one seriously.'

'Bring them all with us when we go. No one's to be captured alive or dead, these horse-fuckers impale anyone.'

For a captured mercenary the choice between death or enlistment on the same terms in the victorious army is an easy one; and so Philo found himself serving Alexander, the man who would push the limits of glory further than they had ever gone before; but those limits were only for himself and his Macedonians and not for the thousands of men of different blood who marched with them doing the hard, dirty work, the thankless tasks deemed too menial for the invincible soldiers of Macedon. So, throughout the campaign, guard duty, punishment raids showing no mercy to all alike, convoy escort and other dishonourable and unenviable assignments had been the lot of Philo and his men. When, at last, Alexander had caught up with the fleeing Darius, high in the Persian uplands at Guagamela, the Greek mercenary hoplites had been placed in reserve, showing just what contempt the Lion of Macedon held for them. It had been this display of contempt that had infused the men's minds so that, as they came to Bactria and Sogdiana, they had decided that they had had enough and now was the time for returning home; home to the sea.

But Alexander had other realms to conquer and, as he set out to cross the mighty Indus river, he had refused to release the disenchanted mercenaries, distributing them instead amongst the new towns he had founded for the Greek colonists flooding east in the hopes of bringing Greek civilization to barbary. And yes, the plays of Euripides had been performed on the banks of the Oxus; and yes, Homer was read in Alexandria Oxiana; and the drachma was the accepted currency in the bazaar of Zariaspa; and the ideas of Plato, Socrates and Aristotle were discussed at symposiums in Alexandria Margiana and Nautaca; but a monkey reciting philosophy is a monkey no less and Philo felt nothing but contempt for the airs and graces of the colonists.

Knowing who Aristophanes was does not mean that you can appreciate his verse, however Greek your blood is, for it was, in general, the poor and uneducated, those who had struggled back in the west, the meek, who had made the hazardous journey east in the wake of the all-conquering army. And the meek make the worst masters, Philo had observed time and

106

time again as the colonists, who now found themselves on top, clashed with the indigenous tribes over rights, land ownership and status. So it fell to him and his men and many others like them, scattered far and wide over the eastern satrapies, to keep the peace and preserve the law. The satraps themselves were not going to do it unless there was a profit or some other gain in it for them because the satraps were the very warlords who had ruled the area before the coming of Alexander and, once he had departed east, they went back to how things were before. So it was that these tribesmen attacking Philo's command were men who should have been fighting alongside him, for they were Batricans loyal to Oxyartes, the local satrap of neighbouring Paropamisadae and father-in-law to Alexander himself.

'Front rank, keep your shields up!' Philo ordered as the last of the horsemen withdrew well out of range, 'and left turn!'

His men, all two hundred and forty of them, exercised the manoeuvre with tolerable proficiency, considering the circumstances, with the front rank rising to their feet, still presenting their shields to the enemy as the four lines turned into a column, keeping between the Bactrians and the caravan.

Philo pushed his way through the formation to take a place at its head. 'Forward at the double!'

The column broke into a jog, ragged at first but then sliding into step as they picked up speed. To their left, the merchants goaded their camels into their long, ungainly strides so that the caravan kept pace with their protectors.

'Stop them!' Lysander yelled from the middle of the formation.

'What is it?' Philo shouted, turning to look back down the column.

Two of the merchants were pelting back towards the three camels that had been brought down in the initial attack.

Idiots. 'Leave them, Lysander,' Philo ordered, breaking from the formation and running back down through the caravan.

Reaching their stricken beasts, the two merchants scrambled to gather up bags, slinging them over their shoulders, all the while glancing up at the column, now more than a hundred paces distant, which jogged away from them at a steady speed.

Philo stood still, letting the caravan pass to either side of him, watching the two men and shook his head as he saw a group of horsemen whoop, kicking their mounts into a gallop. Seeing the incoming danger, the two men snatched up another couple of items and sprinted away.

Philo turned, unwilling to watch the inevitable occur, as the riders closed with the merchants whose greed had just cost them their lives.

'They pay dearly for goods that should cost no more than silver,' one of the merchants commented to Philo as he walked back to his position at the head of the column.

'Their choice.'

The merchant, dark-skinned, hook-nosed and with sunken, but twinkling, brown eyes looking out from beneath a white headdress, inclined his head, one hand across his chest. 'Perhaps. Or perhaps they had no choice as it was all they had and to lose it would mean ruin. In this life we can't always make the choices we would wish to. Good sir, my name is Babrak of Cabura and we Pakthas have a saying which, if I translate it from our Pashtun language renders thus: There is a boy across the river with a bottom like a peach, but, alas, I cannot swim.'

Philo looked at Babrak, wondering just what he was getting at.

'Good sir, we cannot always have what we want and especially if we have deficiencies; it is not the fault of the river that I cannot reach the object of my desire but rather my deficiency in having never learned to swim. Those two men would have chosen life had they been able to afford the loss of their goods; but they couldn't so they had the choice made for them by their own deficiency in coinage. We are not all lucky enough to get to have a taste of the peach.'

It was with resignation to the way of things in the east that Philo sighted the walls of Alexandria Oxiana; the screams of the captured men echoed across the barren land as the sharpened points of stakes began the slow process of rupturing their way up through their innards.

'Philo, there's a messenger from Babylon,' Letodorus, the

garrison commander, said as the column trudged through the town gates into the agora, exhausted from their exertions.

'Tell him to wait until I've bathed,' Philo said, complete disinterest in his voice.

'I think you'll want to hear his message immediately, Philo; even stinking as you are.'

Philo looked at Letodorus, twenty years his junior, and could see that he was in earnest; with a sigh, he turned to follow him towards the garrison headquarters.

'Over a moon ago?' Philo asked the question slowly, trying to digest the momentous news that had caused him to slump down into a chair and reach for the wine jug.

'Yes, sir, of swamp fever, so they say,' the messenger, filthy from travel, replied, eyeing the wine. 'I saw the body before Perdikkas sent me out.'

'So there is no doubt that he is actually dead?' Philo could scarce control the excitement that was mounting within him. 'There can be no mistake?'

'No, sir; Alexander is dead and by now almost the whole empire must know.'

'Gods be praised.'

The messenger looked confused. 'What did you say, sir?'

Philo looked the man in the eyes. 'I said: gods be praised. And I said it because the monster is dead and, perhaps, at fifty-six, my life can start again.'

'But he was glorious; he led us to victory after victory.'

Philo pushed the wine jug towards the messenger. 'Did he? That may have been true for you but for me he did nothing but lead me and my men here, to this prison without bars in this desert land so far from the sea. Now he's gone, we're free.' Philo turned to Letodorus, grinning uncontrollably. 'I think we should call an assembly.'

Letodorus grinned. 'I think we should.'

Philo looked down from the dais, set in front of the garrison headquarters at the edge of the parade ground, at the five hundred Greek mercenaries who made up the garrison of Alexandria Oxiana; sweltering in the heat that tormented them for months on end, their astonishment at the news was palpable. 'And so now we have to decide whether our duty is to this wasteland, guarding it for no other reason than we've been ordered to as a punishment? Or do we do our duty to ourselves and march west to the sea?' He paused to let the question sink into the men's minds; scores of conversations sprung up, animated by the excitement that most of them had expressed when they had been told of the death of the man who had doomed them to this place.

Philo indulged the talk for a few dozen heartbeats before signalling for silence. 'We must not forget, Brothers, that we have had false news of Alexander's death before, almost three years ago, when we heard that he had been hit in the chest by an arrow. We all know what happened to the garrisons who were caught trying to make it back to the sea then: they were executed almost to a man. However, a few were not caught and did get home, thus proving that it can be done. But the difference between then and now is that we know for certain that the tyrant is dead.' He pointed to the messenger, standing with Letodorus to the rear of the dais. 'This man saw his body laid out in state in the great throne-room at Babylon before Perdikkas sent him to us with the news. There can be no doubt that Alexander is no more.' This brought yet another cheer from the assembly. 'And what we must calculate is this: will his death make it easier for us to desert our posts or will whichever uncouth Macedonian who takes up the reins of power be as uncompromising in their treatment of us Greeks as the monster was. And even if they are, my brothers, it still comes down to this basic question: do you want to die here or do you want to die trying to get home to see the sea one more time? I know what I choose, now do you?'

The roar was unequivocal; Philo smiled at the sight of hundreds of full-bearded faces now filled with a hope that had been absent for all the years stranded in the arid limits of the empire. Some were men like himself, homeless; whether from annexation of their lands as in the case of Samos, or from the destruction of their city, such as Thebes. Others were younger sons forced to seek a life of paid military service in lieu of inheritance and the rest were adventurers or outlaws. But all had one thing in common: a love of the sea; the sea that some had not seen for seven years since Alexander had left Egypt and headed into the heart of the Persian empire in pursuit of Darius.

'The sea! The sea! Sea! Sea!' The chant rose over the cheers and soon it echoed around the dun-coloured mud-brick walls of the parade-ground; the visions of a blue expanse of undulating water sparkling beneath a warming sun and cooled by salt-tanged air, or of a sandy beach with soft breakers washing over it or, even, just the thought of standing ankle-deep in its cooling waters and watching a ship sail by, gave volume to the shout until all chanted with one voice, punching their fists into the air in time to the rhythm.

Philo raised his palms and appealed for quiet which came reluctantly, such was the men's excitement. 'Since the Exile Charter was read out at the Olympic Games last year forcing the Greek states to take back their exiles, many of us now have homes to go to. I, for one, am free to return to my ancestral home of Samos and those of you who are also exiles may do the same.' Philo took a moment to compose himself into a sombre, concerned countenance. 'But our homes are far away and we are few, my brothers; we would stand no chance, a small band such as we, trying to make it back over a thousand leagues. We would be prey to the first Macedonian garrison we came across and they would show us no mercy.' That thought took some of the enthusiasm out of the faces of his audience. 'So, therefore, we need strength in numbers. Do you imagine that we are the only garrison out here who yearns for the sea? There are dozens of them and each one is our size, or larger. I move that we should send out messengers to every one of them, suggesting that we go together in the spring. There will be thousands of us, an army. We will make Xenophon's ten thousand seem like a trivial affair. We shall write a tale that will be told through the ages. So follow me, my brothers, follow me and we shall walk out of the desert and come to the sea.'

It was almost rapture that greeted this line; Philo spread his arms and soaked up the adulation. *The gods grant that the Macedonians let us go; having faced their phalanx at Granicus and Issus, I have no wish to do so again.*

Roxanna,
The Wildcat

HER SON WAS strong as he kicked within her; stronger than she had dared to hope. Roxanna placed both hands on her distended belly, the skin stretched tight over it, and waited for the baby to settle. It would not be long now, just a matter of days; two-thirds of a moon at the most. *I could weep with the injustice of it; to give birth a little more than two months after Alexander's death.* She raised her finger over her shoulder to where her slave-girls awaited on their knees, and heard the soft padding of one approaching the couch upon which she lay, looking out of the window, east along the Royal Road towards Susa.

She winced as another kick, stronger than the rest, caused a bulge in her tight flesh; as the baby settled, Roxanna signalled for the girl to come to where she could see her. With eyes to the floor, the slave knelt before her. Roxanna contemplated the girl for a few moments. *I suppose she could be called pretty; she might be able to excite a man.* She looked back down at her swollen stomach, the belly-button pushed out grotesquely, and felt disgust. *Who would want me as I am now; who will ever want me again? Whereas this lucky little bitch will get rutted as much as she wants.* The slap to the girl's face was as loud as it was sudden; she fell sideways to the ground. Roxanna smiled with satisfaction as the girl whimpered, holding her cheek; with an effort, she pushed herself back up to her knees.

Why did I do that? The thought intrigued Roxanna. *Does a queen need reasons?* Again she slapped the girl, who now started to cry.

'Silence!'

With terror in her eyes, the girl sniffed and swallowed as she tried to get a hold of her emotions. Her obvious fear pleased Roxanna, as did the swelling growing on her eyelid. *You won't be quite so pretty tonight, little bitch.* She immediately felt better about herself and took a sip of the sherbet drink, iced and frothy in an engraved glass, enjoying the prickly sensation on her tongue. She frowned, remembering why she had called the girl in the first place. 'Summon the steward of this place.'

With a bob, the girl reversed away from the couch. Roxanna continued her staring out of the window along the empty Royal Road. *Where are you? You should have been here days ago; it's over a month and a half since Perdikkas sent you the summons.* Alexander's Persian widows' tardiness had become a matter of deep concern for Roxanna as she had waited, for the previous half-moon, in the royal hunting lodge two days' journey from Babylon. The lodge had always been used as a staging post in the royal progress along the road to or from Susa. Should her time come before Stateira and Parysatis' arrival at the lodge, Roxanna knew that she would not be able to do as she had planned; that would be a disaster, for if the Persian widows were to reach Babylon then Perdikkas would protect them no matter how much Roxanna threatened him. Again she held her belly as another series of kicks caused her to draw a deep breath. *Quiet, my son, settle down and bide your time. I must administer death to make you safe before I give you life.*

A low cough from the door, behind her, told Roxanna that the steward of the hunting lodge had arrived. She did not look around nor invite him to enter. 'Well?'

The steward did not reply at once.

The fool must know what I'm talking about.

'Begging your majesty's pardon,' the steward said, his soft, eunuch's voice weak with fear.

'No, steward, I do not give my pardon. I asked you a question, so answer it.'

The steward swallowed. 'If it is after the royal progress that you are enquiring, majesty, then I'm pleased to announce that the queens will be here by nightfall. A messenger arrived here within the last hour to instruct me to make the royal apartments ready.'

'I am in the royal apartments.'

'With respect, majesty, you are in one of the royal apartments. There are four more, other than the Great King's personal suite.'

'I shall inspect them and you will find much cause for sorrow if I feel I've been placed in lesser accommodation.'

'Azhura Mazda forbid the idea, majesty. Here, only the best is good enough for the mother of Alexander's child, majesty.'

'Son!' Roxanna corrected.

'Indeed, majesty, Alexander's son.'

I hate his obsequiousness. But he may be of use to me so I'll let it go unpunished – for the time being. 'Very good. Inform me when my royal sisters arrive. In the meantime, have all the uncastrated slaves removed from the grounds and forbid access to my royal sisters' guards; we will enjoy our stay far more if we don't have to be veiled. Send a message to them informing them of the arrangements to which I'm sure they will both agree. I will meet them personally as they arrive.' With a lazy wave, she sent him on his errand.

'We are happy that you have done us the honour of riding out from Babylon to meet us, Sister,' Stateira said. Her pale face, slender and sharp-nosed with huge, dark eyes and full lips, was guileless and her voice genuine. With long legs beneath clinging silk, she stepped down from the travel coach, designed more for comfort than practicality, drawn up in the central courtyard of the lodge; a flurry of eunuch slaves with brightly coloured parasols shielded her from the sun, still strong even as it sunk towards the west. Beyond the open East Gate to the complex, the queens' bodyguard of Persian nobles set up camp.

'Especially in such an advanced state of pregnancy,' Parysatis added, appearing equally as pleased to see Roxanna as her cousin, whom she resembled closely in features and stature.

Beautiful in the tall, lithe and pale-skinned Persian fashion, both of them; but they're nothing but pampered court flowers.

Roxanna's smile was sweet and broad; she did not rise from the wicker chair set beneath an awning next to the raised well at the courtyard's centre. 'My dears, it was the least that I could do as we all share the gloom of widowhood. I wished for us to be acquainted before we grieve for Alexander together as is only right and proper that we should. A man as great as he should have no end of mourning for him; it is down to us to take the lead. Now we are all together we will be able to do justice to this grief.'

With Roxanna's refusal to rise to greet her guests, the battle lines were drawn.

A trace of iciness flickered in Stateira's eyes; she did not approach Roxanna. 'I will gladly have you mourn by my side, Sister. When Perdikkas wrote to us inviting us to Babylon to grieve, we felt nothing but gratitude that our positions should be recognised.'

So, she will not stoop to kiss me and she wishes me to be by her side rather than she at mine; it's as I thought: she considers herself my superior. How right I was to have planned this. Roxanna pointed to the steward, sweating in the full glare of the evening sun. 'My dears, that man has readied your accommodation and I have ordered him to prepare the baths for you to wash away the dust of travel. I trust you will not be discomfited by the exclusion of your guards from the lodge; I thought it would be more relaxed if we did not have to veil ourselves. All the male slaves remaining here have been fully castrated and I myself travelled here with just eunuchs for guards and doctors, as well as my slave-girls and some midwives.'

'An admirable thought, Sister.' Stateira's smile was now fixed. 'You are kind to think of our comfort; we shall enjoy bathing after the rigours of the road.'

'Please take your time, my dears, I have commanded dinner to be served at the setting of the sun but that can always be delayed should you wish.'

'That is most considerate, Sister; we have had little to sustain us on the journey today as we both suffer from a delicate stomach when travelling.'

You poor palace-flowers don't know the meaning of a delicate stomach, but you soon will. 'I look forward to our meal together.'

'And this was our royal grandmother's favourite dish,' Stateira claimed as the steward supervised two of Roxanna's slave-girls with a large silver platter laden with grilled spatchcock quail rubbed with a red spice; the slaves placed it on the low table the three women shared. 'The summaqa brings out the delicacy of the meat, provided it has not been overcooked or over-spiced.'

That's why I had it served this evening. 'I was sorry to hear of Sisygambis' death,' Roxanna lied, helping herself to a grilled bird, placing it on her plate before dipping her greased fingers in a bowl of water and wiping them dry. With a wave she dismissed the steward and the two slaves. 'The whole empire mourns for her.'

Stateira inclined her head a fraction. 'You are kind, Sister. It was a tragedy, but one that our royal grandmother chose to make. The news of Alexander's death was too much for her.' She plucked a quail from the platter and pulled a leg off; the flesh, perfectly cooked, gave way with ease. 'After the death of my royal father, Darius, Sisygambis considered Alexander as an adoptive son; one son she could bear to lose but two was too much for her.' She shook her head with regret and nibbled the flesh from the bone, chewing on it in such a refined manner that her jaw barely moved.

'So she locked herself in her room,' Parysatis said, picking up the tale as she too took a quail, 'and refused food and drink. She was dead within four days, such was her desire to leave this world and be reborn in the light of our lord.'

'I admire her willpower.' Roxanna said, pulling off a wing, skinning it at leisure and then discarding both the skin and the flesh on the side of her plate.

'She was ever a formidable woman,' Parysatis confirmed before taking a delicate mouthful of breast.

Stop talking so much and eat. Roxanna struggled not to appear impatient as she once again washed and dried her fingers. 'Alexander always spoke to me of her with respect and referred to her as his mother. I believe that Olympias, his real mother, got to hear of it; I doubt there will be any condolences sent to Susa from Epirus.'

Parysatis swallowed her mouthful. 'We have heard many stories of the jealousies of Olympias; how will you fare with her?'

Roxanna watched the two queens each take another morsel as she pretended to weigh her answer in her head; she ripped off the second wing, again taking her time to skin it before discarding it on the side of her plate. 'Olympias needs my son more than he needs her; I fully expect her to come to me as a supplicant.' Again she cleansed her fingers.

'You are so lucky to be with child, Sister,' Stateira said, kissing a small piece of the summaqa from her middle finger before slicing a slither of well-spiced breast from her carcass. 'We would that our lord had graced our beds more than just the one time on our wedding night; but he had more pressing concerns.' She popped the meat into her mouth and chewed.

Sucking Hephaestion's cock being one of them; I know because I caught him doing it and he showed no shame. 'He was equally as sparing with his favours in my chamber, my dears; I sometimes would not see him for six months at a stretch.'

Stateira swallowed and again inclined her head at the graciousness shown by sharing such intimate information. 'We are all...' She stopped mid-sentence and stared down at Roxanna's still-full plate. 'You do not eat, Sister?' In alarm, she turned to her cousin. 'Spit it out!'

Parysatis looked at Stateira in incomprehension, her mouth half-full of semi-masticated quail.

'Spit it out, it's poisoned. The Bactrian bitch took the first quail to put our minds at rest and then has done nothing but play with it.'

Parysatis spat the contents of her mouth out into a napkin.

You can spit as much as you like, sweet queens, it's too late. 'I suggest you both lie back and relax,' Roxanna said with false concern, 'I wouldn't want you to get agitated as that would cause you distress. The poison I've used will just numb you; you won't feel any pain as you make the transition and once it takes effect it will be very quick.'

Stateira stuck a finger down her throat and retched; nothing. Again she did it, this time forcing her hand in as far as possible. Another couple of retches were followed by an explosion of vomit that gushed over the table. Parysatis screamed and threw her quail at Roxanna.

'Nothing can save you, my dears; the poison was mixed with the summaqa so you wouldn't taste it and you've had far too much. No amount of spewing or hysterics will help now.'

As one, Stateira and Parysatis leapt across the table at Roxanna, scattering the meal and sliding in vomit, nails flaying and teeth bared as they howled in anger and grief, aiming for her pregnancy. Jumping back, Roxanna avoided the joint attack as the steward and the two slaves she had requested to serve the party rushed back into the room. But the poisoned queens got no further than Roxanna's deserted couch before both began to stumble and then weaken as the sensation in the extremities of their limbs faded.

'I did tell you to remain calm,' Roxanna reminded them. 'I could have used much more painful poisons but instead I chose to show mercy.'

'Mercy?' Stateira questioned, her voice beginning to slur as her lips relaxed. 'Murdering us is mercy?'

Roxanna smiled, it was her best smile that she saved for rare occasions such as this. 'My ancestors would have had you impaled; as would yours have had me. Of course you cannot be permitted to live; whoever married you would have had a claim to the throne and, therefore, been a direct threat to my son.' At the mention of her unborn babe she tensed; a sharp pain shot through her lower abdomen. She bent over with a cry; her two slave-girls ran to her as the steward looked around the room, aghast at the sight of the two dying queens moaning amongst the debris of dinner.

The pain grew, contorting her body with its violence. Roxanna took a series of deep breaths, shaking off the supporting hands of her slaves. 'Leave me, I'll be fine.' She pointed down at Stateira and Parysatis, both of whom had now started to foam at the mouth. 'Steward, they will soon be dead; throw their bodies down the well, I want no one to know of this so do it personally.'

The steward did a swift mental calculation and, realising that there was no way to survive being complicit in Roxanna's plot, fled the room. *Running won't save you, you freak; it'll just get you a more painful death.* She turned to her slave-girls. 'You'll have to do it, get the others.'

As Roxanna watched her slaves drag the dead bodies of Stateira and Parysatis towards the well, across the flagstones of the courtyard lit solely by the rising half-moon, she grasped her belly once more. She supported herself against the wall and took deep breaths; her time was not yet due but the tension and exertion had aggravated her condition. *I must keep strong; I must get to full term to give my son as much chance as possible.* She stood up straight as she heard the splash of the second corpse hitting the water; the sound cheered her and she felt her body relax. She would be fine; she still had time, enough time to get to her carriage and summon the midwives and eunuch doctors who had accompanied her and leave through the West Gate back to Babylon, there to give birth. *Soon, my son, soon is your time. Soon will come the age of the new Alexander. But what if I am wrong?*

It was then that a movement in the shadows caught her eye.

PERDIKKAS,
THE HALF-CHOSEN

'**D**O YOU THINK that you will have it finished by the end of next year?' Perdikkas asked as he and Seleukos admired the framework of the great catafalque that was to transport Alexander's mummified remains back to his final resting place in royal tombs of Macedon. Four paces wide and six long, the frame was mounted, via a suspension system, on two axles, each ending in iron-rimmed, gold-spoked wheels the height of a man. A golden lion's head holding a spear in its teeth adorned each of the wheel hubs.

'With sufficient craftsmen working on the four statues of Nike that will be placed on each corner and then the goldsmiths to work on the gold-leaf olive wreath that will crown the barrel-vaulted roof and the artisans to make the golden columns supporting the roof. Need I go on?'

'Yes, Arrhidaeus; you do need to. I must know.' Perdikkas looked down at the design, drawn with meticulous precision from various angles, that Seleukos was studying.

Arrhidaeus, the namesake of the idiot king before he was renamed Philip, shrugged and continued counting off his requirements on his fingers. 'I need the sculptors for the friezes around the wall and then more for the two golden lions guarding the entrance, and then the painters to depict the various feats of Alexander – all of which we still need to decide. Then I need founders to cast the four great bells that will hang from each corner. More goldsmiths to fashion the hundreds of overlapping gold plates to cover the roof and to make the meshwork of golden ropes that will cover the gaps between the columns. Then I need the men to train the sixty-four mules it will take to pull the thing, each of which will have a gold crown with two golden bells hanging from it as well as a golden collar set with precious jewels, all of which have got to be manufactured twice as we will need a reserve team. If I have all that, then yes, Perdikkas, provided I have all the gold and jewels that are needed, I will be ready by next year – or thereabouts.' Arrhidaeus smiled, showing that he had run out of fingers. 'Oh, and we have to discuss what the sarcophagus will rest upon and what we want for the decoration inside the catafalque.'

Perdikkas wiped the sweat from his brow, brought on as much by the muggy Babylonian late-summer as by the huge expense that seemed to spiral even more out of control every time he visited the throne-room where the catafalque was being constructed next to Alexander's mummified body. 'I've told you that you'll have everything you need.'

'It's one thing to say that, Perdikkas; however, it's quite another thing to ensure it.' He gestured around the vast chamber with its throne at the further end; here and there was a hunched figure bent over a work table. 'What do you see?' He waited a few moments whilst Perdikkas looked, trying, but failing, to work out just what he was meant to be seeing. 'Hardly anything. If you want the funeral cortège to set out for Macedon by the end of next year, then this room has to be full of craftsmen, and the materials for them to work on; and it all has to be here in the next few days and even then I would say it is more likely to be ready in the spring of the year after.'

Perdikkas looked around the room and then back down at the plans. *Why has everything got to be so difficult? How did Alexander manage to organise everything?*

'Delegate, Perdikkas,' Seleukos said as if reading his mind. 'No one can do everything – not even Alexander – delegate. Arrhidaeus here needs craftsmen; they're not just going to come to you so send people out to get them and bring them here, by force if necessary. And do it now, don't wait, never wait unless there is good reason to.'

'But what about the expense? Since Harpalus absconded to Athens with eight hundred talents rather than face Alexander's wrath for his dishonesty, gold and silver are in short supply.'

Seleukos looked at his commander with astonishment; intense dark eyes peered from either side of a thin but prominent nose that bisected an angular face that could have been the model for many an ancient hero's bust, just as his body could have been a model for a statue of Heracles. 'This is the most extensive empire the world has ever seen and you complain about gold and silver being in short supply? Harpalus took a fraction of the wealth so don't use him as an excuse. Give me the word and I'll go out today and bring back enough gold, silver and jewels for Arrhidaeus to complete his work twice over.'

Perdikkas was, as always, impressed by the intensity of the man; his whole energy and the full force of his huge frame was ever invested in all he did. It had been that quality which Alexander had recognised in him that had persuaded him to first make him the commander of the newly formed Elephant squadron. 'Where will you get it all from?'

'Why, here of course. There are scores of temples in the city that contain the wealth of ages. It all belongs to Alexander so I shall take it for his carriage.' He pointed to the base of the vehicle slowly taking shape. 'This has to be the most magnificent thing ever built, Perdikkas; it's for Alexander. Whoever builds it and takes Alexander home to be interred at Argead, possesses his legacy. Macedonian kings have always gained legitimacy by burying their predecessors – even if they assassinated them. If you want that for Philip and Roxanna's boy, if it is a boy and we'll know very soon now, then you won't get it by standing around wondering how to achieve it. Action, Perdikkas, action. It's the same as on the battlefield, except you have more time to think about things. Now, do you want me to go or not?'

'Of course I do. Get going.'

'And the craftsmen?' Arrhidaeus asked.

'Yes. Seleukos,' Perdikkas called after him. 'And the craftsmen; get them whilst you're about it.'

Seleukos looked back over his shoulder, shaking his head. 'Delegation, Perdikkas, is about choosing the right man for each task; I know nothing of tradesmen.'

As Seleukos' footsteps faded, Perdikkas turned back to Arrhidaeus. 'You know what sort of men you want, you go and find them; I want this room full in two days' time.'

'That's the other thing I want to talk to you about: I don't think we should build it in here. For a start—'

'I don't want to hear another word, Arrhidaeus,' Perdikkas snapped, cutting him off. 'It's right and proper that the catafalque should be built here, in Alexander's presence. Now, get on with it and get it done.' Feeling far better with himself than at any time since he had crushed Meleagros, Perdikkas followed Seleukos from the room, pleased that he had managed to assert his authority in a way that he felt befitted the heir to Alexander; for, since his erstwhile comrades had departed for their satrapies, Perdikkas had felt his authority slipping. It was not so much that his commands were being ignored, it was more that he had very few people of consequence to issue commands to. Yes, he had written to Antigonos to order him to help Eumenes subdue Kappadokia; and he had written to Ptolemy forbidding him to expand his satrapy west into Cyrenaica. As well as that, he had written to Krateros commanding him to send the fleet he had commandeered to Tyros so that he, Perdikkas, could take it under his control. But as yet he had not received a response from any of his letters. He looked down at the ring on his forefinger as he strode along the corridor. *I will not be ignored; they may now be satraps in their own rights, but that was a necessity just to keep the peace. I have the overall command.*

With that line repeating itself in his head he burst out into the heat of the palace courtyard full of purpose; he would delegate, as Seleukos had suggested. He would make a good peace-time ruler so that soon all would come to see him as the one true heir to Alexander. *And then I can get rid of the idiot king and have plenty of time to think about how to deal with the eastern whelp, if it's a boy. It should be birthed any day now; pray gods the brat's a girl so I can drown the little bitch without anyone caring too much.*

With this pleasant thought, he walked past the Hypaspists, now under Kassandros' command, working at their weapons training. The thrusts and parries, the shield-moves and side-steps all took him back to his training as a young page of Philip's in the days when Macedon was but a European power. How far it had come and how far he had come; he, Perdikkas, now the de facto ruler of the greatest empire the world had seen. Indeed, it could be argued that he was the most powerful man in the world.

It was with a feeling of great self-importance that he opened the door to his study, in his private apartments, to find his secretary waiting for him, standing by the open window to the courtyard, with a scroll case.

'It's from Antigonos,' the man said, handing Perdikkas the case.

'Thank you, Phocus.' *They write to me for advice,* Perdikkas thought, taking a seat at his desk and breaking the seal of the case, his sense of well-being growing. *No doubt he wants to have my views on how best he can subdue Kappadokia with Eumenes.* He unrolled the scroll; within a moment his smile had faded and he stared in astonishment at the only two words written upon it. He closed his eyes and then looked again to see if he had been mistaken. He had not; there, before his very eyes, was Antigonos' answer to his command to help Eumenes subdue Kappadokia. Just two words: *My arse.*

'My arse! My...arse?'

'I beg your pardon, sir,' Phocus said, his confusion apparent.

Perdikkas scrumpled the scroll in his fist and waved it in his secretary's face. 'Where's the messenger who brought this?'

'I...er...I don't know, sir. He left.'

'Left? What do you mean, left?'

'Well, gone, sir. He went. He...er...delivered the letter and then went straight to the stables to change horses and then left.'

'Didn't he say that he would wait for a reply? All messengers do.' Perdikkas looked at the screwed-up message, his eyes widened in anger. 'They do unless they are warned by the sender that the contents of the letter might cause serious offence and they would be better off being absent when it is read.' He slammed his fist down on the desk; anger flooding into the space left by his punctured self-importance and shattered sense of well-being. 'How long ago did this arrive?'

'An hour or so, sir.'

'Get my brother here; at once!' Throwing the letter after the quickly retreating secretary, Perdikkas again thumped his desk, seething with anger, before holding his head in both hands. *'My arse'? Antigonos dares reply to my direct order to subdue Kappadokia, something that Alexander had charged him to do ten years ago, something he has patently failed to accomplish, with 'my arse'?* His fingers clutched at his hair as the real significance of those two words hit him. *This means war. If not, then I might as well kill myself now. With just two words the old bastard has broken Alexander's empire and everything that I tried to preserve.* He could have screamed for the stupidity of it but instead kicked his chair onto its back, poured a healthy bowl of wine and downed it. *I'll see the old goat taking a well-deserved seat on a stake for this and then he'll have the right to say 'my arse'.* As another bowl of wine disappeared down his gullet, the door to his study opened and Alketas stepped in. 'Don't sit down, Brother. Turn straight around, get a troop of cavalry and chase the messenger from Antigonos; he's about an hour ahead of you. The stables will be able to give you a description of him.'

'You want him back?'

'Not all of him; just his head.'

'Very well, Brother; I won't ask why.'

Perdikkas waved his younger sibling away without replying and reached, once more, for the wine. Bowl replenished, he stood at the window, breathing deeply. Looking out at the Hypaspists drilling as Alketas walked with admirable urgency across the flagstones in the direction of the stables, his footsteps drowned by the exertions of the soldiers, Perdikkas felt his heartbeat lessen as he calmed. *He won't let me down; out of all of them Alketas is the only one I can trust, with the exception, perhaps, of Aristonous who seems to want nothing from me. Whereas Eumenes, Seleukos and Kassandros…well, they would all put ambition before empire and I'd do well to remember that in the coming months and years.*

The cry pierced the air, cutting through the training of the Hypaspists, and drawing all training in the courtyard to a sudden end. Again it shrilled around the high walls of the palace as all who heard it turned to try to identify its source. But to Perdikkas its origin was obvious; he threw down his unfinished bowl to shatter on the floor and strode from the room, his heartbeat regaining pace.

'Kassandros,' he shouted as he came out into the courtyard. 'Bring a dozen men and come with me.' Without waiting for a reply, Perdikkas headed towards the apartments of the woman who could either complicate or simplify matters: Roxanna.

'The queen is indisposed,' a eunuch's soft voice announced in response to Perdikkas beating on the door to Roxanna's suite.

Perdikkas gave the door a mighty kick as Kassandros arrived with twelve Hypaspists, fully armed and sweating from training. 'I know she is indisposed, half-man; she is giving birth. And if you ever refer to her as the queen again I'll cut off any other extremities that you've been left with. Now, open the door or I'll have it beaten down and the whole household executed before the bitch has whelped.'

'I've also always found that being polite is a complete waste of time,' Kassandros observed as the door swung open with obvious reluctance and he followed Perdikkas through.

With a kick, Perdikkas floored the portly eunuch as he tried to bar his way into the main chamber; screams continued to issue at regular intervals from a room to the left as slave-girls and eunuchs cowered in the corners at the sight of armed men bursting into their sheltered domain. 'Is that where she is, half-man?' Perdikkas demanded, pointing at a double door.

The eunuch, eyes wide with fear and sweat seeping from his bald pate, nodded in dumb affirmation.

With another kick to the prostrate half-man, Perdikkas headed straight for the source of the screams and opened the doors.

There was a flurry of midwives, exacerbating Roxanna's birthing screams, as they howled their protests that such a feminine event should be gate-crashed by men – armed men at that.

Roxanna turned her head towards the intruders, her hair lank and clinging to her brow, her chest heaving with effort. 'What are you doing?'

'Where is it?' Perdikkas did not wait for a reply but began an immediate search of the room as Roxanna once again succumbed to the agony of contractions. 'Have your men search the whole place, Kassandros.'

'What for?'

But Perdikkas did not need to specify his quarry as he pulled a curtain aside to reveal a woman nursing a baby. 'For this.' He grabbed it and turned to Roxanna. 'You dishonest little bitch.'

Roxanna screamed again but this time it was at the sight of Perdikkas holding out a naked new-born boy-child.

'Your insurance against the wrong result?' Perdikkas asked, waving the now-bleating babe in Roxanna's face. 'Would you do anything to keep your power? Even try to place a low-born base bastard on the throne, would you?'

Roxanna shrieked again, this time it was a mixture of intense pain and intense rage; she tried to claw at Perdikkas' eyes but, her body heaving with contractions, managed only to scratch the soft newborn flesh of the babe's chest. Perdikkas withdrew the mewling infant beyond her range as Roxanna gnashed her teeth and shook her head in frustration and pain; midwives continued to busy themselves down at the other end.

Perdikkas looked at the squirming little life in his hands and started for the open window.

'Nooo!' a woman's voice yelled over the chaos.

Perdikkas looked down at the flagstones, two storeys below and then turned towards the shout. Across the bed, in which Roxanna writhed, the infant's mother stood, her hands extended towards him, her eyes pleading. Perdikkas turned to Kassandros, who shrugged, and then back to the open window. *How would Alexander punish this attempted deception?* He looked back at the innocent life in his hands and his anger began to ebb. *It was*

Roxanna who forced the woman to give away her child; not the woman herself. That's how Alexander would have reasoned. Roxanna would have killed them both had the babe not been required. With this certainty in his mind, Perdikkas beckoned the woman over to him as a new and even more intense scream issued from the birthing-bed.

She rushed across the room and grabbed her child, cradling it in her arms as if she thought she would never do so again. 'Have one of your men get her out of here,' Perdikkas ordered Kassandros, 'and have her taken to my suite; I'll decide what to do with her later. Just keep her safe from this wild-cat.' Perdikkas looked down at Roxanna, now breathing deep, steady breaths between contractions; her eyes smouldered with unsheathed hatred. He moved to the foot of the bed so as to have a good view between her legs. 'This is where I stay, Roxanna, and you had better hope for your sake and that of your child that you would not have needed to foist the changeling upon us because you won't see out the day if it's a bitch.' He turned to one of the midwives. 'Bring me a chair.' He sat and watched as the dilation grew. *Gods, I hope it's a girl and I could be rid of this murderous easterner. I give her Stateira and Parysatis and this is how she was willing to repay me.*

'What about my men,' Kassandros asked, standing at Perdikkas' shoulder.

'Hmm?' Perdikkas shook his head, as much to get rid of his vengeful thoughts as to dispel the images of birth happening not four paces from where he sat. 'Oh, dismiss them; but you wait here with me as a second witness, one that your father will believe.'

With a curt nod Kassandros did as ordered before returning to his place next to Perdikkas as the crown of a head appeared between bloody lips.

With a growl of bestial proportions Roxanna's body heaved and tensed as women encouraged her and swarmed around with warm, wet towels. Perdikkas looked at the growing protrusion that was shaping into a baby's head and grimaced in disgust. *But I'm not going to shirk my responsibility to Alexander, however disgusting it is.*

He looked up at Kassandros, his normally pale face was white as a funeral shroud. Another set of wrenching groans accompanied by the birdlike encouragement of the woman ended in a howl that was almost a call to the gods, such was its volume. With a gargantuan effort of muscles that Perdikkas did not know existed, Roxanna's body forced the child's shoulders from it; and then, with a shudder, it expelled the rest in a slithering, slimey shot.

Perdikkas leapt to his feet and pushed his way through the crowd as a midwife gathered up the bloodied mess and another went to deal with the umbilical cord. 'Show me its sex,' Perdikkas demanded.

The cord was cut and the babe held upside down by its ankles; a couple of stout spanks on his buttocks provoked Alexander, the fourth of that name, into a gasp for breath and then into full, newborn mewling.

'A boy!' the women shrilled, 'a boy.'

And, with a sinking heart, Perdikkas could see that it was so. He looked over to Roxanna, who smiled in triumph. 'You are a lucky little bitch.' With that he stalked from the room with Kassandros close on his heels.

'That has just made life very difficult,' Perdikkas said as he and Kassandros left the suite, the eunuch on the door keeping a goodly distance from Perdikkas' foot. 'Now we really do have two kings and both of them nothing but figureheads. Two kings and two regents; that is not a recipe for stability.'

'Then marry one of my half-sisters,' Kassandros suggested, quite surprising Perdikkas.

'What?'

'Write to my father and ask to marry one of my half-sisters. That would make you his son-in-law and me your brother-in-law. The two regents tied in marriage like that would be a step towards the stability that we, you, need.'

Perdikkas looked at the lanky man strutting beside him like some sort of avian error and reassessed him. 'Yes, Kassandros, you're right; that would be a good political move for the whole empire.' *It would also isolate Antigonos; with me to his south and Antipatros to his north, we could crush him between us.* His brow furrowed as he contemplated the plan. *Provided Ptolemy to my south is no threat to me.* 'Come with me and we'll compose the letter together, stressing the mutual benefit to such a match.'

The thought kept him preoccupied as he and Kassandros entered his suite of rooms to find the woman and her brat awaiting him in the custody of a Hypaspist and the steward of the apartment.

'Where do you come from?' Perdikkas asked.

The woman shook her head, indicating that she had no Greek.

Perdikkas nodded to the steward who translated and then listened to the reply.

'She's a slave from the royal hunting lodge on the road to Susa,' the steward informed Perdikkas. 'Roxanna forced her to come to Babylon when she was staying there.'

'Ask her if she knows what happened at the lodge.'

The steward did so; the woman looked at Perdikkas, frightened, and then back at the steward, shaking her head.

'Tell her I know she's lying to me and remind her that I can always reverse my decision to spare her child.'

That brought the required result; a stream of gibberish, to Perdikkas' ears, poured from her accompanied by the furious waving of her free arm.

'Roxanna poisoned the two queens and threw them down a well,' the steward explained. 'Then she had the steward of the lodge impaled as she left; the slave-girls who disposed of the bodies she had killed as soon as she got back to Babylon so that there would be no witnesses.'

Perdikkas feigned surprise at the news of the queens' murders; he had assumed as much after Roxanna had left Babylon for a month and Stateira and Parysatis had failed to make the journey from Susa. *So that's how she did it.* 'Ask her how she knows all this if there are supposed to be no witnesses.'

'Because she witnessed it all but then Roxanna forced her to watch her slave-girls having their throats cut,' the steward said over the woman's tears. 'Roxanna then told her that she and her at-the-time-unborn child would suffer the same fate if she would say a word or refused to do as she was bidden.'

So she would have been murdered whether or not Roxanna used her boy so that the last witness would be silenced. This could be a very useful woman to me. 'How did she come to witness this crime?'

The steward listened to the reply. 'She worked in the kitchens and had been out at the well getting water. When they came out with the bodies she had hidden in the shadows but had been discovered. Roxanna was about to have her slaves throw her into the well too until she saw just how pregnant she was; then an idea seemed to occur to her and she changed her mind.'

Perdikkas understood her thinking. 'She realised that she was due any day and if it were to be a boy then it could be of use; but if it were a girl then mother and child would have their throats cut. In a way you have to admire the ruthlessness of that eastern wildcat.' Perdikkas turned to Kassandros. 'You heard all that so you can bear witness to the murder of Alexander's two pregnant Persian queens.'

Kassandros nodded. 'Were they pregnant?'

'That's irrelevant so long as we say they were.'

Kassandros smiled. 'That's a fine weapon to hold over the eastern wildcat's throat.'

Perdikkas turned to the steward. 'Have this woman and her child cared for here where she is safe. And summon Phocos, my secretary; I have a letter to write.'

'Yes, sir. Whilst I get him, Aristonous is waiting with someone in your study.'

'This is Isodorus, one of Cleomenes' agents in Egypt,' Aristonous said without any preamble as Perdikkas entered his study. 'He has just made the journey from Memphis to here in less than a moon to bring you Cleomenes' report on what Ptolemy is doing and I felt that you should hear it immediately.'

Perdikkas looked at the short, brown-skinned man; the skin on his angular face was like leather and his head had evidently been completely shaven before he had set out on his journey. 'Well, go on then.'

'If it pleases you, master,' the agent said, bowing in the most cringing and obsequious fashion.

'It does, get on with it; I haven't had the best of days.'

'My master, Cleomenes, sent me as soon as he saw the truth for himself, a month ago. Ptolemy has assembled a fleet and an army in the newly founded city of Alexandria and, when I left, was about to set sail west to annex Cyrenaica, it having been taken over by a Spartan mercenary called Thribron.'

Perdikkas stared at Isodorus in disbelief; for the second time that day the shock of his orders being flouted hit him like a slingshot. 'But I told him not to,' he blurted, instantly regretting losing his dignity in the company of one so low. 'Who is this Thribron?' *Is it worth me sending him support?*

'He used to be in the pay of Harpalus when he was on the run with the money he stole from Alexander, master. Half that wealth was left in Athens and Harpalus took the other half with him when he fled to Creta. Thribron murdered him there and used the money to recruit a mercenary army to take Cyrene and then the rest of Cyrenaica; he was then betrayed by his Cretan allies and forced out of the city but he eventually defeated his enemies, and held off the Carthaginians and Lybians who came to their aid, and now holds sway in the whole area.'

'And Harpalus' stolen money?'

'Is in Thribron's hands.'

So that's why Ptolemy's going; not satisfied with what he must have found in Memphis' treasury, he wants more. That can only mean one thing. I'd better act quickly.

'What else did Cleomenes charge you to say?'

'Only that he soon hopes to send the money that you have asked for. Ptolemy has put him in charge of the treasury and, having been the satrap, he knows Egypt's finances intimately.'

Because he found every way to extort money from the locals when he was in sole charge of Egypt. I wonder what made Ptolemy give him the same opportunity. 'I'm sure he does. Rest here for a couple of days and I will send you back with a letter to him. Now go.' With a wave, Perdikkas dismissed the agent, slumped in his chair and looked, with weary eyes, at Aristonous and Kassandros. 'Why are all my orders ignored?' He raised his hand, palm out, to stop them from answering what was a rhetorical question; he

133

fully knew the answer. 'It's because I'm not feared and I don't have close allies. So, gentlemen, it's time to work out how to address that.' A knock on the door interrupted him. 'Come in!'

Alketas came in followed by Phocus, the secretary with his writing box.

'All done, Brother,' Alketas said, holding up a dripping sack.

Perdikkas smiled. 'Excellent, thank you, Alketas. That's just what I need to help gain me respect. Come, Phocus, sit at your table, we have letters to write to Antipatros, Cleomenes and Ptolemy; but first to Antigonos to accompany Alketas' little present there. Just two words: Your balls.'

PTOLEMY, THE BASTARD

THERE'S NOTHING MORE *gratifying than a dying enemy; especially a viciously cruel enemy who's dying in great agony.* Ptolemy looked with the inner satisfaction of a job well done at the writing body of Thribron, hanging from his cross in the agora of Cyrene, accompanied by his supporters in the city. *Although I suppose that having lost his ears and nose and had his eyes replaced by his testicles and his tongue by his cock, he's not altogether too unhappy about starting his journey to the Ferryman; I imagine he just wishes it could be a slightly more direct route. Never mind, one can't have everything.*

Attended by his general, Ophellas, Ptolemy sat on a throne set beneath a canopy at the opposite end of the agora from the occupied crosses, as the delegation of Cyrenaeans approached and knelt before him.

Ptolemy listened with little interest as they thanked him for his intervention and affirmed their loyalty to him – the price he had extracted before he had sent his army, under Ophellas' command, to liberate their city from what was no more than an army of unemployed mercenaries out for easy loot. Now the loot was in his hands and most of the mercenaries were in his employ, apart from those he had been forced to nail up to encourage the rest – he had considered using impalement but being of a slightly squeamish disposition and liking to think of himself as a forgiving and big-hearted man, he had opted for crucifixion instead. His major achievement was, however, the recovery of half of Harpalus' stolen fortune, almost four hundred talents of gold and silver; and once he finally managed to prise the whereabouts of the Egyptian treasury, in the next few days, from Cleomenes – who seemed to consider it his personal property – he would be a long way to recruiting and keeping a large enough army and navy to ensure that he was left in peace as he cemented his position in Egypt. *All in all, a very good few months' work.*

The droning of speeches came to an end and it took Ptolemy a few moments to realise that it was his turn to be polite. 'Thank you for your words of love and loyalty,' he said, addressing the leader of the delegation in his most solemn tone that he now reserved for dealing with matters such as this. 'Now you have subjected yourselves to my protection you shall receive a garrison to fend off the Libyans and Carthaginians to the west and in return for that you will pay a tenth of all the value of your Silphium trade, both of the plant itself as well as the animals fed on it, to Memphis.' Ptolemy held up a treaty he had had drawn up during the short two-day trip from Alexandria to receive the city's formal surrender. 'There are two copies; one for you and one that I shall take back to the new city of Alexandria and deposit in the temple of Apsis there. Let there always be a state of friendship between us.'

This sentiment was greeted with much enthusiasm from the delegation and the crowd of citizens looking on – all those who had the good fortune to have chosen the winning side in the recent struggle. Ptolemy watched as the delegation took it in turns to sign the documents before adding his own signature and authenticating it with his seal.

That's one up the arse for Perdikkas; I would imagine that Cleomenes' odious little sneak, Isodorus, is whining to him right about now. I wish I could see the fool's face. I expect he's sitting down to write me a very stern letter. I shall look forward to it. 'I shall leave Ophellas here to act as my proxy; you will treat his word as mine. However, you are free to run your city as you wish.' Leaving that obvious tautology unexplained, Ptolemy rose and took his most regal pose, one arm extended towards his people, the other touching his breast. 'And so I say farewell for I must now return to Egypt where pressing matters await.'

The pressing matter in question was his mistress, Thais. Even after ten years together and three children during that time, Ptolemy was still obsessed by her beauty and her wit and, as he pressed into her again and again, in the slow rhythm that their love-making had eased into over the years, he marvelled that she still held him enthralled. Indeed, he hated being too long away from her, even now. She moaned in her pleasure as the pace of his pressing grew, her pale skin gaining in colour and her tongue, the bringer of such delight, playing with her top lip. Her hair, red-golden, fanned out on the pillow, framing her face, catching the evening sun as it flooded through the open window of the near-complete Royal Palace on the eastern edge of the great harbour of Alexandria.

Together they worked to a shuddering climax, backs arching and features contorting before slumping into each other's loose embrace, panting. With his head on its side, Ptolemy admired Thais' profile, the gentle pout of her lips, the slight curve of her nose, all the little details he knew so well. He caressed her cheek and leant forward to kiss her. 'I'm going to have to take a wife.'

Thais did not open her eyes. 'I know. What are you going to do with the present one?'

'Artacama? I'll keep her, I suppose. What do you mean: you know?'

'I mean: I know. Of course you are going to have to take a wife, it stands to reason, doesn't it?'

'Does it?'

'Of course it does if it's even occurred to you.' Thais turned over and propped her head up with her hand, looking down at him. 'You've just disobeyed Perdikkas' direct order not to move west into Cyrenaica and, whilst you were away, Cleomenes fell into the trap that you set for him—'

'How do you know that as well?'

'Because the venal fool stole so much coin off the caravan that you *told him* was setting out for Babylon with a quarter of

Egypt's wealth as a peace offering to Perdikkas, that it was impossible for him to get it back to his residence here without drawing attention to it.'

Ptolemy smiled at the image of the outrageously fat man and boxes and boxes of coin. 'I knew he would not be able to resist it. I'm told his men took the caravan as soon as it was out of sight of the city.'

'It was quick; the man I had watching his house said he turned up with a loaded wagon on the first night you were on your way to Cyrene. Anyway, you now have all you need to execute Perdikkas' representative in Egypt so you've as good as declared war on him. So of course you're going to ask Antipatros for one of his delicious daughters because you want the old man on your side.'

Ptolemy shook his head in awe of his lover's logic. 'And you don't mind?'

'Of course I don't mind; did you hear me say a word when Alexander made you marry Artacama at the Susa mass wedding? I am one of the highest paid courtesans in the Greek world, of course I don't mind if one of my clients gets himself a new wife.'

'But you only have one client now.'

'He's still a client, even though I've borne him three children. After all, you keep me in more luxury than I ever tasted in Athens. No, take your Macedonian peace-cow, darling, rut her well and fill her belly; anything that makes us more secure here is fine by me.'

Ptolemy kissed her again and swung out of bed; naked, he crossed to the window, took a deep breath of salt-tanged air and looked out over the building site that was Alexandria. 'When you think that eight years ago this was nothing but a collection of fishermen's huts...' He trailed off as the scale of the construction in that time had no words to describe it, such was its magnitude; just the mole, connecting the rocky, barren Pharos island to the mainland, thereby sheltering the harbour, was a work worthy of Titans. But now a city was taking shape on the modern idea of a grid system. Already tens of thousands had flocked to the half-completed metropolis, eager to be a part of what was surely going to be the greatest city in the world; and he, Ptolemy, was now its ruler.

'You should make yourself Pharaoh,' Thais said as if reading his thoughts.

'Ha! That would really give it to Perdikkas up the arse.'

'He might like it; I do.'

'Well, he can wait for that treat. I have a better one for him first: coinage.'

Thais sat up in bed, her arms wrapped around her knees, intrigued. 'Coinage?'

Ptolemy took a coin from a small box on the chest next to the window and tossed it over to Thais. 'What do you think?'

After a few moments her eyes widened. 'No one has ever done that before, that is genius.'

'Yes, until now coins have always had the gods on them, never a mortal man. By putting Alexander's head on my coinage I'm claiming his legitimacy; it's going to be a powerful propaganda statement as these start to circulate around the world. I'll let my rivals get really cross and then I'll make it even worse for them and put my own head on the face.'

'Lucky Perdikkas gets it up the arse twice.'

'And I can guarantee that he won't moan with pleasure nearly as much as you; especially when I pull my biggest surprise on him.'

A knock on the door prevented Ptolemy from expanding on Perdikkas' coming discomfort.

'Come.'

The door opened and a young slave poked his head around it.

'What is it, Sextus?'

'Master, Lycortas says to tell you that he has Cleomenes waiting downstairs.'

'Tell him I'll be there shortly.'

The slave bowed and retreated, closing the door behind him.

'I can barely understand the lad through his thick accent but he's one of the best body-slaves I've ever had.'

'Where's he from?'

'Some town in Latinum, I believe it's called; it's in Italia, north of the civilized Greek part. I don't suppose that Alexander would have even bothered with it had he lived to go west.' He picked up his discarded loincloth, fastened it and then slipped his chiton over his head, stepped into a pair of leather slippers and picked up his belt. Stooping over the bed he gave Thais a lingering kiss. 'I hope you have as much fun in the coming hour as I'm going to.'

Thais giggled and gave an enticing smile. 'I'm sure I can think of something to do but, actually, I think that I'd rather come and watch you deal with Cleomenes.'

Cleomenes shook in outrage; great folds of blubber wobbled on his neck and belly and hung loose from the undersides of his arms. 'I did not attack that caravan, nor did I command it to be attacked.'

Ptolemy made to consider the statement as if it might be the truth and then abruptly changed his mind. 'No, Cleomenes, that's not true, is it?'

'It is the truth; I would swear it by all the gods.'

'I don't think that the gods have much regard for you since you took away age-old privileges from the priests here in Egypt and forced them to buy them back for a huge amount.'

'Alexander needed the money.'

'No he didn't, nor did he need the money that you forced the priests to pay you when you threatened to kill all the crocodiles in the Nile just because one ate your favourite bum-boy. No, Cleomenes, be honest with yourself, you'll feel much better for it; you're an avaricious lump of flab and you've been on this earth for too long. Go on, say it; the truth will refresh you.'

'I did not take the caravan!'

'Tell him why we know he did, Lycortas.'

Resplendent in a long, loose-fitting robe of refined taste, Ptolemy's plump chamberlain, shaven-headed and with an inscrutable expression on his pudgy-lipped face, rose from his seat and motioned a couple of slaves forward. Between them they carried a money chest. They placed it down at Cleomenes feet.

'We found this in the cellar of your new house after we arrested you just now.'

'You searched my house? By what right?'

'By my right, Cleomenes,' Ptolemy crooned. 'Because what I say goes in this beautiful land. Lucky, aren't I? Now open it.'

Cleomenes grunted but opened the box nevertheless and then dismissed the contents with a wave of his hands. 'Drachmas, so what? I have millions and these are just some of them. This goes no way to proving that I was responsible for robbing the caravan.'

'And killing every one of the people riding with it, don't forget.' Ptolemy rubbed his chin in exaggerated thought. 'Do you know what, Cleomenes, I think you could be right: drachmas in themselves would not prove that you robbed the caravan. A very good point. Have a look at one of those drachmas, would you?'

With a shrug, Cleomenes reached into the box and pulled out a coin.

'What do you notice about it, Cleomenes?'

'It's newly minted; so what? I have boxes of newly minted coins legitimately acquired.'

'I know you do; we found the whole treasury in your cellar, eight thousand talents in gold, silver and coin; a small percentage may have been acquired legitimately. However, you've never acquired any like that legitimately, no one's ever acquired any like that because the only boxes of them to ever exist were on that caravan. Look at the face, Cleomenes.'

The fat man did so and his jowls dropped. 'Alexander! I've never seen—' He clapped his hand to his mouth.

'Never seen a mortal on a coin was what you were going to say, was it not? No, you haven't, you're quite right, Cleomenes; no one has ever seen a mortal depicted on a coin because it's never been done before and you just stole the first batch ever to have been minted.'

Porcine, bloodshot eyes blinked as Cleomenes looked around the room in search of aid or a means of escape. 'But Alexander wrote to me saying that if I built a fine memorial to Hephaestion here he would forgive all my misdemeanours past, present and future. You've seen it, Ptolemy, it's going to be a beautiful memorial.'

This is more fun than I thought it would be. 'I know it is but I'm not Alexander, he's dead, don't you know? Nor did I care overmuch for Hephaestion as he was jealous of me for being Alexander's bastard brother – allegedly – and did me down at any opportunity; so I rather think that I've got you there, Cleomenes. I shall write to your friend, Perdikkas, saying that unfortunately you stole all the money that I was sending him as a peace offering and hid it; I was only able to retrieve this one small box as, even under torture, you wouldn't reveal the where-abouts of the rest before you died; so this little box is all you can expect from Egypt, *dear Perdikkas.*'

Cleomenes had gone puce. 'Torture?'

'No, I just said that as a joke. Paris, impale him.'

'Please, no!' Cleomenes screamed.

'Of course not, that was just a joke too. Take his head.' To the wails of a terrified man, Ptolemy took Thais' arm and walked from the room. *Gods I enjoyed that, although sometimes I think I am too forgiving; I would have so liked to see him squirming on a stake.*

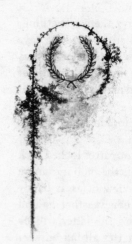

ANTIPATROS,
THE REGENT

ANTIPATROS FELT THE strain; his eyes were heavy from lack of sleep and his joints ached from constant activity. He rubbed his aching head as he stared out of the window at the Macedonian army, bristling with upright pikes, mustering to the north of the palace to the backdrop of shimmering, heat-hazed mountains. Blocks and blocks of men in glistering bronze or hardened-leather or -linen cuirasses, paraded, marching into position under the strengthening sun as, unit by unit, the army took shape under the supervision of Magas, his kinsman by marriage to his niece, Antigone, and his second son, Nicanor. With regret Antipatros shook his head and then studied the letter in his hand one more time, trying to discern any hidden meaning within the words, placed there as a precaution against interception. He could find none. With the barked orders of officers ever-present on the warm air, laden with the scent of wild thyme and resin, he walked to his desk, placed the scroll back down, took a bite of the hard fennel and donkey sausage that was his midday meal and then, sitting, picked up a second scroll-case and unravelled its contents. He read it, chewing on another bite of sausage.

'You look weary, Husband,' Hyperia said, walking through the light curtain that covered his study door; a pleasing floral scent came with her, sparking an interest deep in his belly and he felt his concentration waver. 'Who is it this time? It's been nothing but letters, letters, letters, in the two months since Alexander died; why do they all trouble you?'

'Because people all think that I can give them something; and it's more than two months since he died, twenty-five days more, to be precise.' He indicated to the letter that he was currently perusing. 'This is the only one who asks nothing of me, Aristotle. He gives me information and makes no request in return; that is the sign of a true friend.'

Hyperia sat on the corner of the desk, looking down at her husband. 'What does he say?'

Trying to ignore her tempting aroma, Antipatros looked back down at the neat writing. 'Hyperides goads the mob into more nationalistic fervour, playing upon their view of us as barely civilized northern yokels, and Aristotle believes that he and Demosthenes will soon be reconciled and the latter will be recalled from exile. Indeed, the Exile Charter all but ensures that will occur. He says that once that transpires then war will be inevitable. Apparently Athens has already employed the services of the mercenary general, Leosthenes, and has started to negotiate the enlistment of a mercenary army, which, with all the mercenaries flooding back from Asia, will not be difficult.'

'But with what gold?'

'Ah, that is just it. When Harpalus fled Alexander's return due to his financial excesses, he went to Athens with his ill-gotten wealth and when he was forced to flee from there at least half of it was left behind; Aristotle writes that the haul has just been found and it amounts to over three hundred and eighty talents in silver and gold.'

Hyperia whistled and laid a comforting hand on Antipatros' shoulder. 'That's enough for a very large army.'

'Very large, and, no doubt, growing.' *And that's not the only thing growing at the moment.* He shook his head to try to regain his concentration. 'It may be that they have already assembled a large enough army in the time it took this letter to arrive. Things are moving fast. Aristotle has been accused of pro-Macedonian actions dating back to Philip's time and as a non-citizen he finds it hard to defend himself against them. A certain so-called patriot called Himeraeus tore down the tablet on the Acropolis recording the city's gratitude to Aristotle for his teaching in the Lyceum; the same has happened to the one in Delphi that he set up in honour of his father-in-law.' He pointed to the letter. 'He says here: "I don't care too much; but I don't not care. It's dangerous for an immigrant to stay in Athens." And now, to prove it, his enemies have brought a charge of impiety against him, the same charge they used against Socrates, eighty years ago, and so he's fleeing the city, saying he won't let the Athenians sin twice against philosophy. When my old friend tells me all that then I know that war is becoming unavoidable and it is now certain that it'll be Athens that I have to deal with first.' He indicated to the first letter, discarded next to his lunch. 'That is from Diamades, our paid stooge on the assembly. He's asking for money and free passage to Macedon. The first whiff of danger and the scented dandy is scuttling away as fast as his fat legs can carry him.'

'Forget Diamades, what of Phocion; surely he's been able to keep a level head?'

Again Antipatros pointed to Diamades' letter. 'That's the most telling thing of all: Phocion's been made commander of the newly formed City Guard which means that they plan to take offensive action against us if they feel the need to have a defence force to leave behind.' Antipatros shook his head again, weariness of mind now overpowering physical desire for his wife; he indicated to the open window beyond which the muster of Macedon continued apace. 'It left me no choice but to mobilise now, even before all the harvest is brought in which will be very unpopular but necessary. I have to act fast, leaving tomorrow if I can; if Athens is planning a move north then I must counter by striking south first; I need to get through the pass of Thermopylae before it can be garrisoned against me. If I can join up with our Boetian allies and sack a couple of cities quickly before the end of the campaigning season then that ought to bring the rest of them to their senses.'

Hyperia slipped from her seat on the desk to perch on her husband's lap; with one hand stroking the back of his neck, she kissed him on the forehead. 'Can you be sure of the Thessalians?'

Antipatros ran his hand down his wife's back. 'I've exempted them from any taxes for this year and the next; that should keep them with us. I've just despatched a letter to Menon, their cavalry general, naming the place on the border where we shall rendezvous on the way down south. With their numbers, I can leave a reasonable sized garrison here but I'm still concerned about the security of the kingdom whilst I'm away both from Epirus in the west and also Krateros in the east; I think it's time to write to him and officially offer what he has already taken.'

Hyperia smiled and took his face in both her hands, kissing his nose and then his mouth. 'That is what I came to tell you, Husband; I've just received a letter from Phila: Leonnatus and Lysimachus passed through Tarsus on the way north to their satrapies. She spoke with them; in fact they dined together with Krateros, although she makes no mention of why she was invited.'

Antipatros managed to divert his mind from the breasts so close to his face. 'The first real news from Babylon. What did they say?'

'All the successors to Alexander – as they're now calling themselves, seeing as they all rule parts of the empire in his name – have dispersed and are now in their satrapies, apart from Perdikkas who stays in Babylon along with Aristonous. You are still named regent in Europe and Krateros has been given some grand but meaningless title like Master of the Army or some-such rubbish.'

Antipatros' face brightened. 'So he can no longer lay claim to my position?'

'Exactly.'

'Which means that I don't necessarily have to secure his loyalty by giving him Phila.'

'No, you don't; in fact, now that he has no personal reason to come here, it's best if he stays where he is.'

'And his troops?'

'Those who want to, will come home, the rest will, I'm sure, find employment in the many armies that will spring up in the near future.'

Antipatros nuzzled his face against Hyperia's chest. 'I'm sure they will.'

'I know they will.'

Antipatros was now too busy to reply.

'I said: I know they will.'

Antipatros tore himself away from his sport. 'What do you mean?'

'Well, the main topic that was discussed at this dinner was Antigonos' defiance of Perdikkas.'

With all thoughts of breasts now banished, Antipatros gave what his wife had to say his full attention.

'He has refused Perdikkas' command to help Eumenes pacify Kappadokia; apparently he sent a reply to the written order consisting of two words: "my arse". He saw it as humiliating, in effect a demand for total submission to Perdikkas. Leonnatus, who was also charged to help Eumenes, has yet to declare himself one way or the other; Krateros and Lysimachus have not yet been ordered to help and so are keeping out of the whole issue as neither of them like the sly little Greek, either. So Eumenes has no one to turn to but Perdikkas who will have to support him unless he's to look totally impotent in front of the whole empire.'

Antipatros could see where his wife's thoughts were heading. 'And assuming he does subdue Kappadokia and install Eumenes therein, then he will have to punish Antigonos in some way, otherwise he might just as well slink off into private life because no one will ever take him seriously again.'

'Precisely.'

'So war is now inevitable between these so-called successors; they all will have seen that and their minds will be focused on it; how have they let it come to this, and so quickly?' Antipatros' face brightened. 'Still it does have its advantages: it allows me to prosecute my campaign, whilst leaving the kingdom relatively open to the east, by concentrating the garrison against Epirus.'

'If you're quick, you'll be fine.'

'Oh, I'll be quick, my love; and I'll leave tomorrow. Which leaves me one duty to do before I go that won't be quick.' He cupped her breasts in his hands and nestled his face between them; banishing all the thoughts and cares that weighed him down in the course of his duty he concentrated entirely upon what faced him.

'How many are there facing us, Magas?' Antipatros asked, his brow furrowed with concentration, as he tried with old man's eyes to estimate the size of the rebel Greek army holding the pass of Thermopylae, banners flying and shields presented.

'At least thirty thousand,' Magas, his niece's husband and second-in-command, mounted to Antipatros' right, replied, shading his eyes. In his forties with the bearded, rough-hewn look of the Macedonian uplands, he had been, along with Nicanor, his military mainstay for his entire regency.

Antipatros spat. 'Almost five thousand more than our number.'

'But all Greeks,' Iollas said, with the drawling arrogance of youth.

Antipatros turned to his younger son on his left, next to Nicanor. 'Never underestimate your enemy. True, they may be Greeks, but many of them are experienced mercenaries having fought for Alexander and the Persians before him.'

'But we are well supplied with cavalry, Father,' Nicanor observed, indicating to the dust-swathed multitude of Thessalian cavalry forming up on the deploying Macedonian army's extreme right, taking the higher ground. 'They have very few.'

Thank Aries for the Thessalians. And so Antipatros had prayed since the rendezvous with the Thessalian cavalry and their supporting light troops, on schedule, five days previously at the River Peneios on the border between Macedon and Thessaly. Wild, javelin-armed horsemen, born to the saddle, five thousand of them in their wide-brimmed, leather hats and sleeveless dun and ochre tunics, matching the pelts of their mounts, they boosted not only his numbers but also his men's morale for their bravado and prodigious skill in horsemanship inspired confidence. And it was full of confidence that Antipatros had led his army south through Thessaly, and then west, along the coast, with the fleet keeping pace with him to his left, past the city of Lamia and on to Thermopylae.

But now, nine days after setting out from Pella, marching at a blistering rate, Antipatros had arrived at his first objective only to find it already held against him. *We shall need the Thessalians if we are going to break this army.* He glanced at the sun, falling to his right and then addressed Magas and Nicanor. 'We have four hours until sunset; once order of battle has been formed give the men something to eat and drink and then let's get this thing over with.'

'Your orders, sir,' Magas asked.

'Nothing special; we've the sea to our left and hills to our right. You take the phalanx, Magas, it will roll forward with archers, slingers and light-javelinmen covering the advance; place half the peltasts in the surf on the left preventing any outflanking.' He looked out to sea to the fleet formed up, opposing the Athenian navy also ready for battle. 'Let's hope our lads can stop their fleet getting around behind us.' He turned his attention back to his army. 'The other thousand peltasts station on the phalanx's right flank between it and the Thessalians. Nicanor, have our heavy cavalry in wedges behind them waiting for my signal to charge the break in their line. The Greek mercenaries I'll keep in reserve, I wouldn't like to test their loyalty unless absolutely necessary.'

Nicanor's face clouded. 'If it gets to the stage that it becomes necessary then I don't think we'll be able to count on them at all.'

Antipatros considered the thought. 'You're right. In which case have them sent back down the road a couple of miles; they could be a useful rallying point if it comes to it.'

Iollas' eyes widened in astonishment. 'You don't think it would come to that, Father?'

Antipatros sighed with the weariness of one who would rest but was being constantly thwarted in that ambition. 'I'm seventy-eight, my boy, I have seen most situations in war and the one common factor they have is that there is no predicting the outcome so, therefore, I try to plan for all possibilities.'

'Including the enemy's surrender?' Magas asked, pointing.

Antipatros followed the direction of Magas' finger to where the Greek line was parting to allow three horsemen through, one of whom carried a branch of peace. 'Well, I can't imagine that they have come all this way just to surrender; let's go and hear what they have to say.'

'My name is Leosthenes,' the leader of the group announced as both parties drew up their horses midway between the opposing armies, 'General of the free Greek army.'

Antipatros gave a wan smile. 'That's a novel way of terming a mercenary army; I've never heard of a mercenary fighting for free.'

Leosthenes laughed, it was genuine and infectious; dark eyes glinted with amusement. Although battered by many campaigns and extremes of weather, his bearded face remained handsome in a scarred and rugged way. 'Very good, old man; you have the better of me on that point. Although there are some Athenian citizens and four thousand Aetollian's in our number, I grant you that most of my men don't give a horse's arse for Greek freedom; so long as they have the money to freely plough their own furrows and drink wine freely, they are happy.'

'Men of conscience; admirable.'

Leosthenes shrugged. 'Men of business, certainly. And, right now, their business is to prevent you from passing, which, when you look at the positions, I would have thought a man of your experience could see as being quite likely. So what I propose, Antipatros, regent of Macedon, is this: you take your army back north, leave the Greek cities to govern themselves. I have already defeated your only allies, the Boeotians, three days ago so you'll find no friends south of here apart from a few Macedonian garrisons holed up in their citadels and now under a state of siege. If you go now, then Hyperides and the Athenian assembly will guarantee those garrisons' safe passage home. If you fight, they will all die even in the unlikely event that you triumph on this field. What do you say?'

Antipatros looked across to the rebel army and then up and down the length of his line, as if counting numbers. 'I would say, Leosthenes, that I have more cavalry than you, a lot more, in fact, seeing as you have hardly any. That, along with the superiority in the quality of my infantry, gives me the edge.'

Leosthenes face brightened as if he were pleased to be reminded of something that had almost slipped his mind. 'Ah, yes, I was going to come to that.' He signalled to one of his companions who raised a horn and blew a series of rising notes.

Out to Antipatros' right there was a stirring and then, to the jangle of thousands of harnesses, multiple equine snorts and the stamp of many hoofs, the Thessalian cavalry began to move forward.

Leosthenes looked at Antipatros, a picture of surprise and innocence. 'Oooh, and how did that happen? It looks like I've got the most cavalry now.'

Antigonos took a few moments to comprehend just what was occurring, before turning back in fury to Leosthenes. 'You treacherous bastard!' he spat as the Thessalian cavalry crossed the field followed by their supporting light troops.

Leosthenes looked wounded. 'Come, come, Antipatros; it's not my treachery we are witnessing here, surely you can see that? It's the Thessalians'; they're the ones changing sides, not me. I merely negotiated with their general, Menon, and he seemed to see the logic of my argument. I'm sure it will please you to know that had I not garrisoned the pass in time to block you they would have remained loyal to your cause. At least, that's what they said. But, well, that's Thessalians for you. If you want loyalty, get a dog, I always say. Still, I should know because I've been a mercenary ever since I killed my father when he raised a hand to me just one too many times when I was fifteen. Now, enough of pleasant reminiscences and back to business: if your army is still here in an hour, I'll sound the attack.' With a cheery wave he spun his horse around and trotted back to his lines with one hand on his hip.

'Well, what do we do?' Magas asked as Antipatros turned his mount in grim silence. 'The bastard's got us by the scrotum and is working up to quite a vigorous squeeze.'

'We attack,' Iollas insisted, 'with or without the cavalry.'

'No we don't,' Nicanor said, looking about the field, 'the Thessalians will get around our flanks and take the phalanx in the rear and that will be the end of us.'

Antipatros sighed his deepest sigh of the day. *I really am too old for all this; all I want is to lie with my wife on a rug in front of the fire with a jug of wine and the knowledge of a fine meal being prepared and instead, what do I have: a crisis.* 'So what can we do? We're five days' march from Macedon through now hostile territory and then a further four days to the safety of Pella. We have no supporting cavalry and they now have five thousand to harry us with all the way; we'll lose hundreds, if not thousands and our retreat will be a shambles and a humiliation. And then at one point, Leosthenes will force us to fight, tired and outnumbered. It's unthinkable.'

'What about the fleet?' Magas asked.

'The Athenians' ships will prevent us from embarking; no, that's not an option.'

Magas grimaced at the mental picture of the disaster. 'So what to do then?'

'We make a fighting retreat, step by step. I left a few trusted men in Lamia, three leagues back up the road; as I said: prepare for all eventualities. Although, I will admit that I did not really think that I would need spies to open Lamia's gates for me; it was just a possibility that I foresaw.'

'We're going to take Lamia? What for?'

'So we can tighten our belts and endure a winter siege until help arrives in the spring. This is going to cost me a lot of daughters; I had better get writing letters. They need to be on their way before we're completely closed off.'

Eumenes, The Sly

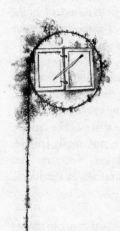

'REMIND ME AGAIN, Eumenes, what was Antigonos' reply to Perdikkas?' Leonnatus said as he and the little Greek stood on the ramparts of the port of Lampsacus looking out over the Propontis to the European shore; below them a trireme approached the harbour, its oars beating in time like the slow, majestic wings of a swan. Salt tanged the air; gulls circled the waterfront, swooping down on any discharge from the dozen ships already in dock.

Eumenes stopped straining his eyes, trying to get a glimpse of the city of Kardia, his home town, somewhere away across a sparkling azure sea, speckled with trading vessels. *If he thinks that he can annoy me with such childish behaviour then he has even more beauty than brain than I'd originally imagined.* He looked up at the dandy general, an expression of mock-concern on his face. 'Oh, Leonnatus, don't tell me that you're losing your memory; I believe that I mentioned his exact words at the beginning of this conversation.'

'Perhaps you did; I have other things on my mind.'

'Do you mean to say that you haven't been giving me your full attention, Leonnatus? In Kardia, where I come from, just across the water, we consider that to be quite rude; mind you, Kardia is quite a distance from Macedon. I believe his reply was: "My arse".'

Leonnatus checked the flick-back of his fringe, patting it into the optimum angle. 'And what makes you think that my reply won't be any different to that?'

'Well, for a start, I imagine Antigonos' arse to be a hairy, sweaty sort of affair, much given to the cultivation of boils, whereas yours is undoubtedly fragrant and smooth and thus wouldn't offer the same sort of insult as Antigonos'.'

'Don't try to be—'

'Clever with you? I can assure you, Leonnatus, I wasn't trying.' Eumenes indicated to the beach, to the right on the harbour, where his cavalry escort was making camp; neat horse-lines and tent-lines signalling the professionalism of the troops. 'I have but five hundred companion cavalry; not nearly enough to secure somewhere as large as Kappadokia. Now, are you going to help me take the satrapy from Ariarathes, as Perdikkas has requested—'

'Ordered!'

'Alright, ordered, but in a nice way. Or are you going to ignore the nice order as Antigonos did?'

'He didn't ignore it; he said "my arse" to it. I don't call that ignoring, do you? I call it refusing.'

I have to admit, that is a reasonable point. Eumenes took a breath to try to stem his growing frustration with the bouffant aristocrat. 'You know perfectly well what I mean, Leonnatus.'

'Do I?' Leonnatus looked back out to sea and appeared to be enjoying the soft breeze despite the fact, Eumenes noted, that it was playing havoc with his coiffure; the trireme slackened its stroke as it passed the mole protecting the port from the ravages of winter seas.

Eumenes decided upon a different tack. 'Since Alexander died, do you think that you've been treated fairly? I mean, at one point you were named as one of the four joint regents and then, for Perdikkas' convenience, you were dropped from that position so that Meleagros could be regent. And now he's dead and yet you never got reinstated.'

'Which is why I'm minded to say "my arse" to Perdikkas. Who is he to think that he can go around giving me orders; me, who has more royal blood in my veins than he has in one finger.'

'You meant that the other way around but, even so, it's not strictly true, Leonnatus, is it? You both have a reasonable claim to royalty and this is just my point: he's giving you orders. But let's just put that aside for the moment and consider why he feels that he can do so.' Eumenes waited a few moments for Leonnatus to ponder the matter before supplying the answer. 'Because he thinks that, in receiving the ring from Alexander, he is the natural leader; that's why. Now the problem with this is that leaders need to earn the respect of the led, something that Perdikkas definitely has not done – witness Antigonos' reply. So how does a Macedonian soldier earn respect, Leonnatus? Give me an insight into the military mind.'

Leonnatus glanced down to check that he wasn't being mocked to see Eumenes with an expression of genuine and unreserved interest. 'By gaining victories.'

'Ah! There you have it: gaining victories. Now tell me, are you gaining any victories sitting here on your fragrant and smooth arse and enjoying a sea view?'

Leonnatus' silence was eloquent.

Got him! 'Now, I would be very happy to serve as your second-in-command and add my paltry five hundred companion cavalry to your army, should you decide to bring it to Kappadokia. In that way, when you finally acquaint Ariarathes' sphincter with the well-sharpened tip of a stake, the glory will be all yours. And then, together – although, with you firmly in charge, obviously – we can go onto Armenia and that'll be two great victories in the space of one year whereas Perdikkas will have had none; then, perhaps, you could think about giving the orders. But if you don't, then it may well be Perdikkas who has those victories and that might well give him the respect he needs to carry on giving the orders.' Eumenes watched the thought travelling across Leonnatus' handsome face, counting down backwards in his head from ten.

'Very well, Eumenes, you have convinced me; I shall bring my men and pacify your satrapy for you. I'm in sole command and you defer to me on every level, agreed.'

'Agreed.'

'And there is one other condition.'

'Name it.'

'That you agree to support me in my endeavours afterwards.'

'What endeavours?'

'That I can't tell you at the moment; but let us just say that should I succeed, and I have every reason to expect that I will, then those who have served me well will have reason to be thankful.'

He's going to try for the throne, the fool; how can he expect to take it when he's only a distant relation to Alexander? 'Of course, Leonnatus, I will have every reason to be grateful to you; of course I'll support you in your *endeavours*.'

'Let's drink on it; I've just received a shipment of wine from my estate outside Pella.'

Eumenes' smile was fixed. 'Ah, Macedonian wine at its best; how super.'

'I've had it chilled,' Leonnatus informed Eumenes as a slave filled his drinking bowl.

They were seated by a huge fire for, despite the relatively warm early-winter air, the palace's stone interior had already grown cold. Eumenes did his best not to wince as he took his first sip; he had already resigned himself to the most brutal of hangovers the following morning. 'Delicious, Leonnatus, what an extraordinary palate you must have to create a vintage of this quality.'

'I like to think so.' But Leonnatus' further opinions on his palate were interrupted by shouting from down the corridor.

'I don't care if he's in conference; I have come across the sea from Kardia to see him and, although I may not look it in these travelling clothes, I am a king and am not used to being denied by people as lowly as you.'

Now, this will be interesting; I mustn't let my loathing show, Eumenes thought as he braced himself for an old acquaintance's entrance.

Within a half-dozen heartbeats a towering, full-bearded, broad-shouldered man stomped into the room. 'You!' he exclaimed, seeing Eumenes and halting in surprise. 'What are *you* doing here?'

'I think that I should be asking that question of you, Hecataeus, seeing as I was here first. However, that lowly fellow you were so polite to was right: I'm here conferring with Leonnatus. Oh, and by the way, Kardia doesn't have a king, just a tyrant, so don't get ideas above your station.'

Hecataeus made to lunge at Eumenes who sprang back, putting a couch between him and his assailant.

'That's enough!' Leonnatus shouted, throwing down his wine bowl and jumping to his feet. 'I don't know who you are but that is no way to treat my guest.'

Hecataeus scoffed. 'Guest! Since when have treasonous weasels been treated as guests?'

'Since murdering tyrants started pretending to be kings?' Eumenes suggested in a helpful manner.

Hecataeus looked with a venomous hatred at his fellow-countryman, fully two heads shorter than him, and then spat at his feet.

'I'm very pleased to see you too, Hecataeus,' Eumenes said, judging it safe to now resume his place. 'It's been fourteen years, I believe.'

Leonnatus raised his hands. 'I don't know what there is between you two, nor do I wish to as it is evidently bitter and personal.' He looked direct into Hecataeus' eyes. 'Now, do me the courtesy of introducing yourself formally and stating your business with me before you go attacking my guest again.'

The big man drew breath. 'My apologies, noble Leonnatus. My name is Hecataeus, the Ki— the ruler of Kardia and messenger from Antipatros to yourself.'

'From Antipatros.' Leonnatus contemplated the news for a moment before inclining his head towards a spare couch. 'Sit, please, Hecataeus, pour yourself a bowl of wine, it is from my own estate and will, I hope, calm your nerves.'

Enrage the beast even further, I shouldn't wonder.

'Now tell me your message,' Leonnatus said after Hecataeus had taken a couple of sips – he had not caught the big man's pained expression at first taste, having been patting his fringe-flick back into order after all the excitement.

Hecataeus nodded at Eumenes.

'You may speak in front of Eumenes; he is my confederate.'

That's the first I've heard of it.

'Very well,' Hecataeus said, looking like he meant the exact opposite. 'Antipatros bids you know that due to the treachery of his Thessalian cavalry he has suffered a reverse against the Greek uprising and is now besieged in the town of Lamia. The knowledge that one of Macedon's greatest generals is so close gives him heart and he prays by all the gods for you to come to his aid. In return he would offer you one of his daughters to make a bond of kin between you.' Hecataeus turned and beckoned down the corridor. Two slaves came through the door struggling with a chest between them. They placed it on the floor and Hecataeus threw the lid open; it was full of gold, silver and jewels. 'Antipatros has sent you this to cover your expenses; he hopes that you will be in sight of the walls of Lamia well before the spring equinox as he will be desperately short of supplies by then.' Looking pleased with himself for such a fluent rendition of his message, Hecataeus sat down; without thinking, he took a large gulp of wine and dissolved into a choking bout.

Leonnatus failed to notice his guest's distress, so deep into thought had he fallen.

The bastard's going to take up the offer, Eumenes thought in alarm, completely ignoring the gasping for air that Hecataeus was attempting. *I need to do something.* 'How can you be sure that this is a genuine appeal for help, Leonnatus? It could be a ploy by Antigonos to ensure that he is not the only one disobeying Perdikkas' orders.' *Gods, that was weak; I can't stop him. Saving Macedon is far more prestigious than subduing Kappadokia; I'm defeated by my own argument. What hideous bad timing; and to be thwarted by this murderous old crook, into the bargain. I'll wager there were two chests when they were delivered to him.*

'Hmm?' Leonnatus gave Eumenes a brief glance, evidently disinterested in his argument, before turning back to the slowly recovering Hecataeus. 'A daughter he says? Which one?'

Hecataeus, still gasping, looked lost. 'He...did...not...spe... spe...specify.'

'Didn't specify. Hmmm. Well, I suppose it doesn't really

make any difference. Tell me, if he is besieged, how did he get this message out?'

'His son, Iollas, left the town soon before it was completely circumvallated. However, he awaits your reply in Kardia as Antipatros wanted me to deliver the message; he felt that it would carry more weight than if delivered by a mere boy.'

Or that mere boy had other messages to deliver in a hurry; I don't suppose old man Antipatros is going to be touting just the one daughter around in return for his deliverance. The old fool; well, that's what you get for trusting Thessalians.

Leonnatus looked down at the contents of the chest. 'Very handsome.' Taking another sip of wine and savouring its bouquet, his face resolved itself into a mask of heroic resolution. 'Very well; I shall come to Macedon's aid since I'm all there is to prevent abject defeat at the hands of lesser men.' He put a hand on Hecataeus' shoulder and looked down his nose at him. 'Tell Iollas to say to his father that Leonnatus will come.' He gave his coiffure a couple of strokes, making sure that he was looking his best for this announcement. 'And I shall bring my army and the wrath of Macedon with me.'

Well, you certainly won't be bringing me; that I can promise. I'll be slipping away at the first chance I get; preferably with the contents of that chest.

'Eumenes, will you accompany me?'

'It will be an honour, Leonnatus; but first, I would like to speak to you in private.'

'What? You can talk in front of Hecataeus, surely; he is a part of this glorious venture.'

Another reason I won't be coming along; he'd slit my throat as soon as he has the chance. 'It's concerning Macedonian politics.'

Leonnatus frowned and then nodded. 'Very well. Hecataeus, would you give us a few moments, please? Join us for dinner an hour before sundown, won't you?'

'My pleasure.' Hecataeus looked with pure loathing at Eumenes and strode from the room, bowling aside his two slaves who waited just beyond the door.

'So what is it?' Leonnatus asked as Hecataeus' footsteps faded.

'Has it occurred to you that Antipatros is probably offering his daughters around to anyone with a following of over ten thousand men?'

Leonnatus considered the matter. 'And what if he is?'

'Do the arithmetic: at the moment he's got three or four marriageable daughters – I lose count, as does he, no doubt – plus at least one great-niece, Berenice, recently widowed, and a couple more just ripening; that's quite a haul of potential kinsmen by marriage he could lure. Now, say he offers one each to all those closest, geographically, to him: you, Krateros, Lysimachus and Antigonos, where will that leave you all?'

'That, little Eumenes, is completely irrelevant.'

'I'd have thought that it was the most relevant consideration of the whole matter in the light of your *endeavours*. And then he will probably give one to Perdikkas and Ptolemy; why not? Let's be generous and treat all alike.'

The smugness that oozed onto Leonnatus' face was nauseating. 'Not if you have no intention of taking one of his fillies. No, my motivation is that in coming to Antipatros' aid, saving Macedon and then going on to crush the Greek rebels I'll gain far more kudos than I would in your little sideshow – which would have served had not this bigger task have come along. Saving Macedon along with what I have been offered will certainly bring my endeavours to fruition and you will do well to help me. I need a mind like yours; someone good with figures.' He pointed down to the chest. 'How much would you estimate that to be, for example?'

Eumenes did not need to guess, he had already weighed the thing in his mind. 'Two and a half talents, give or take.'

'You see, I wouldn't have a clue.'

That's because you're all beauty and no brains.

'Do an inventory of it for me this evening and give me the exact figure tomorrow.'

As if to prove my point: what an idiot you are, but thank you.
'Of course, Leonnatus. But I would just love to know one thing: what is it that you have been promised that will be so helpful to your *endeavours*?'

'Ah!' Leonnatus looked around, ridiculously checking that no one had crept into the room since Hecataeus had left. He lowered his voice. 'I received a letter a few days ago.' He glanced around again before proceeding. 'From Olympias.'

Eumenes could guess what was to come. *If this is true it could make him the favourite to claim the throne with full legitimacy. Perdikkas will be for ever in my debt when I bring him this news; it's Babylon for me and that chest.*

Leonnatus lowered his voice even more. 'Olympias has offered me the hand of Alexander's sister, Kleopatra; I've already written, accepting the match.'

OLYMPIAS,
THE MOTHER

'L EONNATUS!' KLEOPATRA'S VOICE
was shrill with shock. 'When did
you do this, Mother?'

'At the beginning of the month.'
Olympias sounded vague.

'And why, having failed to consult me
before you set such a ludicrous plan in
motion, has it taken so long for you to inform me of it?' With a
stamp of her foot, Kleopatra slumped down into a camp-chair,
her hands balled in her lap. A lamp burning next to her, its smoke
sweetened by incense, was the sole lighting within the leather tent.

'Please don't shout so loudly, the whole army will hear.'
Olympias moved to the entrance of the tent and pulled the flaps
together to afford at least the vestige of privacy. She turned back
to her daughter, keeping her hands on the flaps behind her back.
'The reason that I didn't tell you was because I knew that this
would be your reaction. But think about it, Kleopatra. You're
still young and fertile; you are the only one who could give birth
to an heir that most of the noble houses would agree to. An heir
with no eastern blood, provided the sire was of noble blood
himself. There is no one outside our immediate family with
more Argead blood in his veins than Leonnatus; it's perfect.'

'Perfect for whom, Mother?'

'Keep your voice down.'

'I'll do no such thing until you supply me with a valid reason
as to why I should take that vain, preening dandy into my bed
and allow him to foist a child on me?'

'Children.'

'More than one child? Even worse? He may be a brave soldier, and to have survived the last ten years and come out covered in glory goes some way to proving that, but how can a man who thinks so much about his appearance be a real man? And, believe me, Mother, I need a real man.'

'I do believe you and you may find that he's changed in the last ten years. Just because he likes to model his hair on Alexander's and rubs creams into his skin to keep it soft doesn't mean he's not hard in the bit that really matters.' Olympias let go of the flaps and approached her daughter, her hands to either side of her vision focusing solely on Kleopatra. 'Take your mind from the physical and concentrate on the dynastic. Look at what we know: the eastern bitch has had a boy, yes, he's my grandson and yes I should support his claim but how likely is the claim of a half-caste to succeed? About as likely as the claim of the idiot who has stolen my husband's name; Philip indeed! I should have used a stronger dose on his mother and finished them both off.'

Kleopatra knew her mother only too well to be shocked. 'So that's how it happened?'

'Of course it is. You don't think I was going to let that Thessalian dancer bear a royal child if I could help it, do you? Sadly the runt's body survived the dose even if his wits didn't. But forget him and think of yourself. You are Alexander's only full sibling.'

'And what about his half-siblings? Philip we know about; Europa and Caranus are, thanks to you, no longer a problem.'

'Alexander killed Caranus.'

'Mother, I'm not going to argue about the minutiae of dynastic assassination. My point is there are still two other surviving siblings: Thessonalike and Cynnane.'

Olympias' face clouded. 'Thessonalike would never do anything to get in the way of my ambition; she does as I say. Out of the goodness of my heart I let her live when her mother died and brought her up as if she were my own.' *It's useful to have a spare daughter, even if she's not of my blood; she may one day buy me something of value.* 'As for that Illyrian monstrosity, Cynnane, she's returned home to the north to bring her bitch-whelp up in the barbaric Illyrian tradition; we'll not hear of them again. You are all that's left of pure blood; marry Leonnatus, who shares the same great-grandmother as you, and together you have a better claim to the throne than anyone because your offspring will offer proper stability. What's more, it could happen very quickly as he's now in his satrapy of Hellespontian Phrygia.'

'And you'll try to be the power behind the throne?'

And don't I deserve to be? After all I've done. 'I'll be there to guide you.'

Kleopatra contemplated her mother's eyes as they pleaded with her. She stood, walked past Olympias and threw open the tent to reveal the Eperiot army encamped on a hill, ten leagues over the Macedonian border, as the shadows lengthened from the mountains to the west. Smoke from a thousand cooking fires, harsh voices from ten thousand throats and the equine snorts and bellows from a similar number of cavalry horses and transport mules filled the senses. 'And just how will I explain this to my prospective Macedonian husband: an Eperiot army threatening Macedon's western border while Antipatros, with his main army, is besieged in Lamia?'

Olympias' smile was sweet. 'I suggested in my letter to Leonnatus that he meet you in Pella seeing as Antipatros has got himself all tied up in Lamia. The army came to accompany you as far as the border.'

'And if he refuses my offer?'

'He hasn't.' In triumph, Olympias produced a letter from the folds of her robes. 'This arrived for me today and is the reason why I've told you now. He wrote saying that he accepts the match and would travel with a small escort to Pella as soon as he may.'

'And if he changes his mind when he gets there?'

'I don't think he will with an army on his border and a rebellion to the south, do you?'

'And if you have no personal need for the invasion then how will you persuade Aeacides to turn his army around?'

'I'll travel to Pella with you; I should be safe with both Antipatros and Nicanor cooped up in Lamia. Before I leave I'll tell the runt that if he so much as takes one step further into Macedon then the first thing that you will do as queen will be to organise a regime change in Eperius.'

Kleopatra could not help but smile at her mother's scheming, even though she had known it all her life. 'You've thought of everything.'

Got her. 'So you'll marry him?'

'And produce Alexander's true heirs; yes, Mother, I can see how it would be good for both of us.'

'Then we leave in the morning; if Leonnatus travels by sea then we should arrive at about the same time in Pella.'

'Pella is, of course, utterly provincial after being away for ten years,' Leonnatus observed to Olympias, checking that his hair was in place, as they looked down at the city from the palace.

Her smile was as icy as her eyes. 'For the people of Macedon it remains the centre of the world.'

'Unless they've seen the sights of the east.'

Dionysus, he's worse than I remember. 'You are fortunate in having had the opportunity, Leonnatus. My son would never grant me permission to travel.' *Not that I would have wanted to for one moment and left that toad Antipatros unsupervised.*

Leonnatus looked sideways down his nose at her. 'And where is Kleopatra? I have been here for two hours and am yet to meet my future bride; we have much to discuss. I want our wedding to be the grand affair that two people of our standing deserve. It will take months of planning; the people need to see it and feel awed.'

Olympias felt wrong-footed by the notion. 'Surely the marriage should happen as soon as possible?'

Leonnatus' thoughts seemed to be far away. 'What? Oh, no, no; completely out of the question. In the ten days since I received your offer, I've had time to consider my priorities. For a start, I have to wait for my army to arrive and then I must recruit more locally, especially cavalry, I'm in great need of cavalry. And then—'

'Leonnatus,' Kleopatra cooed, stepping out onto the terrace. 'I have yearned for this moment since you did me the honour of proposing marriage.'

If Leonnatus was surprised at this rewriting of the way the match had been brought about, he had the good manners not to show it. 'The pleasure is all mine, Kleopatra. Walk with me, my dear. We have plans to make.' He offered her his arm, which she took with a coy look up at him from beneath lush, fluttering eyelashes and, with a fearful backward glance to her mother, joined her husband-to-be in a gentle stroll.

Careful not to overdo it, child; he knows perfectly well you're not a virgin as you've got two children and a healthy appetite to prove it.

'Don't they make the most elegant couple, Olympias my dearest?'

Olympias spun round to find Antipatros' wife smiling at her. 'Hyperia, my sweetest, what a lovely surprise.' *Not a surprise for you, regent bitch; judging by your clothes, jewellery, coiffure and make-up, you're dressed for battle.* 'I wasn't expecting to find you here; I thought you would be with your husband.'

'Would that I were sharing his privations with him; I would be such a comfort to him. It's so fulfilling to be a consolation to a man, I do find; I'm sure you remember.'

First blood to you. 'Oh, I do, dear Hyperia; Philip was always very active, even in his later years in his forties. I'm sure you regret not marrying your husband until he was approaching his sixties.'

'Fortunately he still has the energy of a younger man.' Hyperia flattened her dress beneath her belly, revealing the swelling. 'As you can see, my dearest, I'm pregnant again.'

Olympias put on her most astounded look. 'The gods be praised, yet another baby for all your unmarried daughters to fuss over. How are they, by the way, my dear? I hope they are not too wearied by Pella; although it does have so much to commend it.'

'Oh, they won't be here for that much longer, but thank you for your concern. We've had much interest in them of late: Ptolemy in Egypt has written requesting the honour of marriage into our family, as has Perdikkas. I still manage to communicate with my husband, despite his present…difficulties.'

Humiliation.

'We've decided that Krateros should be offered the hand of Phila—'

'I'd heard that he had already taken it – or was I confusing it with another part of her anatomy?'

Hyperia's smile hardened even further so that her back teeth were now showing. 'And we're expecting them to come to Pella for the wedding.'

'How lovely; but tell me, which of your daughters had you in mind for Leonnatus, for I'm sure that the poor love must be so bitterly disappointed.'

'Originally Eurydike, but since Leonnatus' refusal we've decided that she should go to Ptolemy and Nicaea to Perdikkas.'

'It's a bitter taste, that of rejection.'

Hyperia composed her face into a countenance of regret tinged with triumph.

This is her killer-blow expression; I must have walked straight into her trap.

'Alas, it is, but fortunately in this case the rejection has been tempered by an honourable offer of service: Leonnatus is to take his army south to relieve my husband and extract him from Lamia.'

Olympias felt the full force of the body-blow, just as Hyperia had meant her to. *But surely he wants Antipatros to fail and preferably die in that siege? How can he be so stupid?* And then a second strike almost took the wind from her lungs as she saw, now, exactly what Leonnatus had done. *Never ever underestimate him again; the bastard has accepted Kleopatra over Eurydike because she holds the key to the throne. That done, he will then make a deal with Antipatros for him to support his claim should Leonnatus extricate him from Lamia.*

Hyperia gave a slight nod and a half-wink as she saw the implication of the deal sink in. 'I'm so happy for you and your good news of Kleopatra's engagement to Leonnatus, my dear. Now, I must be going as I have so much to organise for my girls.'

Olympias watched her walk away, horror-stricken. *My daughter may become Macedon's queen but I won't have any influence as Antipatros will still be the real power. And if I cancel the wedding then I'll be no further forward and I'll also run the risk of falling out with Kleopatra who's my quickest route to power. Somehow I've got to stop this.* She examined her options, chewing on her cheek. *Wait, Leonnatus said he was in great need of cavalry; well, well, perhaps I should get some for him.*

PERDIKKAS,
THE HALF-CHOSEN

WAS THERE NO end to the difficulties that beset him?

Perdikkas glanced down at the ring; how many times since he had received it from Alexander's dying hand had he asked himself that, Perdikkas wondered as he contemplated the latest piece of news from an extremity of an empire convulsing?

Perdikkas looked at the merchant with world-weary eyes, finding his long robes and elaborately wound headdress even more outlandish than Persian costume. 'Are you sure, Babrak?'

'Yes, good sir, when my caravan was escorted into Alexandria Oxiana, the messenger was waiting to tell Philo. The first thing that he did upon hearing the news was to call an assembly of the garrison at which they voted to abandon their posts and return home. They seemed to have a fixation with seeing the sea again.'

Perdikkas sighed and rubbed the back of his neck. *Well, I can't blame them for that. I'm starting to wish for the same thing; what with the news of Cleomenes' execution and Ptolemy's virtual declaration of independence by minting those hideous coins – why didn't I think of that? And then the uncertainty surrounding Krateros. No, the sea sounds like a good place to be, right now.* 'But they hadn't left their posts by the time you continued your journey?'

'Some had, good sir. The last I heard was that they had secured the agreement of nearly all the garrisons in Sogdiana and most of the Bactrian ones; those that could make it before the weather closed in had come to Alexandria Oxiana; it is called thus because it's on the Oxus—'

'Yes, we all know where Alexandria Oxiana is,' Alketas butted in, 'we were there when Alexander founded it and a more desolate place for a city he could not have chosen.'

Perdikkas gave a quick glance to Kassandros, who had been left behind in Macedon, and, seeing the well-aimed insult hit home and Seleukos' and Aristonous' shared look of amusement, wished that there could at least be some unity between his closest comrades. 'Go on.'

Babrak bowed and touched his forehead with the tips of his fingers. 'Indeed, my good sirs, I apologise for giving offence with such a basic geographical reference. Well, quite a few of the garrisons had arrived by the time I had completed my business and was ready to move on; I'd say that there were at least five thousand men in and around the city in camps, with more coming in all the time; it was a great boost to trade and the reason why I did not need to tarry long in the city.'

Perdikkas looked to Seleukos, inviting his opinion.

'They're being sensible this time,' Seleukos said, leaning back in his creaking chair with his long legs outstretched and crossed before him. 'Last time, after they thought that Alexander had succumbed to that arrow in India, they went piecemeal and were picked off one by one; although some did get back, enough were killed to discourage the rest. This time though...'

Seleukos did not have to finish his sentence; all in the room knew what was now at stake and Perdikkas closed his eyes as he contemplated it. *The very existence of the eastern empire. If our eastern garrisons desert then there will be no one to prevent the satraps breaking away from my rule. That in turn will lead to the Massaegetae and the Sakae, as well as other northern tribes, testing the borders in search of new lands.* He groaned out loud as the danger in his mind grew. *And then the Indian kingdoms; how they would love to take back what Alexander took.* 'Is there anything else, Babrak?'

'No, good sir, that's all I know.'

'Thank you; you've done well.' Perdikkas threw a purse of gold to the merchant and dismissed him.

'I have one boon to ask before I leave your mighty presence, good sir.'

'Name it.'

'When my business here is done, I shall be heading to Sardis in—'

'We all know where Sardis is,' Alketas again broke in, 'we conquered it.'

Babrak bowed and touched his forehead once more. 'Good sirs, my manners are far inferior to your geography; I forget myself. Where have you not been?' He turned back to Perdikkas. 'Would it be possible for you to give me letters of introduction to Menander who is the satrap there and to Krateros who is, I believe, if the rumours are true, in Cilicia, which is…forgive me, good sirs, you all know perfectly well that it is on the way, as you conquered it.'

Perdikkas shooed the man away. 'Yes, yes, now be off, we have important matters to discuss; see my secretary, he'll draft them and I'll sign them.' Again it was Seleukos to whom he looked as Babrak withdrew with many bows and much touching of his forehead.

'A big rebellion needs a big response,' Seleukos said with his customary directness. 'We need to learn how to control the eastern fringe of the empire and I would suggest that terror and awe in equal measure would be the right tools.'

'So kill them all before they start out in the spring.'

'Then how will you know that you're killing the right men? If you do that then you would have to kill every Greek in every garrison whether he was planning on deserting or not, which wouldn't be at all helpful. No, wait until they set out and they have reached their full strength and then kill them all; every one of them, including their women and children. That should send a clear message to everyone in the eastern satrapies as to who is in charge.'

'Peithon's the man for the job,' Aristonous said after a few moments of contemplating the massacre that would have to occur if these former comrades were to be deprived of their dream of the sea. 'They will have to pass through Media, his satrapy.'

'But there may well be upwards of fifteen thousand of them,' Seleukos pointed out, 'perhaps twenty. His satrapy army is no more than fifteen thousand. To be completely sure of victory, which we have to be in this situation, he will need an army of twenty-five thousand.'

'Then I will have to lend him the troops,' Perdikkas said.

But it was Kassandros who voiced the snag that lurked in the back of all their minds. 'If you give one man twenty-five thousand troops to intercept and destroy an army of mercenaries, twenty thousand strong, how can you be certain that the man won't just end up with an army of forty-five thousand? After all, when twenty thousand mercenaries see an army of twenty-five thousand of their former comrades in front of them, they're not going to charge them, they're going to surrender to them; so unless they are murdered in cold blood they are going to end up enlisting in the army that was sent to stop them, if only to survive until the next time they get a chance of heading home.'

Gods, why is everything so difficult? Why can't I have the empire exactly as Alexander had it? Perdikkas looked around his comrades' expectant faces. *I need to be seen to be making decisions just as easily as he did.* 'Kassandros, get Peithon here to Babylon as soon as he can; it's just under a hundred leagues to his residence at Ecbatana, using the relay a message can be with him in under two days so he could be here in five. Alketas, see to it that the Greek mercenaries here in Babylon are up to date with their pay; I don't want any cause for discontent here when they hear about what's happening out in the east.' Perdikkas turned to Seleukos as Alketas followed Kassandros out of the room. 'Start working out where we can strip the troops from to give Peithon enough to stop this.'

Seleukos got to his feet. 'Leaving you enough to deal with another event elsewhere should one occur?'

Perdikkas frowned his incomprehension. 'Another event? Where?'

'Well, with the way things are, it could be anywhere. Ptolemy, Antigonos, maybe even Krateros, of whom we have had no news for a few months now; who knows what he's thinking of doing with his ten thousand veterans. Any one of our potential enemies could take advantage of you denuding yourself of too many troops.'

It should have been me that pointed that out. I must think faster, I don't want people wondering whether I'm getting out of my depth; if I can't lead them then who can? 'Of course leave me enough to deal with something else; I thought you meant there was already another event occurring.'

'Indeed, sir,' Seleukos said, his face a rigid mask, as he turned and left.

'If you want to keep that very able and ambitious young man's loyalty,' Aristonous said, when they were alone, 'then I would advise you not to pretend that you've already thought of something that he suggests or points out.'

'Of course I'd already thought of it!' Perdikkas snapped. 'Seleukos is not the only one with brains.'

'No, he isn't,' Aristonous agreed, getting to his feet. 'I possess some as well; and if you wish to carry on receiving my wisdom then I'd suggest you refrain from shouting at me, especially when you're lying.'

It was with a face of exhaustion, and a numb feeling within his whole being, that Perdikkas watched his most loyal supporter leave the room at an agitated pace. He tried to stand and call out an apology but the words would not come and, instead, he slumped back into his chair, rubbing his knuckles into his eyes. *Perhaps it should be me who goes east to deal with the deserters; at least then I'd be doing something that I can do: campaign. Something that I know I'm good at.* It took a couple of heartbeats to realise the stupidity of the thought. *If I were to go east then there would be no west for me to come back to. So what to do then?*

It was at times like this, when depression, supported by a nagging sense of imminent failure, weighed heavy upon him, that Perdikkas took himself to the place that made all the pressure seem worthwhile. And so it was with a great lifting of his spirits that he walked into the throne-room, now alive with meticulous activity, and beheld Alexander's catafalque, already fully constructed but bare of decoration. 'You've made progress since last I was here, Arrhidaeus,' Perdikkas said, beaming with pleasure at what had become his pride and joy.

'Yes, sir; as you can see the roof is now on,' Arrhidaeus replied, looking up from a plan he was studying. 'That was the last piece of construction and today we begin the decoration which will take the whole of next year and more; I have started the sculptors on their tasks. Once they finish then it will be the turn of the painters and, lastly, the gold- and silversmiths.'

Perdikkas felt his depression fading as he surveyed the vehicle ahead of which he would make a triumphant return to Macedon as the custodian of the corpse of a god and the regent of the two kings who are his heirs; this is what would make his position secure. 'Very good, very good, Arrhidaeus. So we're still looking at a spring departure the year after next?'

'Provided the mules are all trained in time, then yes. I'm hoping to be ready to leave at the equinox.'

'And that would get us to Macedon when?'

Arrhidaeus shrugged. 'It's hard to tell; we would be in Syria a month after we left and then from there it's difficult to estimate because of the state of the road.'

'Good, good; I'll get someone to work on the problem. I'll need to know exactly when I have to leave to be in time for it entering Macedon for the first time. I cannot miss that moment.'

'First of all, you're going to have to get that thing outside,' a voice from behind said.

Perdikkas turned to come face to face with Eumenes, dusty from the road. 'What are you—'

'Doing here? I've come to see you as, once again, you need my help; in return for which I need yours.'

'Why do I need your help?'

Eumenes pointed at the main double doors to the chamber. 'Well, for a start, you're going to need someone to point out that you need to enlarge those.'

Perdikkas looked at the beautiful waxed cedar-wood doors,

towering to three times the size of a man. They looked quite big enough to him. 'Why?'

'If you want to lead Alexander's funeral cortège in triumph back home, you first have to get the catafalque out of this room.'

Perdikkas looked again at the doors and then at the catafalque as a sick feeling developed in his stomach. *I can't even do that properly; I've ordered the catafalque to be built in a room where the doors are too small to get the thing out. What an idiot! Yet why had no one else noticed? Seleukos, Aristonous, lots of people have seen it; Arrhidaeus looks at it every day. Have they all noticed but say nothing because they're enjoying a joke at my expense. Are they all laughing behind my back?* 'Arrhidaeus!'

Arrhidaeus looked up from his plans, startled by the venom in the shout. 'Yes, sir?'

Perdikkas walked towards him with menace. 'Why didn't you tell me that the catafalque would be too big to get out of the doors?'

Arrhidaeus stood up to his full height, pulling his shoulders back. 'I tried to, Perdikkas; I said that I didn't think we should build it in here but you wouldn't listen.'

'But I didn't know that it would be too big.'

'Because you didn't give me a chance to tell you.'

'But what will we do?'

'That's your problem; you're the one who insisted that I should build it in here. I'm building it; you get it out. Now, if you don't mind, *sir*, I need to get on with my work.' With exaggerated finality, Arrhidaeus bent back down to pore over his plans.

Perdikkas made a move towards him and then checked himself. *Stop; you've lost enough dignity already.*

'A wise choice,' Eumenes said from behind him. 'Pointless to alienate him even more, seeing as you were the idiot who insisted on building it in here; he may just end up saying "my arse" to you as that seems to be rather fashionable these days.'

Perdikkas spun round to face the little Greek. 'I'm fed up with the sound of your smug little voice.'

'Well, that is a shame, Perdikkas; because I was about to tell you something very interesting that you need to know. However, out of deference to your sensibilities, I won't. Although I do think you should listen to me; had you listened to Arrhidaeus you wouldn't be a laughing stock now. But, hey, that's your decision.' He turned and began walking towards the rear door of the chamber.

The little bastard's right; I'd be a fool not to hear what he's got to say after he's travelled so far to tell me. Swallowing what remained of his pride, Perdikkas walked quickly to catch up with Eumenes. 'I'm sorry, Eumenes.'

'Sorry, are you? Goodness me, I might have to sit down; I don't think I've ever witnessed a Macedonian being sorry. How does it feel? Do you need to sit down as well?'

'Very funny. Now tell me what you've come to say.'

'Let's get out into the open where we're safe from being overheard.'

'Are you sure,' Perdikkas said as they crossed the great courtyard of the palace complex. 'Leonnatus is really going to marry Kleopatra?'

'He told me so himself.'

'And she accepted?'

'It was the other way around; she, or rather Olympias, made the offer and Leonnatus accepted. I think that way around it appealed to his vanity more.'

Perdikkas was in no mood for levity. 'But this is serious; if he does that then he could claim precedence over me.'

'Of course he would; he would be king.'

'King?'

'Naturally. The army in Macedon as well as his satrapy army, the one that he's taking with him to relieve Antipatros, would proclaim him as such as soon as the siege of Lamia is lifted and the Greek rebellion in the west crushed.'

'But what should I do?'

Eumenes sat down on the base of the fountain at the centre of the courtyard. 'You defend yourself against possible attack without being provocative.'

'You think that Leonnatus would attack me; surely Antipatros would dissuade him as I'm due to marry one of his daughters.'

'But have you yet? At the moment there is no tie of kin between you and him so he wouldn't feel obliged to hold Leonnatus back should he decide to invade. And, let's face it, Perdikkas: war is now inevitable – if you want to keep your position, that is. And your life, come to think of it.'

Perdikkas sat next to Eumenes and contemplated the statement, slowly nodding his head. 'Antigonos, Ptolemy and now Leonnatus; you're right, Eumenes, war is inevitable so I would do well to prepare for it.' He frowned. *Is this the event that Seleukos was talking about? Had he already foreseen the conflict between us; us who had once been brothers? Why did they not just accept me as their leader? After all, I have the ring.* 'So you advise that I prepare for a possible attack without being provocative?'

'Oh, so you were listening.'

Perdikkas gave the Greek a look that caused him to incline his head and hold a hand up in apology. 'So tell me.'

'The way I see it is like this,' Eumenes said, taking his time as he formulated his argument in his head. 'You can forget Ptolemy for now as he's busy getting a firm grip on Egypt. As for Krateros, no one knows so he is a variable in the arithmetic. However, what you can be sure of is that if Leonnatus were to invade, with or without Antipatros, he would come across the Hellespont into his satrapy and then south, linking up with Antigonos on the way, as he has no love for you as his last communiqué revealed.'

'My arse, yes; I wish we could just forget about that. But you are probably right. So what do I do?'

'You have an army up there waiting for them.'

'But that would be provocative; they could say that it was me who started the war.'

'Not if the army was doing something else, something that didn't look at all as if it was just waiting to repel an invasion.'

'Like what?'

'Like subduing Kappadokia.' Eumenes raised his hand to stifle Perdikkas' protest. 'Think of it: Kappadokia borders both Antigonos in Phrygia and Leonnatus in Hellespontine Phrygia. The Royal Road runs through it so if, whilst you're defeating

Ariarathes for me, you hear that an invasion is imminent, you will be able to move fast along that road to wherever you need to be. And all the time it looks as if you're pacifying a satrapy rather than planning for civil war. And, for good measure, send an army to settle the Armenian situation; it's right next to Kappadokia, so could easily reinforce you should you need it.'

Perdikkas contemplated the matter. 'Yes, Neoptolemus could do that.'

'I had someone with at least a vestige of competence in mind.'

Perdikkas shook his head. 'I need to bind him to me by giving him the chance of some glory. He'll be fine.'

'No, he won't.'

Perdikkas ignored the remark, contemplating instead the beauty of the scheme. *I'll be back doing something that I really can do; I'll be back in the field leading soldiers. I'll be able to get my self-esteem back and the respect I'm owed from my peers. Yes, the slimy little Greek is right and so what if he too gains from the deal; the main thing is that I'll feel better about myself. And, if I install him in Kappadokia, with Armenia pacified, I'll have someone in the north to look after my interests if I ever have to go south to face up to Ptolemy. And, besides, what else could I be doing whilst waiting for the catafalque to be completed?* Perdikkas smiled and clapped Eumenes on the shoulder. 'You are the slyest of little Greeks.'

'Why, thank you, Perdikkas.'

'And you are also the shrewdest. I'll do it; I'll bring my army to Kappadokia for you.'

ANTIPATROS,
THE REGENT

'MAGAS!' ANTIPATROS BELLOWED, straining to make himself heard over the violent clash of a rare assault on the walls of Lamia. 'Magas! Get men to the West Gate! This was a feint; they're bringing a ram up. Get artillery and oil over there. Now!'

Antipatros' second-in-command held his hand up in acknowledgement as yet another ladder crashed against the parapet. Leaving the threat to be dealt with by the chiliarch commanding the troops on that section of the southern wall, Magas raced off, sprinting down the stone steps to the street below and then on, through the town to the main gate in the western wall.

Satisfied that the assault on the gates would be taken care of, Antipatros stabbed his pike back down at an Athenian hoplite mounting one of the many ladders thrust up against the city's south-facing wall. Forcing his weapon down again and again, Antipatros grunted with exertion as the point cracked repeatedly into the hoplite's shield, held over his head as he clambered up, using only his right hand for balance. The ladder bent under the pressure of Antipatros' attack and the weight of other men below the hoplite, but the man kept coming, invulnerable beneath his shield, blazoned with the ghastly face of Medusa, red tongue protruding, eyes wide and snake-hair writhing. To either side of him, Antipatros' men battled with the blood-hungry Greeks scaling the walls: dropping bricks, stabbing with pike or spear and pushing away the ladders not yet too weighed down by assault troops. Ceaselessly they had slogged thus since the horns had sounded the attack soon after dawn, before most defenders had broken their fast and so it was with empty bellies that they fought – not that they ever had their fill anymore; with the siege in its fourth month and the price of cats, dogs and rats at a premium, breakfast was a meal that was often not much more than a distant memory.

Gods, I could eat a whole dog, Antipatros reflected as he felt his stomach churn and he emitted a sour-tasting burp. *I'm too old to be fighting on an empty stomach. How does that man keep on coming?* Again he slammed his pike down onto the Athenian's shield, this time feeling it wedge itself into the leather-bound wood. He pushed down with all his weight, forcing the hoplite to halt his ascent. An arrow whipped past his head as Antipatros strained on his haft, prying the hoplon down and away from the Athenian's head. 'Get him!' he shouted to the man to his left; he hurled a lump of stone down from above his head to crash onto the horse-hair pluming adorning the Athenian's attic helmet. With a cry, barely heard over the chaos of the assault, the hoplite plunged from the ladder, dislodging the man under him and freeing Antipatros' pike; with a quick stab he took the eye of the suddenly exposed soldier below as the man to his right pushed at the ladder top with a pitch-fork, toppling it backwards with ease now that so much weight had been lost. Back it fell to crash down onto the upraised shields of the troops awaiting their turn in the assault, hundreds of them with more in reserve behind in the no-man's land between the walls and the siege lines. No sooner had it been repelled was the ladder retrieved by willing hands and rushed forward under a hail of javelins from one of the units of peltasts that Antipatros had interspersed with his heavy infantry along the wall.

Gods, why won't they desist? They're only a diversion after all; do they really want to get themselves killed as a mere diversion? He risked a glance to the west to see that the ram in its leather-roofed housing had now disappeared around the corner on its slow trundle to the main gates. 'Take command here,'

Antipatros shouted to the chiliarch; he winced as a slingshot glanced off his helmet with a deafening clang and, crouching low, made his way to the steps leading down from the wall.

'Relieve them as soon as there's a lull in the fighting,' Antipatros ordered the full-bearded officer commanding the reserve waiting at the foot of the steps. 'I imagine they'll withdraw soon as they're just about to achieve their objective of getting a ram to the gates.'

With a curt nod acknowledging the officer's salute and, detailing two men to escort him, Antipatros stalked off through the narrow streets of Lamia towards the main gates.

Despite the fact that the city was under siege and, indeed, was even now being assaulted, life proceeded, as far as possible, as normal. Craftsmen carried on their trade in open-fronted workshops, using stockpiled materials kept aside for exactly times such as this. Cobblers stitched sandals, blacksmiths beat on their anvils, washerwomen scrubbed on ridged boards bringing a sense of unreality to Antipatros as he walked past them, having just been killing men not more than a couple of hundred heartbeats previously. But then he reflected that the people of Lamia must be well used to war due to their geographical position astride the only feasible route for an army travelling between the north and the south. *How many of them still have hidden supplies of food, I wonder. It's getting very close to the point where I shall have no choice but to start raiding people's homes so that I can feed my men.* With this gloomy thought, and ignoring the anti-Macedonian taunts aimed at him by faceless men in the crowds, Antipatros walked into the agora alive with market stalls selling most things that would be expected other than food – at least openly for, despite his edict that all foodstuffs were to be distributed through his quartermasters, Antipatros knew that meat and grain could be obtained under the counter in the agora. 'No, I don't want to buy one of your hats,' Antipatros snarled at an importunate trader's son, shrugging off the lad's hand as he tried to grab his shoulder and following it up with a clip around the ear.

'Macedonian savage!' the boy shouted, ducking away into the safety of the crowd.

'Uncouth barbarian,' another disembodied voice called out; it was followed by a volley of similar cries reflecting the Greek disdain for their northern overlords.

Brooding on the fact that the people of Lamia would soon have every Macedonian in the city murdered in their beds if it were not for the business that a besieged army brought, Antipatros fended off another couple of market-stall holders and pushed his way through the jeering crowds into the wide thoroughfare that led from the agora to the main gates.

'How are they holding?' Antipatros asked Magas as he arrived at the gate-tower to the resounding report of the iron-headed ram pounding on wood.

'They'll hold for a while,' Magas replied, pointing at the reinforcing metal bars wedged into place all the way down the gates, 'long enough for us to get above the gate and fry a few of the bastards operating the ram. Get your arses up there!' he bellowed at a body of men wearing thick gloves and carrying eight steaming cauldrons of heated oil between them. 'Run, don't walk!' He turned back to Antipatros. 'The archers can't penetrate the leather roof of the housing so I'm going to try and set fire to it and roast the buggers out.'

'That'll do it. It beats me why Leosthenes ordered such a large-scale attack having just sat on his arse for the last few months trying to starve us out with no more than an occasional assault more for appearance's sake and to keep his men sharp.'

'Perhaps he was bored and thought that a large-scale attack might pass the time.'

Antipatros winced as another blow thundered onto the gates and was relieved so see them standing firm. 'It's an expensive way to do that. His losses are already in the hundreds.'

'Less men to pay; they're mostly mercenaries after all, aren't they?'

'Most of them, yes; but he's using the Athenian citizens as the diversion and they're taking the brunt of the casualties.'

Magas shrugged as they mounted the steps in front of the

men struggling with the hot oil. 'Then perhaps he's been told to get a move on by his political masters.'

'That's what I was wondering; and the only thing that I can think of that would cause them to do that is if they know that either Leonnatus or Krateros are on their way to break the siege.'

'Or both.'

'Indeed.'

The tower above the gates was crowded with archers, mainly Cretan mercenaries who had been long in Antipatros' pay; a couple of light bolt-shooters stood at either corner.

'Move! Move!' Magas shouted, kicking men out of the way. 'Hot oil coming through. Hot oil! Hot oil, you slugs.' He barged his way to the parapet. 'Get your men back,' he ordered the Cretan officer, 'and then stand by to pick them off as they run. That goes for you artillery lads as well.'

Antipatros grabbed a discarded shield and holding it in front of his head leant over and looked through a crenellation down onto the ram. Huge it was, the trunk of an aged tree grown tall and thick; its iron-bound head visible as it crunched forward from under its leather housing to pound once more on the gates.

Slingshot cracked onto Antipatros' shield and he stepped away from the edge as the cauldrons were brought up to the parapet. 'That'll do no good, Magas. The crew is completely protected by the roof. The oil will just slop down to either side.'

'Which will be fine. Now, pour them!'

The first four cauldrons were tipped forward, disgorging steaming oil that would take the flesh off all whom it touched, except, as Antipatros had predicted, it touched no one, such was the durability of the leather roof.

'Now, you four!' Magas shouted.

With a growing sense of urgency as the rhythm of the ram increased, the last cauldrons of oil were tipped onto the ram below; Antipatros risked another look down as the Cretan officer brought his men back now that the parapet was again clear. The leather roof was slimed with the oil but all beneath it were untouched; however, the incline leading up to the gates was forcing the oil to flow down the length of the housing.

Grim beneath their broad-brimmed leather hats, the Cretans nocked arrows and awaited further commands as fire-raisers ran forward.

'Now!' Magas shouted.

Half a dozen burning torches were lobbed down and, within a few moments, Antipatros was rewarded with a waft of searing flame as the oil exploded into an instant inferno covering the roof and dripping down the side like a flaming curtain. Shrieks erupted from within the housing and, an instant later, the first of the crew pelted out from its rear. Bowstrings thrummed as the Cretans, masters of their weapon, picked off man after man fleeing the flames. Screams rose through the air as the crew toward the front of the ram were forced to try their luck diving out through the curtain of dripping flame; oil caught their tunics and hair and clung to naked skin, blistering and peeling as all the while, from above, the arrows thumped in with unerring accuracy. For more than a few, writhing on the ground, consumed by fire, the thump of a shaft in their chests was a mercy; Antipatros noted with approval that the archers never let a burning man suffer for long as all who had ever partaken in a siege knew the fear of fire from above and had witnessed the agonies of a burning death: a death deserved by no man in war, not even one's enemy and especially not a fellow mercenary.

'That's cleared the bastards out,' Magas shouted, his eyes wild with the thrill of victory as the Cretans continued taking down anyone within range.

Antipatros surveyed the field through the smoke of the burning ram: between the gates and the siege-lines the Greek units waiting to storm through the broken gates were now pulling back; the din of the attempted escalade of the south walls had lessened. It was as he was about to turn and walk away, with a view to seeking the comfort of some sour wine and a meagre portion of twice-baked bread, that a cavalry horn screeched through the air. Straight in front of the gates, two hundred paces away on the siege lines, a horseman appeared, crouching low on his mount. To Antipatros' left was the source of the call: with cloaks billowing out behind them a unit of two dozen cavalry swept across the siege lines, aiming to cut off the lone rider.

'Give him cover,' Antipatros ordered the Cretans and artillerymen.

It was the bolt-shooters, with their superior range, that released first, sending missiles half the height of a man hissing towards the pursuing cavalry as the horseman urged his mount on to greater exertion between two units of withdrawing hoplites; such was his speed and surprise that none of the infantrymen challenged his progress.

'Stand by to open the postern-gate,' Antipatros ordered the captain of the guard below.

With bulging arm muscles, the artillery crews wracked back the torsion-arms of their pieces and slotted bolts into the groove. The release catches were triggered and the arms slammed forward into the restraining uprights, hurling the missiles forward. Shading his eyes, Antipatros followed their trajectory, marvelling at the accuracy of the crews against a moving target; one bolt slammed into the ground in the midst of the cavalry tripping a beast, which in turn brought down another, whilst the second plunged into the rump of a galloping horse, causing it to rear, forelegs thrashing at the air in its agony, as the rider tried, but failed, to cling to its back. But still they came on in their bid to prevent the first man to break the siege since the circumvallation was complete. Again the crews strained to reload their weapons as the Cretans began to nock arrows, for the Greek cavalry was approaching their range. With another two dull thumps the bolts accelerated away, one to pass right over the nearing Greeks as the second took a rider completely from his mount; a white mount, Antipatros noted, recalling that of Leosthenes on the day they had parleyed. The Cretans began to send shaft after shaft at the approaching cavalry who soon reined in and kicked their horses away as another two artillery bolts hissed into the ground behind them, causing no damage. Antipatros strained his eyes as the retreating horsemen stopped at the body of their fallen comrade. Hardly daring to hope – if the downed man were Leonthenes – that his cause had

had such a piece of luck, in his excitement he almost forgot the approaching horseman. 'Open the gate,' he called, tearing his eyes away from what he was now sure was the Greek mercenary general prostrate and motionless on the ground one hundred and twenty paces hence.

Below, the postern-gate creaked open and the horseman rode through, his mount sucking in huge gulps of air after its intense gallop. The rider leapt from the saddle and, removing his helmet, looked up at Antipatros. 'Hello, Father,' Iollas said, 'I've got good news and bad news.'

'That is good news,' Antipatros said, chewing thoughtfully on a wrinkled apple, one of the few treasures his son had been able to bring with him in his small travelling bag. He looked at the rudimentary map lying on his study desk. 'So I could expect him in the next ten days, taking into account the nature of the road at this time of the year.'

'I'm afraid there is also the bad news, Father.'

Antipatros looked at his younger son, resignation in his eyes. 'In my experience there always is. Go on.'

'Leonnatus' army is still in Hellespontine Phrygia and is not expected to cross into Europe until close to the spring equinox and that crossing will take longer than usual as there are very few ships to be had—'

'Because Krateros has commandeered every vessel in the eastern Aegean for the navy that Alexander wanted; and now he hoards them for himself.' In his younger days Antipatros would have exploded at this news but now he found he could accept the way of things far easier. *Well, it is what it is, I suppose; at least Leonnatus is coming and I can boost the morale of my men with that news.* He looked at Magas and Nicanor, both also enjoying a wrinkled apple. 'So a couple more months to hold out, then? We can do it, eh?'

Nicanor crunched on his apple core. 'I would say so, Father; but knowing that relief is on its way will make it easier, even if we are down to boot-leather.'

'Boot-leather and tree bark,' Magas elaborated.

Antipatros considered the situation as he finished his apple, core and all. 'Give the order to search all houses for food, Magas, and bring it here under guard. I don't want anyone hoarding in the next two months and I'll need my men fit to break through the lines when Leonnatus' army appears.' He turned back to Iollas. 'Is that the only bad news?'

Iollas grimaced, shaking his head. 'I'm afraid not, Father. Leonnatus has refused your offer of a bride.'

Antipatros did not understand. 'Then why is he coming to my aid if he's not wanting a formal alliance by marrying into my family?'

'He's not in a position to accept the proposal as he's accepted an offer of marriage from Kleopatra.'

Antipatros almost choked on his mouthful; a spray of semi-masticated apple splattered onto the map. 'That's that bitch's doing!' He slammed his palm onto the desktop. 'I can smell her reek from here. I can see exactly what Olympias has done and I shan't let her succeed. She's trying to make Kleopatra queen and have Leonnatus usurp my place. I imagine his price for breaking the siege will be my backing for him to become king. I expect the demand will come any day.'

Iollas pulled out a letter from his bag. 'I suppose this must be it, Father. Leonnatus gave it to me as I left Pella.'

Antipatros scanned the writing before screwing the letter up and hurling it into a corner. 'It's bribery!'

Iollas retrieved the letter and read the contents. 'I'd say that was pragmatic politics, Father.'

'And what do you know about pragmatic politics at your age?'

Iollas handed the letter to Nicanor. 'Just that if I have something that you need, like an army for example, then I would be foolish to give it to you without getting something in return, especially if my army was the only one around.'

'Ah! But it's not,' Nicanor said, putting the letter down on the desk. 'There's Krateros; and he's got an army and a fleet. Did you see him?'

Iollas nodded. 'I did. I stayed with him for a while as he contemplated your request, Father.'

Antipatros was interested. 'And?'

'And he didn't come to any decision.'

This time Antipatros could not contain himself. 'What! He's sitting over in Cilicia with more than ten thousand veterans and with one of my daughters catering for his every need and he can't come to a decision about helping his future father-in-law?'

'I'm afraid that's about it.'

'Then what is he doing?'

'That's something that is only known to Krateros.'

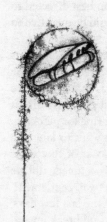

KRATEROS,
THE GENERAL

'FORTY-TWO TRIREMES OR larger, general,' Kleitos the White informed Krateros as they looked down from the satrap's palace onto the full to bursting river harbour at Tarsus. 'Seventy-three biremes, thirty-five lembi for scouting and running swift messages and one hundred and twenty-three transport ships, forty of which have been converted into horse transports able to take sixty-four horses each; enough to get your cavalry across the Hellespont in one go.'

Krateros looked with admiration at the host of ships moored, three sometimes four abreast, on the many jetties constructed along the Cydnus River as it passed the great city of Tarsus on its way to the sea, just four leagues distant. 'Very good, Kleitos; but who said that I would be wanting to transport my army across the Hellespont?'

'No one did, general; but if you do then you have the ships for it.'

'And if I don't?'

'And if you don't you would still have the ships for it.'

Krateros suppressed a smile. *That's exactly the sort of soldier I need serving me; I'm lucky to have him, even if he does feel the need to dress up as Poseidon and wave a trident about.* 'What say you, Polyperchon? Should I claim Phila as my prize as Antipatros offers and go north and, with the use of Kleitos' horse transports, take Europe, or shall I keep my Amastris and, with a Persian wife, take Asia?'

189

The wizened soldier looked at his commander with a shrewd eye. 'I should have thought that was a question best directed to the ladies concerned, general, as only they would be qualified to press the finer points of their case.'

Krateros laughed, it was genuine and hearty, and slapped his second-in-command on the back. 'It's not the finer points of the good ladies' cases that concern me, my friend, I am well aware that both of them are not afraid to attend to detail in the finest degree. It is which of their homelands is most ripe for plucking, Europe or Asia? It being given that we don't want to languish here in Cilicia for ever; now we've rid the coast of the pirate menace there would be very little to keep us occupied, and we all know what happens to a bored army, don't we, gentlemen?' He looked up to the sky, the heavy clouds of the last few days' overcast weather were beginning to brighten and break up and there was a definite lessening of the chill that had afflicted the coast over the winter months. 'Spring is coming and, along with it, the campaigning season; there are thrones to be won, my friends. I have earnt the right to one; but the question is: which?'

And that was the problem that had beset Krateros ever since the news of Alexander's death had reached him: which way to turn? Both directions had their plus and minus points and he had a woman to help him in whichever way he chose to go.

Phila, as Antipatros' daughter, would give him the support of the old man still besieged in Lamia. Assuming that his, Krateros', sources were correct – and there was no reason to think otherwise as the information fitted with the arrogance of the man – Antipatros would welcome an ally against Leonnatus who would, no doubt, use his new royal connection to make himself king. That would be an eventuality that all who had surrounded Alexander would wish to avoid: the arrogant, preening dandy with his coiffure aping the great man himself would not be a king of unification: few would be able to stomach such a man lording it over them; and, besides, he was not the possessor of the greatest military mind.

And then there was Amastris, his Persian bride forced upon him by Alexander at the mass wedding in Susa; the cousin of

Alexander's wife, Stateira, she would be a great asset with the Persian nobility should he decide to turn east and face down Perdikkas. But that would mean condoning the very thing that he had fallen out with Alexander over and was the ultimate cause of his being sent back to Macedon to, ostensibly, relieve Antipatros: the fusion of Macedonian and Eastern blood. Nevertheless, the East was the greater prize; of that Krateros was certain for he had seen the riches with his own eyes.

It was Polyperchon who broke the contemplative silence. 'Macedon may not be as rich as the east, but it is far more secure. The Greeks will be broken again; Epirus has not been a serious threat for over a century; the Illyrians spend too much time fighting amongst themselves as do the Thracians – when Lysimachus is not purging them, that is. I'd say the choice was obvious: divorce Amastris, marry Phila, become Antipatros' son-in-law and then all you would have to do is crush Leonnatus between you and he would have no choice but to make you his heir.'

'But that would mean Macedonian fighting Macedonian; that must never happen. And besides, what about Kassandros?'

'What power does Kassandros have? The command of the younger Silver Shields that have replaced the veteran three thousand here with you; what good will they do him? He's leagues from Macedon, he's weak and, what's more, he is not one of us, Alexander made him stay behind. Kassandros could never win Macedon from you or anyone; he's untried, he's never led an army; in fact, he's hardly ever been in battle, for that matter.'

Kleitos grunted his agreement, although Krateros rather thought that it was more for his personal desire to return home than from any strategic analysis of the situation. It was at times like this that Krateros knew there was only one person he could turn to for unbiased advice, even if it went against her best interests.

'My father will resent Leonnatus forcing him to support his claim as king in return for lifting the siege of Lamia,' Phila said as she and Krateros relaxed in a warm bath sprinkled with rose petals imported from warmer climes further south; a slave plucked sweet chords on a harp in the far corner of the room, concealed by a wooden screen. 'And neither will he countenance Kleopatra becoming queen and thereby letting Olympias back into the centre of power; so he will be your ally whether or not you assist in raising the siege with Leonnatus.'

Krateros lay his head back on the rim and spread his arms to either side, gazing up at the richly coloured, geometrically patterned ceiling; he closed his eyes, enjoying the warm of the water and the position of his big toe. 'So what you're saying, Phila, is haste would make a confrontation with Leonnatus all but inevitable.'

'Yes; at the moment Leonnatus is strong, so if he succeeds in raising the siege of Lamia without losing too many casualties, then preventing him from taking Macedon will lead to civil war, which you would avoid at all costs.'

Krateros chewed his lip as he considered the argument. 'So, therefore, if I do go west there is no need to hurry.'

'Precisely; don't waste your men doing something that Leonnatus can do by himself. Let him take the casualties and, hopefully, come out weaker from the experience; and therefore more likely to negotiate.'

'And if he fails altogether and your father remains trapped in Lamia?'

'That's the best scenario: Leonnatus' stock will be so low that none of the noble houses would accept him as king and neither would the army. It would then be your turn; and you won't fail.'

I never have before. 'And I could demand that Leonnatus lends me whatever's left of his army in order to save Macedonian honour from rebellious Greeks.' He wiggled his big toe and was rewarded with a giggle followed by a small sigh. Despite the arduous afternoon in her chamber, Krateros could never get enough of Phila, either of her body or of her mind. Her intellect was of the highest calibre that he had ever come across in a woman, and, indeed, there were few men who could claim to being her equal. It was said that her father used to consult her from a very early age, before she had even blossomed into womanhood, such was her analytical ability. 'And if he does free your father without losing his strength?'

'Then my father will go back on his word supporting Leonnatus' bid for the crown and call on your support to help resist him.'

'Leaving Leonnatus the choice of backing down or being reviled for striking the first blow against a fellow Macedonian.'

'Exactly.'

Krateros grinned. 'In that case it won't be me breaking an agreement when Antipatros turns on Leonnatus; it will be your father and on his conscience alone. I will just be supporting what I see as the best thing for Macedon.'

Phila smiled at him; wet auburn hair stuck to the pale skin of her cheeks and green eyes twinkled with mischief as she, too, probed, gripping him between her feet. 'Oh, I'm sure he'll get over it; although he's never gone back on his word to anyone before, not even Olympias; it will come as quite a shock to Leonnatus.'

'Yes; it'll probably really ruffle his coiffure. I'm looking forward to seeing his expression when he learns what your father has done.' He tried another couple of manoeuvres with his toe. 'You are sure that he will break a promise.'

'Mmmm?'

Phila's concentration was wavering so he repeated his question.

'Hmmmm. Well, if he doesn't Leonnatus will have to kill him, Olympias will insist.'

'So I go west, when the time's right, despite it being the poorer prize?'

'At the moment it's only a point in the south that I'm interested in.'

He withdrew his toe.

'Hey!'

'So I go west, despite it being the poorer prize?'

'You know my views on holding the east and they haven't changed once in the last seven months: no one person can hold it so there will always be war. Take the smaller prize and live in peace and honour so none will be able to say: it was Krateros who began the Macedonian civil war.'

'You advise that even though that might put me in direct conflict with your brother, Kassandros.'

'You asked me for my considered opinion on the subject, not for my personal feelings; anyway, he's my half-brother and not a very nice one at that.' She grabbed his foot, pulling it back to where it had been so comfortable. 'And, besides, he has no power and is unlikely to get it so he's no threat.'

Krateros relented to her pleasure and enjoyed the benefit of the stroking and rubbing of her feet as he slowly settled his mind, once and for all, to abandoning all thoughts of being Alexander's heir; let the lesser men fight it out, he would take Macedon. It was now no more than a question of timing: when would the time be right?

The first part of the answer came from the north in the form of a ship.

'It took him three days to get here,' Kleitos told Krateros and Polyperchon, having introduced the triarchos of a sleek little lembi, newly arrived in Tarsus that morning with the dawn.

'So Leonnatus' army started crossing on the morning you left, Akakios?'

'Yes, general; Kleitos sent me up to patrol the Hellespont and to make a run for here as soon as they moved. It will take them time as they have very few ships available; no more than two dozen at the most.'

Krateros did some mental calculations and then nodded to himself. 'In which case, they will probably all be across by this evening, or midday tomorrow at the latest.'

'That will put them in Pella in five days' time,' Polyperchon said without needing to think about the journey.

'Allowing time to provision them for a campaign, Leonnatus should be able to make his move by the spring equinox or thereabouts.' Krateros tossed a weighty purse at Akakios. 'You've done well; get your men, wine and women before you go out again.'

The triarchos' face lit up, revealing teeth that most women would shy away from without considerable financial incentive. 'The gods keep you, general.'

'Send more ships to patrol off the coast of Thessaly, Kleitos,' Krateros said as Akakios withdrew, 'I want to know as soon as Leonnatus moves south.'

'Yes, general. Should I get the rest of the fleet ready to sail?'

'No, not yet.'

Polyperchon frowned. 'What are we waiting for?'

'Two things: Kleitos, have we heard from our patrols off Samos and Pireaus yet?'

'Only that the Athenians have still got a couple of squadrons patrolling off Lamia keeping Antipatros' fleet from getting behind their army. Their main fleet, however, has still to sail, general; as soon as it does we'll know when and where to.'

'Very good. Once I know that then there is only one other thing to worry about: Perdikkas.'

EUMENES, THE SLY

EUMENES HAD ALWAYS enjoyed a good confrontation, and this was one of the best he had witnessed as neither side were able to compromise since there was no middle ground; it was down to a battle of wills. *If I were a gambling man I'd have a denarii on Perdikkas,* Eumenes mused as he leant against the open window of Roxanna's suite, looking down at the army of Babylon mustering in the palace courtyard in preparation for its march north to Kappadokia.

'If the king is to accompany the army,' Roxanna almost shrieked, such was her outrage, 'then the idiot will stay here.'

'The *idiot*, as you term him, is also a king!' Perdikkas' exasperation manifested itself in his voice raising an octave. 'And when the army goes on campaign it goes with both kings; it goes to war as The Royal Army so that it has complete legitimacy.'

'My son is all the legitimacy the army needs as he is the one true king.'

'Philip is equal in standing to your son, Roxanna, and you are well aware of the fact.'

'I am aware of no such thing. I am the queen and I have given birth to Alexander the Great's child; his actual child with Alexander's actual blood in his veins. Tell me, Perdikkas, what blood does the idiot have flowing through him, eh? Tell me that.'

How are you going to get out of that one, Perdikkas? Eumenes turned to fully catch Perdikkas' reply and his expression as he made it.

'Philip has the royal blood of the Argead dynasty, which is all he needs to be elected king by the army, as he was, Roxanna; remember? A king of Macedon is made by the army not by some eastern bitch that happened to get fucked by Alexander because Hephaestion wasn't around anymore.'

Good point.

'I was his wife! It was time he paid me his full attention.'

Perdikkas ducked under the vase she hurled with admirable dexterity; it crashed against the wall just two paces from Eumenes.

'Hephaestion took up far too much of Alexander's time; and he could never bear Alexander's children.'

Well, it wasn't for want of trying, that's for sure. Eumenes frowned and then held his forehead between his thumb and middle finger, suddenly deep in thought. *What did she just say?*

'Roxanna,' Perdikkas said with finality, 'I'll waste no more time on this; both King Alexander and King Philip will travel with the army. The only question is whether you want to come as well.'

'What do you mean?'

'Exactly what I said: do you wish to accompany your son when he travels with The Royal Army or would you prefer to stay here? The choice is yours but, frankly, I would be much happier if you chose to stay.'

Roxanna's eyes, the only visible part of her veiled face, stared at Perdikkas in disbelief. 'You would part a babe from his mother?'

'Don't give me that. You don't breastfeed him or change him or rock him to sleep, in fact you do nothing for him, so I doubt very much he'll miss you when I send soldiers in here to take him.' Perdikkas neatly ducked another vase.

'You don't have the right!'

'I am his regent; I decide what is best for him and I deem it best for him to travel with the army.' He turned to go, indicating with a jerk of the head for Eumenes to follow.

'I'll kill him before I allow you to take him from me!'

Eumenes gave a slow smile of comprehension. 'No you won't, Roxanna, because you know that would mean your death as well. But you will do as Perdikkas commands or he will let it be known that it was you who poisoned Hephaestion.'

Perdikkas looked at Eumenes in confusion. 'I will?'

'Liar!' Roxanna screamed.

Eumenes dodged a well-aimed slipper. 'Am I, Roxanna? You just gave yourself away. Now, we all know how you poisoned Stateira and Parysatis, Perdikkas has a very interesting witness kept safe for future reference—'

'It was Perdikkas that agreed to me doing it; he summoned them to Babylon.'

Perdikkas dismissed the suggestion with a wave of his hand. 'Nonsense.'

'You did!' The second slipper flew from her hand hitting him directly on the chest.

'What Perdikkas did or didn't do is irrelevant,' Eumenes insisted. 'The fact is that we know you poisoned them and seeing as you are a proven poisoner then it is not hard to see you poisoning your rival for Alexander's attentions. And you just all but admitted it, Roxanna. Perdikkas said something like: "A king of Macedon is made by the army not by some eastern bitch that happened to get fucked by Alexander because Hephaestion wasn't around anymore." And then you said: "I was his wife! It was time he paid me his full attention." Implying that it was you that had decided it was the time to have Alexander's attention and to get it you had to kill your rival. You poisoned Hephaestion and you can deny it as much as you like but it all fits.' He paused to give Roxanna a false smile. 'We will keep this between ourselves, shall we? So long as you do as you are told, obviously. If you don't, Roxanna, we will let the army know just what you did; Hephaestion was a great favourite of theirs so I wouldn't expect that being the mother of Alexander's child will be of much help to you when they find out, especially a child that you planned to replace had it been a girl. Don't forget we still have the slave girl as a witness to that piece of eastern treachery.' His smile broadened. 'We march at dawn tomorrow. Come, Perdikkas.'

Dodging an ivory comb, Eumenes turned and left the room

with a bemused Perdikkas trailing behind him, scratching the back of his neck.

As the doors to Roxanna's suite were closed behind them, Perdikkas looked down at Eumenes. 'How did—'

'I work out that Roxanna had poisoned Hephaestion? I didn't; it was intuition based on the way she phrased "It was time he paid me his full attention." Although I seem to have hit the mark; I imagine she'll be joining the march tomorrow as if it were exactly what she had wanted to do all along.'

Perdikkas' jaw muscles clenched in anger. 'The little bitch; I should have her executed for that.'

'I wouldn't, she may prove to be of some use other than skirmishing with whatever objects come to hand.'

'It's not funny, Eumenes.'

'I never said it was.'

'It could be argued that she is the cause of all this mess—'

'Because had Hephaestion not have died Alexander might have had a stronger will to live? I doubt it; he still had half the world left to conquer. I think that would have been motive enough for him.'

'Do you think—'

'She killed Alexander? No, she would have been much more now had he have lived. If you think she's a handful at the moment, just imagine what she would be like hiding behind Alexander's throne? But anyway, it's a waste of time speculating about what might have been; it's reality that we need to concentrate on. Have you heard from Peithon yet?'

'The last I heard was that he had taken the troops I gave him from here back to Media and he was waiting in Ecbatana for news of Philo's departure. He has spies out watching the road and he claims to have made contact with some of the deserters who are willing to have second thoughts – for a price, naturally.'

'Naturally. And our insurance that Peithon does the right thing and doesn't just double the size of his army?'

'Seleukos is on his way and will trail Peithon's army without his knowledge. Although I'm not sure that Peithon has the gumption to rebel.'

'It's not just Peithon that I'm worried about; what if his army quite likes the thought of going home and thinks that these Greeks might be on to a good thing?'

Perdikkas stared in horror at Eumenes. 'Gods, I hadn't even considered that.'

Of course you hadn't, that's why you always need my help; I just wish you would admit it, just the once. 'An army of forty to fifty thousand deserters would, I believe, grow very quickly as it headed west. Seleukos will see to it that the right result is achieved; by the time we've dealt with Kappadokia you won't have anything to worry about with either Peithon or this Philo.'

PHILO,
THE HOMELESS

T HE EQUINOX WAS approaching; the snows had melted in the valleys of the east but lingered still on the surrounding peaks. Philo looked west, from a high window, across the lands they would traverse if they were to reach the sea. Barren and brown after a winter beneath the snow, the terrain was as uninviting as he had ever seen it, yet on this day, for once, he did not resent it; for this day was the last day he would feel trapped by the endless wasteland stretching further than could be imagined. This day they would begin their march to the sea.

Philo felt the excitement of the moment jittering in his belly and he had to hold his hands firmly on the window ledge to stop them from shaking, such was his tension. Rising up from below came the din of excited voices, thousands of them, as the Greek mercenaries of the eastern garrisons mustered on the parade ground of Alexandria Oxiana. Into their *taxeis*, units of five hundred to a thousand men, they formed, having loaded their possessions onto the long line of wagons waiting, on either side of the bridge spanning the Oxus, together with the camp followers and those families that were to be taken back.

There must be five or six thousand civilians, Philo guessed as he tried to estimate the number of useless mouths he would have to feed on their journey. *I should have forbidden the bringing of hangers-on.* But even as that thought crossed his mind, he knew it would have been an impossible order to enforce: how would he have stopped them? Order his men to attack anyone who tried to follow the column? Have them kill their own women and children? Of course they would not have obeyed and he would have lost face and authority; so they were lumbered with the civilians and would, doubtless, be slowed by them. Casting the problem from his mind as an unnecessary consideration seeing as there was naught he could do about it, Philo turned and looked around his room for the last time; it was almost completely bare save for a bedframe, a table with an earthenware bowl upon it and a chair, all of which he would be leaving behind. *Who will use them next, I wonder? Or will the town get sacked by a people who have no use for such things?* Deciding that he did not care what happened to Alexandria Oxiana after he had gone, he picked up his leather kit-bag, shield and helmet and strode from the room, leaving the door wide open, without a backwards glance.

'We're just about there, sir,' Letodorus said as Philo emerged onto the parade ground. 'We've eighteen taxeis with a total of just shy of twelve thousand all told.'

'Have all the couriers come back in?'

'Almost all; they have promises of another seven or eight thousand men joining us on the way; now that they know our route, they shouldn't have any difficulty in locating us.'

'That's very good news, Letodorus; safety in numbers is the key to our success. It would take a brave man to attack an army of twenty thousand seasoned mercenaries trying to get home; with luck they'll just watch us pass and feel thankful that their men don't try to join us.'

Letodorus looked less than convinced. 'Let's hope that's their attitude, but my guess is that we will have to fight at some point.'

Philo sighed and let his kit-bag drop to the ground and rested his shield on it. 'Do you really think that they would be prepared to lose hundreds, maybe thousands, of men just to stop us?'

'The Macedonians will be mightily pissed off with us and my experience of Macedonians is that when they're mightily pissed off they tend to hit people without wondering about the cost, if only because it makes them feel better.'

Philo considered this for a few moments. 'Well, there is nothing we can do about it except be prepared for that eventuality and therefore keep scouts out to all sides of the column so that we don't get any nasty surprises.'

'Very good, sir.'

'I'll address the men before we set off,' Philo said, mounting the dais at the centre of the parade ground, his helmet tucked under his arm.

He stood, looking down at all the bearded, expectant faces waiting for him to speak and felt the weight of leadership settling on his shoulders. Many times he had led men into battle but never had he led men on such a desperate journey across nearly three thousand miles of, what must be assumed to be, hostile terrain. He knew that they would not be able to trust anyone but themselves and those that join them on the way. *But if we do this then we will eclipse Xenophon and this paltry ten thousand who barely covered a third of that distance.*

'Friends,' he declaimed as silence became manifest, 'or should I say brothers, for we are to be like brothers over the coming months, supporting each other, looking out for ourselves alone and trusting one another. And that is how it must be if we are to reach our goal of the sea.'

At the mention of their ultimate aim the parade ground erupted into thunderous cheers; helmets were waved in the air, bronze sheening in the growing sun and horse-hair plumes, red, white, black and golden rippled in the breeze.

Philo let them cheer for a while before holding up his hands for silence. 'We may be allowed to walk free, there will be enough of us to make anyone think twice before challenging our progress; however, I will not lie to you, my brothers, there is a chance that we shall have to fight our way to the sea.'

Again, at the mention of the sea, cheering broke out and helmets waved.

'But I promise you this,' Philo continued as soon as he could make himself heard, 'that if we have to fight, then we will do so, no matter who they send against us; not even if we know the faces staring at us from over their shields, brothers from another age, for they will no longer be our brothers if they stand in our way. No one will stop us if we remain united in our purpose. We will walk out of this wasteland to which we were condemned for the crime of wanting to return home. But now the monster who condemned us, despite the service we had rendered him, is dead and good riddance to him for it leaves us free once more. So follow me, my brothers, follow me to the sea.'

To a massive roar, Philo took his helmet, almost full-faced with eye-holes and a shortened nasal piece between the enclosing cheek-pieces and resplendent with a high, full plume; with an exaggerated swagger, he placed it on his head. Down he came from the dais and, picking up his kit-bag and shield, marched with purpose through the throng of cheering mercenaries towards the town's west gate.

Past all the wagons he marched, then across the stone bridge over the slow-flowing Oxus, with his men surging behind him, until he was at the head of the column. There he halted, throwing his kit-bag onto the leading vehicle; he raised his clenched fist into the air and pumped it thrice.

To the largest cheer of the day, he brought his arm down to point west and with that gesture he took the first step to the sea. And the taxeis followed him, filing past the wagons until just the rear guard remained, letting the baggage train move off before them.

It was wearisome and it was endless the march west; the road – for there was one to follow – was more of a track this far out east; a track made by messengers and the caravans travelling to and from India and the half-believed, veiled lands beyond. Soon the road veered south towards Zariaspa and despite the change in direction every step was still a step towards freedom and the harshness of the terrain that the road traversed was softened by that thought.

On the second day they came to Zariaspa where another three and a half thousand mercenaries awaited them and it was with tears of joy and hope that Philo and his men greeted their new brothers; men like themselves, toughened fighters who had known of little else but a life in the field since they had come of age. Men of all ages cheered as they joined the column; some, even, in their seventies, with over fifty years of battle-scars earned fighting for Persia and Macedon to prove it, marched in step to younger men, new to the east and liking not what they found. And once the new arrivals had taken their places, Philo again set his face to the west and led his followers off the road; for the road meandered and would carry on south and then east as it made its way through the tall peaks of the Parapanisus Mountains and then on down into Arachosia where it would again turn to the west before veering to the north crossing into Aria and from there to Parthia. And it was in Parthia, just to the south of the city of Susia, that Philo planned to re-join the road having led his men across over a hundred leagues of wild country that was the heartland of Bactria, crossing the Margus River at Alexander Margiana and then the Ochus River at Siraca.

Food and water became scarce the further they travelled from habitation and the Bactrian tribes that called the wild interior home were not of the sharing habit; however, due to their numbers, the tribes left Philo and his followers alone, content just to shadow them across their lands and pick off any foraging party or group of scouts unwary enough to stray too far from the main column. On they went through the sun and the wind and the rain; now and again smaller bands of mercenaries would join them, deserters from the northern border garrisons, looking for a better life than the bleakness of plains, uplands and deserts and the constant skirmishing with the Dahae and Massaegetae, the bloodthirsty horsemen with a hatred for all but themselves.

Within a few days the weather brightened, but it was still too early in the year for the midday sun to be an issue and so it was from dawn to dusk they marched without a break even for the midday meal, of dried bread and hard cheese, eaten on the foot. Stragglers were few and those that did fall by the way were picked up by the wagons of the baggage train, for none would leave a brother to the cruelties, known or imagined, of the Bactrians.

Philo thanked the gods each day for the improving weather for although there was not much rainfall in this arid land, neither was there an excess of heat to make burning thirst a curse. Smaller rivers were forded and almost drained as thousands of water-skins were filled and the beasts hauling the wagons drank their fill; then another score of leagues would need to be covered on that small, precious supply until the next stream was encountered.

Thus they travelled, a column almost a league in length but dwarfed by the vastness of the terrain, topped by an overbearing sky; thousands of men made to seem but a small snake slithering across the desert floor by the magnitude of their surroundings.

And it was with great relief that Philo beheld the walls of Alexandria Margiana built to guard the bridge over the River Margus close to the western borders of Bactria; here another four thousand mercenaries waited, their bags packed and their posts deserted. Now they had over half of the eastern and northern garrisons in their number and those that remained were nearly all behind them and, therefore, no longer a threat.

'Two days, Letodorus,' Philo said as the mercenaries set up their camp on the western side of the Margiana Bridge. 'Two days we shall stay here to rest and then we shall attempt the next stage.'

Letodorus grinned, his beard and skin covered with the dust of travel making the whites of his eyes seem brighter than the norm. 'To be honest, sir, I didn't think we would get this far unmolested and with so many of our lads still on their feet. I'm told that only a couple of hundred have been unloaded from the wagons to stay here after we leave.'

Philo sighed as he contemplated the fate that may well lie in waiting for those unable to carry on. 'Poor bastards; leave what money you can with the town's suphetes, that might just buy them some compassion and prevent them from being slaughtered and robbed.'

'I doubt it.'

Philo sucked the air through his teeth. 'Yes, I'm afraid I do too; but what can we do? If we wait for them to convalesce then others will fall ill. So we leave in two days, come what may.'

And at dawn on the second day the camp was struck, the column formed and the journey west to the sea continued. Soon they had crossed the border from Bactria into Parthia and the terrain began to rise and fall and the vegetation grew lush. Foraging became easier, both for abundant game and fruits and because of a lack of wild tribesmen ever willing to have sport with the foraging parties. On they walked, over rising hills, before coming down into the verdant valley of the Ochus River, with the town of Siraca astride its banks. Here they did not tarry, for the journey had been but five days from Alexandria Margiana; paying a fraction of the colossal toll demanded by the town elders, who were left in the certain knowledge that they were lucky still to have a town to be the eldest in, Philo led his men along the west bank of the Ochus for a further two days as the terrain slowly rose until the flood-plain between the Ochus and the impressive hill range to their right was less than a third of a league wide. But it was here that Philo remembered from his journey out east, with Alexander's army, that the road slipped through the hills as it came up from the south and then again turned west to head for the sea by way of the Caspian Gates.

And there it was, just where he remembered it to be, and his men celebrated that night as, from now on, their journey would be easier. No more would they stumble across rough land; now they would follow a road that had existed for almost two hundred years since Cyrus the Great had ordered its construction.

'Now we can afford to send scouts much further in advance,' Philo said to Letodorus as they ate a stew of rabbit and wild garlic in his tent on their first evening back on the road. 'They should be relatively safe here in Parthia but make sure they travel in groups of no less than twenty. Keep them a couple of leagues to our flanks and as far along the road as they dare go.'

'They'll leave at first light, sir,' Letodorus said, licking gravy from his fingers and then wiping them on his chiton. 'I'll order them to go as far as the border with Media.'

'Do that. How far do you estimate that to be?'

'About a hundred leagues; light horse like our scouts could

cover it in five days and be back with us three days later provided we keep moving at this pace.'

'Oh, we will, Letodorus; I've never known a body of men march so willingly.'

It was exactly eight days later, as Letodorus had predicted, that the scouts rode into the evening camp.

'There is nothing ahead of us, sir,' their leader reported, sipping with pleasure on the best wine that Philo could find. 'We went past Hecatompylos and then on to the border, nothing to be seen, sir. So I divided my men and sent ten further into Media and came back with the rest.'

Philo slapped the man on the shoulder in approval of his actions. 'You've done well. Rest for the night and then go back out in the morning to replace the men you sent on.'

It was three nights later that the scout officer returned and, with a voice grim with foreboding, reported to Philo: 'Peithon has brought an army east, almost twenty-five thousand, I should reckon. He's chosen his ground; he's waiting for us just beyond the Caspian Gates.'

ANTIPATROS, THE REGENT

'THE BRIDGES ARE all ready,' Magas said as Antipatros inspected the work-party in the agora at Lamia. 'Two hundred of them as you requested, sir.'

Antipatros surveyed the piles of ten-paces-wide, two-paces-long flat wooden constructions piled in tens down the centre of the agora. Gone were the market stalls for they had all been commandeered to build what Antipatros believed to be the key to extracting his army from the siege: the means to bridge the siege-lines. Indeed, most of the wood in the city had been stripped to build the bridges: doors and window shutters had been ripped away, there was hardly a piece of furniture worth its name left and almost all the inhabitants now slept and ate – if they ate at all – on the floor. Even roofs had been dismantled for their valuable beams and wood considered insufficiently strong for construction had been burnt to keep the ravages of a Thessalian winter at bay.

But now, soon after the equinox, the weather had improved and each day Antipatros knew that the time for escape was nigh, for surely the roads were passable once more. 'Very good, Magas; now all we need is for Leonnatus to appear.'

'It had better be soon; I had reports of the first townsfolk dying of starvation yesterday.'

Antipatros rubbed his shrunken belly. *Once they start to go, the rate speeds up remarkably.* 'How many yesterday?'

'Three.'

'And today?'

'Five.'

Tomorrow will be eight and by the end of the month we'll be on fifty or more a day and then the men will start dropping too. Hunger had gnawed his insides for many days now but it had been for his men that Antipatros had been concerned, not himself; in the situation that he had found himself there was nothing that he, personally, could do for if they were to break out it would be through the strength of his men – as many of them as possible. And so he and his officers had reduced their rations to a level less than the ordinary soldier. The townsfolk received no rations whatsoever anymore but were too weak by now to rise up in rebellion against the besieged garrison who had confiscated all the foodstuffs they could find. Already there were more than dark rumours of murder and cannibalism; Antipatros had been confronted with the evidence.

'Have all the bridges moved to the North Gate, Magas,' Antipatros said, pushing from his mind the image of a roasted human thigh with slices already carved; the two men who had been caught attempting to sell it for a small fortune had been crucified in the agora. The remaining portions of the body, however, had not been found and Antipatros rather suspected they would never be; someone had made himself rich. 'We'll break out in that direction and head for rough country when the time comes; my guess is that they will expect us to take the East Gate and so follow the road, but I won't give their Thessalian cavalry the pleasure.'

'We'll find the rough terrain just as hard going, sir, and the phalanx will have trouble keeping a tight formation.'

*And that is the risk that I have to take if I'm ever going to sit and have a quiet meal with my wife again. Gods, I'm too old for this; I should be warming my feet by the fire with a cup of spiced wine and a grandchild on my lap and instead...*he looked around at the desolation that Lamia had become and, sighing, shook his head at the misery of it all. *Instead I need to break out of here and then I need to make the rebels pay for what they have done otherwise I'll* *never find peace by my hearth.* 'We'll manage, Magas; we always do. Keep the picked men at their training with the bridges and keep a lookout to the north and the east.'

Scratching at his lice-infested beard, Magas turned to issue the orders to move the bridges as Antipatros walked away, hands clasped behind his back, stooped with fatigue, anger rising inside of him as he contemplated the six months and more he had endured in this place. And yet he was still alive which, had it not been for one piece of luck, one fortunate shot, he very much doubted that he still would be. For the killing of Leosthenes, on the day Iollas had broken through, had saved them as Antiphilus, his replacement, was not of the same calibre and seemed to prefer to do nothing other than let his men die of disease rather than force an end to the siege. And it was in this that lay Antipatros' hope, as many of the contingents from the rebel cities had returned home, sick of a long winter siege and concerned now with the welfare of their farms. The mercenaries had, in the main, stayed; but the fact was that the rebel army was almost a third of its original size. And, as the horns sounded from the lookout towers, the following day, announcing the sighting of Leonnatus' relieving army, Antipatros had for the first time in months a real spark of hope within him; soon he would be home with his wife; soon he could rest and regain his strength in order to subdue Greece in such a way that he would never be put through this ordeal again in the few short years that remained to him.

'How many would you reckon, Nicanor?' Antipatros asked as he, Magas and his two sons strained their eyes, looking at Leonnatus' army deploying from column to line as it arrived along the coast road.

Nicanor shaded his eyes. 'All I can see is not enough cavalry; he can't have more than fifteen hundred with him but they do look to be all lance-armed heavies.'

'Well, at least he has some because we can't do this with just infantry. Fifteen hundred should be enough to keep the Thessalian light cavalry from taking the phalanx in the flanks; those bastards never like to get too close to the tip of a lance.'

211

Antipatros turned to look down into the town where his men were forming up in pike-bristling columns along the wider thoroughfares; rank upon rank of them, emaciated, hollow-eyed with louse-ridden matted hair and beards, but still alive. *Still alive! Thank the gods for that and let us trust that they still have the energy to unleash the hatred that has grown within them over the winter.*

'They're moving!' Magas shouted, bringing Antipatros back to events beyond the wall.

Antipatros slammed a fist into his palm. 'I knew they would have to. They can't risk not bringing their full strength against Leonnatus now that so many have left them.' He beamed at his three companions, the smile lighting up his grey-skinned face for the first time since the hunger began to bite, moons ago. 'Well, gentlemen, it's time we said goodbye to Lamia. Magas, you and I shall lead from the front, me with the pioneers and you with the phalanx. Nicanor and Iollas, you bring the peltasts and archers and secure the phalanx's northern flank.'

The gates were stuck, having not been used for the duration of the siege and it took the force of many men to get them slowly grating open. Speed now was of the essence and Antipatros resented each hold-up. 'Put your hearts into this, lads! We need to be on the other side of the siege-lines in some sort of order before the bastards realise what's happening and set their cavalry upon us.'

With a chorus of strained grunts and groans, the two heavy wooden gates ground open, pace by pace, until the exit was as wide as could be.

'Clear the way, boys!' Antipatros shouted at the men on the gates; they filed back to either side revealing what Antipatros prayed would be their way out of Lamia. He raised his sword in the air. 'Now!' he bellowed at the hand-picked pioneers handling the bridges. Without waiting to see if they were following, Antipatros turned and ran, on weakened legs, through the gates and into the no-man's land beyond. Rough and furrowed it was from countless attacks but, thankfully, it was dry; muscles burning and lungs straining, Antipatros led his men across the two hundred paces of deserted ground uncontested. Gasping for breath and with a pain in his side that he thought would cripple him, he reached the first line of trench-work along the wall constructed of stakes twice the height of a man.

A single arrow slammed into his shield as he jumped down into the trench, taking him unawares, but no other threat came close as the skeleton crew manning the lines fled through tunnels under the wall in the face of such numbers. For numbers there were as each bridge was carried by eight men on four crossbars; they fanned out as they crossed the ground so that there were one hundred bridges in a row, with the other hundred directly behind them as they arrived at the siege-lines. Down the lead men jumped to take the front of their bridge above their heads and then walk it to the other side of the trench, there to secure it in position with wooden pegs. Once fixed at both ends the teams waiting with the bridges behind sprinted across and on over the ten paces to the wall of embedded stakes. Using their bridges now as rams they swung them into the uprights, slowly getting into rhythm and shouting with each strike as archers, under Iollas, and the peltasts, commanded by Nicanor, formed up behind them, leading the rest of the army now streaming from the town.

With a cheer, the first of the stakes began to topple, jerking forward with each crashing blow from the rams.

'Keep going, lads!' Antipatros shouted again and again as he patrolled up and down the line. *If we can get the wall down without the main rebel army being alerted, then, by the gods, we stand a good chance of being able to form up before the Thessalians are sent to slaughter us.*

And it was with great relief that Antipatros watched the first gaps begin to appear in the wall that had contained them these last months; down the stakes came and, as they fell, the pioneers stepped on them and with their weight and that of the rams they laid them horizontal. On the pioneers ran and Antipatros ran with them, racing for the next trench just paces away. The archers came behind, arrows nocked, to pick off any resistance in the second trench with the peltasts prepared to storm it if necessary; but there was none and the rams became bridges again and were soon secured in place.

And thus the army of Macedon, so long prisoner within the town of Lamia, burst through the circumvallation and crossed the trenches to either side of it. More and more Macedonian infantry flooded over the bridges, their officers bellowing at their men to form up on them once across; unit by unit the phalanx started to take shape and then grow as file after file was added on the rough ground beyond the breached siege-lines.

'This is more like it,' Antipatros roared at Magas. 'This is what we want, my friend: a phalanx facing the rebel army and us forming up behind it. They will not enjoy this one bit.'

Magas grinned, showing what was left of his teeth, now mostly rotted through malnutrition. 'An ideal opportunity; let's make the most of it.'

And it was with his heart pumping, and feeling more alive than since he had last bedded his wife, that Antipatros ordered the advance as soon as his phalanx had completely formed up.

With a cheer from thousands of throats, the army of Macedon moved forward to catch the Greek rebels between it and Leonnatus.

Antipatros could now see, half a league away, the two hosts facing each other, the pike-armed phalanx of Leonnatus opposing the long-thrusting spears of the Greek hoplites; skirmishers swarmed back and forth between the armies with bows, slings and javelins doing little harm to anyone but their opposite numbers. Being short of cavalry, Leonnatus had placed his southern flank on the coast and his fifteen hundred cavalry, with him and his standards leading them, on his right flank as the ground began to dip into a depression before rising up to the coastal hills; the Thessalian light horse formed up opposite them.

With the uplifting thought that his future was now back within his control, Antipatros took his place next to Magas at the centre of the front rank of the phalanx as it rumbled forward, with the siege-lines around Lamia covering its right flank and loose formation peltasts and archers under his sons on the rising ground to its northern flank to prevent the Thessalians getting around should they turn their attention to the army behind them.

But the Thessalians showed no sign of trying to outflank either enemy.

'What are they doing?' Antipatros asked as horn blasts rose from the Thessalians; they peeled off to the north, heading across the depression, and then started to climb the hill.

'I'm buggered if I know,' Magas replied, sounding equally as confused.

'Whatever it is, they don't seem to be threatening either us or Leonnatus.'

'You don't think…'

Menon is capable of anything so why not defect back to us, now that he can see the tide has turned against the Greeks since we broke out of the siege. 'I'm beginning to think that I do, the treacherous bastard.'

'Surely it's only treachery if it is against us; if he's coming back over to us then it's loyalty; even if it is expediency on his part.'

'I'll still make him pay for deserting us in the first place. He's responsible for me not seeing my wife for months.'

'Well, he's pulled his men back up the hill and left the Greeks exposed to Leonnatus cavalry.'

And it was so, Antipatros could well see: the Thessalians had withdrawn, exposing the entire northern flank of the Greek formation to Leonnatus. *But if he moves on it then he still has the risk of the Thessalians charging down the hill onto his flank.* And then a thought occurred to Antipatros, a thought that did not sit uncomfortably with him having experienced Menon's treachery at first hand. *Unless this has been planned well in advance and Leonnatus has already negotiated with Menon and bought him off as Leosthenes did. That must be the truth of it as Leonnatus would never walk into such an obvious trap; surely?*

And, as Leonnatus brought his cavalry forward to threaten the Greek flank, exposing himself in turn to a Thessalian charge, Antipatros became convinced that it was, indeed, the case. 'Sound double-pace!'

The horns blew, the officers bellowed and the lumbering formation broke into a quick march, pikes still at the upright.

Something isn't right, Antipatros realised as he saw no movement within the Greek ranks to counter either his move or that of Leonnatus.

Why aren't half of them turning to face us?

It was the whoops and battle-cries of a cavalry charge that provided Antipatros with the answer as the Thessalians, near on five thousand of them, streamed down the hill, leaning back in their saddles against the incline, dust rising from twenty thousand thundering hoofs, straight towards Leonnatus and his companion cavalry.

'Is that treachery or Leonnatus' stupidity?' Magas asked as the Macedonian cavalry realised the imminent danger they were now in and tried to turn.

'Halt!' Antipatros yelled; the signallers blared and within twenty paces the phalanx had come to a stop. 'Left turn!'

The phalanx obeyed the order piecemeal, as it rippled to either end.

'What are you doing?' Magas asked as the first screams of the dying rose from the cavalry battle not more than a third of a league away.

'Even if they do manage to extract themselves from the trap they'll be so badly mauled they won't be of any use to us.' Antipatros pointed at the town and then up the hill. 'So, unless we want to retreat back to the relative safety of a besieged town, we need to take the higher ground and wait this out to see what happens.'

So they climbed, their ranks disordered by the rough ground littered with boulders and scrub and treacherous gullies; but climb they did, for every man knew the alternatives: death or retreat to the living hell they had been subjected to. But it was the heavy infantry who climbed; the archers and the peltasts, troops far more suited to the ground because of their dispersed order, formed a screen between them and the Thessalians. And when they were a couple of hundred paces above the two armies below, Antipatros brought them to a halt facing down the hill with the skirmishers before them and the peltasts split on either flank.

'Leonnatus seems to be managing to extricate himself,' Antipatros observed as soon as he once again had the time to observe the progress of the battle, 'but he's left a lot of dead in that depression.'

'Marshy ground, by the looks of it,' Magas said, 'see how the horses are struggling.'

Antipatros' eyes narrowed. *That was a complete set-up and Leonnatus fell for it; how could he have been so stupid?*

The Thessalians mauled the final units of retreating Macedonians with showers of javelins, bringing many down even as they closed on the safety of their own lines. It was a ragged formation that rallied behind the phalanx, at least a third down in number and with no sign of Leonnatus' banners.

'They dare not attack without cavalry support,' Magas said; a quiet descended over the field as each side assessed its options.

It's time we tried to get out of here. 'They could stand there for the rest of the day; in fact, I hope they do. Whilst they stare at each other we'll get behind Leonnatus and then he can fall back on us and we'll crawl home together.'

It was an eerie sight, Antipatros thought as his troops slipped away on the higher ground: two armies standing facing each other in silence with the sea sparkling to the south and east in spring sunshine and a ruined town lying raped to the west; to the north the sky grew dark. It came as no surprise to Antipatros when, with a guttural cry from thousands of men, their hoplites moved forward. *They must be confident to attack pike-armed troops; I've not heard of that done since Chaironeia, fifteen years ago.* But the phalanx pulled back as the Thessalians again probed its flank; even with the now-rallied cavalry doing its best to protect it, the risk of standing to receive the charge was too high and so, step by step, the army of Leonnatus retreated as, beyond the siege-lines, a ship set sail from the small port that served Lamia, heading in the direction of Athens.

News of Leonnatus' defeat and my escape will be in Athens by tomorrow; that'll give them far more cause for concern than celebration, although they will savour their small victory. What could have made someone as experienced as Leonnatus do something so stupid?

'Olympias,' Leonnatus whispered. His strength was barely enough to form the words as he lay on a camp-bed in a rain-sodden tent, half a league from the battlefield. His and Antipatros' armies had manged to link up on a hill soon after the threatened downpour broke, forcing the Greeks to break off; they, however, had kept the field and could, with justification, claim victory.

'Olympias?' Somehow this did not surprise Antipatros; the witch was capable of anything. He looked down at the remains of Leonnatus' right arm, hewn off above the elbow and bound in bloody linen; blood-soaked bandages also swathed his head where half his scalp had been sliced away. *Even if the doctors could save him he won't want to live like that, not someone as vain as he.*

Leonnatus looked up with his one remaining eye. 'Yes; I trusted her.'

Well then, you deserve exactly what you got, idiot. 'To do what?'

'I needed cavalry and she said she would provide it; I believed her because I was to marry her daughter.'

'And she told you that she had persuaded Menon to change sides?'

'Yes.'

'Did she also tell you that Menon had already changed sides once before?'

Leonnatus closed his eye. 'No.'

'And you hadn't heard just how I ended up getting shut into Lamia?' *If you did you ignored it, thinking that it was just an old man's foolishness, you arrogant bastard.*

'I...er...I don't know.'

Antipatros could see that the younger man was fading fast; his blood loss had been immense when his men had brought him, scraped from the carnage in the marshy depression, and the doctors had given him little hope. 'And when you saw Menon retreating up the hill it never occurred to you that he might double-cross you?'

'I'd sent him gold.'

'Gold! You can send him as much gold as you like, he'll still be a Thessalian – as you found out the hard way.'

'And it was the death of me. Will you…will…'

His voice now was almost inaudible and Antipatros had to lean in closer.

'Avenge me?' He looked up again, a pleading look in his eye.

Antipatros put a hand on his shoulder and squeezed. 'I will; either me or one of my sons, if I am not spared. But if it makes it any better for you, as you travel to the Ferryman, she did not do this to get at you; the bitch did it to stop you from relieving me. The last thing she would want is me in Macedon if she has managed to marry Kleopatra to you; you would have been king.'

Leonnatus was too weak to reply but his expression was one of understanding before it relaxed into death with a sigh.

The bitch; I'll have her this time. At least I've got cavalry enough to ensure that we can get home relatively unscathed. That's going to come as a nasty shock to her. 'Magas!'

'Yes, sir,' Magas said, getting up from a chair in the shadows of the tent.

'Magas, we leave in the morning. A fighting retreat, screened by cavalry, with the wounded on wagons, although I doubt they'll try anything if this weather keeps up. I don't want any news of Leonnatus' death or our escape travelling to Pella before us. In fact, I don't want any news at all of our movement going ahead. I want to arrive in Pella and give the surprise of her life to Olympias.'

OLYMPIAS,
THE MOTHER

'I CALL UPON ROARING and revelling Dionysus. Primeval, double-natured, thrice-born, Bacchic lord; wild, ineffable, secretive, two-horned, two-shaped, ivy-covered, bull-faced, warlike, howling and pure; you take raw flesh and feast, wrapped in foliage, decked with grape clusters. Resourceful Eubouleus, immortal god sired by Zeus when he mated with Persephone in unspeakable union. Hearken to my voice, O blessed one, and with your fair-girdled nymphs breathe on me in a spirit of perfection.' So sang Olympias, standing next to a white bull, as the spring festival of Dionysus reached a climax at midnight on a wooded hill to the north of Pella.

Adherents to the cult, both male and female in various stages of intoxication, were grouped around her in the darkness, holding torches and swaying as a drummer, unseen amongst the shadowed trees beyond the gathering, delivered a gradually increasing beat. The women held up prodigious phalluses, made of fig-tree wood, glistening from recent usage; the men held a thyrsus, a wand of giant fennel covered in ivy and topped with a pine cone, pumping them in the air to the beat of the drum.

A double-headed axe flashed in the hands of a giant of a man, wreathed in ivy, with spilt wine sticky on his belly and sporting a huge erection. Down the blade sliced to thump through the bull's neck, severing the spinal column and exploding blood, dark in the torchlight. All four legs buckled as one as a shudder wracked through the beast; it fell, eyes wild and rolling, wound pumping, as a basin was placed to catch the precious fruit of sacrifice.

'Euoi! Euoi!' the congregation chanted over and over as initiates into the cult were brought forward for the final stage of the three-day initiation. The men, having enacted Dionysus' life, death and rebirth, symbolically being dragged down to Hades to undergo an ordeal in the caves further down the hill – an ordeal that none would ever speak of again – were given cups of wine mixed with the blood of the bull; this drunk, they were presented with their thyrsus and allowed to join the main body of the worshippers.

The female initiates were then brought forward, all prepared as Ariadne, the bride of Dionysus. Ritually, they were flagellated, Olympias herself brandishing the whip and causing more hurt than was strictly necessary. This done they received the cup of mixed wine and blood, many with tears of pain rolling down their cheeks and with welts reddening on their backs and buttocks; swallowing hard and fast, they drained their drinks and received from Olympias their fig-tree wood phalluses.

And now the orgiastic climax of the ceremonies could begin as the man who had sacrificed the bull was ritually stoned to death in an enactment of the ancient practice. Pipes shrilled and the drumming became frenetic as wine was devoured in vast quantities.

Olympias swilled her fill, her mind on the mystery of the ritual as she worked herself into a frenzy of religious passion, hair wild and feet stamping to the differing beats; all her cares and worries suspended as she focused solely on the magnificent erections of all the males present.

A goat was forced into the throng; it kicked and bucked in terror and lowered its head to butt its way out of danger. Screaming with bloodlust, the worshippers barrelled after the beast, quickly cornering it and wrestling it to the ground. Teeth ripped at its flesh, tearing it apart; limbs were wrenched from its body as its bestial shrieking rose to an unheeding sky.

Ripping a portion of raw flesh from the ravaged animal, Olympias stuffed it into her mouth; chewing maniacally, she danced, with one hand waving free, holding her phallus. Wine appeared and she washed the chewed meat down as more pipes sounded and the drumming became a blur. Over she was bent and, without preamble, entered; back she pushed herself, writhing on the rod within her, her cries escalating as the religious rapture grew until it burst with orgasmic delight, thrilling her senses and sending flashes across her vision as seed exploded inside her, potent and life-giving. She felt the withdrawal but within an instant was mounted again as if there were a queue waiting. She squeezed herself to more enjoy the bliss of a forced entrance as she watched other couples in similar trysts; others danced around the copulation, swigging from wineskins and tearing at handfuls of raw meat, fur still attached, blood still dripping.

On she thrust, back and back, harder and harder as each new penis or wooden phallus brandished by a woman, pleasured her, until she could bear it no more and screamed her ecstasy to the god who had bestowed such great gifts of sensuality, again and again until, with a final scream, she knew no more.

'You look terrible,' Kleopatra said as she came into Olympias' bedroom.

Olympias raised her head and looked around but the pain became too much and she slumped back down onto the pillow; she ran her hands over her body. 'Who dressed me?'

'I did, someone had to. You were brought in naked with blood running down your legs and semen matting your hair.'

Olympias put her fingers to her head. 'It's still there.'

'Of course it's still there; I wasn't going to do any more than the bare essentials as you were fighting and screaming like a Harpy even when I was wiping the blood off you. And then you tore three shifts before I could get you dressed for bed so, no, I thought I'd leave the sperm to you, seeing as it suits you so well. And you wonder why I refuse to join your cult, Mother?' Kleopatra held up a bronze mirror to her mother's face. 'Look at you and look at me and ask yourself who has the most dignity: the one with clean skin, combed hair, no bruises and a fresh dress on, or the one awash with spunk?'

'It's done for the glory and praise of our lord Dionysus, Kleopatra; in thanks for the joy of wine and the other gifts he brought us.'

Kleopatra threw the mirror down to go clattering across the floor. 'Well, if getting fucked by half of Pella helps glorify Dionysus, then you've done him proud.'

Olympias winced and held her hands over her eyes. 'Yes, whatever, but please don't shout and stop throwing things around. How did I get back here?'

'I don't know and I don't care! It's the same every year on the first full moon after the spring equinox. You shame yourself for three days and then turn up in such a state that the slaves can barely hide their sniggering—'

'I'll have the tongue out of any one of them I catch sniggering!'

'They're all sniggering at you but are too careful to show it; just remember that next time you feel the need to praise Dionysus.'

Olympias waved a lazy hand at her daughter. 'Stop it now, I'm your mother. Must get ready; how long until the regent's council meets?'

'It met yesterday.'

'Yesterday! How long have I been asleep?'

'You've been *unconscious* for a day and two nights.'

'But the council?'

'The council met without you and decided to approve my marriage to Leonnatus.'

'What about his claim to becoming king?'

'They didn't discuss it.'

'Didn't discuss it! Why not? If I had been there they would have discussed it.'

'You wouldn't have been allowed in.'

'Of course I would have, I'm the queen.'

'You still wouldn't have been allowed in. I wasn't and when I said that they had no right to bar me they told me that they had every right as it was the regents' council and not mine or yours; and if I insisted in taking a seat then they would all leave and go back to their estates.'

'Then reassemble them and I'll show them who's in charge.'

'They've all gone back to their estates and won't return until Antipatros arrives back.'

'Well, they'll have a long wait then.'

'I wouldn't call two days a long wait.'

Olympias looked at her daughter, trying to work out if she was joking.

'That's right, Mother, two days.'

This can't be true.

'He escaped from Lamia.'

'But he wasn't meant to. Leonnatus was supposed—'

'Leonnatus is dead.'

'Dead!'

'Dead.'

'How do you know?'

'The spies you had with Leonnatus' army came in last night and, seeing as you weren't able to, I debriefed them.'

'It might not be true.'

'Of course it's true. That's why Antipatros didn't send a message back to Pella; he wanted to surprise you, it's obvious. Had Leonnatus survived then he would have sent news of his glorious victory before him as that was the sort of man he was. No, Leonnatus is dead all right.'

'But how can that be?'

'The Thessalian cavalry caught him and his companions in the flank. How stupid can you get?'

'But Menon was meant to—'

'Yes, Mother? What was Menon meant to do? What have you been up to with your plots and scheming?'

'Menon was meant to pretend to change sides and then take the phalanx in the flank so that it would be forced to withdraw and be unable to come to Antipatros' aid. Leonnatus would then have had to withdraw back to Pella leaving Antipatros exactly where I want him.'

'Well, Mother, that didn't go at all well, did it? Antipatros broke out from the siege and Menon attacked the cavalry instead, killing my husband-to-be and completely ruining our plans. And when Antipatros gets back—'

'Does he know what I did?'

'I don't know, Mother. I do know that he did talk to Leonnatus before he died.'

'Then he does know.'

'Why? Did you tell Leonnatus of your plot? Why would you do that?'

'Because I couldn't persuade him not to relieve Antipatros so I thought I'd sabotage the attempt. Leonnatus needed cavalry so I got him cavalry by intriguing with Menon. I told Leonnatus that Menon would bring his five thousand Thessalians over to him. Once he knew that then he was ready to march south. Obviously I had to make him think that Menon was really changing sides; I told Leonnatus to send him three talents of gold as he approached the town as that was Menon's price.'

'Leonnatus would have mentioned that detail to Antipatros before he died, I'm sure.'

'So that's why Antipatros is trying to catch me by surprise. Well he won't. Get packing, Kleopatra.'

'Where are we going? Back to Epirus?'

'No, there's no power to be had there so we'll search for it elsewhere; we're going to take a ship to Asia, immediately.'

'What about my children?'

'I'll send Thessonalike back to Epirus, she can look after them until we return.'

'And we're going to do what?'

'If you can't marry Leonnatus then let's make the most of a bad situation and marry you to either the man who has the respect of all the army or the man who controls both the kings.'

Kleopatra considered this for a few moments. 'Yes, you're right, Mother: Antipatros won't relinquish his hold over Macedon, so the only people left who could force him into it is either Perdikkas or Krateros.'

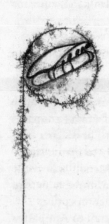

KRATEROS,
THE GENERAL

'AND YOU SAW these things with your own eyes, Akakios?' Krateros asked as they walked with Kleitos along the quayside of Tarsus' river port. A stiff breeze thrummed the rigging of the fleet crowding every berth as gangs of slaves toiled to victual the ships. Sailors scrubbed, caulked and made other running repairs to their vessels, readying them for sea. Triarchoi barked orders, urging their crews into more haste as they all knew that departure was imminent; Polyperchon had marched north with the main body of the army, with the exception of Antigenes' Silver Shields, nine days previously. It had been the joint news that Leonnatus was heading to Lamia and that Perdikkas was coming up from Babylon that had spurred Krateros into action; but now there was fresh news.

'I didn't see Leonnatus dead with my own eyes but I spoke to a man who had,' the triarchos replied, stepping over a coil of rope, 'but I did see the Athenian fleet sailing north as we came through the straits of Euboea. We were lucky they didn't spot us.'

'At least a hundred and fifty vessels, all told.'

'Yes, general; mostly biremes and triremes, nothing bigger.'

'And that was three days after Antipatros began his withdrawal north?'

'Yes, general, and it took us three days to reach you.'

'And Antiphilus, the new Greek general, has not followed Antipatros?'

'No, general, he remains in Thessaly.'

'So the Athenian fleet has overtaken him which means that they are not working in tandem.'

'They're heading for the Hellespont,' Kleitos said, slapping a slave carrying a heavy sack on his shoulders out of the way with his trident.

Krateros nodded. 'That was my thought too. They want to stop any reinforcements crossing back to Europe. It's what I would do. The sight of a Macedonian army retreating for the first time in years and the news of Leonnatus' death will give heart to all the Greek cities as well as to Epirus and the Illyrians. I would wager that even now ambassadors are travelling to every leader who has cause to hate Macedon with a view to gathering an alliance that will invade our country.' He brooded on the matter in silence as they continued along the bustling quayside. 'How long before you're ready to leave, Kleitos?'

'If we embark the Silver Shields overnight then we could sail tomorrow.'

'Good. It's three days to the Hellespont, if we have favourable weather. Polyperchon should arrive with the army in Abydus in seven days' time which will leave us four days to defeat the Athenian fleet and clear the channel so we can cross to Europe.'

'Plenty of time, general,' Kleitos said, his eyes gleaming at the prospect of action again after the defeat of the pirates. 'The thing about the Hellespont is that it's very narrow so although that makes it easy to blockade it also makes it very easy to catch a blockading fleet as they have very little space in which to manoeuvre.'

Krateros clapped Kleitos on the shoulder. 'Very good, my personal Poseidon; I'll give Antigenes orders to begin embarkation at sunset.'

'The lads are refusing to go, general,' Antigenes said in response to Krateros' order.

Krateros peered at Antigenes, mouth open in disbelief. 'Refusing? They can't; Macedon is at stake.'

Antigenes was apologetic. 'Well, I'm afraid that they have, general.'

'But why?'

'Most of them are in their sixties, some even in their seventies, and they feel that they're too old to go back to Macedon and start families there. They want to stay.'

'And do what?'

'They want to join Perdikkas; they think that you were wrong to refuse his call for assistance in Kappadokia.'

'It wasn't a call, it was an order and he has no right to give me an order. And besides, Macedon itself is now under threat so, in hindsight, I was absolutely right to refuse him.'

'Well, the lads want to join him.'

And there is nothing that I can do to stop them as I've sent the rest of my troops north with Polyperchon. I'll just have to make the best of it. 'Very well, Antigenes, take them to Perdikkas and go with my blessing. If you want to do something that will make the political situation easier and help avert the unthinkable, then tell Perdikkas that it was me that sent you in response to his order.'

Antigenes smiled, understanding the significance of the lie. 'I will do, general. I wish you success against the Athenian fleet.'

'Masts ahead!' the lookout shouted down to the deck as the Macedonian fleet rounded the first point in the Hellespont, revealing the port of Abydus less than a league away.

'How many?' Kleitos called back from his position between the steering oars in the stern of the ship.

There was a pause as the lookout, clinging to the masthead above a full-bellied sail, shielded his eyes and gazed along the narrow straits; dun and deep ochre hills fringed the blue ribbon of strait, just over a league wide at this point; the fields of Ilium lay on their starboard side. 'Between seventy and a hundred.'

'That's just half of the fleet,' Kleitos said to Krateros.

'If they're blockading Abydus, where are the rest?'

'They could be blockading Cyzicus ahead in the Propontis?'

'Perhaps.'

Krateros felt worry begin to gnaw at his belly; he turned to look back west. 'Or they could be behind and preparing to trap us in this channel.'

Kleitos shared a concerned look with Krateros. 'Then we had better finish this part of their force off quickly. We'll get straight at them, lads!' he roared, shaking his trident in the air. 'We've got the wind in our favour. Poseidon will do battle!'

The crew cheered their Poseidon as the deckhands ran to action stations and the marines and archers took up position in the bow of the trireme. Below, the rowers rushed to their benches and readied their oars for the moment when the sail would be furled and the ship returned to human power.

'Signal to the squadron commanders to follow my lead,' Kleitos ordered his second-in-command. Ripping off his tunic he made his way to the prow of the ship, naked but for his sandals, and stood there, seaweed in his hair, with his trident pointing at the Athenian fleet as it became aware of the size of the fleet rounding to point.

Krateros remained by the steersmen, mindful that there was little or nothing that he could do in the coming battle, he was a land general not one of the sea. He took off his kausia and wrung the water from the sodden wool; rolling the woollen sides back up, he looked to larboard and starboard: the narrow channel was alive with ships; triremes, biremes, lembi and transports, a fleet of two hundred and forty in total, all with sails set, faded by the salt air but made pregnant by the wind. As Kleitos' signal relayed around the fleet the frontline squadrons, ten ships in each, took their triangular formations and held position with Kleitos' lead squadron at point; behind it, a second line of eight squadrons, held in reserve, kept a thousand pace distance.

On they drove with a full wind in their sails, churning the sea with rams protruding from their bows, leaving white water frothing in their wake. Gulls circled and swooped, screeching their mournful cries, excited by the sight of so many craft and the prospect of food; a grey-white globule of slime landed close to Krateros' foot and he wondered if it was good luck or bad to be shat upon by a bird.

Spray flew past Krateros' face as the ship rode up on the swell and then crashed back down, slapping the surface on the other side of the wave, the rhythm slow but exhilarating as the fighting ships of the fleet began to pull away from the slower, more wallowing transports.

Another third of a league was covered and the Athenian fleet had begun to deploy for action, their oars spreading like wings as they turned and heaved out into the channel from Abydus. From this distance, Krateros could not tell how many lines they had but what he did know was that the Athenian navy had been the best in the world a century ago and he prayed to Poseidon, the real one, that despite the Macedonian superiority in numbers, it was not still the case.

With no more than half a league separating the two fleets, the Athenians had fully deployed into lines; again their oars spread and dipped as they began the toil of picking up speed against the wind.

Sails raised and full, many blazoned with the sixteen-point sun of Macedon, the Macedonians came on; the rowers resting and drinking from skins of fresh water in preparation for the lung-bursting exertion that lay ahead. Deck crew tightened sheets and hauled on lanyards to harvest every last morsel of power from the gods-given wind as they surged towards the enemy with a naked, trident-wielding imitation of Poseidon, strewn with seaweed, at their head.

Kleitos' physique was as sculpted as Poseidon himself as he strutted and posed with his trident in the prow of the ship, roaring his defiance at the oncoming fleet and promising to send each and every one of them to the bottom of his dark and wet realm. Behind him the marines and archers made their final checks to their equipment and gave entreaties to their favoured gods.

With less than a third of a league now separating the opposing forces, Kleitos turned and ordered the sail furled and oars to be dipped. Sailors scrambled up the mast and along the yard to release the sail from its bindings; down the great sheet came with many hands pulling on it to prevent it from flapping in the wind. As soon as the rest of the first line of the fleet saw Kleitos' move they followed in a ripple out to either side from the centre. Sails tumbled and ships sprang wings; the pipes of the stroke-masters shrilled, taking their timing from the leading vessel. The oars dipped as one and a huge groan of masculine exertion emanated from each ship; without losing speed, the fleet surged on.

Using his trident to set the pace, pumping it in the air in a slow, deliberate rhythm, Kleitos judged the closing distance between the fleets. Now Krateros could make out individuals on the decks of the Athenian ships: deckhands, marines with bronze helms, their cheek and nasal guards almost completely obscuring the faces and plumes standing tall as, with muscle-bulging arms, they hefted javelins and held their round shields up. Archers, standing to either side of the marines, nocked arrows and, with wetted fingers held up, gauged the windage. *This is where we have the slight advantage with the wind being in our favour,* Krateros told himself with the detached interest of an observer. Having only seen small actions with a pirate ship or two and never partaken in a full-scale naval encounter he had become fascinated by the imminent prospect. *You never know, but even at this stage of your life you could learn something new.*

At four hundred paces, Kleitos increased the rhythm of his trident and the ship leapt forward, to the shrill of the pipe, into attack speed. All along the line the others did the same as triarchoi now began to single out enemy ships as their targets.

It had become apparent to Krateros that Kleitos had no real plan other than 'up and at them' and it would be every ship for itself as the two fleets crashed together.

Before them was a trireme with its hull painted red and with two dark eyes to either side of its prow; its ram, visible intermittently, was crowned in bronze and its prow was adorned with a wooden image of Athena, tall and proud, holding a spear and shield. Kleitos roared with pleasure and, pointing at the vessel, turned to shout at the triarchos, Paris, a weather-beaten old veteran, quite the antithesis to his mythological namesake: 'That's ours, Paris! Take her as best you can. Poseidon will fuck Athena!' Leaving the details of the attack to Paris, Kleitos turned back to the oncoming enemy and increased the beat so that the ship, followed by the rest of the fleet, surged into ramming-speed.

And the arrows flew, rising from the decks of both fleets like flocks of sparrows taking to the air; up they rose to their apex before falling to bring fear and death to the enemy. But the wind played its part and the first Athenian volley fell short, perhaps killing a few enemy fish at most; the Macedonian archers, however, had more success as their volley was blown into the oncoming ships and the first cries of pain floated across the water. Again the bowstrings hummed and the hiss of many shafts passed up into the sky. Volley after volley the archers loosed as the Athenians found their range and an iron-headed hail began to thud down onto the Macedonian decks.

Krateros, his shield held before him, affected to ignore the danger thumping in from above as fire pots were brought up from below and placed amongst the archers, who, for the moment, continued with high, arching shots.

The stroke-master's pipes were now at the fastest beat possible for the huge-hearted rowers, powering the ship on and on; with less than fifty paces until impact. The archers switched to fire arrows as in the short flight they were less likely to extinguish. Multiple strands of smoke now streaked across the sky joining the two fleets together as if they were ropes hauling the enemy in. Flames caught and buckets were deployed as all on board each ship now kept a close eye on the nearing foe. With but thirty paces to go all thought of fighting fire or loosing arrows disappeared as each man, with firm handholds, braced for impact.

With the Athenian trireme now less than twenty-five paces away, head on, Krateros involuntarily closed his eyes as he held fast to the rail and Paris shouted: 'Now!'

The steersmen slammed their steering-oars to larboard; the huge trireme responded immediately, slewing to starboard, crossing the path of the oncoming Athenian, now aflame amidships.

'Again!' the triarchos cried and the steersmen now slammed their oars the opposite way so that the trireme regained its original course but now heading straight at the Athenian's larboard oar-bank. 'Ship larboard oars!' Paris roared down to the rowers.

The reaction was instant as all knew the fate of an oarsman who failed to withdraw his sweep in time. But the Athenian triarchos did not react with such alacrity and, with Kleitos roaring a victory hymn to himself, the bow raked down the enemy's oars, cracking them back into the chests and faces of the rowers, breaking ribs and pulverising features as they snapped like dry twigs broken up for kindling. The screams of the injured rose from the belly of the ship as archers and marines pumped their missiles onto the crowded deck; arrows and javelins flew back in reply, punching men back to fall twisted to the ground.

Oblivious to shafts hissing all around him, Kleitos grabbed a grappling hook and, whirring it about his head, hurled it across the gap to latch onto the enemy gunwale; with fleet hands, he tied the end of the rope to a cleat as the oars continued to shatter below and smoke from the burning deck engulfed both triremes. With a sudden jerk the rope tautened, belaying the ship's progress and pulling the two warring vessels together with a grinding of wood on wood. Marines hurled themselves over the rail, shields up and spears thrusting overarm as the archers kept a constant hail of barbs streaming into the foe, feathering their shields until the proximity of their comrades forced them to seek other targets.

It was with a cacophony of battle-cries that the two sets of marines clashed, shield slamming into shield as spears thrust down in explosive overarm jabs; the screaming began; the wounded and dying fell. Krateros considered joining the melee, out of interest, as Kleitos, still naked but now protected by a shield, jumped onto the Athenian ship and, barging through the fighting, took the triarchos in the throat with his trident. As the Macedonians pushed the Athenians back in a flurry of overarm strokes, Krateros decided against joining; *I'll just get in the way. It's a younger man's occupation and, besides, they seem to be doing well enough without me.*

He looked about as smoke wafted across the deck; not twenty paces to starboard another two ships entered into a deadly duel. And then more and more, to either side, collided, raked or rammed with sudden reports of the cracking of shattered timber and resounding hollow thumps, magnified by the drum-like interiors of the stricken vessels, in quick staccato succession. Clash upon clash ensued as the front lines of the two great fleets collided and entwined, some ablaze, belching fumes, each conflict existing within its own private world.

But not all the Athenian ships had engaged; indeed, it had never been their commander's intention for all to do so, for, having been apprised by scouts of the previously unheard-of fleet making its way to the north, he had determined to trap and destroy it despite it being of far greater size. Thus it was that, as he looked back to the second line, Krateros saw beyond it the rest of the Athenian fleet speeding, under full-sail, around the point to complete the trap.

Where possible, the Athenians forced their way through the first line of the Macedonian fleet to face the reserves coming up fast behind so that they would have to fight in two directions.

Krateros saw the move and immediately understood the plan. *Hold our first line whilst destroying the reserve, then the odds will become more even; this Athenian commander is definitely worthy of his predecessors.*

And so, through the first line many of the Athenian ships went, but at the expense of others manoeuvred into combat by the Macedonians. The sea now swirled with blood and churned with men thrashing their limbs in desperation, trying to stay afloat. Through the smoke and confusion, a second wave of Athenian ships hove into view before them as Krateros' trireme and the Athenian, still coupled in a deadly embrace, began to rotate.

'Paris!' Krateros shouted, pointing at an oncoming bireme bearing down on them as they drifted side on to it.

'Starboard oars!' the triarchos shouted down to the rowing deck, recognising immediately the danger Krateros foresaw. Within a few heartbeats the stroke-master's pipe shrilled and the sixty double-banked oars of the starboard side pulled as one; the upper oars, longer and worked by two men and the shorter single-man oars of the lower level strained back through the water, the oarsmen putting all the strength into the pull for they could see through the oar-ports the approaching threat. On the bireme came, bearing down on what, its triarchos could well see, was a helpless victim. At ramming speed it shot through the waves; the Macedonian rowers lost courage as the deadly ram foamed the sea, heading inexorably towards them. Oars clattered down as they were abandoned and men scrambled for the companionways up to the main deck and daylight.

Krateros watched, in morbid fascination, the Athenian close at a speed he felt was impossible for a sea-borne craft to achieve. At the last moment he crouched; the ship jumped back, crunching into the entwined Athenian trireme, as the ram forced its way through its timbers into its belly with the multiple mighty reports of splintering wood. On the bireme came as its ram cleaved through the innards of the Macedonian, showering wicked shards that killed and maimed, until the prow smacked into its beam and the ship juddered to a halt. All three vessels were now conjoined and rocked together so that none aboard could keep his footing. Krateros rolled along the deck, back and forth, with the violent swell of the impact and its aftermath. It took a few heartbeats for the motion to steady; Krateros stumbled to his feet as rowers flooded up from below, their wet tunics and many bleeding wounds telling of the destruction wreaked by the ram.

'She won't last!' Paris shouted.

'On to the trireme!' Krateros ordered the surrounding crew as they recovered their senses and realised their peril; the bireme began to back oars to extricate itself from its unnatural union.

Knowing that, to survive, leadership was paramount, Krateros rushed to the larboard rail and, drawing his sword, jumped the gap onto the Athenian. The deck, shrouded in smoke, was slick with blood; men, felled by the recent collision, rolled about, clutching at one another in to-the-death struggles. With a sharp downward thrust, Krateros skewered an Athenian marine as he tried to gouge out the eyes of a Macedonian; behind him, rowers and deck crew streamed across from the stricken ship. 'Take over the oar deck!' Krateros screamed at the first oarsmen to make the crossing. Understanding the importance of the task they scrambled around for discarded weapons – knives, swords or javelins – and charged down the companionway to do battle with the opposite numbers already much depleted by the raking.

Through the carnage, Krateros found Kleitos by the mainmast, slitting the throat of an archer, his trident now lost. 'We need this ship,' Krateros shouted in his ear, 'ours is going down.'

Kleitos looked round, his eyes unfocused. 'What did you say?'

Krateros repeated his assertion and drew Kleitos back from the blood-frenzy of the fight; he looked around. 'Macedonians, to me!'

The surviving marines and archers formed up on their leader, ready for one last effort as more crew, along with the triarchos, fled the sinking ship, now visibly lower than the Athenian. A small band of Athenians grouped together in the bow, bloodstained and weary; from below came curdling screams as the Athenian rowers were put to the sword, outnumbered now by their Macedonian counterparts streaming down into the gloom of the oar-deck.

It took a couple of heartbeats for the Athenians to realise the gravity of their predicament and, almost as one, they dropped their weapons and fell to their knees.

'Tie them up,' Kleitos ordered, picking up a sword and striding over to the grappling hook; with one blow he severed the rope and the two ships parted, the Macedonian stern now heavy in the water.

'I'll get the oar-deck in hand,' Krateros shouted as Paris barked orders at his crew to quench the flames and to clear the bodies and debris away.

Corpses littered the floor down in the shadows of the oar-deck. 'Get the dead over-board and see how many oars you can salvage from the larboard side,' Krateros ordered the stroke-master.

'And the wounded, general,' the stroke-master indicated the many oarsmen with crushed chests and pulverised faces, lying moaning beneath the benches.

Most were beyond help, Krateros could see. 'Slit their throats and dump them through the oar-ports as well; do it now!'

The stroke-master did not need to be told that they were helpless until they could manoeuvre; he turned and barked orders at his men. Throats were cut, bodies were slithered into the sea and oars were redistributed.

Krateros ran back onto the deck to see their erstwhile ship's bows rise from the surface as, with the whistle of expelled air, the ship slipped, stern-first, under the waves leaving a foaming, bubbling sea to mark its passing.

The fires were now under control and Kleitos, his trident recovered, strode around encouraging the men and placing them in stations as Paris and the steersmen awaited news from below. Krateros drew breath as he looked around. All he could see were ships: fighting, burning, sinking, fleeing or just drifting through the smoke and debris. Looking back west, he could see many of the Athenian vessels, having broken through the Macedonian first line, head straight at the reserve line as the second half of the Athenian fleet closed in on it from behind.

Comprehending the magnitude of the engagement and the consequences should the Athenians take the day, Krateros ran over to Kleitos. 'We have to link up with the reserves and then hold position here so that I can get the army across to Europe.'

Kleitos nodded and looked around, counting ships that were still serviceable in the now-fractured leading line. Many were still involved in boarding or repelling boarders; one group, at least a dozen vessels in all, were all joined, ragtag, creating a small island upon which an imitation land-battle was being played out, but through the fumes its outcome was unclear.

'All's ready below,' the stroke-master called up the companionway.

'Not before time,' Kleitos said, almost to himself; he pointed his trident west towards the reserves as the first of the Athenians crashed in amongst them. 'Paris, get us underway and signal to all who can to follow us.'

Against the wind and with depleted oars, the huge trireme

struggled to accelerate as the groans of exertion rose from the rowers with each slow-pulled stroke.

Leaving the battle-locked vessels behind, the captured trireme slowly got under way, taking those Macedonian ships unengaged with it; three to four dozen in all. *But will that be enough?* Krateros judged it to be four to five hundred paces to where the reserves were being set upon by the Athenians who had broken through; how far behind the second half of the Athenian fleet was, he could not tell.

On the trireme powered, with Kleitos back in the bow, as it gained momentum through debris-strewn waves, the stroke-master's pipes almost drowned out by the roars of the rowers as they strained their last, knowing that the fate of their comrades rested on the speed with which they could come to their aid.

With fists, white-knuckled, gripping the rail and Kleitos now singing the Hymn to Poseidon again next to him, Krateros watched the distance between the two lines lessen. *If we lose this and I can't get my army across this year then we will lose Greece; and if we lose Greece, then what will be next? The east for sure. And then we'll start fighting each other.* Krateros shook his head at the previously unthinkable that was becoming more of a possibility with every ship they lost.

Four hundred, three hundred, down the distance came; now Krateros could hear the screams and shouts from the fighting blown with the wind across the surface. Closing with the enemy ships, he realised that there was a fundamental difference this time: they would attack them in the rear as they were already engaged to their front or side and were unable to turn to face the new threat.

Aiming the ram at a slight angle between the steering oars of the Athenian before him, Paris kept the steersmen on a true course as the archers began to release volleys, alerting the Athenians to the danger grinding in from their rear.

But there was nothing that they could do as they were already engaged, leaving their sterns – or beams if they had drifted around – as they struggled with their foe.

Up the tempo of the stroke-masters' pipes went as Kleitos signalled, trident pumping hard, for all ships to accelerate to ramming speed for the last fifty paces. And it was with a sound that dwarfed the most violent thunder-crack as a storm broke at the height of Zeus' anger, that they hit the Athenians. But it was not just one thunder-crack, it was many in a staccato beat of destruction as rams shattered, splintered and split Athens' wooden walls. Down Krateros tumbled as the ram forced its way into the trireme's stern at an angle so that it would not slide off. In it thrust and with it came a huge explosion of water that surged through the captain's small cabin, washing the thin walls away and exposing the length of the oar-deck.

'Reverse stroke, reverse stroke!' Kleitos bellowed over to Paris. 'She's done for. It's pointless losing lives boarding her.'

And so it was that many of the Macedonians found themselves in a similar position, reversing their oars and withdrawing their rams from gaping wounds flooding with water.

Krateros pulled himself to his feet as the trireme backed away from its victim now spewing seamen as they abandoned a fast-sinking ship. The archers, for the fun of it, carried on their strafing, sending many twisting into the waves, blood arcing from unnecessary wounds. And, as more of the Macedonian ships backed water, a hole began to appear through which the Macedonian reserve line started to flood as they extracted themselves from their duels moments before the second Athenian fleet hit them. Some were caught, suffering the same fate as their opponents, holed in the stern or raked from behind but many more burst through to the comparative safety beyond as floating wrecks and wallowing vessels hampered the navigation of the newly arriving Athenian support. Back Kleitos' galley and many others went, facing the new arrivals as the Macedonian reserve rallied on them and turned to face their pursuers forming a long and formidable battle line unhampered by wreckage.

A silence fell as the two fleets faced each other with just the wind thrumming stays and flapping loose material to be heard as all drew exhausted breath.

It was the Athenians who blinked first.

'They've had enough, the soft Greek bastards,' Kleitos cried as the first ships began to back away. 'But hold fast, lads, we'll let them slink off for today.'

As the last Athenian spun about and rowed away to the west, Kleitos turned his fleet about and headed into the Abydos, passing many a ruined vessel on the way in.

'I would reckon we sank over fifty of them if I can believe this report from the triachoi,' Kleitos told Krateros, waving a scroll, as they sat, an hour later, on some steps, leading down from the quayside, with their feet in the water, 'and captured a couple of dozen more. Compare that with our losses of twenty-six ships sunk and eight more in a bad way, then I would say that was a good day's work.'

Krateros was too tired to do anything but yawn.

'Krateros?' a voice said from the top of the steps.

He turned around to see Polyperchon astride his horse.

'Polyperchon? Is the army here?'

'It'll arrive in two days; I rode ahead because I heard that the Athenians had blockaded the port and I wanted to see the situation for myself.'

'Good man, quite right.'

'Well, I can see the situation and I'd say it was reasonably favourable.'

Krateros smiled at the understatement; he turned to Kleitos. 'Get going as soon as you can and catch the rest of the Athenian navy; leave me the transport ships and I'll get the army over to the other side as soon as it arrives. We'll meet up at Aenus on the Thracian coast in four or five days and then move west in tandem and, with Antipatros, crush the Greek rebellion in the west.'

PHILO,
THE HOMELESS

AND AT THAT time the Greek rebellion in the east faced its greatest challenge as Philo led his men towards the narrow pass, just to the south of the Caspian Sea, through which all armies must pass unless they wish to endure the baking heat of the waterless desert to the south. For ten days they had travelled, knowing that Peithon held the pass against them. Messengers had been sent to the satrap of Media offering gold in exchange for him allowing their passage but the answer had been negative.

'He said that he will only negotiate with us if we return to our posts and then it will be for a pardon not safe passage,' Letodorus informed Philo upon his return from Peithon's camp on the farther side of the pass. They were standing looking at its wide entrance silhouetted by the westering sun; hills rose sharply to either side of it and then constricted it as the pass climbed before opening out onto the fertile uplands of Media, four leagues hence. 'I tried everything: flattery, threats, bribery, even appealing to his sense of justice, which is, of course, very Macedonian and therefore has no room for Greek complaints.'

Philo considered his options; they were limited. 'So we either return to the east or we use the southern route and see how many of us survive.'

'Very few of the women or children, that is for certain.'

'And when we do emerge from the desert, weak and depleted,

who's to say that there won't be an army waiting to finish us off?' *If I were Peithon I'd be wanting us to take the southern route; he'll lose fewer men defeating us.*

Letodorus shook his head, his face grim. 'That's how I see it too; so really it's just a choice between fighting or going back.'

'If I order the men to turn back then I might as well slit my own throat.'

'And mine.'

'Yes, and yours, my friend. Did you manage to get an idea of his numbers?'

'Difficult, but I would say that he has less than us, fifteen thousand foot at the most.'

'That's heartening, but he can choose his ground as we emerge from the pass and, if he's militarily competent, which he is, then our superior numbers won't count for anything.'

'That's how I see it.'

There's nothing I can do to change anything; I must concentrate on the facts and not wish for things that I haven't got and cannot have. 'Then that's how it will be.'

'So we fight, Philo?'

'Yes.'

'I told Peithon we would.'

'And?'

'And he regretted that it was to be the case and said that he hated to waste good men. He then asked if we would be willing to join with him.'

'Join with him? Against whom?'

'Against anyone he feels like fighting. It seems that, being so cut off since Alexander's death, we've missed a lot of what is going on and, judging by what Peithon was saying, the empire is not going to hold together much longer.'

'And he's thinking that he might be able to carve a little bit of the east off it?'

'Something like that.'

'And what did you say?'

'I said that the men want to go home to the sea and not swap one master for another; there's no appetite for staying out here.

Then he offered more silver but I told him that silver was not the issue, the sea was the issue.'

'Did he understand?'

'Of course not.'

'So he's expecting us.'

'Yes.'

'Then we mustn't disappoint him. Muster the men before dawn; we'll be through with a couple of hours of daylight left if we hurry; more than enough time to crush Peithon.'

There was an eeriness about the pass as it climbed through an otherwise impenetrable landscape of ridges, ravines and sheer cliffs. *Perhaps it's the thought of all the dozens of armies that have passed through over the centuries,* Philo considered as he felt wonder that the very name, The Caspian Gates, should have such a resonance to it; and that, once again, it was proving to be pivotal in yet another passage of history. Ten abreast they marched along its length, the width of the pass at its narrowest so that there would be no slowing at bottlenecks. The metallic jangle of the men's equipment rang through the rocks and echoed back off tall, jagged cliffs, unceasing as if an endless herd of bell-carrying goats was being driven through the pass. Few spoke as the eeriness grew and a sure sense of being spied upon entered their minds; men looked up with nervous eyes, afraid that at any moment a volley of arrows or a fall of rock would come from above, the work of the unseen enemy who, all were soon convinced, lay in hiding awaiting their opportunity to strike. Such was the ruggedness of the terrain that very little in the way of scouting could be achieved.

The sun rose and soon beat directly down upon the column; with no breeze, the air grew stifling within the pass and sweat dripped down men's backs and glistened on tanned brows. The stench of unwashed tunics rose from the column, thickening the already close atmosphere and adding to the sense of oppression that all now felt.

Philo took a long swig of water from his skin and looked to the burning sky as the sun passed its zenith; carrion birds circled with a lack of urgency, seemingly certain that such a great passing of the living would leave in its trail plenty of the dead to feast upon.

Weariness grew with each passing step as they reached the halfway-point; Philo dared not call a pause to the march for fear of not making it to the other side in time to confront and beat Peithon's force. 'Spending the night in the pass would be to expose ourselves to a night attack,' he told a delegation sent to the front in order to plead with him to call a halt for the day and to finish the journey on the morrow. 'To win we need to break through this evening; if we don't then all our suffering up until now will have been for nought. Have faith, Brothers, and we will reach the sea.'

The delegation fell back to their places in the column with promises to quell any dissension should it start to rise up in the ranks.

Soon after the delegation left, figures on horseback appeared, shimmering in the heat-haze ahead.

'Bring them straight to me, Letodorus,' Philo ordered as the scouts galloped in. 'I'm anxious to know the worst.'

'He knows we're on our way, and will arrive late afternoon,' the leader of the scouts told Philo. 'He's drawn his army up into position and is now feeding and resting his men so that they are in peak condition when we arrive.'

The scout's face gave Philo no doubt that the man thought arriving that day to be the height of foolhardiness; he ignored it. 'Did you manage to get a look at their disposition?'

The man thought for a few moments, organising his mind. 'His phalanx, eight to ten thousand strong, is, unsurprisingly, on the flat ground, directly opposite the mouth of the pass, with a screen of archers and slingers in front of it. The main bulk of his cavalry, the heavy lancers, are on his right flank with peltasts in support and then some local levies, to bulk up the numbers, well to the rear out of the way. The rest of his peltasts and his horse-archers are on the left flank with light javelin-armed infantry acting as a screen.'

'Horse-archers? How many?'

'Just under a thousand, I should guess. But the strange thing is that beyond them there is a small hill which he seems to have neglected to occupy. If we could—'

'If we could seize that then we would have control of that half of the field.' Philo felt the thrill of a burgeoning hope.

'I'll do it, sir,' Letodorus offered. 'I'll take the three thousand men in my taxies and double-time them out of the pass and be on that hill before Peithon knows what's going on. The horse archers won't try to get in amongst us, they'll just send in volleys from a distance and we're used to that from the caravan escorts. The peltasts and their light infantry won't bother us one bit. We'll take it.'

Philo could see it in his mind's eye. 'Yes, Letodorus, I think you will. That will be a sight to give courage to all the men when they see you up there. Do it and do it quick.'

Letodorus gave an easy smile and squeezed Philo's shoulder. 'I will and when you come out of the pass you won't believe your eyes.'

The heat was fading from the sun as it fell towards the west; Philo watched the last few units of Letodorus' command disappear to the right as they left the pass and accelerated away. He looked behind and raised his fist in the air. His men, all of whom had been doing last-moment checks to their equipment in preparation for battle, drew themselves up and took deep breaths. This, they were all aware, would hurt. Down came Philo's fist and away he jogged with the first company racing with him. One by one the units broke into double-time, following their general out from the Caspian Gates to face an enemy far more prepared than they could hope to be.

Sucking in lungfuls of air as he ran with full kit, Philo left the mouth of the pass to see the might of the Macedonian army arrayed before him. Its phalanx dark and brooding and bristling with thousands of pikes, sixteen feet in length and tipped with honed iron, covered most of his vision, such was its size. To his left he could see the wedge formations of the heavy cavalry, their lance points glinting gold, backlit in the westering sun. He prayed that they would not be released whilst he tried to deploy his men and the gods answered his prayer and he raced away with his men streaming behind to form up the first unit on his extreme left flank. It was not until he had reached the requisite position and the first unit's officers took over command that Philo turned to see how Letodorus was doing. His heart leapt as he saw his second-in-command's men had indeed taken the hill; they swarmed all over it and now controlled all that sector of the field for to succeed there Peithon would have to fight a bloody battle to evict them.

With confidence flowing through his being, Philo turned his attention back to his deployment before, with a sickening feeling surging up his gorge, he jerked his head back to look at the hill once more. He almost choked as he saw how Letodorus' men were formed up: they were facing his troops, not Peithon's.

Treachery had won the day.

The implication of Letodorus' betrayal filtered, without pause, through the whole army; the deployment slowed to a crawl and then stopped altogether.

'Comrades! Comrades!' The shout came from the Macedonian lines; a rider on a white horse rode forward until he was midway between the two sides. 'I am Peithon, one of Alexander's bodyguards. Many of you know me.' He paused to ride up and down the Greek line so that all could see that he was indeed who he claimed to be. As he approached where Philo stood, he slowed and pointed at him. 'Philo! You know me; who am I?'

It's over; I've nothing to gain by aggression. 'I can vouch for you, Peithon; what do you want?'

'Nothing that you Greeks cannot afford: I want you and I want you alive.'

'Alive to do what?'

'Alive to be grateful to me for sparing you. Look around you, Philo: you can't retreat, we would just massacre you as you tried to flee back down the pass; and you can't go forward without a battle which, since Letodorus and his men saw sense, you have not got a hope of winning. So what's it to be, Greeks? Life or death?'

246

There was no need to debate the matter for all knew that Peithon had assessed their situation perfectly. *If I am to retain any authority over my men I need to lead the way.* Philo stepped forward and, with great exaggeration so that all could see, cast down his shield and spear and then pulled his sword from its sheath and dropped it at his feet.

A mighty cheer rose from the rebel army as the men realised that they would live and that the dream of the sea was not entirely dead; they had glimpsed death but knew now they would not be dying this day. Spears and swords were discarded and they walked forward to greet the opposing army, many of whom they knew from shared campaigns. It was with a carnival atmosphere that the two sides came together, embracing and clapping one another on the shoulders whilst striking up conversations of hardships and battles and memories of comrades no longer alive.

'Come with me, Philo,' Peithon said, in a tone that brooked no refusal.

The Macedonian camp reeled with drunkenness as night fell and the two sides celebrated their new-found friendship. The laughter and shouts filled the air, loud even in Peithon's leather tent where Philo looked at Letodorus, disgust in his eyes, as they awaited the Macedonian general. 'Why did you do it?'

Letodorus shrugged. 'The normal reasons: greed and self-preservation.'

Philo spat. 'I thought we were friends. I thought that you actually cared about getting home.'

'I do; it's just that when I saw Peithon's army I realised that I wouldn't be able to get home in such a large company; there would always be armies waiting for us even if we beat this one. Whereas a small group of half a dozen men with money would stand a far better chance; and I now have that money thanks to Peithon's generosity.'

'Thanks to your treachery, more like.'

Letodorus looked hurt over his cup as he took a sip of wine. 'That is not fair. I've saved all our lives. Most of the lads will get sent back east with Peithon as their benefactor; he'll take over paying their wages and they will become his men.'

'And you?'

'I shall enjoy my retirement – by the sea.'

'You bastard.' Philo went for his sword only to remember that it had been taken from him after he had surrendered.

Letodorus tutted and patted the hilt of his sword which he had been allowed to keep as a mark of Peithon's trust. 'Really, Philo; and what good would that do even if you were armed?'

'It would make me feel a lot better.'

'And Peithon would have you executed. Wouldn't you, Peithon?'

'What?' Peithon said, emerging through the entrance, the noise of carousing coming with him.

Letodorus repeated his assertion.

'I wouldn't think twice about it, Philo; you're a Greek. But I'd rather that you served me.'

'Doing what?' Philo asked, not taking his eyes off Letodorus.

The noise from the camp grew ever more raucous as the shouts and yells of drunken fighting began to impinge on the general merriment; Peithon cocked his head to listen for a moment and then ignored it. 'I plan to take the east and with your men I could hold it.'

'And what if we don't want to stay there?'

'Then you will die here.'

Philo considered his options as the sounds from outside grew more heated. 'What will you pay us?'

'The normal rate plus your lives; so a great deal is the answer.'

Screams rang out from close by. Peithon again cocked his head and this time decided to investigate. Philo and Letodorus followed him out into a camp studded with flaming torches and fires in whose light hundreds of figures struggled. Philo's eyes took a few moments to adjust to the gloom and paled as the massacre became apparent. 'Stop them, Peithon. That is nothing but murder.'

Peithon looked, astounded, as his Macedonian troops lay into the unarmed Greeks with whatever weapons they had to hand. Swords, knives, spears or javelins, they cared not for all killed equally well and it was upon killing that they focused. 'I didn't order this. What do I have to gain by it?'

The look in Peithon's eyes made Philo believe him; he watched in horror as throats were slit and bellies pierced; one veteran shrieked as both hands were severed as he raised them to ward off a blow to the face; another sat on the ground staring down in horror at the pile of slimed intestines in his hands until a sweep of a blade sent his head spinning, spiralling dark drops of gore in the torchlight. Here and there small groups of Greeks had joined together to mount some form of resistance but as they had all been disarmed these efforts were doomed to failure and they were cut down without mercy, hacked and stabbed by the very men they had been sharing food and drink with only a short while ago.

And it was through this murder that there strode a body of men, all heavily armed and using their shields to protect the officer, swaggering with a tall plume on his helm and a fine cloak, in their midst. On they came towards Peithon's tent, pushing aside all who got in their way.

'Seleukos,' Peithon said, almost under his breath, as the officer approached him.

'Yes, Peithon,' Seleukos said with a charming smile. 'It really is and aren't you so pleased to see me?'

'Did you order this?'

Seleukos looked around as if he were trying to ascertain exactly to what Peithon referred. 'Oh, you mean the justice being meted out to the deserters. No, Peithon, I didn't order it, I just reminded a few of the officers of their duty to the kings and to Perdikkas; I think they must have been the ones who ordered it. It's just as well that they did as I would have hated you to make the irrevocable mistake of bringing scum like this into your army.'

'I—'

'Don't try to deny it, Peithon, you haven't got the intellect to lie convincingly; you're a plain speaker. Always have been and always will. Now, this is the deal: we kill every one of them...' He paused as he looked at Philo and then Letodorus. 'Except, perhaps, these two here; Perdikkas might well like a quiet word with them. And then you replace the eastern garrisons with your men and take what's left of your army back to Ecbatana; I'll return the troops that Perdikkas lent you back to him in Kappadokia. You will then stay in Ecbatana and behave yourself, doing whatever Perdikkas needs you to do and, if you're a very good boy, Perdikkas might one day forgive you for trying to steal the east from him. Don't deny that was what you were planning to do.' He turned to Letodorus and made a great show of recalling his name. 'Letodorus! Is that not so, Letodorus?'

Letodorus was eager to be of help to the new master of the situation. 'Yes, Seleukos; he told us that he wanted the whole east for himself.'

'And how much was he willing to pay you?'

'You would have to ask Philo that, as he was the one negotiating with him since I had refused the offer categorically.'

'You lying bastard!' Philo shouted. His fist lashed out into his erstwhile second-in-command's face, crushing the nose; such was his anger at the betrayal and murder of his men even now going on around him. He dived at Letodorus, one hand grabbing his throat and the other the hilt of his sword; his momentum pushed them both to the ground, struggling in a tangle of limbs. Squeezing tight his grip on the throat, Philo yanked at the sword, pulling it free and, with one swift jab, rammed it up under Letodorus' ribcage. Blood slopped from Letodorus' mouth and a look of pain and surprise contorted his face.

It was the last thing Philo saw.

KRATEROS, THE GENERAL

KRATEROS LIFTED HIS new wife's veil, pushing it back over her head, and, intoning the prescribed words, completed the transfer of Phila, attended by her sisters, Eurydike and Nicaea as well as her cousin, Berenice, from Antipatros' family into his own. The old regent and his wife were the first to offer their congratulations as Krateros displayed his bride to the crowd of dignitaries witnessing the wedding in the cavernous great hall of the royal palace in Pella.

'I hope you father many sons on her,' Antipatros said to his new son-in-law with a knowing smile. 'If she takes after her mother then she's fertile ground.'

'Father!' Phila exclaimed, her cheeks reddening. 'Don't talk in such a way in front of our guests.'

'Well, it's not as if you're a virgin,' Eurydike muttered, causing Nicaea to snort with suppressed laughter, covering her mouth

'Shame on you, Husband,' Hyperia admonished, pretending not to hear her second eldest daughter's remark. 'That is not the sort of talk for a wedding.'

Antipatros slapped his wife soundly on the buttocks, causing her to cry out in outrage – but not without a little twinkle in her eye, Krateros could not help but notice. 'Nonsense, my dear; that's exactly how to talk at a wedding, it's all about procreation and the fun we have doing it and all this talk of it has put me in the mood, so stand by for boarders directly after the wedding feast.'

251

Krateros laughed despite himself and received a sharp dig in the ribs from Phila; he composed his countenance into one of sombre dignity. 'I pray that our alliance will prove equally productive for both our families.'

'I'm sure it will,' Antipatros replied, looking down out of the corner of his eye at his wife's breasts.

'As a sign of the mutual trust that is now between us and also as a mark of respect of a son for his father, I place my army and navy, when Kleitos returns, under your leadership in the forthcoming campaign against the Greek rebels; I also offer my services as your second-in-command.'

This got Antipatros' attention; his wife's breasts momentarily forgotten, he looked at Krateros with gratitude. 'You, at least, understand that working together is best done not by committee but with a hierarchy in place. That is a very generous gesture that will make teaching the Greeks a lesson far easier for both of us.'

It avoids civil war and will make me commander of your army, and what's left of Leonnatus' and mine when you die, in the next couple of years, old man, whatever your son, Kassandros, might think. 'That is my wish.'

'Order is what we need, with a strong and clear line of command.'

'I agree, which is why I've made the offer. The main problem that Perdikkas has is that most of our colleagues have refused to submit to his will; so I'm hoping that if I put myself at your disposal that'll send a signal to other commanders that there is no shame in serving worthy men and we might attract a few more to our banner.'

Antipatros immediately understood the implication. 'Forge an alliance against Perdikkas? But I'm soon to send Nicaea to him to be his wife.'

'Which will put him in the same position as me; look at what I've just done.'

'But he would never put his forces under my control.'

'Perhaps not, but he will see the respect in which I hold you and realise that if I'm willing to submit to you but not him then others may well do the same if he carries on trying to make himself the new Alexander.'

'In other words there'll be less chance of war if he just marries my daughter and minds his own business.'

Krateros inclined his head. 'Exactly. I think that most of us can now see that there will never be a united empire again and that the best that we can hope for is that it splits into its constituent parts with as little blood-loss as possible; only that way will we have a chance of holding what we have and keeping the tribes to the north and the east from trying their luck.'

'And so I settle for Macedon with you as my heir apparent?'

'*Father*-in-law, let's discuss that at the wedding feast.'

The male guests were in bullish mood as, led by Nicanor and Iollas, they toasted, once again, the sexual prowess of the groom and, despite all knowing that it was not the case, the purity of the bride; slaves scuttled around the tables refilling cups and bringing out yet more courses on platters and in bowls, beautifully decorated with athletes, gods and warriors.

Krateros, for the first time since leaving Cilicia, allowed himself to get drunk, not worrying that it may affect his performance on his wedding night; with Phila segregated with the rest of the women in a dining area of their own, there was no one to gainsay him. And besides, she was well aware, by now, of his prowess.

With it being almost a year since Alexander's death had rocked the world, Krateros felt a relief that he had swallowed his pride and sided with Antipatros, a man of proven political adroitness who would prove a useful ally against Perdikkas. With Leonnatus out of the way, a piece of luck he could never have wished for, he, Krateros, was the obvious choice to take over as regent of Europe after Antipatros' death; and, unlike kingship, eligibility for the regency was not hereditary; Kassandros would have no claim to his father's position. *Yes, all in all this is a very smart move; what's a little dent to the pride when I'm positioning myself for the long-term goal of control of the west; let Perdikkas keep Babylon and the east; Eumenes is most welcome to Kappadokia and no one will ever manage to shift Ptolemy from*

Egypt. No, I'll settle for this. He raised his cup and drank a toast to himself, relishing the prospect of the coming campaign and the chance to get some real soldiering done again, free, in the main, from politics now that Antipatros would shelter him from its reach. *And what is more, it will be Greeks who I'm fighting and not my own kind.*

'We'll leave Polyperchon here in Pella as acting regent with Nicanor in command of the garrison, when we go south,' Antipatros slurred, 'between them they've got the ability to beat off Aeacides if the little bastard tries to flex Epirus' muscle again. Although, now that witch Olympias has disappeared, I doubt he will with no one to stiffen his cock for him.'

'Have we heard where she ran to?' Krateros asked, allowing his cup to be refilled yet again.

'Buggered if I know. She can stay lost for as long as she likes for all I care; it's one less problem to cope with.'

Krateros lifted his cup. 'Here's to having no problems.' He downed the wine in one and the rest of the revellers joined him.

He did, however, have one outstanding problem: now that he had laid claim to Hellespontine Phrygia after Leonnatus' death, he wished to know the minds of Antigonos and Menander, the rulers of two of the satrapies bordering it. Lysimachus, the ruler of the third, had let his army pass through his territory of Thracia without charging too exorbitant a price for the forage it required; Lysimachus himself had even joined him for dinner as he waited on the northern side of the Hellespont for his army to be ferried over. Here it had become apparent that the satrap of Thrace had no designs on expanding his territory to the south but, rather, was concentrating his efforts on subduing the wilder Thracian tribes to the north. They had parted with gifts of friendship but Krateros had not been fooled for he knew that should Lysimachus be successful then he would have a potentially huge army of his wild, new subjects; he was a man to be watched in the future.

But what of Antigonos and Menander? And Assander in Caria, for that matter? Would they be content for him to quietly grow his power? Would they see what his real long-term objective was now that he had manoeuvred himself into Antipatros' favour? He had little doubt that they would, but would they take action?

His musing on the complexities of gaining power were broken into by a rumpus at the door as yet another toast was drunk. 'Where is he? Where is he?'

Krateros knew that voice only too well and when the three-pronged tip of a trident came through the door there was a cheer from all present.

'Krateros!' Kleitos called across the room. 'I've come to give you the best wedding present yet.' He paused to strike what he considered to be his most god-like pose, trident raised over his head and one hand on his hip. 'Two days ago I defeated the Athenian navy at Amorgus in the Cyclides as they tried to secure the strait; all their vessels are either destroyed or captured. There is nothing between here and Piraeus.'

That report brought the biggest cheer of the day; it was the news that all had waited for.

Antipatros turned to Krateros as both their cups were recharged. 'I think you might just have time to get my daughter pregnant before we march south.'

'Indeed; but first some more wine,' Krateros said, raising his cup. 'To the fleet and Kleitos.'

The fleet had shadowed the army down the Thessalian coast, speckling the azure summer sea, sails filled with northerly breeze and accompanied by squadrons of gulls feasting on the trail of detritus cast in its wake. But, unlike the previous time the Macedonian army had marched south, there was nothing to fear from the sea; the fleet's presence was purely to keep the army, fifty thousand strong and comprised mainly of infantry, supplied so that it wasn't slowed down by a lengthy baggage train. Speed was now the key; speed in order to catch the rebels before they heard that Antipatros had marched south.

And speed had proven to be an ally as Krateros, Antipatros and Magas listened to the commander of the light cavalry unit freshly returned from scouting inland. 'A shit-hole that goes by the name of Krannon, sir; it's about six leagues due west from here. It's home to about a couple of dozen old men, a few hags with half a dozen teeth between them and the communal goat that the men take turns with; all the young lads are with the rebels and the young women are servicing them – you know how fond they are of their sisters and cousins around here?'

'Yes, yes,' Antipatros said, waving a hand, disinterested in the scout's many observations on local practice. 'So what is there at Krannon for Antiphilus and Menon?'

The scout, tanned leather for a face and breath powered by raw onions and garlic, took off his broad-brimmed sun hat and scratched at a scabby, bald pate. 'Well, it ain't for the agriculture, that's for sure; most of the farms are overgrown because of the war. However, the ground does suit us: apart from the hill where they've camped, it's flat.'

'Flat?'

'Yes, sir, flat.'

Antipatros tossed the man a coin and dismissed him.

'We've caught them out in the open,' Krateros said as the scout left the tent.

Antipatros was not so sure. 'Have we? Or are they trying to make us think that we have?'

'Either way, if we can get there by tomorrow late afternoon we could face up to them and have it done once and for all.'

'If they come down from their hill,' Magas said, 'the lads don't like to fight uphill if we can help it.'

Krateros shook his head. 'If we catch them on that hill then they'll have two choices; try to withdraw in good order, in which case we harry them all the way to Thermopylae and trap them there, or they come down and fight because if they stay on that hill they'll starve, we'll see to that.'

Antipatros sat down with a sigh. 'The flat ground will be good for their cavalry.'

'Most of it is Thessalian light javelin skirmishers, just a quarter of it is heavy and all of it javelin-armed, no lancers at all; even if they have retained the five thousand that deserted you they're no match for our two thousand heavy lancers and one thousand lights. If we can tempt them into doing something rash and neutralise them, then it'll be a straightforward infantry slogging match, the sort the lads love.'

'I hope so. Anyway, do we have a choice in the matter? Not to engage them now would just mean the campaign will drag on until the harvest and then we'll start getting disgruntled men.' Antipatros paused for a thought. 'Mind you, so will they; and their men are more likely just to go home.'

'Don't take the risk. Remember, a lot of them are mercenaries without farms and a harvest to get in.'

Standing, Antipatros slapped his thigh, his mind made up. 'You're right. Magas, have the men issued with two days' supplies; we'll march at an hour before dawn and we'll march hard and fast. Krateros, I want you to command the cavalry and I'll see to the infantry. We'll deal with them quickly.'

But it was not to prove so easy and Krateros was growing weary; the only orders he had issued to his cavalry command for the previous eleven days were to form up in the morning, the lancers just to the rear of the right flank of the phalanx, and the lights slightly in advance of its left flank; and then, six hours later, he would dismiss them back to the camp, the rebels having, once again, refused to come down from their hill and do battle.

'I don't blame them,' Antipatros said, yet again, as his senior officers met in his tent after another day standing on the plain waiting for the rebels to break camp and face them. 'We outnumber them by fifteen thousand, if our spies are to be believed; I wouldn't come out against such odds.'

'They'll have to soon,' Krateros said, wiping the dust from his face with a towel. 'We're being provisioned by our fleet but they have nothing. We've cut their supply line and it's apparent that none of the messages they sent, asking for reinforcements, are being responded to; no one's coming to their aid and the longer this goes on, the more they'll haemorrhage men.'

'Then why don't they surrender?' Magas asked, slumping down onto a chair.

'Would you without a fight?'

Antipatros rubbed his temples. 'We'll try to get them to commit to a fight one more time tomorrow.'

'And if they don't?'

'If they don't, it leaves me with no option but to advance up their hill, handing them the advantage, and give them the simple choice: stand or retreat.'

And it was to stand that the rebels chose as their far outnumbered hoplite phalanx waited in the rising sun for their Thessalian cavalry, under Menon, to attempt to expose the Macedonian phalanx's right flank as it moved into position, coming to a halt just fifteen hundred paces from the base of the hill.

Krateros rolled his shoulders and adjusted his posture in the saddle, his thighs gripping the flanks of his mount and his feet hanging free; he felt the weight of the lance in his right hand and enjoyed the glinting of the sun reflecting off its honed point as he surveyed the field from just behind the phalanx. Ahead of him was a first line of peltasts sent forward to cover the right flank of the infantry formation. Looking behind him, he satisfied himself that all his cavalry, in a column along the rear of the phalanx, had complied with his last order.

'Stay close to me,' he told the signaller behind him, 'this will require timing.'

With ranks redressed after its initial deployment, Antipatros gave the order for the Macedonian phalanx, almost half a league wide, to advance. Trumpets sounded along its length and, like a great beast rising from its slumber, the huge body of men slowly began to move, not quite evenly, so that the formation stretched here and there before contracting back into line as each individual gained a steady pace of march.

Krateros hung back with his men, following the tactic that he and Antipatros had discussed as they had broken their fast that morning on fresh bread and olives: the objective was to win the encounter with as few casualties as possible.

'If we don't have too much cause for vengeance,' Antipatros had told him, 'then I can give most of the cities reasonable terms.'

'Why would you want to do that?' Krateros had asked.

'You'll see when I come to deal with the Athenian delegation.'

The regent had winked in a conspiratorial manner but had enlightened him no more.

But Krateros cared not for the niceties of post-war diplomacy; it was on the present fight that he was focused and this was the first proper land battle he had participated in for four years, since Alexander had defeated the Indian king, Porus, at the battle of the River Hydaspes. He would do as Antipatros had commanded and hold his men back, deliberately exposing the phalanx's flank in order to tempt the Thessalians into a rash move. But, when he did let his men go, he was not going to ask for restraint; far from it, he was going to enjoy himself and expected his men to do so as well.

And so the lumbering beast marched on, over the flat ground that suited it best; the unison crunching of leather-shod feet, almost a physical phenomenon as it rose from the plain, shook the very earth. The file closers at the rear worked hard to keep their charges level and at the same pace whilst the file leaders, veterans to a man, kept their eyes on one another to ensure that none got out of line.

Krateros pulled on his bridle to steady his horse, made skittish by the passing of so many men and the sight of cavalry forming up just a thousand paces away across the field of battle. Then, to his surprise, he saw that the rebel phalanx was now coming completely down off its hill in a move that he immediately understood and was grateful for. *They've fallen for it. They must be coming down in support of their cavalry but I would have kept at least twenty paces of the higher ground and had the lads piss down the hill to make it slippery to a frontal attack. They would still be close enough for their cavalry to rally.* He strained his eyes to see if something was not as it appeared to be. *We'll need to be careful; you don't give up that sort of advantage without a good reason.*

The Macedonian phalanx was now linking up with the peltasts in the first line. Together they pushed on, the peltasts at the lazy lope they favoured as the phalangites marched with rigid step. Beyond, the Thessalians, screened by jogging archers and slingers, trotted forward, making as if they were to attack the peltasts frontally. Krateros wiped his forehead, sweat was now seeping from beneath his kausia as the high-summer sun grew in strength. *It'll be a scorching day; the battle may come down to who has had the most water for breakfast; there'll be no fresh supplies once we've joined.* Pushing the thought from his mind, he waited for the moment to order the first deployment of his cavalry.

A shrill horn screeched above the mass footsteps of the phalanx and the rebel archers and slingers broke into a run with the Thessalian cavalry keeping pace behind them. With a hundred and twenty paces between the two sides the skirmishers released shaft and stone to hiss into the dispersed formation of the peltasts. Down went a few, the rest loped on, crescent shields raised and javelins hefted, waiting for the moment that they should come into range. Missiles continued to hiss in from the skirmishers, clacking into shields and ringing off helms, but doing, otherwise, very little harm.

And then, with a hundred paces between the forces, another series of horn signals rent the air; the Thessalians broke into a canter, penetrating the skirmish lines and breaking into a gallop aimed directly at the peltasts. The moment that Krateros had been waiting for had come and, taking off his kausia, he thrust it above his head; at a repeated signal, echoing throughout the formation, the cavalry trotted forward in column out from behind the shadow of the phalanx and, once clear of it, turned to form line, now a good five hundred paces from the rear of the peltasts.

On came the Thessalians, closing the gap with the Macedonian forward line, ninety, eighty, seventy paces; the peltasts released their first volley. High flew the javelins and at that same moment the Thessalians, in a display of prodigious skill which few could have attempted, swerved as one to their left, racing along the frontage of the peltasts so that almost all the volley fell short.

Krateros smiled to himself as he gave another command and the horns rang out; it was as he had hoped. *They haven't seen us and are trying to get around the peltasts to take the phalanx in the flank; they're in for a nasty surprise.* He looked along his lines as each unit formed a wedge, like teeth in the maw of a giant wolf.

A second javelin in their hands, the peltasts took the required quick steps, arched their backs, with their right arms extended behind them, and released again, catapulting the projectiles on by flicking the leather loop at its centre with their forefingers. No sooner had those javelins launched than the Thessalians once again changed direction to charge forward, whooping and urging their mounts to lung-bursting excess, for they aimed to gallop underneath the volley. For the most part they did; the rear ranks suffering some hits but those horses and men tumbling to the dust had none behind them to impede. And on they came still, almost fully intact and displaying no lack of cohesion, directly at the peltasts who began to show signs of wavering as individuals looked to their rear or fumbled with their third javelin.

Krateros immediately saw the implication of the move. *They're desperate; they're happy to take unnecessary casualties trying to break the peltasts in the hope that their rout will demoralise the phalanx before they hit it in the flank.* Krateros' heart sped. *We're going to have to charge through our own disordered, fleeing troops.*

The phalanx marched on, closing with its opposition, and the Thessalian charge neared home and, sure enough, unsure of what to do, the peltasts wavered; some knelt behind their shields, those equipped with long thrusting spears braced them against the ground, others hurled their final javelin and turned to flee whilst more than a few just stared at the infantryman's nightmare hurtling towards them.

And Krateros' time had now come.

It was as the first of the peltasts went under the hooves of the lead horses, two hundred paces away, that Krateros turned to his signaller. 'Sound the charge.'

Up went the notes and, with a cheer and much equine snorting and jangling of harness, two thousand of Macedon's finest cavalry broke into a walk. Krateros immediately signalled once more, the horn blared and the lancers eased into a trot as the Thessalians broke through those of the peltasts who had stood their ground, leaving a trail of dead and wounded in their wake as they drove those routing before them. But the sight of superior cavalry now coming into a canter was not what they had bargained for; they had hoped to be given a chance to crash into the soft underside of the phalanx and reap havoc against undefended infantry who could see their comrades in flight, being run down and butchered within a few score paces of them.

As Krateros brought his lance from its upright position and held it overarm ready to stab down upon the first enemy he reached, the signaller called the gallop and eight thousand hooves pounded the ground to the chorus of war-cries practised over the years throughout the known world. The Macedonian Companion cavalry were at full charge with one objective: Thessalian blood.

And, with less than a hundred paces between them, the Thessalians turned and fled.

With wind in his face, a cry in his throat and a lance in his fist, Krateros urged his horse on as, at the point of the central wedge, he led the cavalry to slaughter. With no time or chance to manoeuvre, they rode down the fleeing peltasts and trampled those already wounded or broken beneath thunderous hooves. With eyes showing white with battle fever, nostrils flaring and slack-lipped mouths foaming, the great beasts of war pounded the earth as they pursued their prey, now less than fifty paces from them with the swirling dust of swift retreat rising in its wake.

Ever on, Krateros led his men, gaining on the enemy and clearing them from the phalanx's flank as it, in turn, collided with the rebels, thrusting pikes, with ease, past the long spears of the hoplites, to stab and push.

With a lunge, Krateros lanced a straggling Thessalian in the kidneys, arching him back with a scream, to fall on his neck and disappear under a wall of horseflesh and dust. And again he jabbed as the wedges to either side of his also made contact, scooping up the fleeing Thessalians between their teeth, chewing them to bloody shreds.

But, with a glance to his left, Krateros saw that the slaughter could not go on; they had left it too late. The rebel phalanx had, at first contact, begun its ordered withdrawal back up the hill and Antipatros was not to be tempted; he immediately broke off rather than fight an elevated foe. Krateros' reaction was instant. 'Withdraw! Withdraw!'

The signal rang out and was carried along the line; most heard and reined in their mounts but for some the blood-lust was too intoxicating and they rode on stabbing at the enemy's exposed backs; few of them returned to their comrades as they rallied to the rear of the phalanx, now parked, immovable at the base of the hill, defying the rebels to try their luck once more.

'And about time,' Antipatros said as, a couple of hours after midday, the heralds came down the hill. Krateros waited with him having left his cavalry to tend to their mounts. Behind them, the phalanx had withdrawn five hundred paces but remained in formation, eating bread and dried meat brought up from the camp.

Krateros noted, with interest as he sat beneath a canopy on the field of victory, that neither Menon nor Antiphilus had chosen to come in person. Although it had not been crushing, just five hundred, or so, of the rebels dead, as compared with a few over a hundred of the Macedonians – mainly the unfortunate peltasts – it had been decisive: the rebel commanders knew that their troops would be unwilling to fight again.

Now it was time to negotiate terms.

'Absolutely not,' Antipatros said with the smile and the light voice of a reasonable and patient man. 'I cannot treat all the rebel cities in the same way; some are guiltier than others. Lamia, for example, only joined the rebellion after I managed to extract my army from it; it did so, I presume, because it had no choice in the matter, seeing as the rebel host was billeted on it.' He looked at the two heralds with a troubled and confused expression. 'Tell me, gentlemen, should I treat Lamia as I would treat Athens, the city that started the rebellion? Would that be fair on Lamia? Or should I treat Athens in the way that Lamia deserves? Would it be fair on little Lamia that Athens, which has been the cause of all this woe, is punished so lightly? Would that be justice? I think not. No, go back to your masters and tell them that each city will be dealt with according to its guilt. Tell Menon of Thessaly that I am willing to overlook his treachery if he and his men come down to me now, otherwise I will start the destruction of the nearest Thessalian towns and keep going until he comes to his senses. And let it be known to the mercenaries that they can find employment in my army if they are down from the hill by an hour before dusk. The contingents from the cities will stay in your camp until a temporary truce has been finalised.'

The senior herald, a man with a strong Athenian accent, looked nervous at the pronouncement. 'And what about Athens?'

Antipatros feigned confusion. 'Athens? What do you mean, what about Athens?'

'What will you do with Athens?'

'Do? What do you expect me to do about Athens? What did Alexander do to Thebes when it led a rebellion?'

The herald swallowed. 'He razed it to the ground and sold its citizens into slavery.'

This time it was surprise that Antipatros affected. 'Did he now? Every one of them?'

'I believe so.'

'You believe so.' Antipatros considered the statement. 'So you would prefer it, as I'm sure would every citizen of Athens, if I didn't do to Athens what Alexander rightly did to Thebes, am I right?'

Again the herald swallowed. 'Yes, sir.'

Krateros watched with concealed amusement as Antipatros worked himself up into a state of indignant ire; he was not disappointed as the regent leapt to his feet and pointed a jabbing finger at the herald.

'Then you'd better tell your leaders to come and fucking beg me! I spent the winter locked up inside of Lamia, eating rats, rotten grass and the stuff between my toes because of Athens. I didn't bed my wife for six months because of Athens; six months! Can you imagine how I felt? Six whole fucking months! Now, if Athens wants me to show some sort of leniency then I want to sit down with Phocion and Demades and hear what they have to say concerning Athens' behaviour and that of Hyperides and

Demosthenes. And I will do that, when they're ready, amongst the ruins of the agora in what's left of Thebes. Perhaps that will focus their minds. Now fuck off!'

Krateros watched the startled heralds bow and scuttle away until they were out of hearing range before bursting into laughter. 'You've just made yourself the most unpopular man in Attica. There is nothing an Athenian hates more than being told what to do.'

'And I wasn't the most unpopular man before?'

'I think Alexander still held that, even though he's dead, because of his Exile Decree forcing Athens to return Samos to its rightful owners.'

'Perhaps so, but I'm happy to take the mantle from him and teach these fucking Greeks a lesson.'

'If they come to the Thebes talks.'

'Oh, they'll come all right; I'll make sure of that.'

'How?'

'Once I've settled with Menon and Antiphilus I'm going through the Pass of Thermopylae threatening to storm every rebel town I come across; those that surrender will have no harm done to them and be forced to accept a Macedonian garrison. But those that don't, well...' He turned to Krateros and smiled. 'Well, they'll remind the Athenians exactly what happened to Thebes.'

Krateros continued to chuckle. 'You're a man after my own heart, Father; Alexander knew the power of coercing the strong by demonstrating his intent on those less so. It saves Macedonian lives in the end. Let's hope they understand the lesson as I've never been that partial to a siege.'

PERDIKKAS,
THE HALF-CHOSEN

'THE SIEGE WILL be lifted only, and I repeat, only,' Perdikkas said, enunciating each word as if he were talking to a deaf old crone, 'when Ariarathes opens the gates and comes out *on* his knees and pleads for forgiveness from the two kings.'

The spade-bearded Kappadokian herald kept his nose pressed into the dust as he lay prostrate at Perdikkas' feet, beneath a canopy overlooking Mazaca, the city that the rebel satrap, Ariarathes, had chosen as his seat, in central Kappadokia. 'But lord, King Ariarathes begs you to allow for his advanced years, he is—'

'Eighty-two, and has swollen knees,' Eumenes cut in, standing behind Perdikkas' chair, 'we know; you have said so before. You have also, before, been told that Ariarathes is not a king and yet you've just referred to him as such. I find it puzzling that a man should be so willing to have his tongue cut out.' He signalled to the guard standing next to the herald; the man drew his knife.

'My apologies, great lords, it was a slip of the tongue.' In his alarm, the herald completely missed the comic value of what he had just said as Eumenes and Perdikkas shared a look and burst into laughter; the man raised his eyes a fraction to see what the cause of the mirth was.

Perdikkas slapped the arm of his chair and brought his features back to a serious countenance. He signalled to the guard to put away his knife. 'No need for that.'

'Yes,' Eumenes agreed, still chuckling, 'it would be a shame to silence for ever such a comic talent.'

Perdikkas looked down at the man, who immediately averted his eyes. 'Now get up and deliver my message to the traitor.'

Eumenes cast a look over towards the besieged city; much smoke rose from the siege-lines as the Macedonian troops prepared their midday meal. 'And be grateful that, due to your masterful word-play, you have a tongue to do it with and won't be relying on acting it out – mind you, with talent like yours I'm sure you would be able to do it in a way that would have everyone falling about with laughter.'

'Evidently not,' Eumenes said as he looked at the herald writhing upon a stake set upon the city walls a short while later.

Perdikkas slammed his fist into his palm. 'Why does everyone defy me?'

'They don't defy *you*, Perdikkas; it's not personal – at least, in Ariarathes' case it's not personal – it's pride. Would you go kneeling to him if the roles were reversed?'

'Of course not, a Macedonian kneels to no one.'

'Oh, of course, I'd forgotten; silly me. Well, it's pointless me trying to explain in that case; we'll just have to go and kill everyone in there because of one old man's pride and your inability to see the cause of it. But before we do, I'm off to find some lunch.'

Perdikkas watched the little Greek walking away, frowning. *Why does one of the few men I trust always have to be so aggravating?* He sighed and turned back to the city, contemplating his options in this, the climax of his swift Kappadokian campaign.

And it had been swift, gratifyingly so. Having set out from Babylon, in a large fleet of river transports under the command of his brother-in-law, Attalus, a month before the snows were due to melt in the lower lying parts of Kappadokia, Perdikkas had managed to get to Thapsacus, on the Syrian border, and, from there, retrace Alexander's footsteps to the sea and then north into Cilicia, through the coastal plain of Issus – the site of his second major victory over the Persians – and onto Tarsus. Finding Krateros newly departed with most of his troops,

267

Perdikkas' disappointment had been compensated by Antigenes and the Silver Shields pledging themselves, at Krateros' request, to his cause – it was a welcome sign of respect. Upon hearing the news that Krateros had taken his entire navy north and then on to Europe with the intention of joining, in an alliance sealed by marriage to Phila, Antipatros' war against the Greek rebellion in the west, he had written, yet again, to the ageing regent asking for the hand of one of his other daughters.

It had not been until he had followed the Carinalas River up into the belly of Kappadokia and had begun a spring offensive against the rebel satrap that an offer of a different kind had caught up with him in the form of a letter from Olympias who was now, to Perdikkas' surprise, in Sardis. He had had the messenger killed so that the queen would not know when or whether he had received the letter thus buying himself time to think on his reply.

As he had chased Ariarathes over rough country, defeating him in two major encounters, Perdikkas had contemplated the consequences of renouncing his proposal to marry into Antipatros' family and take up, instead, Olympias' offer of marriage to Kleopatra. Now, here at Mazaca, in the shadow of the great Mount Argaeus, the subjugation of Kappadokia was about to be completed and, with Neoptolemus now dealing with Armenia to the east, it would be time for Perdikkas to turn west to put down a rebellion in Pisidia, right next to Lydia and its capital, Sardis.

Now that he had cornered Ariarathes in his capital, the decision could not be put off much longer.

But I'll have to confide in Eumenes soon; I'd be a fool to take a decision like this without taking his advice. The sly little Greek has the rather unpleasant habit of being right; that's another reason I find him so aggravating.

Resolving to put the matter off until Ariarathes was safely impaled on a stake, Perdikkas sent a summons for all his senior commanders to join him in his tent. 'And I'll take my midday meal there!' he shouted after the messenger.

'We don't need to scale the walls or try to knock down the

gate,' Eumenes informed the briefing in reply to Perdikkas' request of suggestions upon how to do just those two things.

Perdikkas looked at the Greek in surprise. 'No, Eumenes? Then how are we going to get into the town, fly?'

Eumenes considered the suggestion for a few moments. 'We could, I suppose, but seeing as not even Archimedes ever invented a way of doing so and it would certainly take us some years of experimentation to come up with a viable system and, even then, look at Icarus and the problems he had. No, I wouldn't advise it, especially if we would rather take the town tomorrow.'

'Tomorrow?' Alketas exclaimed.

Eumenes smiled at Perdikkas' younger brother in the condescending manner he reserved for Macedonians of lesser rank and intellect. 'Or tonight, if you would prefer, Perdikkas?'

Gods, the man is aggravating! 'If we could do it tonight, then why didn't we do it last night?'

'For a start, you were still negotiating; secondly, you didn't ask and, thirdly, and this, gentlemen, is the crucial point.' He paused to look around the half-dozen Macedonian officers all hanging on his every word. 'I wasn't ready.' He turned back to Perdikkas. 'But now I am.'

'Ready to do what?'

'Get us into the city, of course, like you've just asked.'

'How will you do it?'

'Well, I'm not going to do it personally, why risk yourself when there are others who will gladly do it for you? No, no, I've got other people to open the gate.'

Perdikkas checked his rising temper. 'The gate?'

'Yes; I thought that would be the easiest way of getting into the town; it's a tried and tested method.'

'Who's going to open the gate for us?'

'You let me worry about the treachery. It's an area in which, as a non-Macedonian, I can shine; you Macedonians can get your men ready to lead them into the town, once I've got the gate open, and then you can do what you do best: massacre everyone. I think we all might shine tonight.'

A shadow flitted towards him; Perdikkas' fist closed about his sword's grip. He tensed but stopped himself from drawing the blade lest it should ring out or reflect even some of the dim light from the torches burning above Mazaca's gatehouse, just fifty paces away. Behind him, the two hundred picked men from the Silver Shields, under Antigenes' command, waited motionless in the moonless night, with all extraneous kit removed and rags tied around their sandals; Perdikkas was determined that there should be no surrendering the advantage of surprise.

The shadow neared, gradually resolving into a human shape that knelt down next to Perdikkas.

'Well, Alketas?' Perdikkas asked under his breath.

'Eumenes assured me that the gate would open; we just have to be patient.'

'Patient? I've been being patient for half the night already; how much longer does he want me to be patient for?'

'Until the gate opens, I suppose.'

Perdikkas glanced at his younger brother. *Cocky little bugger.* Hunching back down, he tried to exercise the virtue that Eumenes had requested. As he did so, he reflected upon how the little Greek had managed to make contact with whomever it was betraying the town, seeing as the gates had been firmly bolted ever since the arrival of the Macedonian army before them.

He was no nearer solving the conundrum when a brief, curtailed cry brought him out of his reverie; the torches on the gatehouse were thrown, one by one, down behind it. Another shout, hollow in the night, rose from behind the gates, before the grinding of wood against wood heralded the removal of the heavy bar on the inside.

Perdikkas turned to Antigenes. 'Ready?'

The veteran commander nodded; the movement was just visible now that most extraneous light had been extinguished.

It was at the first creak of hinges that Perdikkas drew his sword, hefted his shield and ran forward; behind him the picked men, hunched, dark shadows on a dark night, followed with minimal noise.

Another scream, and then another, rent the air as the gates ground open, making Perdikkas kick harder to cross the open area before the town. The gates, silhouetted by the light of the torches thrown down behind them, gaped; dim figures could be seen struggling beyond them.

Faster Perdikkas ran, caring not about volume now that they were in. It was at full pelt that Perdikkas led his men into Mazaca, crashing into the guards, roused from slumber by the death cries of their comrades on duty. Surprised by such a sudden appearance of the enemy, the defenders lacked armour and helms and only the few lucky ones had had time to grab a shield; down they went in the face of the Macedonian rush, quicker than they could be reinforced. Through the arch went Perdikkas and on into the market place beyond, from which three streets led, as a great shout rose from behind him; the main body of the attack was now charging after his assault group. Crashing his shield into the bearded face of a befuddled defender, Perdikkas slashed his sword at the raised spear of another guard, taking three fingers and the tip of the thumb from the man as the blade slid down the haft. He fell back with a scream and four spurts of blood as the sound of racing footsteps echoed from down the main street ahead, leading from the market place into the heart of the town.

'Form up! Form up!' Perdikkas cried as his men surged in behind him. 'Antigenes! Get them into formation!' He pointed down the street at the oncoming relief force. 'They'll cut us to pieces if we're not supporting one another.'

Shouting at his junior officers to instil discipline into their men, the veteran commander kicked and pushed his Silver Shields into line as arrows hissed through the night, thumping into silver-covered wood and clattering off stone walls.

Fifty abreast and four deep the Silver Shields stood across the market place as the Persian garrison emerged from the main street, releasing arrows as they ran. From behind came the clatter of the Macedonian column jogging through the gate and Perdikkas felt relief in knowing that his numbers now would only grow. 'Forward!' he shouted from the centre of the front rank, pointing his sword at the enemy as a brace of arrows thudded in quick succession into his shield.

The Silver Shields, each man in his sixties and a veteran of countless fights, moved as one towards the Persians as more battle cries came from the two streets to either side of the market place. Perdikkas looked left and then right as scores of shaded figures streamed from the two side streets. 'The lads behind us will deal with them,' he shouted at his men as they strode forward. 'We'll just concentrate on the bastards in front of us.'

With their spears ready for an overarm thrust, the Macedonians closed with the foe as arrows continued to slam in, bringing down a number of the old soldiers whose luck had finally run out. It was with his weight on the left leg that, as the two forces collided, Perdikkas made his first thrust, low, beneath his shield, and was rewarded with the jolt of metal cutting through flesh. Harder he forced his thrust as he twisted his wrists left and then right, releasing the suction of the wound and shredding the gut; blood slopped over his hand and onto the ground. Down came a storm of spear thrusts onto the Persian line as they, in turn, hammered their weapons against the Macedonian shield-wall; both sides shoved against each other to a chorus of cries and grunts and metallic ringing.

Lost in his own microcosm of violence, Perdikkas could do naught but heave on his shield and probe with his blade as the stench of urine, blood and faeces assaulted his nostrils and the din of battle rang in his ears and reverberated about his head. Close on either side of him, comrades in arms were immersed in their own personal struggles whose success was vital to the safety of the unit as a whole. It was with a sense of triumph that he managed to take a step forward as the pressure on his shield lapsed for an instant; he felt the line coming with him and the Persians pull back. 'We've got them, lads!' he roared as he crunched the tip of his sword into a shield, jolting it to one side; a spear thrust from behind, over his shoulder, took the exposed man in the chest.

But the euphoria welling up within him died a quick death at the sound of hooves pounding along the stone street. Looking up, he could see nothing beyond the shadowed, bearded faces of the enemy as they renewed their struggle, buoyed by the sound of cavalry behind them, coming to their aid. There came cries from the right, portending he knew not what but from their tone they seemed to be Macedonian shouts of distress rather than triumph. Cursing the gods for the fickleness of their favour, Perdikkas redoubled his efforts, shouting at his men to do the same. *If we falter now, we're dead men.* Why was it that, when he was so close, fate always seemed to slap his face? He gritted his teeth and worked his right arm, stabbing and stabbing as he battered his shield forward. The sound of the cavalry closed, their noise now rising with ease over the infantry struggle. Perdikkas braced himself for the inevitable hit to the flank of his unit and then its almost instant disintegration as powerful beasts smashed through its ranks. Grimacing, he thrust again, wondering if it might be the last blow he would strike in his life; but, as his blade was deflected by that of an enemy, a shudder went through the Persian formation and a wail, shrill in its distress, rose from their left flank. Perdikkas glanced up to see the horses wading into the foe, rearing as their bearded, betrousered riders jabbed down with javelins and swords on those beneath them and those beneath them were, like them, Persians. Through the cavalry cut, dealing out death wherever it chose as the Macedonians pulled back letting their unlikely allies do their work for them. Perdikkas watched with growing amazement the skill of the riders as they manoeuvred their mounts within a tight confine to cut down at the now fleeing infantry.

And then the man leading the charge caught Perdikkas' eye and he did a double-take as he knew him well but had never imagined to see him like this; for it was a small Greek who led the cavalry and Perdikkas knew then that he now owed his life to Eumenes.

'Kappadokians, actually, not Persians,' Eumenes informed Perdikkas as they made their way back to the Macedonian camp, leaving Alketas and Antigenes to mop up the few last bits of resistance in Mazaca and hunt for Ariarathes. 'They were the men who opened the gates for me.'

'For us,' Perdikkas corrected as the first rays of dawn glowed pink on the snow tipping the mountains to the east; his breath steamed in the early chill.

'Indeed. Anyway, they claim to be the finest cavalry unit in the satrapy and, from what I've seen, they may well have a point. And to answer the question that you're about to ask, it's because they could see that Ariarathes' days were numbered and I was the coming man in Kappadokia. They reasoned that it would be better to live serving me than to die serving Ariarathes; I have to admit that I couldn't refute their logic, so I gladly accepted their offer to betray their former master.'

Perdikkas acknowledged the salute of the captain of the guard at the camp's gates. 'And just how long do you think it will be until they offer to betray you to someone else?'

Eumenes did not need to consider the matter. 'The day after I lose my first battle, I would have thought.' He turned enquiring eyes to Perdikkas. 'Would that seem to be about right to you?'

Aries, he's aggravating; but still, I should ask his advice.

'Kleopatra, without question,' Eumenes said after Perdikkas had laid the facts out over a breakfast of dried fruits and fresh bread next to a glowing brazier in his tent. 'She brings power and legitimacy; Nicaea just brings an old man as an ally.'

'But choosing Kleopatra would make that particular old man an enemy.'

Eumenes spat out a date stone. 'So what? What's he going to do? Invade Asia and make war against the regent of the two kings who is also married to Alexander's sister? I think not, Perdikkas, he would have no legitimacy and, besides, he would be tainted with the odium of civil war. Antipatros is old enough and wise enough to realise that you have made the move for dynastic reasons and not to deliberately insult him. He will let the slight go and concentrate his efforts on securing his position in Europe and he's welcome to it – until such time as we feel it should be incorporated back into the empire, that is.'

Perdikkas contemplated Eumenes' opinion over a slow-chewed mouthful of bread.

'And another thing,' Eumenes said, 'Antipatros has already given Phila to Krateros and, if the rumours are true, has promised Eurydike to Ptolemy, which puts you in a club with three members. Kleopatra is exclusive.'

'Alketas says I should stick with Nicaea.'

'Your brother is a fool but you and he are evidently unaware of the fact, otherwise he wouldn't be giving you advice and you certainly wouldn't be asking him for it, let alone taking it. Answer me this: if you marry Nicaea who will Kleopatra marry?'

'I could marry them both; Alexander had three wives, after all.'

'You are not Alexander.'

I know but I could be and I should be as I hold his ring. 'But even so.'

Eumenes pointed a finger at Perdikkas. 'Now listen; I've been trying to help you since he died and arsing hard work it's been too, but if you take one piece of advice from me it should be this: to marry both Kleopatra and Nicaea will get Nicaea killed quicker than you can fuck her.'

'Killed? How?'

'Poison, I would think. That is Olympias' favourite weapon, I believe. She is not going to allow a daughter of Antipatros' to share power with her daughter and thereby with her. And if Nicaea dies in those circumstances then you really would have the threat of a legitimate invasion by the old man in revenge for his daughter. And, believe me, there would be more than a few who would sympathise and side with him. So forget that idea and answer the question: who will Kleopatra marry if not you?'

Perdikkas looked as blank as his mind was for suggestions.

'Lysimachus so that she can share in the joys of keeping the northern tribes at bay?' Eumenes suggested in a helpful tone. 'Peucestas in his trousers in order to learn Persian? Peithon, perhaps, for his towering intellect.'

Perdikkas shrugged. 'I don't know.'

'Well, it won't be any one of them, I can assure you of that; nor would it be me, despite the fact that I get on extremely well with the woman and her mother was once heard to say something not altogether disparaging about me. No, she won't marry anyone; she'll just sit in Sardis as a prize for whoever dares to make a bid for empire. Kassandros, for example.'

'She wouldn't marry a son of Antipatros!'

Eumenes contemplated an apricot before popping it into his mouth. 'Really? I'd say that would be the neatest solution to the whole problem; not that you would be around to witness it as you would be very dead.'

The aggravating little bastard's right again. I ought to marry Kleopatra, but I dare not repudiate Nicaea; there must be a way of doing this that no one has yet seen.

A tall, dust-covered figure in a stained travel coat, pushing past the guard at the entrance of the tent, drew a halt to Perdikkas' thought-process. 'Seleukos.'

'Here's another possibility for Kleopatra,' Eumenes said, not entirely to himself.

'It's done,' Seleukos announced, pulling off his cloak and throwing it over the back of a chair. 'Over twenty thousand mercenaries killed. Murdered, in fact; it was as I – I mean we – suspected: Peithon made a deal with them and was going to take them into his army.'

Eumenes raised his brow. 'Peithon showing initiative? Well, well, well.'

Perdikkas ignored the comment. 'What did you do with him?'

Seleukos poured himself a drink and sat down. 'Nothing. I told him to give the bodies a decent funeral and not to be a naughty boy again. He's to stay in his satrapy until you summon him. I sent his troops to replace the garrisons out in the east until we can recruit more mercenaries to take up the posts; and brought those that you had lent him with me.'

Perdikkas sighed and shook his head. 'Is there no one I can trust?'

'You can trust me,' Seleukos replied and then looked at Eumenes. 'You might even be able to trust this sly little Greek, although I wouldn't. But I'll tell you one person in whom you've misplaced your trust and that is Neoptolemus; he's completely fucked things up in Armenia. I came through the satrapy, following the Royal Road back from Media.'

'I won't say I told you so,' Eumenes muttered.

Perdikkas scowled at the Greek and then turned back to Seleukos. 'What's he done?'

Seleukos tore off a hunk of bread. 'He's pissed off his lads by not paying them and they're refusing to fight for him; he, in turn, is now refusing to pay them until they fight for him. Don't ask me why, I don't know; all I know is that there is a Macedonian army in Armenia sitting around doing nothing whilst local petty potentates strut around without a care in the world. I had to bribe my way through the country.'

Perdikkas slammed his fist down onto the table, spilling all three cups. 'Then you had better get back there and sort it out, hadn't you?'

'Bollocks.'

'Bollocks? Are you refusing an order?'

'I have just arrived after being out in the east for months and I'm not about to go to Armenia to sort out someone else's mess.'

'I'll go,' Eumenes put in quickly.

Perdikkas and Seleukos looked at the Greek in surprise. 'You?' they said in tandem.

'Yes, me. Me and my Kappadokian cavalry. It'll give us a chance to get to know one another.'

Seleukos waved a dismissive hand. 'Better you than me.'

'Yes, I think so too,' Eumenes agreed, looking to Perdikkas.

Well, it gives me a way out of a nasty situation; I suppose I should be grateful to the aggravating little man. 'Very well, then, Eumenes,' Perdikkas said as the guard came through the entrance of the tent. 'Take them east whilst I deal with Pisidia.' He looked at the guard. 'What is it?'

'They're bringing Ariarathes in, sir.'

'Ah, some good news at last; summon the kings.'

'Can I really have him killed?' King Philip asked, excitement in his voice and drool on his chin.

'Keep your voice down, your majesty,' Perdikkas said out of the corner of his mouth as the tall, imposing figure of Ariarathes was brought before the assembled army. 'If he does as you ask then you must show mercy.'

'Mercy?' The term evidently did not mean much to the king.

'Slit his belly open and laugh at his suffering,' Roxanna hissed, holding her infant son.

Perdikkas ignored her as he had ignored the fact that she had come despite his command that only the infant and his nurse should be present. 'Ariarathes,' Perdikkas declaimed as the rebel stood before him next to a sharpened stake implanted in the ground. 'The army of King Philip and King Alexander has defeated you in the field; however, the kings are merciful.' He gestured to Philip. 'Your majesty?'

Philip shook with eagerness as he recalled his line. 'Kneel!' he shouted, far too loud for regal dignity.

Ariarathes spat on the floor and then laughed, deep and hollow. He looked at Perdikkas. 'What's that? Is that what you Macedonians now call a king? That and that babe in arms?' He spat again. 'I'll not kneel to that.'

'Slit his belly open!' Roxanna shrieked.

'Quiet, woman!' Perdikkas said without turning to her. 'You will kneel or die, Ariarathes.'

'I know, Perdikkas. That is why I chose not to kill myself. I wanted to show you the contempt in which I hold your drooling idiot and your suckling babe. Alexander's heirs? Pah!' He looked at the stake. 'I chose the most painful of deaths.'

The bastard is making me look stupid even as he dies but I can't go back now. Why is it never straightforward? 'Very well.' He nodded to the guards. 'Impale him.'

Ariarathes did not struggle as his robes were ripped off and made not a sound as he was lifted into the air and the point of the stake was placed in his anus so that his toes could not quite touch the ground. The guards let go of him; he did not try to support his own weight as the point slipped into him and his toes tipped the ground, but, rather, spitting once more towards the royal party, he pushed himself down onto the stake sending it searing up through his entrails to burst his heart. He was dead by the time it exploded out of his left shoulder.

'Well, that went well,' Eumenes commented to Perdikkas as they walked away from the impaled body. 'He came over as a hero, refusing to be ruled by an idiot and a baby. Very clever. Let's hope you have better luck in Pisidia.'

'Shut your aggravating mouth and get yourself to Armenia,' Perdikkas snapped, in no mood for Eumenes. 'Antigenes, give the order to break camp.'

'Yes, sir.'

'And send a messenger to Menander in Lydia and Antigonos in Phrygia, telling them to meet me in Pisidia in a month's time with three thousand men each.'

Eumenes stared in horror at Perdikkas. 'Antigonos? You are not serious, are you?'

Perdikkas frowned. 'Why not? I'm giving him the chance to make up for disobeying my order to support you in Kappadokia and show his loyalty to the kings.'

'You're also giving him the chance to give you the same answer as he did last time; what will you do then?'

What will I do then? Well, then we will be one more step closer to war.

ANTIPATROS,
THE REGENT

'YOU WALKED AWAY last time because you couldn't stomach the idea of unconditional surrender.' Antipatros looked between Phocion and Demades, completely ignoring the third member of the Athenian delegation, the ageing philosopher and one-time friend of the recently deceased Aristotle, Xenocrates. 'For the sake of our long acquaintance and mutual respect, Phocion, I did you the kindness of not bringing my army into Attica so that your people would not have the burden of feeding it. But remember, I can reverse that decision any time.'

The three Athenians sat in a row on a low bench opposite Antipatros and Krateros in their comfortable chairs; around them the overgrown ruins of the Theban agora, weed-strewn and choked by creepers and home to two rival packs of wild dogs, served as a reminder of Macedonian ruthlessness to a defeated enemy.

Phocion, of an age with Antipatros, wrinkled under a full white beard but with the bright eyes of a younger man looked at Demades, twenty years his junior, portly, clean-shaven and with the oiled hair and bejewelled fingers of an ageing dandy; the two men shared a moment and then, reaching a silent agreement, turned back to Antipatros.

'It was a kindness, Antipatros,' Phocion said, 'and one that we hope you do not reverse.'

Xenocrates cleared his throat and stood to make a speech. 'I demand that—'

'Sit down!' Antipatros snapped. 'I'm talking to Phocion.'

'But I demand that—'

Antipatros raised his voice. 'When I was trapped in Lamia, Phocion, your general, Leosthenes, would not listen when I offered him terms; in fact, he said that it's the victor who sets the terms and I had to admit, grudgingly, that he was right. So, now you've been back to Athens, to report on our first meeting, and they have sent you to me again, I assume that you are willing to hear my terms; the terms of the victor.'

Xenocrates went puce with indignation. 'Barbarian! I demand that—'

'Enough!' Ignoring the insult, Antipatros pressed on, keeping his focus on Phocion. 'Firstly, that Athens should reduce the number of people allowed to partake in its democracy; from now on only men with property worth over two thousand drachmas will be allowed to vote.'

Phocion stiffened. 'But that–'

'Will make the city an oligarchy, I know; oligarchies are easier to control. People with less property have less to lose and are, therefore, more likely to vote for rash and destructive policies. The wealthy have more interest in keeping the peace.'

'But I demand that—'

'A Macedonian garrison of five hundred men will be installed at the Munychia fortress in Piraeus and, finally, Athens will pay all the costs that Macedon has incurred during the course of the war plus a fine of fifty per cent of those costs. Those are my terms.'

Phocion and Demades again shared a look as Xenocrates started making his list of demands, ignored by all.

'The garrison,' Phocion said, talking over Xenocrates. 'Is that an absolute necessity? Macedon has always spared Athens that humiliation in the past.'

'Phocion, I am willing to grant you anything, except what will destroy us both. If Athens is left unguarded and revolts again then you will be as much their enemy as I, for it is you who is negotiating with me and not Hyperides or Demosthenes.'

'Sadly, I believe you have a point, old friend.'

'And as for Hyperides and Demosthenes, I will send the Exile-Hunter after them; he and his Thracian friends enjoy that kind of sport and I can think of no reason to deny them it. How many lives have been lost because of their demagoguery?'

'Too many and I won't plead for mercy on their part but I will plead for one favour.' He turned and looked up at Xenocrates, who was still declaiming. 'Would you please be quiet; we're trying to talk.'

Xenocrates stopped and looked down at Phocion. 'But I demand that—'

'You can demand as much as you like,' Antipatros said, 'but no one will listen.'

Xenocrates looked down his nose at Antipatros. 'You are treating Athens too generously for slaves and too cruelly for free men. That Athens, the centre of civilization, should be treated thus by barely literate barbarians from the hills is intolerable.'

Antipatros rolled his eyes, weary of Athenian snobbery. 'Your opinion is your own to have and yours to keep; please don't bother me with it again. Now, Phocion, what was that one favour?'

'That Athens may keep Samos.'

Antipatros shook his head. 'Alexander's Exile Decree stands and you will remove your colonists from the island so that the original inhabitants and their descendants can return.' He got to his feet to indicate that the meeting was now over. 'But I will provide lands in Thrace for all those who have nowhere else to go and those in Athens who will lose their franchise and do not wish to stay in a city in which they have no stake; I think that is more than fair.'

'It's far more than fair,' Krateros said as he and Antipatros walked through what had once been a city gate, beyond which a rough-looking group of men were waiting. 'I would have installed a Macedonian tyrant and completely got rid of the vote.'

'But you have been in Asia for more than a decade, Krateros, and have forgotten that things work differently here in Europe. I need Athens to have a semblance of freedom to give the other cities hope; if we treat them all like slaves then they will have nothing to lose and, frankly, I'm too tired to have to keep on dealing with rebellion; I just want to go home to my wife.'

'You sent for me, Antipatros,' the leader of the waiting group said; he possessed a round, almost boyish face with humorous eyes and topped by luxuriant black curls.

'Yes, Archias; I have three jobs for you and your...er...associates.' Antipatros surveyed the half-dozen men, red-bearded and dressed in fox-fur hats, high boots and foul-smelling tunics and cloaks; each carried on his back the long-handled curved blade favoured by the Thracians, the rhomphaia, feared by all who had had the misfortune to stand against it.

'I am yours to command.' Archias smiled, revealing surprisingly white teeth; but then he had once been a tragic actor and knew the value of keeping up his appearance, Antipatros reflected.

'Hyperides and Demosthenes are to be killed; I'll give you one talent in gold when you come back to Macedon with the news.'

'Where will I find them?'

'No doubt they would have gone into exile and, as you are an exile hunter, I leave that to you. You can sail to Athens with the garrison that I'm sending there and then I'll have one of the ships put at your disposal to seek them out.'

Archias inclined his head. 'I will bring you their tongues seeing as they have caused you the most trouble. And the third job?'

'I have brief business in Corinth and then will head back to Macedon. When you get back to Pella I want you to accompany my son Iollas who will be escorting my daughter Nicaea to Asia to marry Perdikkas.'

The Exile-Hunter frowned and looked at Antipatros questioningly. 'Perdikkas? Why would you want to marry a daughter to him, a mere regent like yourself, when there is a king to marry, if you don't mind me asking that is?'

Antipatros was, for a moment, rendered speechless by the impertinence of the question. 'I don't think that it is any of your business, Archias.'

'Fair enough, sir; I only wish to point out that there remains an unmarried king and, as Sophocles so wisely pointed out in Phaedra: Fortune is not on the side of the faint-hearted. I would have thought you aim too low and...' He discarded the thought with a flick of his hand. 'But have it your way. I'll be back in Pella in ten days.'

'He has a point, you know,' Krateros said as they watched the Exile-Hunter and his men walk away. 'Perdikkas is Philip's regent; his son can never be a king, just like yours or mine. Why not marry her to Philip? She might well produce an Argead heir that could reunite the whole empire eventually.'

'The man's a fool and I'll not have him drooling over my daughter.'

'Well, he's going to drool over someone one day, and that someone will be in a very good position to advance her family.'

'Perdikkas is the better choice. With you, he and Ptolemy all married to siblings we have a chance of avoiding war. Only a fool would marry a fool.'

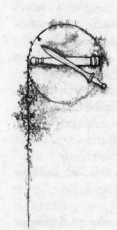

ADEA, THE WARRIOR

THE BLADES RANG metallic as they parried; with a fleet movement Adea thrust the knife in her left hand down to block that of her foe as they struggled with swords in their right hands, now locked together, hilt to hilt. A jump to her left with a kick into the belly of her opponent, a man twice her age but no bigger than her, took Adea free of the impasse, her sword flashing through the air to parry another attempted stab from the knife which had darted around her the entire encounter. Sweat dripped into her eyes but, resisting the temptation to wipe it, she pressed an attack with repeated cuts of her weapon, forcing her opponent back and back, towards where her mother, Cynnane, sat watching her fight with rapt interest.

Another quick jump, this time to the right, brought Adea to a three-quarter profile to her sparring partner; he flicked another lightning jab of his dagger that she caught on her sword forcing his left arm out wide, pushing with all her considerable strength as she ducked beneath a swipe of a sword and thrust the blunted tip of her knife onto her sparring partner's chest, above his heart. 'My kill, Barzid!'

'Indeed, mistress,' Barzid said, breathless from the frenetic exercise. 'And a good one, worthy of a princess. That is the tenth time in a row you've bested me; I have nothing more to teach you.'

Adea looked over to her mother, who smiled approvingly.

'Barzid is right,' Cynnane said, rising to her feet and walking towards her daughter. Tall and broad-shouldered with a heavy brow and a prominent, bulbous nose, Cynnane could not be called beautiful in a classical way. However there was something about the power in her almost masculine body that men found attractive; since Alexander had murdered her husband, Amyntas – his cousin and therefore a direct threat – upon his succession, she had not been lacking of suitors. However she had different tastes and rejected all of them in order to focus on bringing up her daughter in the Illyrian way: to be a warrior.

And Adea, at the age of fifteen, was certainly that. A thumb's-breadth taller than her mother and as tall as most men if not quite so broad, Adea was a killer and it was time for her to go to war.

Cynnane held Adea's face in her hands, tilted it down and kissed her forehead. 'Are you still willing to do as we planned?'

Adea looked her mother in the eyes; she nodded slowly. 'I will, Mother. Although I still feel that it would be better for you to do it. You can still bear children and the king is only your half-brother. You are, after all, Alexander's eldest sibling and that would make it far more likely that you are listened to, even if you are a woman.'

Cynnane smiled and kissed her daughter again. 'We've been through all this before: I am the product of a Macedonian king and an Illyrian princess; you are the product of a Macedonian princess – me – and a Macedonian nobleman, the cousin to Alexander, who had as much right to the throne as he did, which was why he was killed. You, my sweet girl, are far more qualified to be the wife of the half-wit king. Had you been a boy it would have been you they would have placed on the throne, not a babe and an idiot.'

Adea took a deep breath and steeled herself against the coming ordeal. *How will I find the strength to go through with this when I know that everything about Philip will disgust me?*

Cynnane could read her daughter's thoughts. 'You'll only have to let him do it once or twice, Adea. Barzid has covered you, so you know how it is; it won't come as a surprise to you.'

'It's not that, Mother. Barzid was kind enough to show me what men do to women, that doesn't bother or interest me; like you, I prefer my own kind, as you know. What I fear is that just the sight of him will revolt me: I remember seeing him as a child, seeing his weakness, his slobber, his piss-stained tunic; I fear I'll vomit as he covers me.'

'I'll make sure that I'm in the next room, sweet girl, and I'll have a tasty morsel waiting for your pleasure once he has finished. Don't worry yourself, Adea, I'll always be there for you.'

And Adea knew that to be the truth, for her mother had never left her side in the fifteen years of her life. They had been inseparable, eating, training and sleeping together, even when Cynnane had a lover in her bed and then, recently, when Adea had followed her mother's lead and taken a slave-girl to dominate. Their life together had focused upon Cynnane passing on everything she knew to her daughter to forge her into a warrior princess in the traditional Illyrian fashion; here in the fastness of their mountainous country, safe from the poison potions of Olympias, Adea had become all that her mother had hoped she would and now, together, they planned for power.

It had been Adea's idea at the beginning, a year after Alexander's death; Cynnane had been railing at Olympias' scheme to regain power by marrying her daughter, Kleopatra, to Leonnatus and it had occurred to Adea that, for once, Olympias' scheming was not as ambitious as it could be: why aim for a companion of Alexander's when his half-brother and heir was unmarried? She had never thought that it would be her who would be the one to marry Philip when she had suggested it to her mother; she had barely even become a woman at the time and had absolutely no interest in men whatsoever. But she had submitted to her mother's will and agreed to take the place that she had suggested Cynnane occupy. But it was with great reluctance for she feared to enter the world of men; indeed, Barzid was one of the few that she had come into contact with and, after, at her own request, he had shown her what it was like to be covered, she would have rather that it remained that way.

It was with a heavy heart that Adea finally resigned herself to the actuality of what they were about to embark on. She took her mother's hands in both of hers. 'When do we leave, Mother?'

'As soon as Barzid has assembled an escort worthy of a queen; he is summoning one hundred of the bravest warriors of the southern Illyrian tribes all mounted and with a spare horse each. We will need to travel fast and far for there will be many who would try to stop us. For that reason we'll need to avoid Macedon and take the northerly route and come down to the Hellespont through Thrace and we need to be there before autumn if by the end of the year you are to be Macedon's next queen.'

ANTIPATROS,
THE REGENT

'FINALLY, SOME PEACE,' Antipatros said as he rolled off his wife, his heart pounding with the recent exertion and his skin sleek with sweat. 'With the Greek rebellion in the west dealt with, I can clear my head of the cares of defending the kingdom for an hour or two.' He lay on his back with one arm behind his head and one around his wife and looked at the ceiling, trying to think no thoughts.

'Has it been that bad?' Hyperia asked, laying her cheek on his shoulder and running a finger over his chest.

'At my age I should be taking my ease and not fighting wars and imposing punitive peace terms.'

'Then why not relinquish the regency?'

'And who would take over?'

'Krateros?'

'I've thought about it but not yet, he's been away from Europe for so long that he's forgotten the politics. Perhaps in a couple of years' time he'll be ready; I'll just have to carry on until then.'

'What about Kassandros, then?'

'Kassandros! If you think that then you don't know your step-son's character, woman: he's venal and power-hungry, possibly the worst combination. And added to that is his sense of inadequacy due to Alexander leaving him behind – something that I think he was right to do – which would make him the most unjust ruler and put everything that I have worked to achieve over the past dozen years in jeopardy.'

'Why do you say that against your own son?'

Antipatros considered the question, closing his eyes and stroking Hyperia's shoulder. 'The truth is that I have never liked him; he was a deceitful child and more arrogant than he had cause to be. And I believe him to be a coward; why, he hasn't even killed a wild boar on a hunt and so therefore still has to sit up at table rather than recline and yet he seems to feel no shame. All in all, I'm pleased that Perdikkas has kept him in Babylon with a prestigious command, enough to satisfy his vanity and to keep him out of my way. No, my dear, I can't give up the regency just yet, not until I've found someone strong enough to keep Kassandros from stealing it.'

'Then you'll die as the regent because there's not a stronger man than you in all Macedon.'

Antipatros smiled, feeling a great affection for his wife now that the urgent need to bed her had been satisfied; indeed, he had made his way directly to her chamber upon his arrival back at Pella, not one hour previously, despite the fact that Archias the Exile-Hunter had returned from his errand in the south and was waiting to see him. He turned and kissed her as he braced himself for asking the question which they both knew would come. 'Are you ready to say goodbye to Nicaea and Eurydike, Hyperia; the time has come for them to leave for their husbands and it'll be many years before you will see them again, if ever.'

'It's not so much me that I'm concerned about, it's you. You are probably never to see them again; I, at least, have the advantage over you in youth.'

She's right; but still I must go through with it if we are to have peace. 'We'll have the consolation of keeping Phila here. And Nicaea we may well see again; but Eurydike in Egypt? Well, I doubt that very much.'

'So do I and that is why I've made an arrangement without your knowledge.'

Antipatros looked at his wife, curious.

'I know that Eurydike is going to be completely isolated from her family so I've arranged that her cousin, Berenice, goes with her to Egypt as a companion.'

Antipatros squeezed Hyperia's shoulder in approval. 'That is a fine idea; Berenice is happy to go?'

'Yes; now that her late husband, Philip, has left her widowed with three small children, it appeals to her sense of adventure. Her mother, Antigone, and I both agree that it is for the best.'

'And what has Magas got to say about it?'

'Berenice has always respected her father, but now that the man Magas had chosen for her is dead, she feels that her life is her own to lead.'

'She has always been a headstrong girl, just like Antigone.'

'She knows what she wants and she thinks that she won't find it here; to tell you the truth, it was Berenice who suggested it and who was I to say no when it meant support for Eurydike?'

'And with Iollas accompanying Nicaea, both the girls should feel less cut off from the family.'

'But I will miss you so much, Father,' Nicaea said, putting her arms around Antipatros' neck and kissing his cheek.

'As shall I, Father,' Eurydike said with a tear in her eye, kissing his other cheek as Iollas looked on.

He hugged them each in return, his gaze falling through his study window onto the fleet that would bear his daughters away, preparing for sea down in the harbour to the south of the city. 'And I you; but we all must do our duty despite personal feelings. Your marriage to Perdikkas, Nicaea, and yours to Ptolemy, Eurydike, will go a long way to ensuring peace in our lives and even further into the future if you both produce strong sons. These are fragile times, my girls, and family alliances such as I'm making will save much suffering. Now ready yourselves for the morning for then we really do say goodbye for what may well prove to be a very long time.' He stroked their cheeks and smiled with saddened eyes and then indicated that they should leave him.

Turning as Nicaea and Eurydike left his study, Antipatros picked up a scroll from his desk and handed it to Iollas. 'When you get to Babylon, give this to Kassandros.'

'What does it say?'

'No doubt you will read it anyway, so I may as well tell you.

I want him to stay in Babylon and watch out for his half-sister, I wouldn't want an *accident* to happen to her. Perdikkas may be marrying her but I would be a fool to trust him completely, especially after she's borne him an heir.'

Iollas looked at his father in shock. 'You don't think that Perdikkas would...'

'I would just feel better if Kassandros would stay in Babylon and, er, make his presence felt, shall we say.' *And keep well out of my way here in the north.* 'It will keep Perdikkas' mind focused on his ties with our family. Now go and prepare for the journey and send Archias in as you leave.'

Archias placed the two small boxes on the desk and grinned. 'A man's life blood is dark and mortal; once it wets the earth what song can bring it back?'

'What?'

'Agamemnon, by Aeschylus.'

'Indeed.' Antipatros winced at the cloying smell of decay emanating from the boxes; he did not wish to open them but knew that it was expected of him by the Exile-Hunter; if he paid the man to kill for him then he could at least bear witness to the proof of those kills.

'That is Hyperides', Archias said as Antipatros opened the first box to reveal a severed human tongue, part-shrivelled in the heat. 'His was the shorter of the two. He tried to seek sanctuary in the shrine of Aeacus on Aegina.' Archias gave a grim laugh. 'As if some long-dead demi-god could prevent justice being meted out. I left his body exposed for the birds.'

Antipatros nodded and opened the second box; he gasped. The tongue was swollen and almost purple in colouring.

'Poison,' Archias informed him. 'The old rabble-rouser managed to take matters into his own hands. He had taken sanctuary in Poseidon's shrine on Calauria; neither I nor my men were keen on breaking that boundary, what with so much sea to cross in the coming months.'

'Yes, quite,' Antipatros said, concentrating far more on the body part that had been the cause of so much violence. *Two wars that tongue started and never once did it apologise for either of them.*

'So, realising that we had the place surrounded and he could choose between starvation, a rhomphaia or poison, he took the latter.'

Antipatros closed the lid. 'You and your men have done well, Archias.'

'My money?'

Antipatros scooped up a heavy purse from the desk and threw it to the Exile-Hunter. 'That's for the tongues. I'll pay you half the money for escorting Nicaea and Iollas to Babylon now and then Kassandros will pay you the other half when you get there.'

'Kassandros? I know of no one with any reason to trust him.'

Antipatros sympathised with the opinion. 'He will pay. I've written to order him to; it's in the letter that Iollas carries. Come back to me when you're done; I'll have plenty of work for you in the coming months.'

'Then we had better get going.'

'The fleet will sail at dawn tomorrow.'

'What do you mean: the Asian fleet will stay in the east?' Krateros exclaimed, astounded, as he and Antipatros arrived at the harbour the following morning.

'Exactly that, Krateros: the Macedonian fleet will stay here in the north along with those vessels captured from the Athenians, and the fleet that you commandeered in Asia will return there with Kleitos the White. Half will stay in Tarsus and the other half will go onto Alexandria.'

'But it's my fleet.'

'No it isn't; it's Alexander's seeing as he commissioned you to assemble it; now he is dead, it belongs to the empire. And even if it were yours, you've put it and your army under my authority.'

'But that's…that's…'

'Politics, Krateros, politics. If I keep the entire fleet here then it will make me look the aggressor.' Antipatros turned to Krateros and took him by the shoulders. 'We must avoid descending into war. I must avoid it – at all costs. And the best way to do that is to give Perdikkas and Ptolemy half the Asian fleet each as a dowry for Nicaea and Eurydike; then we'll all have the same.'

'But Kleitos is my man.'

Antipatros smiled and patted Krateros on the shoulders. 'So he is; now he's going to stay in Tarsus and serve Perdikkas but it wouldn't surprise me if he always remained your man.'

Understanding dawned on Krateros. 'You sly old fox; Kleitos will come over to us should Perdikkas try to use the fleet against us.'

'Or go the other way and attack Ptolemy.'

'Thus ensuring Ptolemy's gratitude and loyalty.' Krateros grinned and shook his head in wonder. 'You're giving Perdikkas nothing, aren't you?'

'Not true, my friend; I'm giving him – and Ptolemy – very generous dowries for my daughters.'

Antipatros could not restrain the tears as he, Hyperia, Phila and Krateros stood on the quay of Pella's harbour and watched the trireme cast off, taking his daughters to an uncertain future. Nicaea, Eurydike and Berenice would travel together as far as Tarsus where Nicaea was to disembark with Iollas and their escort to travel overland to Babylon in the cooler winter weather. Eurydike with her companions, Berenice and her three children, would then complete the voyage to the new city of Alexandria and the realm to Ptolemy.

Will this spending of my daughters be enough? Will history thank me for it or will I be seen as a romantic fool who thought that family ties could prevent the breakup of the greatest empire ever seen?

Phila wept as copiously as her mother, each hanging onto the other in a way that seemed to make it impossible for them both to remain upright.

Berenice's farewells with her mother and father, Magas and Antigone, had been equally as tearful, although the three children, Magas, Antigone and Theoxena were too young to understand the full implications of the journey; Theoxena, indeed, was still a babe in arms.

A few of the citizens had turned out to wish the women farewell but not as many as the significance of the occasion warranted; not many of the ordinary folk of Pella could grasp the high-stakes politics that this move represented and the likely consequences should it prove to be insufficient.

It was with a silent prayer to Zeus to hold his hands over an uncertain world that Antipatros tore his gaze from the receding ship; but it was half-hearted as he had lived long enough to know that it was chaos that ruled, not the deities. On sighting Polyperchon walking at speed towards him with disaster written on his face, Antipatros halted his petition to father Zeus mid-prayer – the deity had evidently not even begun to listen. 'Well?'

'I've just had reports from two separate sources in the north.' Polyperchon swallowed as he considered how to frame the news. 'The witch, Cynnane, and her daughter have left Illyria keeping to the north of us, heading for Thrace and thence into Asia.'

Antipatros' eyes widened. 'Where're they going? Whom do they plan to marry?' He glanced back at the ship now disappearing into the channel that connected the harbour with the open sea. 'Not Perdikkas or Ptolemy, surely?'

Polyperchon shook his head. 'In a way, would that it were one of those two or both of them even but this is far worse. Cynnane plans to marry her daughter to the fool, Philip.'

Antipatros put his hand to his forehead. *A child from that union – if it were possible, and it may be – would cause years of uncertainty and Adea, married to Philip, would be able to speak with his voice. That cannot happen.* 'Send a message to Lysimachus and have him apprehend them as they cross his territory. How many in their escort?'

'A hundred or so, all cavalry.'

'Tell him two hundred will be sufficient; but make sure that they know not to kill them; just turn them back. Killing Alexander's eldest sibling and her royal daughter would be the height of folly.'

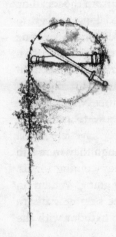

ADEA, THE WARRIOR

THEY HAD FOLLOWED the course of the River Strymon for two days now, staying on the flood-plain on its western bank as the six-paces-wide stream bent to the south towards the sea. During the twelve days they had been travelling from Illyria, through the lands of the Agrianes, to the north of Macedon, and then bypassing Philippopolis and skirting to the south of the Haemus Mountains and on into Thrace itself, they had seen very few people; Adea was starting to hope they would escape Europe unnoticed.

Cynnane and Barzid had driven the mounted column on at the fastest pace possible over the varying terrain, every man swapping between his two horses four or five times a day to get the most out of each beast. They had made broad detours around any habitation larger than a collection of hovels and those people they had come across, hunters in the main, had been more frightened of them than curious, disappearing as fast as they could. They were almost, now, at the end of the first stage of their journey.

'What do we do when we reach the sea, Mother?' Adea asked, rubbing her saddle-sore rump as she changed horses for the second time that day.

'I've brought money; a lot of money. Barzid has it distributed about the men to carry. It, along with the price of the horses, will be enough to get us a ship.'

'Where to?'

Cynnane did not answer her daughter's question, but, rather, shielded her eyes against the late morning sun and gazed south. 'Barzid! Tell me what you see.'

Adea swung herself up onto her second horse as Barzid strained his eyes and looked south. There were figures, unmistakably, figures on horseback, but how many she could not reckon.

'Cavalry, mistress,' Barzid announced. 'More than we have; I would say twice our number. They are on the opposite side of the river and coming this way.'

Adea could now see them distinctly although they were still just dark shadows at this distance. 'Are they coming for us, Mother?'

Cynnane shrugged. 'That I couldn't say but we have to assume they are. Antipatros would have heard by now of our flight and, of all people, he would want to stop us.'

A glint off one of the heads of the lead riders confirmed what they all thought. 'He's wearing a helmet,' Barzid muttered. 'They've come dressed for battle.'

Cynnane reached down and unhooked her helm from the saddle. 'Then we had better do the same; running is not an option.'

'We have not come to fight you,' the leader of the opposing cavalry shouted as they drew near. He had led his men across the river and was now on the western bank a little more than two hundred paces away. 'We bring you a message from Antipatros, Regent of Macedon, and Lysimachus, in whose satrapy you now find yourselves; and it is this, Cynnane: turn back and go home to Illyria and no harm will come to you. Carry on and you and your daughter will be seized, all the men escorting you will be killed and you will both be taken as prisoners to Pella, treated according to your rank but never to be released. Those are your choices.'

'He's forgotten one,' Cynnane mused.

'Ride through them and kill as many as we can,' Barzid suggested.

'Preferably all of them.'

Adea looked at her mother, surprised by her confidence. 'But there are twice as many of them than us.'

'Then we all have to kill two each; make it three to allow for our casualties.' She looked about her and her face brightened. 'In fact, our spare horses can do their share.' She turned in her saddle to address her followers. 'These men before us wish to stop us from reaching the coast. They are telling us to go back, back to Illyria! Do Illyrians ever slink home just because a Macedonian tells them to?'

The rumble of disapproval from her men made it clear that they did not.

'They say that if we do not do as they wish they will kill all of you and take me and my daughter prisoner. Will you let that happen?'

The answer was an unequivocal negative.

'Then this day we fight?'

This time it was positive.

Drawing three short javelins from the holster on her mount's rump, she thrust them in the air and pointed at the enemy with her other hand. 'These are for those men! Make every one count and they will all be lying dead before the sun reaches its peak!'

Another cheer rent the air.

'Ride with your spare mounts next to you and watch my arm; when I lower it, let the spares go and slow your own so that the spares run on ahead. Are you set, men of Illyria?'

Pulling javelins from the holsters as they controlled their skittish horses, the Illyrians shouted their readiness to their queen as her steed reared, its forelegs scratching the air. With a tug on the beast's reins, Cynnane brought it under control enough to kick it forward, accelerating it into a canter as excitement pulsed through her followers; with whoops and cheers they urged their mounts onwards, the spares running at their sides, towards the Lysimachid foe twice their strength as they, too, broke into a charge.

Adea flushed with excitement, squinting against the rushing wind, as the pace accelerated into a gallop; she leant forward over her horse's neck and gripped hard with her thighs, hanging onto the reins with her left hand and with her spare mount's lead and javelins fisted in the other as the distance between the two sides rapidly closed.

With a hundred paces between them, the opposing sides were at full tilt, pounding the ground so that it trembled with their passing, their hoof-beats rumbling in the air: massed drums beaten at random.

And it was as a frenzy rose within her that Adea saw her mother lower her arm; she let go her spare mount and thwacked it across the rump with the flat of her javelins, propelling it forward as she tugged a fraction on the reins to slow her horse back to a canter. On they surged, the riderless animals, eyes white and ears down, each immersed in the momentum of the herd, as over their heads hissed the first Illyrian javelin volley to scythe into the Lysimachid cavalry. But the volley received no reply as the foe, terrified of the oncoming wall of uncontrolled horseflesh, hurled their missiles directly at it, sending a score crashing to the ground and bringing others down in a chaos of screeching beasts.

With a massed exhalation, the Illyrians flung the second wave of javelins; it rained down on the enemy, punching men back and downing their mounts an instant before they ploughed into the terrified, unguided equine mass. Up they reared as they shied at the last, lashing out with cracking forelegs or bucking like a thing possessed, snapping limbs and knocking men cold. Into this carnage Adea and Cynnane and their men charged, hurling their final javelin at anything that still stood as they whipped swords from sheaths and kicked their reluctant steeds on. Wading into the Lysimachid disorder, Adea slashed down at a half-horsed rider, opening his shoulder and sending him slithering earthward; screams of man and beast raged about her and fire burned behind her eyes as again and again she jabbed and hacked, now almost motionless as the momentum of the charge was nullified by heavy congestion. But on they pressed, their advantage now supreme as the Lysimachid cavalry struggled to escape the entanglement thwarting its flight.

Again she killed and again Adea screamed to the heavens with the joy of it, for no fear did she feel in the heat of the fight, just the thrill of release of all lessons learned in long years of schooling.

As abrupt as it started, so did it end; the killing work had been done and slowly did men return from the dark place within that revels in the close company of death. Adea came with them, slowly at first but soon she could focus further than the confined space in which she had struggled and it was a shock to the eye to behold: all about lay dead and dying men and horses and over them was swathed a uneven coating of muddied gore and from them rose a dissonance of pain. And through all this, her mother and Barzid roved, searching; but for what Adea knew not.

'He's here!' Barzid shouted. Cynnane raised her head and kicked her blood-spattered mount towards him; curious, Adea followed.

It was the commander of the Lysimachid cavalry prostrate on the ground, both his legs at an impossible angle and his belly disgorging viscera. Barzid jumped down to him and lifted the man's head; his eyes flickered open but failed to focus.

Cynnane looked at the dying man. 'Can you hear me?'

His eyes searched for the voice and they came to rest on Cynnane.

'Perdikkas? What news of Perdikkas?'

His mouth moved but no sound came forth.

'Perdikkas?' Barzid urged in his ear. 'Perdikkas? Where is he?'

'P...P...Pisidia,' was the weak reply.

'Pisidia.' Cynnane mused as she skewered the dying man's throat with her bloodied blade – an act of mercy. She turned to Adea. 'Your husband-to-be is with Perdikkas in Pisidia. Come, Barzid, get the men ready, we need to ride to the coast and find a ship that will take us to Tarsus.'

PERDIKKAS,
THE HALF-CHOSEN

MUD-BRICK WALLS WERE no
match for the stone-throwers
arrayed against Perge, the final
town in Pisidia to hold out against
Macedonian rule. Shot fizzed in arcs into
its defences, crumbling them away into
rubble and dust.

Perdikkas breathed deep of the autumnal air, savouring
life as he prepared to deal out the same justice he had dealt
Termessos, the only other town that had refused to surrender
after his lightning strike west into the rebel heartland as
Menander brought his men south from Sardis: death to all
males over twelve and enslavement of the rest. It had been a
profitable month and a half, made even more so by Antigonos'
silent refusal to join the campaign. *This time I really can't ignore
Antigonos' insubordination; either I attack Phrygia and be the
aggressor or...*

He brought his concentration back to the present and looked
along the lines of the Silver Shields, armed for an assault with
thrusting spears, swords and shields and grinned back at a few of
the veterans who caught his eye. He turned to their commander,
standing next to him. 'The lads are going to enjoy this one,
Antigenes. Termessos whetted their appetite and this is half as
big again.'

'Yes, plenty to go round,' Antigenes agreed as they watched a
huge lump of the masonry fall away, leaving the rooftops of the
houses within exposed through the dust.

But rather than thin out as the wind blew it away, the dust seemed to thicken and swirl above the buildings until, with a sudden flash, flames burst from the rooftops.

'They're setting fire to the place,' Perdikkas observed in the neutral tone of a disinterested observer.

'Perhaps they feel that if they are going to lose their homes then they might as well ensure that no one else can have them; I suppose you can't really blame them.'

Perdikkas was forced to agree. 'Still, we should try and save as much of the town as possible; it would be good to settle some of the lads here once they've had their fill. At least three of those breaches are viable, Antigenes; take them in.'

With a salute, Antigenes re-joined his command and within a few heartbeats the horns of assault sounded; but as they died away a great, high-pitched wailing rose from Perge: the sound of many people in great pain; and as the wailing grew, so did the flames.

Perdikkas listened for a few moments and then, startled, broke into a run. *They're burning their women and children; they're cheating me out of a fortune.* 'Antigenes! Hurry, the bastards are killing themselves!'

But Antigenes had realised what was occurring and already had his men doubling to the walls; those with ladders held them aloft. From behind, the stone throwers had raised their aim so that they now strafed the top of the wall in the hope of keeping the defenders down. But men who know that, whatever happens, they will perish this day care not if their head is taken from them by a projectile, especially if it means buying time for their families to die and save them from a life in fetters; as soon as the Silver Shields were within range, the wall was lined with archers and slingers, two or three deep. And their volleys darkened the smoke-wreathed sky as a new element assaulted the senses; the tang of burning flesh. With shields raised over their heads the Silver Shields raced on, furious that their sport was being ripped from their grasp. Through the arrow and shot storm they waded, their shields thundering with impacts as, despite the massive losses received, the defenders kept their missiles coming. With hideous regularity, artillery stones cleaved through the ranks on the wall, imploding chests and exploding heads into mists of blood, but still they stayed, emboldened by the death-cries of their loved-ones who would now be for ever free.

And then the Silver Shields made the wall, for nothing would stop them such was their ire. Up the ladders they shot as rubble from the damage was rained down upon them, felling some and glancing off the shields of others as they pushed for the breaches, just eight feet or so above them, now crowded with men.

Like feral dogs the defenders fought to delay the inevitable for they knew that the town must surely fall as nothing, not even the walls of Tyros, could hold back the military might of Macedon. Rung by rung, the veteran Macedonians scaled the walls and Perdikkas ran to join them, his fury raging as the inferno within the town grew, flames and smoke soaring skyward.

As the breaches were gained so did the defenders thin out and Perdikkas was soon able to push his way into the town. Standing on the wall he beheld a sight he had never before seen and understood just why the defence had reduced from fierce and frenzied to almost nothing in the space of a very few heart-beats: satisfied that their families were now charred husks, the men were throwing themselves into the conflagration; with no hesitation they ran and leapt into the flames as a chosen few fought off attempts by the lead Macedonians to prevent such mass immolation. In they jumped, singularly, in couples holding hands or in long chains all together, whooping as they went, and once in the whoops turned to screams of blazing agony as their combusting bodies writhed in the inferno.

'That is the bravest but most stupid thing I've ever seen,' Perdikkas said as he halted next to Antigenes who stared, open-mouthed, at the horror unfolding. 'We would have given them a clean death.'

'I don't call impaling clean,' Antigenes muttered, unable to tear his eyes away as a father and his teenage son, arms around each other, ran headlong into a house; the roof flared and then collapsed in a fountain of sparks and licking flame. 'Besides, even if they knew that we would execute them relatively painlessly, I think their sense of honour would have still led them to share the fate they had forced their women and children into; I know I would've.'

Perdikkas sucked the air through his teeth, shaking his head in disbelief. 'Well, it's done now and we can think about heading back to Babylon for the winter. Call your men off, there's no point in risking their lives if the bastards are jumping into the fire all by themselves. All senior officers are to report to my tent as soon as convenient.' With another shake of the head, he turned and made his way back to the camp.

'I want you, Alketas, to go to Tarsus and wait for Nicaea,' Perdikkas said, pacing around his tent with his hands clasped behind his back.

'And what about you?' Alketas asked as he, Seleukos and Menander warmed their hands around a brazier.

'Me? I'm going back to Babylon so that I can receive her in state. I'll be travelling by the relay system; Seleukos and Antigenes will bring the army behind me using Attalus' fleet. You come as fast as you can once you have Nicaea.'

'And what are you going to do about Antigonos?' Seleukos asked, rubbing his hands together.

'I'm going to summon him before the army in Babylon to face trial.'

Seleukos laughed. 'Summon Antigonos! My arse, he'll say, and just ignore you.'

'Yes, I know; he didn't come the last two times so I have no reason to expect that he'll come the third time; but at least I'll have done everything correctly so if I do have to fight him next year then I'll have right on my side.'

The laugh froze on Seleukos' face. 'You can't let it come to that, surely?'

'I'd prefer not to but in disobeying me he disobeys Alexander's ring and therefore Alexander himself; it cannot go unpunished.'

'You'll also have everybody else who matters on your side,' Menander, the satrap of Lydia said; in his fifties, balding and running to fat, he was the least martial-looking of the gathering, preferring the luxury of his palace in Sardis to the ardours of the campaign tent. 'Your soon-to-be father-in-law, Antipatros, will support you and I'll back you as will Lysimachus in Thrace and Eumenes in Kappadokia; Ptolemy is too far away to matter. Antigonos is a fool and a dead man.'

Perdikkas could not hide his pleasure at this assessment. 'I think he may well be.' He paused and looked at Menander as if gauging him. 'I'm going to make a change in Lydia, Menander and I think you'll understand why.'

'Will I?'

'Yes, I'm sure you will. You see, now that Kleopatra has taken up residence there, I feel that, as Alexander's full sister, she should be shown honour so I plan to make her the satrap.'

'Satrap!' Menander exploded. 'Over me! Is this how you repay me by putting a woman in my place? A woman? A woman can't be a satrap!'

'She's no ordinary woman, she's Kleopatra.'

'She's still a woman. Do you expect me to take orders from a woman? Would you? Would anyone?'

Perdikkas looked at his brother and Seleukos, neither of them had any measure of support written on their faces. 'You won't have to take your orders from her. I'm going to move you to Hellespontine Phrygia.'

'Hellespontine Phrygia! That's Krateros'.'

'No it's not, it was Leonnatus', but he's dead, as you know.'

'And Krateros claimed it as his own when he passed through early this year.'

'It wasn't his to claim.'

'You tell him that.'

Perdikkas lifted his hand. 'I have the ring, and it was through that authority that I made the distribution of the satrapies after Alexander's death and it's through that authority that I'm moving you to Hellespontine Phrygia. You're still a satrap. You still have power.'

'But I'm very happy where I am, Perdikkas. And, let's be frank, there isn't much that you can do to make me move, is there?'

'I've already written to Kleopatra to inform her of my decision.'

'You really don't see it, do you, Perdikkas?' Seleukos said. 'You really don't understand that the ring in itself doesn't give you Alexander's authority. You can't go acting in this sort of high-handed manner, ordering your equals around; as Ptolemy so rightly pointed out, you were only half-chosen.'

That's going to follow me for the rest of my life unless I do this thing. I have to make this happen if I want Kleopatra to accept that I must marry Nicaea, in order to bind Antipatros to me, before I can marry her. To return to Macedon with Alexander's corpse and Kleopatra as my bride will surely make me look like Alexander's chosen heir. 'Well, it is done; and it can't be undone.'

'I don't accept it,' Menander stated in a firm voice. 'I will be staying in Sardis and she can think what she wants.'

'Whether you accept it or not, my decision stands and I'll have the documents drawn up to that effect.'

'You're a fool, Perdikkas,' Menander spat as he stormed from the tent.

'Well done, Perdikkas,' Seleukos said, 'with one blunderous move you've managed to upset Menander and Krateros as well as insult all Macedonians by giving a woman power like that. How long do you plan to stay alive?'

Perdikkas had no time for this argument. 'I'm leaving for Babylon immediately to check on the progress of Alexander's catafalque. You're dismissed.' He turned his back on them.

'No, I'm not dismissed, Perdikkas; I've decided to leave.' And, with an exaggerated inclination of the head, he did.

'Alketas,' Perdikkas called a moment after his brother and Seleukos had left the tent.

'Yes?' Alketas replied, putting his head back through the opening.

'Do you think I was right to do that?'

Alketas walked back in and shrugged. 'It's done now. What I wonder is: why was it done and I think I know the answer.'

'Go on.'

'You want Kleopatra to be in your debt.'

'Perhaps.'

'You're planning to marry her even though you're going to marry Nicaea, aren't you?'

'Kleopatra will make me king.'

'Then marry her now.'

'That will make me Antipatros' enemy.'

'And marrying his daughter then repudiating her won't?'

'Marrying his daughter, getting her pregnant and then taking a second wife will secure both him and the crown.'

'That sounds like one of Eumenes' ploys.'

'It's not, actually; it's all my own. And I know for a fact that it's one that the sly little Greek would not approve of, so, seeing as he's away in Armenia, he won't have to find out until it is done.'

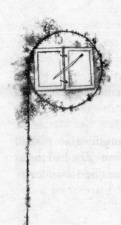

EUMENES, THE SLY

WHAT HAD SURPRISED Eumenes the most was how much he had enjoyed the campaign. The years of acting as secretary to, firstly, Philip and then Alexander, had kept him away from the field and it was not until Alexander's last year that Eumenes had been entrusted with a command; even then it had been for small-scale, supporting actions. Now, however, he was operating independently and all tactical decisions were his own to make; and that had been what he had relished the most for he seemed to have a natural talent for soldiering.

'Parmida,' Eumenes said as he and the commander of his Kappadokian cavalry surveyed Carana, a small walled town high up the Euphrates, just five leagues from its source, 'you take half the men, cross the river and skirt around the town to the north and I'll come round from the south with the rest. We'll send patrols out ahead to spring any ambushes. I'll see you on the other side. If there's no sign of any military activity we'll accept the town's surrender and then move on down the river safe in the knowledge that there is no threat to our rear, and head home to Kappadokia.'

'If it is your pleasure, general, then so be it,' Parmida replied formally in heavily accented Greek.

'It is my pleasure and it will be made doubly pleasurable by the knowledge that Neoptolemus will be spitting with rage and jealousy that we've manged to achieve in three months what he failed to do in six.'

And so it was with a warm feeling that Eumenes led two hundred and fifty of his cavalry on a reconnaissance of the southern reaches of the town, for this was the last community that had expressed any hostility to Macedonian hegemony and it had unconditionally offered its surrender. One by one the towns had surrendered to Eumenes as he had led his Kappadokians around Armenia with a speed that caught all by surprise. The process had been made far simpler by the fact that the Armenians had not been united and had proved to be, instead, a collection of feuding petty-lordlings who could be dealt with individually, the relatively few men he had in his command being sufficient. He had been unable to get more troops as Neoptolemus had flatly refused his request as he sulked in Amida, the town astride the Royal Road in the south of the county, cursing his mutinous, still unpaid, men who continued to refuse to fight for him.

But Eumenes had not needed reinforcements as speed had made up for paucity of numbers and Neoptolemus' jealousy had grown with each of his successes as his plan to hamper him by denying him troops backfired. And now Armenia was brought back within the Macedonian sphere of influence with the Armenian satrap appointed by Alexander, Mithranes of the royal Orontid House, installed back in the capital, Armavir.

Riding the rough country had become a joy to Eumenes and as he skirted around the south of Carana, overshadowed by Mount Abus' snow-capped peak, he almost regretted that the campaign was coming to a close and that he would be returning to mainly administrative tasks back in his own satrapy. The half-circuit complete, Eumenes drew up his men in front of Carana's western gate as Parmida led his troops splashing across the Euphrates, no more than ten paces wide at this high point.

'Anything, Parmida?' Eumenes called, admiring, as always, his high-helmed men, splendid in their embroidered tunics and trousers and soft-leather boots and with intricately decorated javelin holsters hanging from their saddles.

'Nothing, general; I think we can take them at their word that there are no soldiers in the area.'

Eumenes pointed at the town's gates. 'Go and tell them to open up, then.'

It was with a holiday atmosphere that Eumenes led his cavalry into the town and received its surrender and pledge of loyalty to Mithranes; people lined the streets, waving and cheering as if they had never supported the rebel lord, Arakha, whose impaled body they proudly displayed in front of what had been his palace – his many wives and children had shared his fate, their skewered corpses surrounding his.

The messenger arrived soon after Eumenes had finished a speech praising the people of Carana for their heroic and selfless despatching of the rebel and so many innocent women and children.

Making his excuses to the local dignitaries, Eumenes walked away from the grisly array of bodies. He looked at the seal and did a double-take. *Olympias! What does she want, I wonder?* He broke it and then unrolled the scroll and read:

Eumenes, you are one of the few people whom I can trust as you have always showed loyalty to my son and his father before him. My offer of marriage of my daughter, Kleopatra, to Perdikkas, made after our arrival in Sardis, has been received with luke-warm enthusiasm and now I hear that Nicaea, the daughter of that toad Antipatros, has arrived in Tarsus and is beginning the overland journey to the Euphrates and thence on to Babylon where she will marry him. Perdikkas has made Kleopatra the satrap of Lydia, much to Menander's disgust, as a signal that he favours her and yet he continues along the path of marriage to the daughter of a mere regent. If this wedding does take place then my offer to Perdikkas is void for I will not bear the shame of my daughter being a second wife. Nor will I allow Kleopatra to accept him if he repudiates Nicaea; a man who can do that once could easily do it again when expediency calls. I would be grateful, my dear Eumenes, and deem it a personal favour if you would travel to Babylon and explain my position to him face to face. If he and Kleopatra are to claim the throne of Macedon together it must be now; if not, it is never.

There is one other very interesting development that I thought you should know: my spies inform me that shortly after Nicaea arrived in Tarsus and her sister Eurydike departed for Alexandria in Egypt, another ship came from the north; in it were two women and around seventy Illyrian warriors. They sold their ship and used the money to buy horses and engaged a guide to take them overland to Babylon once they found out that Perdikkas had headed back south. The women are believed to be Alexander's and Kleopatra's half-sister, Cynnane, accompanied by her daughter, Adea. It is thought that they are travelling to Babylon so that Adea can marry the idiot now known as Philip, the third of that name. I believe this to be true as it is what I would have done had I been in Cynnane's situation. You must prevent this and I do not care how. Olympias.

Eumenes looked up at the sky. *It's not often that I see things in the same way as Olympias.* He took a deep breath, then reread the letter. 'Parmida!' he shouted as he finished.

'What is it, general?' Parmida asked, coming up to him.

'Tell the men to mount up, we're leaving immediately.'

'Where to?'

'Down river until it becomes navigable; I need to get a ship and be in Babylon as soon as possible.'

But as soon as possible turned out to be eight days sailing or rowing day and night, despite the fact that he commandeered the fastest vessel he could find in Melitene, the town guarding the Royal Road as it crossed the border between Armenia and Kappadokia. But eight days he hoped would be quick enough as he watched the huge blue-tiled walls of the great city, astride the Euphrates, grow closer, for he knew that he would not be too far behind Nicaea and well ahead of Cynnane and Adea seeing as, according to Olympias, they would by travelling overland all the way.

Through the harbour gate Eumenes' ship glided, dwarfed by looming walls, centuries' old, leaving the main course of the river behind it. With a brief suggestion to the harbour-master as to where he might like to look for his docking fee, Eumenes made his way through the bustle of the quayside and surrounding streets, to the palace complex. His sudden appearance out of the north caused the commander of the guard to gape in surprise as he stepped through the opened gate. 'I wasn't told to expect you, sir.'

'Where's Perdikkas?' Eumenes demanded, caring not what the man did or did not expect.

'He's in the throne-room.'

With a curt nod, Eumenes headed across the expansive central courtyard as fast as his short legs could go without breaking into an undignified run and resisting the temptation to stop and look at the glorious catafalque, parked beneath a voluminous awning, ready to transport Alexander's mummified corpse back to Macedon.

It was into a sombre atmosphere that Eumenes walked as he entered the throne-room, through the doorway that had been much enlarged. Although crowded, very few people moved as all attention was focused upon the solemn ceremony taking place. It was at the very moment Perdikkas, standing next to Alketas and a smug-looking Kassandros, removed Nicaea's veil and kissed her, thus completing the marriage ceremony, that Eumenes could see what was going on. 'You fool!' he roared, breaking the mood of the chamber. 'You massive fool, Perdikkas, now you have lost every last hope of keeping the empire united.'

Perdikkas looked up in shock at the outburst to see the small Greek whom he thought to be hundreds of leagues away. 'What are you doing here?'

'Trying to prevent you from doing what you have just done and also to warn you of a huge danger approaching.'

'What danger?'

'Not in front of all these people, Perdikkas, outside.'

'Cynnane?' Perdikkas' eyes narrowed, puzzled. 'But I thought she'd returned to her mother's native Illyria.'

Eumenes struggled to keep his voice level as they walked out into the palace courtyard. 'Things change, Perdikkas, as even you really must have noticed by now. Cynnane has come to Asia and is on her way here to marry her daughter to King Philip.'

'Well, I won't let her.'

'No? Not even when the army demand that Alexander's half-brother takes his half-niece as a bride and thus ensure a real Argead heir – assuming that the union bears fruit, that is.'

'I'll talk to them and persuade them that it won't be the best course for the empire.'

'Do you think the common soldier would understand that Adea marrying Philip will create another rival to both you and Antipatros, thus bringing the likelihood of war even closer. No, Perdikkas, they won't; they will just see Alexander's bloodline being thickened and, believe me, they will like the idea of that, because one day the hope is for a second Alexander.'

Perdikkas contemplated this as they approached the catafalque. 'Then I have to stop her from getting here; kill them both, I suppose.'

Oh, the military mind at its finest. 'Perdikkas, try to keep your stupid ideas to just one a day; and I would say that you've used up your quota already for today by marrying the wrong woman. You can't go around killing off Alexander's family without the army ripping you bodily apart with its bare hands. Give me some men and I'll go and find her, take her back to Tarsus and put her on a ship.'

Perdikkas shook his head. 'No, Alketas can do that; I need you to go to Sardis.'

'It's too late, Perdikkas; Kleopatra won't marry you now.'

'She has to in order to keep Alexander's legacy together.'

'I know and, believe me, it's what I want too; that's why I advised you to marry her in the first place. Olympias wrote to me to say that if you went ahead with the marriage to Nicaea then her offer was void.'

Perdikkas looked surprised. 'Kleopatra wrote the same to me.'

Eumenes could not believe what he had heard. 'If you knew that, then what possessed you to go through with the wedding to Nicaea?'

Perdikkas looked at Eumenes as if he were unable to grasp the obvious. 'I need Antipatros as much as I need Kleopatra if I am to unite the empire.'

It's pointless arguing in the face of such stupidity; all I can do is try, for Alexander's sake, to fix what this idiot has broken. 'Very well, Perdikkas; you send Alketas to turn Cynnane back and I'll travel to Sardis to see if I can possibly change Olympias' and Kleopatra's minds.'

Perdikkas clapped Eumenes on the shoulder. 'If anyone can, you can, my sly little Greek.'

'Less of the "little", Perdikkas; less of the "little" and more of the "sly",' Eumenes mumbled as he stopped to admire Alexander's catafalque.

'It begins its journey tomorrow,' Perdikkas said with unmistakable pride in his voice. 'It's going overland along the Euphrates, leaving it at Thapsacus and crossing to the sea, I hope it'll be there by spring; from there it goes up the coast to Tarsus, then on to Sardis and then up to the Hellespont where I plan to join it with my two brides for a triumphant return to Macedon, late summer, there to claim the regency over the whole empire and expect to be offered the crown.'

The man's delusional. 'I'll watch it leave Babylon and then start my journey back up the River to try to clean up your mess.'

The entire population of Babylon turned out to watch Alexander's body take its leave of the city, the following morning at the second hour. In their tens of thousands they thronged in the broad streets, lined with the villas of the wealthy, leading from the palace to the North Gate as the sixty-four mules hauled the elaborate vehicle by to the accompaniment of the jangle of many bells and the protests of the beasts as their minders goaded them with sharpened sticks. At the head of the procession rode Perdikkas with King Philip and Arrhidaeus, the designer of the catafalque who had been charged with accompanying it all the way to Macedon; with him went two *ilia* of two hundred and fifty Companion cavalry.

Eumenes, riding behind Perdikkas with Alketas, Kassandros, Seleukos, Attalus and Antigenes, was obliged to give Perdikkas grudging respect for the beautiful job that had been done in creating the catafalque. Within it, Alexander's body lay in a sarcophagus with a curved top made of small glass pieces, held together by lead; refracted, he was visible to all who stared down on it in wonder. Lying on a bed of preserving herbs and spices, with his blond hair arranged neatly on the pillow and eyes closed, he looked to be gently sleeping; one could not help but whisper in his presence for fear of waking him. His hardened-leather battle cuirass, with a rearing horse inlaid in silver on each pectoral, had been buffed to a sheen and his hands clasped the sword laid on his chest. Eumenes had been moved to tears as he gazed down on the man who had achieved more than anyone had or would; kissing the tips of his fingers he had laid them on the glass above Alexander's forehead.

And so Alexander commenced his final journey; as the procession left Babylon, and they watched it disappear into the distance, Eumenes turned to Perdikkas. 'How will you know when it reaches the Hellespont?'

'I have told Arrhidaeus to send couriers back every ten days to keep me notified of its progress. It'll be slow but it will get there.'

Eumenes looked at the fortune in gold and silver rumbling up the dusty road and wondered if he would have given a larger guard than five hundred men.

'You should be leaving,' Perdikkas said, breaking through Eumenes' train of thought. 'I need Kleopatra's consent as soon as possible.'

Eumenes sighed at the virtual impossibility of the challenge and the political necessity that it should be achieved. 'Very well, Perdikkas, hopefully you'll have some news from me in a month or so. In the meantime, don't let Alketas do anything stupid with Cynnane and Adea.'

ADEA, THE WARRIOR

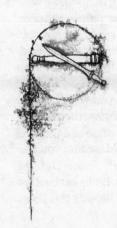

THE DAYS HAD blurred into an endless procession of barren land interspersed with mean mud-brick villages as the guide had led Adea, Cynnane and their mounted escort across the desert, from the coast to the Euphrates. Now that they were following the course of the river, the vegetation had become more verdant despite the fact that winter was upon them; in these southern climes winter held no fear for the traveller, indeed, it was their friend. Even with the passing of the winter solstice the sun still burned down on Adea's head and sweat dampened her tunic as the column moved south at a slow walk to conserve the horses' energy as they had insufficient money for spares – and not nearly enough for a river transport for seventy.

By day they travelled and each night they camped on the Euphrates' bank, dipping wearied limbs in the water as their tired horses drank their fill. But although it was slow, progress was made every day; they had now passed through the satrapy of Assyria and on into Babylonia, ten leagues from the river-port of Is and just fifty from Babylon itself. And it was here, just past the border, that the sight that Adea had been dreading appeared.

'How many this time, Barzid?' Cynnane asked, shading her eyes and looking at the line of cavalry that barred their way a thousand paces ahead of them.

'The same as the last time: two hundred, perhaps two hundred and fifty.'

'And this time we are only seventy and have no spare horses.' Cynnane turned to her daughter. 'Death is a better option than being turned back here; I think that it's time we appealed to the soldiery of Macedon and won their hearts.'

Adea felt her stomach clench at the thought of public speaking, knowing that her skills lay far more with the physical rather than the rhetorical.

Cynnane smiled at the look of unease on her daughter's face. 'I'll do the talking; you just sit next to me and look the part.'

'How do I look the part, Mother?'

'You are an Argead of the Royal house of Macedon; you fear nothing and nobody. You are immovable.'

Feeling less than immovable, Adea rode next to her mother as they approached the Macedonian cavalry blocking their way; Barzid held their escort back behind them to emphasise that they came in peace and expected no violence.

Pulling their mounts up just ten paces from the commander of the unit, Cynnane and Adea, with neutral expressions, surveyed the four-deep formation of shieldless, lance-armed cavalry, with long-plumed bronze helms and hardened-leather muscled-cuirasses; their weapons were all lowered, ready to strike.

'Who bars the road to Cynnane, daughter of Philip, the second of that name, of Macedon, and her daughter, Adea?' Cynnane's voice was loud and pitched high so that all could hear.

'I do,' the commander replied, stating the obvious.

The muttering of surprised voices and curious looks as the men gazed at the two women came as a relief to Adea. *They didn't know who they had been sent to intercept; mother's announcement has come as a shock to them.*

'I meant: what is your name?'

The commander looked about, sharply, as a few sniggers came from the ranks. 'Alketas, son of Orontes, and brother to Perdikkas who demands that you go no further.'

Cynnane lifted her chin and looked down her nose, wrinkled in scorn, at Alketas. 'I go where I like in the empire of my brother, Alexander.'

It was the mention of that magical name and the reminder of just how closely related Cynnane was to him that changed the atmosphere completely; Adea now sensed that the men completely agreed with Cynnane's assertion that she should be allowed to pass unhindered.

Alketas, too, perceived the swing in the mood and then saw the proof of it as many of his men lifted their lances upright. 'Perdikkas holds Alexander's ring and he has commanded, in Alexander's name, that you go no further and return whence you came.'

Cynnane shook her head as she dismounted; she walked a few paces along the ranks of cavalry, away from Alketas and drew herself up, taking a deep breath. 'Men of Macedon, you know who I am, the eldest daughter of Philip; had I been born a man I would be your king, even now. But I was given a woman's body and accept a woman's role which is to breed.' She pointed back to Adea. 'And this is my daughter, sired upon me by Amyntas, also of the Argead house; her name is Adea and in her veins runs blood almost identical to that of Alexander's.' She paused to allow the magnitude of that claim to sink in; the mutterings grew as it did. 'She has come to put an end to the uncertainty surrounding the succession. She has left her home in the north to travel south to Babylon in order to marry my half-brother, her half-uncle, the new King Philip. Their union will produce a pure Argead heir without the taint of eastern blood. An heir for the whole of the army, the whole of Macedon even, to unite behind; he will be an heir who will avert the possibility of war because he will be the undisputed heir to Alexander's throne. We come to give you a Macedonian heir and yet you bar our way. What means this, soldiers of Macedon? Why do you try to stop a mission of peace?' One hand on her hip and one on the hilt of her sword, she stood and cast her gaze along the lines of faces, questioning with her look the motive within each man for such action. Most averted their eyes, either staring at the ground or looking to Alketas to come up with a reason why they were being asked to do something so obviously against the common good of all Macedonians.

Adea kept her face neutral, smiling within. *She's got them; our captors will become our escorts and Alketas will either accept the fact or die.*

Cynnane began to walk forward, her steps measured and strong. It was as she was about to pass between the muzzles of two horses that their riders moved them aside; behind them their comrades did the same, creating a passage through the formation.

'Close your ranks!' Alketas roared as Cynnane disappeared between the first two horses. He repeated the order to no effect and, thwarted, yanked his mount to the left to gallop around his command.

Adea kicked her horse forward and followed her mother through the Macedonians to be greeted with respectful nods and the hints of smiles that softened hardened faces.

Cynnane had reached the hind legs of the last rank as Alketas drew his horse up in front of her in a skidding cloud of dust; he swung the beast round to face her and lowered his lance so that the tip of it pointed to her heart.

'You shall not pass,' the Macedonian commander said, his eyes fixed with determination.

'I go where I want, Alketas,' Cynnane said, walking forward.

'Go back, I warn you.'

'And I warn you, Alketas, let the sister of Alexander pass.' She continued to advance until the tip of the lance pressed against her chest, just beneath her left breast; she continued, pushing at the weapon so that a little blossom of blood appeared on her tunic.

'Halt! I command you,' Alketas screamed, desperation in his voice, pushing the lance against her.

And still Cynnane kept straining forward, even as the honed tip slipped between her ribs; on she pushed and harder still did Alketas resist as Adea looked on in horror.

She's prepared to sacrifice herself for me. 'Mother, no! Stop!'

But her cries fell on deaf ears as Cynnane raised her eyes to Alketas and jerked herself forward again, grimacing with the pain of iron slicing through flesh and muscle. Alketas looked down at her, horrified at what she was doing, but kept his arm braced, nonetheless. His men had all turned in their saddles and were staring aghast at the confrontation.

Another push and the lance blade was half in; it was past the point of no return and Cynnane sensed that; she grabbed the haft with both hands. 'Alketas, let…me…pass!' Her arm muscles tensed and, holding the lance firm, she drove her body onward so that the iron exploded her heart; its final beat spraying blood through the wound onto the shaft. Her whole frame juddered, the muscles in her legs rigid. With a guttural cough, gore slopped from her mouth as, again, her body spasmed.

Adea screamed as Alketas, terror written across his face, released the lance as if it had suddenly become red-hot. Down Cynnane fell as her legs buckled beneath her, slumping onto her side, the lance protruding from her chest as her tunic reddened.

Adea leapt from her horse; Alketas looked at the corpse in horror as a deep growl rose from his men.

Kneeling, Adea took her mother's head in her hands and turned her face towards her. She met with a glazed and vacant stare. 'Mother! Mother!' She broke into a series of wretched sobs, each more racked than the last, before kissing Cynnane's cheek and putting her mouth next to her ear. 'Mother, you swore that you would always be there for me.'

But Cynnane did not hear her whisper.

Adea looked up at Alketas; hatred in her tear-clogged eyes. 'You've killed her; you killed my mother.'

Alketas gasped and looked up at his men as they rode towards him, encircling him and Adea, still cradling her mother's head. 'Get back into your ranks!' But the command was ignored as lances now fell to point at his throat. 'Get back into your ranks!' But still they advanced towards their trapped commander.

It was at that moment when Adea realised, through her grief, that to take full advantage of the sacrifice her mother had made, she needed to act like a queen and not a distraught girl. She rose to her feet, raising her hands above her head in an appeal for quiet. *Now is my chance to secure my position and get myself a Macedonian bodyguard at the same time.*

The men stilled their horses and looked at the teenage girl with her dead mother at her feet.

Adea pointed at Alketas, her nerves about speaking to a crowd forgotten. 'This man has murdered the sister of Alexander; the woman who gave me life. I can feel your anger; my own is strong within me. However, we must not give in to our feelings but, rather, we must act to honour her memory. To murder Alketas is to stoop to his level.' Adea paused, her heart beating swift as mixed emotions, grief, anger, hatred and excitement swirled around her. Taking a deep breath, she continued: 'Let it be Alketas who takes my mother's body before the army in Babylon and explain why he killed her; let it be him who asks for their forgiveness as they wail for the loss of Alexander's sister. Seize him and bind him but do him no harm. Build my mother a cata-falque and we will lead it to Babylon with Alketas tied to its rear so he has to stare at the body of the woman of the royal Argead House of Macedon whose life he took. And you, brave men of Macedon, may guard me against any other attempt to turn me from my purpose of providing you with a full-blooded heir to Alexander's legacy.'

It was with vigour that they cheered her as Alketas was pulled from his horse, protesting his kinship to Perdikkas, and bound and gagged. And it was in the fellowship of brothers that they welcomed Barzid and his men and together they converted one of the Macedonian's supply-wagons into a catafalque and lay Cynnane's body in it.

So it was that Adea, now accompanied by three hundred and twenty mounted warriors, led her mother's body towards Babylon with Alketas stumbling along behind the wagon, a constant target for jibes and phlegm. And as they passed the great catafalque of Alexander, heading in the opposite direction, Adea offered up a prayer for the dead siblings and asked that her union be fruitful with the new King Philip.

Roxanna,
The Wild Cat

IT WAS A warm feeling that grew in her belly as Roxanna heard the furore break loose in the Palace. Wails of grief pierced the night and many running footsteps echoed off the high walls and ceilings of the corridors. In fact, Roxanna was feeling better than she had since the deaths of her two Persian rivals as the moment of her triumph neared.

It had taken a lot of planning and not a few purses of gold in bribes to secure the method and access but eventually she had been ready. To find a poison that could evade the detection of a food-taster had been the first problem as the tasteless ones tended to cause instant symptoms and a speedy death. Eventually she had come up with a potion that would work slowly if applied over three days consecutively.

But administering the dose at three different meals had proved difficult; eventually she had one of her women seduce and coerce a slave in the victim's apartments and the deed was done. Today was the night of the third day and the slave already lay dead in a shallow grave, throat cut, so he would never be able to reveal who had murdered Philip, the third of that name.

It was with a smile on her lips that Roxanna imagined the agony that the idiot king would be in, as sweet music tinkled within her room failing to mask the uproar without.

Now there would be nothing but the bastard Heracles, the discharge of that bitch Barsine, in the way of her son, Alexander, and he would be easy to get to. *I'll have that bitch too, whilst I'm about it.*

That was also a pleasant thought and Roxanna's smile broadened and her feeling of pleasure intensified. She had left the bastard for last, fearing that, had she poisoned him before Philip, Perdikkas would have immediately suspected her of aiming for the king next and would, therefore, have made the security arrangements around the drooling fool even more stringent. One more killing and all her rivals would be out of the way and there would be nothing to stop her taking power through her son who was now a boisterous toddler of two years and four months. Of course she would have to wait patiently as the little beast grew up and, of course, she would have to endure the insolence of Perdikkas as he continued to refuse to acknowledge her position as Alexander's queen and therefore the singular most important person in the world after her son – now that Philip was in his death throes, that was.

Taking a peach from the bowl on the table before her, she guessed that he would die sometime in the mid-afternoon in two days' time, provided that the physicians did not guess what was killing him, and only then in the very unlikely event that one of them knew the antidote would Philip's life be saved.

No, he's as good as dead and I can sleep peacefully tonight.

The crash of doors kicked open startled Roxanna; her peach, one bite missing, dropped to the floor and the musicians in the corner of the room squeaked to a halt.

Perdikkas stormed towards her saying nothing; his expression spoke his thoughts eloquently enough. Seleukos and Aristonous surged into the room behind him, swords drawn.

'What are you doing?' Roxanna hissed. 'How dare you barge into my rooms like that? A queen is never intruded upon.'

'A queen can go fuck herself,' Perdikkas said through clenched teeth as he grabbed her arm and hauled her from the couch. 'But before she does, she will administer the antidote to whatever it was that she managed to give Philip.'

'I don't know what you are talking—'

The sharp slap across her cheek cut off her protestations.

'Don't play me for a fool, Roxanna. Philip has been poisoned and I know you to be a poisoner and you have the most to gain by his death – at least you thought you did.' He turned to Seleukos and Aristonous. 'Grab the boy and take him to my rooms.' With an unpleasant grin he slapped Roxanna across the face again. 'That's to clear your head so that you understand exactly what it is I'm threatening you with. You will make sure that Philip survives and is in no worse a state than the sorry one he already finds himself in. If you do this, I might, just might, not tell the army about the attempt on his life and who was responsible for it. If you don't save him, the army will be informed that the tragic disease that carried off the elder king also, alas, spread through the palace and took the younger king as well and in her grief his poor mother, the kind and beautiful Roxanna, hung herself; and to prove it I will display the rope marks around your corpse's neck. Now, do you fully understand me?'

'You can't do this.'

'I can and I am,' Perdikkas replied as the screeching, writhing form of Alexander, the third of that name, was carried out of his bed chamber by Aristonous as Seleukos beat back a gaggle of women with the flat of his sword, laying a couple out cold on the floor.

Roxanna screamed at the sight and then spat in Perdikkas' face. 'If I refuse you and you kill my son and me you'll be left without a king. Ha! I have you there.'

Perdikkas tightened his grip around the slender arm and wiped the spittle from his face. 'Wrong, bitch; I would still have Heracles; a bastard maybe, but Alexander's bastard.'

Heracles! Perhaps I should have killed him first. I'll know for next time.

'Or, perhaps, I'll decide that I do not need a male relative of Alexander's. Who knows? One thing is for sure and that is you and your son are both dead if Philip dies. So which is it to be, Roxanna? Hurry with your decision because I've lost my patience and would be very happy to string you up here and now.'

Roxanna let her body relax in a show of surrender. 'Take me to him, but first I need to get the antidote.'

The phial, opaque turquoise, sheened with the soft glow of lamplight, shook in Roxanna's hand as she held it close to the dying king's mouth; Philip groaned with his eyes closed. That she should be forced into undoing all her good work, the life of her son being used to coerce her, was intolerable; Perdikkas was intolerable; her situation was intolerable; was she not queen after all? And yet here she was, saving the life of a drooling fool for whom death was too good.

She pulled the phial away and heard a child's whimper come from behind her; she turned to see Perdikkas standing with his hand gripped around her son's neck, his knuckles white. Too young to understand what was going on, Alexander had still sensed the tension of the situation and realised that he was in a degree of personal danger; tears streamed down his face and he looked around for the comfort of one of his absent nurses.

'Do it!' Perdikkas ordered.

Roxanna held the phial to him. 'You do it.'

Perdikkas squeezed Alexander's neck even tighter by way of reply.

'I'll do it!' Tychon, Philip's personal physician and full-time companion, cried in desperation, both his hands holding those of his charge.

Roxanna hissed at the Greek. *There's no choice. Next time I'll plan it better and get Perdikkas at the same time.* Resigned, she pressed the phial against slack lips and, with care, tipped the contents into the king's mouth.

Philip spluttered but the liquid stayed in; he swallowed.

'How long will it take?' Perdikkas asked, walking over to the bed and peering down at the king.

'I have to give him the antidote on three consecutive days.'

'Three days!'

'Yes, that's how I administered the poison.' Roxanna anticipated the next question. 'No, the slave that did it is dead; I wouldn't be so stupid as to leave an accomplice alive, would I?'

Perdikkas grunted. 'Then this is where you stay, Roxanna; you stay until Philip is well.'

'You can't make me.'

Perdikkas looked down at her. 'When will you get it into your head that I can do anything I like with you? You're nothing to me. You stay here; there'll be an armed guard on the door. I'll take the boy with me to ensure your continued interest in the treatment.'

Roxanna's nose smarted from the continual inhalation of air infested with the stench of urine rising from Philip's bed. The shutters on the windows remained closed against the mid-afternoon heat raging in the courtyard beyond. She looked down at her erstwhile victim and it was with a mixture of relief and rage that she watched Philip's eyes flicker open an hour after she had administered the final dose. They looked around and then fixed on Tychon, who had not left his side for the last three days of the treatment.

'Tychon,' Philip said, his voice weak, 'will I be well now?'

To Roxanna's amazement, Tychon had tears in his eyes. 'Yes, master, you will be well now. All will be well now.'

How can anyone care so about such a piss-stinking monstrosity? Not wanting to witness more of this stomach-turning display, Roxanna got to her feet as Perdikkas barged through the door.

Philip turned to him. 'Perdikkas, I will be well, all will be well; Tychon said so.'

Perdikkas strode over to the bed, took the king's face in one hand and examined his eyes. 'You seem to be fine.'

'Oh, I am fine, Perdikkas,' Philip assured him as shouting erupted in the courtyard. 'I would like steak and my elephant.'

But Philip's request was ignored as Perdikkas, disturbed by the noise, went to the window and threw the shutters open. He froze. 'God's below,' he whispered, so that Roxanna could just hear him. 'Alketas, what have you done?' He turned and sprinted from the room.

Roxanna watched him in alarm before walking to the window and looking down. As she did so, a girl standing on a wagon with a corpse at her feet, surrounded by a huge crowd of soldiers, both mounted and on foot, raised her arms in the air in a request for silence.

'Soldiers of Macedon.' Her voice surprised Roxanna by the strength and masculinity of it. The girl pointed to a man roped, kneeling, to the rear of the wagon. 'This man, Alketas, whom you all know, wishes to explain to you why he killed my mother, Cynnane, the sister of Alexander.'

Roxanna chuckled to herself, pleased to hear of the death of another of Alexander's family. *And at Alketas' hand, as well; those Macedonian pigs won't like that.* Her smile grew broader as Alketas was kicked and punched; shouts turned from outrage to outright anger.

The girl once more appealed for calm; by the time it was manifest, Alketas was bloodied and prostrate.

'My mother was bringing me here for you, soldiers of Macedon.'

'Wait!'

Roxanna looked down, to see Perdikkas pushing through the crowd with two Macedonian officers following him. *With luck they'll rip both him and his brother to death.* Roxanna's mood had greatly improved.

'Wait,' Perdikkas shouted, breathless from shoving and pushing his way through. 'What are you doing with my brother?' He pointed at the men surrounding the wagon. 'Get back, all of you. Docimus, Polemon, push them back.'

'He killed Cynnane!' many voices replied as the girl stood by the corpse, with her hands on her hips, saying nothing, as the two officers cleared a way for Perdikkas.

'Touch us and you're dead men,' Docimus, the elder of the two, shouted with menace in his voice as he and Polemon manhandled a path through the crush.

That would escalate things. Roxanna smiled, her eyes cold.

Perdikkas reached the wagon and looked up at the girl. 'Believe me, Adea; I told him that neither of you were to be harmed.'

Adea looked down at her mother's corpse and indicated to it with an open palm. 'And yet there she lies!'

Rough hands again grabbed Alketas and pulled him to his feet as a flurry of punches cracked into his ribs and face. He doubled over as Docimus and Polemon tried to reach him.

A growl of anger surged through the crowd, now thousands strong and growing all the time as men poured through the gates, the news of the murder of Alexander's sister spreading throughout the city.

'Take your hands off my brother!' This time the voice was female; Roxanna searched the crowd for the source to see a tall woman in her mid-thirties, possessed of beauty and confidence. *Atalanta! This gets better and better; to have the sister killed alongside her brothers would be more than I could ask.*

'Who are you to treat my brother like that, girl?'

Adea fixed her eyes on the new arrival. 'I am the daughter of a murdered mother and the granddaughter of Alexander's father, Philip, and I demand justice.'

'You can demand all you like but if one more hand is laid upon my brother then it will be me demanding justice of you. Now let him go.' Atalanta walked towards Alketas, the men parting for her, despite their anger. Reaching him, she raised him up, untied his bonds and led him by the hand back through the crowd. 'Let us pass.'

None hindered their passage but all growled their anger.

Again Adea appealed for quiet as Atalanta took her brother to safety. 'I came here for one purpose and now, Perdikkas, if you want my forgiveness and if you want me to intercede with the soldiers of Macedon and ask them to spare your brother's life when he is not under the protection of his sister, then you will not stand in my way. Give me justice.'

Perdikkas looked around as he sensed the ill-will surrounding him. 'Very well, Adea, I will give you justice; what is it that you want?'

A cheer erupted and spread throughout the gathering; helms were flung in the air and weapons shaken above heads.

Roxanna felt jealousy writhe within her as she beheld a female getting the sort of praise that she could only dream of and was confused as to what its cause was.

She did not have long to wait as Adea brought the celebrations to a lull. 'Soldiers of Macedon, I have come here to marry the new King Philip.'

Roxanna felt as if a fist had punched her in the belly. She turned and looked at the man whom she had attempted to poison and then been forced to cure; his countenance was childlike and bewildered.

Adea's voice drew her attention back to the courtyard.

'I have come to be your queen; I shall take the royal name of Eurydike and provide you with a true heir of pure Argead blood.'

With bile in her throat, Roxanna staggered away from the window. *Over my dead body, you little bitch.*

ANTIGONOS,
THE ONE-EYED

'AND YOU'RE SURE she's dead?' Antigonos asked, his one eye boring, alternately, into those of Babrak, the merchant, across the desk opposite him; Philotas and Demetrios sat in a couple of chairs by the window, bright with sun reflected off a snow-bound landscape.

Babrak hunched his shoulders and spread his hands. 'Well, obviously, I didn't see the body myself, great lord, it happened a hundred leagues down the Euphrates on the Babylonia border; but that's what Arrhidaeus told me when I met Alexander's catafalque on my journey north from Egypt. The two funeral cortèges passed each other so he saw her; he said she was killed by Alketas.'

Antigonos looked over to Philotas. 'On Perdikkas' orders, one must assume. Alketas has never had the gumption to do anything by himself. And Perdikkas expects me to appear before the army in Babylon when he orders summary executions of Alexander's family without a by your leave? My arse! My damp, hairy arse, I will.' He glanced at Perdikkas' summons that had lain on his desk, unanswered, for the past four months. 'Well, that finally puts my mind to rest over sending him the same answer as the last time he tried to give me an order.' He took the summons and ripped it up. 'I'm afraid to say, my boy, that war seems inevitable if Perdikkas is behaving like this.'

'And where will that leave us?' Demetrios asked.

Antigonos wiped a tear weeping from his missing eye. 'That is a very good question.'

He tossed a purse to Babrak. 'Thank you, old friend, I'll see you next time you pass my way.'

Babrak got to his feet and touched his forehead. 'It will be a different world the next time we meet, great lord, I feel the wind changing for the worse, like a boy losing the bloom of youth and becoming a man.'

'What? Oh yes, I see; you could be right, Babrak, you could be right.'

'But war brings business opportunities, so I won't complain.' With a bow Babrak left the room.

Antigonos reflected on the statement for a moment and then turned to Philotas. 'Well? Where *does* it leave us?'

Philotas did not need to consider the question. 'It all depends upon what position Eumenes takes in Kappadokia. Perdikkas can rely on Peithon's support in Media after that business with the mercenaries and Peucestas' support in Persia but no one else except, perhaps, the sly little Greek. If Eumenes stands with Perdikkas, we'll have a fight on our hands; if he comes over to us then Perdikkas is a dead man.'

Antigonos scratched his beard and looked at Philotas. 'You're right, old friend, we need to talk to Eumenes, even though I refused to help him in Kappadokia.' He looked out of the window at the blanket of snow covering the Kappadokian uplands in the distance. 'Who fancies a trip into Kappadokia at this time of year?'

'He's not in Kappadokia at the moment, Father,' Demetrios informed them. 'When I arrived in Tarsus he had just passed through, coming from Babylon.'

'Passed through? Where was he going?'

'Sardis was the rumour, according to Barbek.'

Antigonos' one eye widened as the implication hit him. 'Sardis? Well, it wouldn't be to see Menander because, as far as he's concerned, Menander should be in Hellespontine Phrygia and not Sardis, so he's going to see Kleopatra and if he's coming from Babylon he's doing so at Perdikkas' instigation.' The enormity of the implication hit Antigonos like a slingshot. 'The sly little Greek is negotiating a second marriage for Perdikkas!

He's killed Cynnane and now plans to break with Antipatros, repudiate Nicaea and marry Kleopatra; the bastard's going for the crown! King Perdikkas, my arse. When Antipatros hears this it will force him to go against Perdikkas.' He grinned, his one eye gleaming. 'Right, gentlemen, I don't give a fuck about the weather; I need to get to Antipatros to set things in motion. Philotas, you stay here and gather all the troops you can; Demetrios, you help him. I need to find a ship prepared to sail in the winter. It's finally come to it: we've got a war to fight.' *Phalanx against phalanx; gods, this will be good. A lot of the lads will die because of it but I'm going to enjoy it to the full.*

Antigonos' one eye blazed as he stared at Antipatros. 'Then you'll have to make a truce with them and pull the army back to Pella, ready to cross the Hellespont as soon as the weather turns.' He slapped the camp table to emphasise his point.

Antipatros pulled his sheepskin cloak tighter about his shoulders and stared into the flames of the brazier, his eyes tired and his expression hang-dog. 'I had barely enough time to get my wife pregnant again before the Aitolians decided to rekindle the Greek rebellion and I had to come south again to this... this...' He indicated, through the tent flaps, to the bitter snow-streaked hills of Aitolia, south-east of Thessaly, and the hilltop town under winter siege. 'And just as I'm a couple of months away from starving the bastards out you're saying that I should pat them on the backs and tell them not to be so naughty again and then, rather than going back to the comforts of my wife, I launch a war that could take me away for a couple of years; at my age? Is that really what you're suggesting?'

'That's exactly what I'm suggesting.'

Antigonos looked over to Krateros and Nicanor, who both nodded their support.

'Fuck the Aitolians, Father,' Nicanor said, 'we can deal with an army of goatherds anytime. Perdikkas is going for the crown. He's about to personally humiliate our family by taking Kleopatra as a wife, either repudiating Nicaea or relegating her to second wife, and he has just ordered the murder of a member of the royal house—'

'Whom I hate.'

'Personal feelings have nothing to do with it,' Antigonos snapped; he raised a hand in apology for his harsh tone. 'You taught me that more than forty years ago, when I was twenty.'

Antipatros sighed. 'Was that so long ago? Philip wasn't even king then and I was approaching forty and thinking about starting to take life easy.' He shook his head. 'And now, forty years later, you want me to start the biggest war of my life?'

'You have to,' Krateros said with as much sympathy in his voice as he could muster. 'Perdikkas won't rest until he has us all in his thrall. He thinks that he can take Hellespontine Phrygia from me and give it to Menander; for Ares' sake, who does he think he is? Thank the god of war that Menander is an honourable man. But killing Cynnane is unforgivable.'

'We don't know that he ordered Alketas to kill her.'

'It doesn't matter whether his fool of a brother did it by a mistake or because he was ordered to, it's still Perdikkas' deed. But it's his wooing of Kleopatra that's the most dangerous thing. If he marries her he will claim the crown and then who will be back in power?'

Antipatros slapped his forehead. 'Olympias.'

Nicanor blew into his hands and rubbed them. 'Yes, and our family will be dead; all of us.'

Antipatros looked at his son, his eyes weary. 'Will there never be any peace?'

'What? For you personally or for the empire?' Antigonos asked.

Antipatros heaved another sigh. 'Well, I suppose I have no choice in the matter, I can't let that witch Olympias back into Macedon, her vengeance will be a bloodbath.' He lifted his eyes from the flames and strength seemed to flood back into them, his decision made. 'Alright, gentlemen, we take an army over to Asia to defeat Perdikkas and any others who stand with him.' He stood, dropping his cloak to reveal full armour underneath, walked to the entrance of the tent and, looking at the besieged town, took a deep breath of icy air; it steamed from his mouth as he spoke. 'I'll make a deal with those vermin up in the town which they will, no doubt, take as a victory because I'm withdrawing without taking their filthy little hovels. But so be it, although I think that one day I'll come to regret it.' He turned back into the tent. 'Antigonos, go back to Asia and rally support: Menander and Assander will be with us, remind Kleitos of his loyalties and try to persuade Neoptolemus and Eumenes to see sense. Krateros, you and I will prepare the army for a long campaign; we'll cross to Asia as soon as the weather warms in a month or so. I'll leave Polyperchon in Pella as my deputy and you'll stay with him, Nicanor, with enough troops to fend off an attack from Epirus; my guess is that as soon as the witch hears that I'm moving east she will slink back from Sardis and start intriguing with that weakling Aeacides again to persuade him to have another go at taking a few towns from us.' He smiled, grim and determined. 'I shall write to Ptolemy and ask him whether he would be so kind as to make a nuisance of himself; let's make things as difficult as we can for Perdikkas.'

PERDIKKAS,
THE HALF-CHOSEN

'WE MARCH NORTH immediately,' Perdikkas stated, looking at each of his senior officers seated around the table in the throne-room. 'The whole army, north, now. If the information is correct, and I completely trust Eumenes and his spies, then we must be at the Hellespont to stop Antipatros and Krateros from invading.' He turned to Archon, the satrap of Babylonia. 'Assemble every ship large enough to carry troops in the harbour. Antigenes and Seleukos, muster the army ready to move.' He pointed at two middle-aged officers in turn. 'Docimus, I want you to go to Peithon and Polemon, you go to Peucestas and tell them to bring their armies to Tarsus; we shall rendezvous there and carry on north together. Aristonous, I want you to hurry to Tyros and join Nearchus and take whatever ships he's managed to gather and secure Cyprus; I won't have that island used as a base for naval operations against us as we go north.' He looked across the table to his brother-in-law, Attalus. 'Take Alketas, keep him out of trouble, Atalanta can go with you. Travel north as fast as you can to Tarsus, send messages to Eumenes and Neoptolemus to take their armies to the Hellespont in support of Kleitos and the fleet; then take any ships still in Tarsus south to Aristonous whilst Alketas musters Cilicia's army and waits for me to arrive with the main force. If Alexander's catafalque arrives, tell Arrhidaeus to wait and then it can travel with us as we move north; they won't dare stand against us if we're escorting that.' He turned to Kassandros. 'I want you to stay in Babylon and look after things here whilst I'm away.'

Kassandros scowled. 'As a hostage? It is my father, after all, who you're marching against.'

'Which is why I feel it best that you stay out of it. You are not a hostage; you are the commander of the garrison of Babylon.'

'Which one of my officers will you give the order to kill me if my father beats you?' He nodded at Archon. 'Or will that nonentity of a satrap finally be given a task of some responsibility other than being your shadow?'

'It will never come to that.'

'So it has crossed your mind then?'

Of course it has; you would do exactly the same. 'You are in command of the army in Babylon.'

Kassandros snorted.

Wiping the sweat from his brow, Perdikkas tried to calm his nerves. Ever since the message had arrived from Eumenes, less than an hour previously by messenger relay, stating that Antipatros had concluded a very un-advantageous peace with the Aitolians and had pulled his army back to Pella in preparation for an assault on Asia, Perdikkas had been in a state of nervous excitement. If all his efforts to avoid war were come to naught and his authority as the bearer of Alexander's ring was to be constantly flouted, then so be it: he would call their bluff and they would back down because, ultimately, he had The Great Ring of Macedon. It suited him perfectly: he was not the aggressor, he was faithfully defending Alexander's legacy and the rights of the two kings; he would march against fellow countrymen with a clear conscience and the sure knowledge that right was on his side. Eumenes, Kleitos and Neoptolemus would hold the Hellespont against Antipatros and Krateros and once he arrived with Alexander's catafalque, he would cross it himself. *Let's see if they dare make war on Alexander's corpse. They'll come begging my forgiveness and it will be forthcoming if they pledge their loyalty to me over Alexander's dead body.*

Yes, it was playing into his hands, this foolish move of Antipatros; and why was he doing it anyway? He, Perdikkas, was the old man's son-in-law after all; even if the regent knew about his intriguing with Kleopatra, he had still not married her; indeed, Eumenes had written a few days previously of his disappointment at being unable to change her mind and persuade her to marry him. *But that will change now; when she sees the real possibility of war breaking out she will realise that the only way to prevent it is to marry me and give Macedon and the empire a legitimate king and queen.*

'What shall we do about the two kings and their two growling bitches?' Seleukos asked, using the term that they had all come to use to refer to the royal party since the marriage of Adea, or Queen Eurydike as she was now known, to Philip. The union had instigated a feud between the new queen and Roxanna that had provided amusement for all during the previous couple of months.

Perdikkas winced at the thought of what he would have to do in order to ensure that one did not kill the other during the campaign. 'Well, I can't separate them, leaving one here and taking the other, as they both have to come to Pella with Alexander's corpse; so they had better both come along now so I can keep an eye on them.' *Until such time that I don't need them and then I'll let Roxanna do for her rivals and then... oh, how I'll enjoy that.* 'Are there any other questions?'

'Just two,' Seleukos said. 'Ptolemy? What about Ptolemy?'

'What about him?'

'It occurs to me that if the whole army of Asia is off facing the whole army of Europe then the whole army of Africa is free to do whatever it likes.'

Perdikkas dismissed the notion with a wave of his hand. 'Nonsense. Ptolemy is very happy with Egypt; he's going to do nothing to attract my attention or cause any enmity between him and me. He'll keep out of this. And the other question?'

'What about the Greeks? Might they not take advantage of a Macedonian civil war?'

Perdikkas smiled, triumphant, and held up a letter. 'That would be a good point were it not for the fact that Demades wrote to me from Athens demanding that I depose Antipatros; they're still smarting from the terms he imposed on them. They won't do anything either whilst I'm dealing with him.'

Seleukos nodded and steepled his hands. 'I notice that you keep on saying "I", "me" and "my".'

'I mean, "we", "us" and "our", obviously.'

'Do you? Do you really?'

'Of course I do; now if there is nothing else, gentlemen, then I suggest that we get busy moving north. With luck we'll catch up with the catafalque somewhere near Tarsus.'

'Damascus!' Perdikkas exclaimed, unable to believe his brother's answer to his question as he disembarked the trireme that had speeded him and Seleukos up the coast to Tarsus ahead of the main army. 'Who told Arrhidaeus to take the catafalque to Damascus? It's in completely the wrong direction.'

Alketas looked blank, his eyes darting around the ships docked in the river port as if inspiration could be found in one of them. 'I don't know; I'd assumed that you had.'

Perdikkas grabbed his brother by the collar. 'Assumed! Why would you assume that I told Arrhidaeus to take the catafalque south when we all know that it's going north, back to Macedon? I even told you to expect it in Tarsus, didn't I? So then why, when you heard that it's going south, did you not send troops after it to discover just what the fuck was going on?'

Alketas grabbed Perdikkas' wrist and, squeezing it, pulled it off him. 'Because, Brother, you never tell me anything; you just give me orders, orders, orders and if I arrive in Tarsus to be told that the catafalque was last heard of passing through Damascus, I just think that you've changed your mind again without telling me and so I get on with the orders that you last gave me and muster the army and make sure that Eumenes, Kleitos and Neoptolemus are guarding the Hellespont. And that has all been done but do I hear you thanking me? No, all I hear is whining on about the catafalque going to Damascus.'

'Through Damascus,' Seleukos pointed out. 'That's what you just said, wasn't it? You were told when you arrived here that "the catafalque was last heard of passing through Damascus". Which means that it's still going south.'

Perdikkas caught Seleukos' train of thought. 'How long ago did you hear the news, Alketas?'

'The day I got here, eight days ago.'

'It could be in Hierosolyma by now and then...' Seleukos left the sentence unfinished.

Perdikkas slowly turned to Seleukos, his face growing pallid. 'Does that mean what I think it could mean?'

Seleukos nodded.

Perdikkas almost staggered as if he had been belly-punched. 'Ptolemy! The bastard; he couldn't have.'

'It very much looks like he has. Where else could it be going?'

'But how did he do it?'

Seleukos looked at Perdikkas in surprise. 'Do you think that Arrhidaeus enjoyed the way you treated him? When you gave him the blame for building the catafalque in a room where the doors were too small to get the thing out, do you think that he just let it pass? For the abrupt manner in which you dealt with him, do you think that he just said to himself: "Ah, well, that's just his way; good old Perdikkas."? Do you think that the first agent who approached him with an offer to hijack Alexander's catafalque got a swift rebuttal or do you think that Arrhidaeus embraced the idea because he was so heartily sick of you?'

Perdikkas looked in horror at Seleukos and then Alketas and then back again. 'Are you both blaming me?'

Seleukos shook his head and gave a grim smile. 'It's not about blame; it's just an honest appraisal of the facts. Now, the question is: not why it happened but what are you going to do about it?'

Perdikkas held his head in his hands as if he were in severe pain. *Deprived of Alexander's body I can't cross into Europe without it seeming like an invasion; it all rests on having it and Kleopatra. I shall write to her yet again and ask her to reconsider as well as tell Eumenes to go to see her again and press my suit. Neoptolemus and Kleitos will have to hold the Hellespont together.* 'This must be kept a secret; not a word to anyone, understood?'

Seleukos nodded. 'Of course; if word of this gets out then our cause is considerably weakened.'

'Exactly. We must trust that our forces in the north can hold the Hellespont whilst we take the army south, Peithon and Peucestas can follow; together we will get the catafalque back and, before we head back to Macedon, we'll deal once and for all with Ptolemy.'

PTOLEMY, THE BASTARD

MEMPHIS WAS A city that Ptolemy could only tolerate in the winter months; in all other seasons, it was his opinion that the ancient capital of Egypt was a blisteringly hot place fit only for mad dogs and natives. But he had made an exception this once, bringing his very pleasing new bride, Eurydike, and her delectable cousin, Berenice, south from the cool sea-breezes of partially constructed Alexandria to this baking furnace situated at the base of the Nile Delta. He had also brought Thais, for, despite the pleasures of his new wife, there were certain things that only Thais could do with the enthusiasm that was required for complete satisfaction, especially in this heat. But it was with good reason that he had made the journey, for he was about to witness the arrival of the one thing that would give him a legitimacy that his peers lacked: he was about to take custody of the mummified body of Alexander.

He smiled to himself as he processed along the Sacred Way leading from the heart of the palace past the vividly decorated Temples of Ptah and Amun, fronted by high, seated statues of the gods, towards the High Steps from which he would greet his former king. Peacock-proud in his tall-plumed helm and purple cloak and with beautiful women following him, Ptolemy had a good feeling for his new realm; it suited him perfectly, as he always knew it would. *Give me another couple of years or so and I could think about proclaiming myself Pharaoh. I'd enjoy the expres-*

sion on Perdikkas' face when he hears that; I'll wager that it'll top the look he gave when he heard that my cavalry had intercepted the catafalque in Damascus.

Despite the dignity of his progress he allowed himself a little chuckle at the ease with which he had accomplished the thing. Arrhidaeus had been good to his word – and his, Ptolemy's, gold – and had brought the catafalque south to Damascus where Ptolemy's troops had joined the procession, distributed more gold to the escort, and then guided it through the city and on to the port of Tyros. Here, secured by a huge bribe to Nearchus, the satrap, five ships waited to carry the catafalque, mules and all who wished to join Ptolemy's service, back to Egypt – not a man was left behind.

'You sound pleased with yourself, Husband,' Eurydike said from behind his right shoulder.

'I have cause to be, Eurydike, although I rather think that your sister's husband wouldn't agree.'

'Which one, Phila's or Nicaea's.'

Ptolemy thought for a moment. 'That's a good question; it was Nicaea's to whom I was referring but Krateros might not approve of my actions either, despite Antipatros writing to me to ask if I would be so kind as to make a nuisance of myself on Perdikkas' southern border. Well, I think I can say without any doubt that I've done my father-in-law proud.'

And now I shall do myself proud by making this a national issue; manufacture a crisis and then solve it yourself thus making yourself the hero of the nation and the one destined by Egypt's ghastly gods to rule the kingdom. If I really am Philip's bastard then he would also be proud.

It was to rapturous applause that Ptolemy appeared at the top of the High Steps overlooking the parade-ground, laid out by a long-dead Pharaoh for the exercising of his chariot-based army. Broad and wide it was and full of Macedonian soldiers as well as their native comrades who had been recruited as a part of Alexander's drive to integrate the nations under his sway – Ptolemy had found the programme far advanced upon his arrival and thanked Alexander daily for providing Egypt with such a mighty army. Before him were twenty thousand men, just a third of the entire force available to him and, because of what he had done, he was sure that he would be using them in anger very soon.

Beyond the soldiery were the little people of Egypt, the farmers and the tradesmen who kept the fields tilled and the markets stocked; here they were today, in holiday mood, to witness the return of the greatest man of the age to their land. And they cheered with all their heart the man who had made it happen for Alexander's return was a miracle decreed by the gods themselves: Ptolemy had let it be known that he had divine inspiration. He had circulated the rumour that, in Babylon, he had consulted the oracle of Bel-Marduk, the chief god of the city, as to where the king should be interred; the oracle had replied: 'There is a city in Egypt named Memphis; let him be interred there'. Being a devout people the Egyptians fully endorsed this religious act and considered it to be also the will of all Egypt's gods, not just Bel-Marduk. Ptolemy had merely played the part of the gods' pious servant and he had played it to the full. Now, as the gates to the complex opened, revealing the magnificent catafalque of Alexander, he prepared himself to play the next scene with gusto. The ships that had transported his prize from Tyros, in but three days, lay tied up on the quays lining the banks of the Nile. To the east, shimmering in the heat and back-lit by the midmorning sun, lantern-sailed fishing boats plied their trade up and down the river that was the life-blood of Egypt.

Horns rang and drums sounded; forward the sixty-four mules were goaded, pulling the precious load behind them, into the lane created between the soldiers, leading directly to the bottom of the High Steps which now filled with the priests and priestesses of the various cults in the city. All were in their finery, both male and female: high and low headdresses, long robes or short kilts, some barefooted, some elaborately shod, some heavily made-up and some clean-faced. Whatever their appearance, they all had one thing in common and that was the hymn to Alexander, composed especially for this day, that rose in their throats; a slow dirge of great dignity befitting for the mourning of one so great as he made his return to the city he had liberated from hated Persian rule.

On came the catafalque and more mournful grew the song as the priests' ranks grew, each one adding their vocal to the chant, the women's notes shrilling high and sad, bolstered by the mass of young boys stationed to either side of the High Steps, as the men's deep tones carried the tune that brought tears to the eyes of many and a lump to the throats of all.

As the catafalque came closer to the foot of the High Steps, Ptolemy stepped forward, removing his helmet, and began to descend, symbolically going to greet Alexander, as if summoned, rather than show disrespect and being seen to receive him. The priests and priestesses parted, allowing Ptolemy to progress, one slow step at a time in accordance with the solemnity of the occasion, down to the ground level as the mules came to a halt with the entrance to the temple on wheels directly aligned with the bottom of the steps. Up into the catafalque Ptolemy climbed, his head bowed; the priests and priestesses ceased their hymn and there was a hush throughout the huge crowd.

All waited as Ptolemy spoke to Alexander in the name of Egypt.

Four candles burnt within, each in front of a bronze mirror set at the corners, augmenting the daylight that seeped in through the golden netting hung between gold pillars supporting the roof. Ptolemy squeezed his eyes closed and then slowly reopened them a couple of times to accustom himself to the relative gloom. As his vision cleared, Ptolemy drew an involuntary breath and then looked around the gold-encrusted interior in awe. *Not only have I got Alexander but half the wealth of Babylon as well.* For, although the exterior was constructed in a fortune of gold, the interior was equally as rich and even more refined; studded with precious stones of all hues. Two golden lions, with ivory claws, guarded the coffin with rubies for eyes and diamonds for teeth. Wealth glistered all about him and Ptolemy almost forgot the reason he had entered. It was with a start that he looked down through the opaque covering of the coffin onto the sleeping face of Alexander. *I have to hand it to Perdikkas; he did a good job; he looks beautiful. He really is going to resent this. I'd better mobilise immediately; if I were him I wouldn't waste time preventing Antipatros and Krateros crossing into Asia, plenty of time to deal with them once he's dealt with me.* He looked closer at Alexander's life-like face. *That's what you would do, isn't it, old friend? One lightning campaign and then move against the second front so fast your enemy cannot believe that it's you. Just like when you crushed the Thracians and then arrived at the gates of Thebes so quickly that they thought it was Antipatros, not you.* Ptolemy smiled at the memory as he caressed the glass above Alexander's face with his fingertips. *Why did you die so young and leave such chaos behind you?*

Shaking his head, he pulled himself out of his introspection, back into the present; he had a purpose to this theatre and now was the time to perform. He turned, walked out of the catafalque and, to absolute silence pregnant with anticipation, ascended the High Steps.

'Alexander has come to his chosen resting place and it pleases him,' he announced, without preamble, as he reached the top and spun to face the crowd. Heralds throughout the crowd relayed his words in Greek and Egyptian; the roar of rapture spread like wind-blown fire.

Holding his hands high to embrace them all, Ptolemy celebrated with his people the return of the king. For scores of heartbeats they cried out their joy until Ptolemy felt they were ready for what he had come here to say. Appealing for quiet with as dignified a series of gestures as possible, he soon brought the crowd under control.

'We have done what the gods and Alexander wished; no more, no less,' he declaimed once silence reigned. With an abrupt hand-signal he stilled any cheering of this statement. 'But in doing so we will have incurred the wrath of mere humans; people who now wish ill of Egypt. Therefore, Brothers, we must act to prevent their success. We must act to save Egypt and Alexander; we must preserve the will of the gods and keep his body here. We must take the army north and block the

Nile Delta crossing at Pelusium; in short, we must prevent the invasion of our sacred land of Egypt.'

With a mighty eruption the crowd roared their approval of their new ruler's rhetoric. On they cheered, hands waving as the soldiers punched the air with their shields.

'Religion and nationalism,' Ptolemy said to his women, applauding behind him. 'A heady brew at the best of times but I think I've broached this cask at just the right moment.'

He turned back to the crowd, acknowledging their cheers as it slowly developed into a chant. 'Soter! Soter!' they repeated again and again, bringing a smile to Ptolemy's lips.

'They're calling you their saviour,' Thais said as the word became distinct.

'So, they think I'm their saviour, do they? Ptolemy Soter, that suits me fine. A saviour can do no wrong; when I move Alexander out of this furnace up to his mausoleum in Alexandria and make that city my capital they won't argue with my will.' He looked back to the crowd and, with arms open again, tried to look as pious as he could. *But first we take Perdikkas.*

OLYMPIAS,
THE MOTHER

'**P**ERDIKKAS IS STILL the route to power,' Olympias declared.

'Your route or mine, Mother?' Kleopatra mused, not quite to herself, as a bejewelled pin was inserted into her hair and nimble fingers worked to secure the final tress.

'I heard that.'

'Good, because it's a pertinent question.'

'You'll be the one marrying him, of course.'

'Then surely I'm the one who should be making the decision; not you.'

Dionysus, the child is difficult. 'I'm only offering advice.'

'Biased advice based on your desire to have your vengeance on every noble family in Macedon for any perceived slight they may have dealt you in the past. Now please, Mother, Eumenes is arriving soon and I need to get my thoughts in order.'

'But—'

'No buts!' Kleopatra snapped as her slave-girl held up a silver mirror to her face so as she could examine her coiffure. She patted either side of her head, ensuring that the elaborate construction was secure, gave the briefest of nods and held out her wrists for the application of perfume. 'I need to know what has changed so much that Eumenes is back barely two months after he was last here appealing on that fool Perdikkas' behalf. So be practical and help me, Mother; help *me*, not you; understand.'

'Us.'

Kleopatra rubbed her wrists together and then sniffed them. 'Us, then. But just help, alright. What's changed to make Perdikkas seem so desperate? What do we know?'

'The bitch Cynnane is dead and her whelp is married to the fool; now Adea or Queen Eurydike, as she now styles herself, has more claim to the throne than Perdikkas, except if he's married to you. She's a real threat to him.'

'And, therefore, someone who needs to die should I decide to change my mind.'

'Someone who needs to die whatever you decide and, believe me, I shall work at it.'

'I don't doubt it.' Kleopatra stood to allow slave-girls to attend to the fall of her dress and the positioning of the pearls around her neck. 'So, what else?'

'Antipatros and Krateros have marched for the Hellespont and are probably halfway there by now having secured passage through Thrace from Lysimachus in a deal that remains a secret. That non-entity, Polyperchon, is deputy-regent in Macedon. Polyperchon! Who is he?'

'Yes, yes, but what else?'

Olympias swallowed her anger and then looked blank. 'I don't know. Antigonos is back in Asia and Assander, satrap of Caria, has sided with him. Menander remains here, professing his support for an anti-Perdikkas alliance but doing nothing one way or the other. Perdikkas has surprised everyone by taking his army south towards Damascus and Peithon is just behind him. And that's all the latest news we have.'

Kleopatra did a couple of half-twirls, left and then right, admiring the flow of her dress behind her as it swayed. 'Something has happened, Mother, believe me. Something important, otherwise Perdikkas would have come himself instead of suddenly heading south and asking Eumenes to deputise for him when he should be watching the Hellespont.'

She's right, but I can't put my finger on exactly what it is. But, yes, things are coming to a head and I feel that it's time for me to return to Epirus. 'You look every bit a queen.'

'Thank you, Mother. And now I shall listen to what Eumenes has to say and decide whether I shall make Perdikkas a king.'

'It is the only way to prevent conflict,' Eumenes insisted, looking up from a low stool at Kleopatra, seated on the high-placed satrap's chair. 'Look around the empire, Kleopatra, and you'll see that the world is descending into chaos. A Greek rebellion out east was barely contained; a Greek rebellion in the west put down for the moment but resentment still simmers. Antipatros and Krateros are marching to Asia with Antigonos, Assander and Menander as allies and with Lysimachus' tacit support. Our world, as we know it, will be at war if we don't produce one strong leader, right now. Perdikkas, leading Alexander's catafalque to Macedon, with you by his side, will be seen as that leader; he could claim the crown and the Argead house will still reign in Macedon through you.'

'But would he be strong enough to keep the crown?' Kleopatra asked.

'Antipatros will have to accept his authority, despite the foolish insult that Perdikkas has offered over Nicaea.'

No he doesn't, Olympias thought, standing behind her daughter's seat. 'And say he does and Perdikkas is crowned king, what of Philip the fool and my grandson, Alexander?'

Eumenes considered the question for a few moments. 'I won't pretend that it is not a delicate situation. Perdikkas is well aware of the strength of feeling that surged through the empire when the tragedy happened to Cynnane. But I will be frank: there is no place for Philip in this scenario. Fortunately Roxanna has already made an attempt on his life which Perdikkas has covered up. Should Perdikkas be crowned king then the hapless Philip will, indeed, become a victim to that eastern bitch's potions as will his new young wife. Roxanna will pay the price and your grandson will be an orphan. Who better to adopt him than his aunt and her husband; the king and queen gain an heir who is also Alexander's son. I think that everyone will see that as being the most stable of outcomes.'

'What if I want to have a child myself?' Kleopatra asked. 'And what if that child is a boy? Perdikkas might prefer to see his bloodline inherit.'

Eumenes made a gesture of helplessness. 'What happens so far in the future is out of our hands. It is the now we have to worry about; how we secure the Argead bloodline now.' He paused and considered the two women, his expression grave. 'For all my adult life I have served your family; first Philip who raised me up to a position of influence – even though I wasn't a Macedonian – and then Alexander; my loyalty is to the Argead royal house and to it alone. Nothing and no one will ever change that; I will fight to my last to ensure its survival. This course of action is the way I can see a peaceful solution; one that ensures the continuation of the line with very little blood spilt – just that of a fool, a wild-cat and a vixen. What are they compared to the deaths of thousands of men and an uncertain outcome which may, even, be the complete extinction of your house? Sometimes I think that because I am an outsider, a Greek at that, indeed, a sly little Greek, I can see more clearly what needs to be done: swallow the insult he offered by marrying Nicaea and marry Perdikkas, Kleopatra, and take Alexander to Macedon, inter him there and then claim the crown between you. Think on that, ladies. I have pressed my suit for Perdikkas and have nothing else to add other than this.' He picked up a small walnut-wood box by his feet and opened the lid. 'I have here Alexander's diadem and I will give it to you to give to Perdikkas as a wedding gift should you decide to accept him.'

Olympias' eyes flashed with power-lust at the sight of such a symbol of authority; Kleopatra slowly nodded her head as she recognised what Eumenes was offering.

There was a period of contemplation as the two women considered Eumenes' argument.

Olympias glanced at her daughter. *He's getting to her; the little Greek can be very convincing. My daughter the queen, my grandson the heir-apparent and a fool, an eastern bitch and a vixen out of the way; very neat. Eumenes, I couldn't have asked for more. So where is the catch?*

Kleopatra turned to Olympias. 'If I do this, Mother, you promise me that you'll go immediately to Epirus and have Aeacides' army threaten Macedon's western border, drawing

Polyperchon away so that Antipatros has no hope of reinforcements and nowhere to run to. That should focus his mind and help him submit to us.'

'That was exactly what I was going to do whether you decided to marry Perdikkas or not.'

'I can always trust you to meddle.' Kleopatra stood and walked down to Eumenes, offering him both her hands. 'Very well, Eumenes, I will do it but here are my conditions: firstly, Nicaea remains his wife so that there is no cause for vengeance on Antipatros' or Kassandros' part and they agree to give up Iollas as a surety of their good behaviour.'

Eumenes inclined his head. 'Agreed.'

'Secondly, that I am present at all the negotiations with Antipatros; I think they will be more cordial with a feminine influence.'

'Again, agreed.'

'And, finally, that we do it as soon as possible, before there is a chance that blood is spilt and we pass the point of no return. To that end I suggest that Perdikkas comes to Sardis immediately, with Alexander's catafalque; whatever he's up to in Damascus has no bearing on the important issue of securing peace in the north.'

Eumenes' grip on her hands lessened. 'That might not be so easy. Perdikkas could come, but...' He looked down, evidently uncomfortable.

They are hiding something.

Kleopatra frowned. 'Perdikkas could come but not Alexander's catafalque; is that what you're saying?'

'Yes, but I'm assured that it is a temporary situation.'

And then Olympias saw it. *Ptolemy.* 'Ptolemy! Ptolemy hijacked it.' She knew it to be the truth. *It's what I would have done.*

Kleopatra let go of Eumenes' hands as if they had suddenly become things of burning heat. 'Is that true?'

'You didn't know?'

'We knew something was wrong, but I didn't imagine that it would be that catastrophic. If Ptolemy has Alexander then

351

Perdikkas will never get him back. Without his body we shall be just another contender for the throne with no better claim than the other two. The deal is off.'

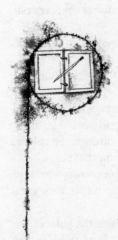

EUMENES, THE SLY

T*HEY DIDN'T KNOW. Gods! How could I be so stupid? Still it's done now and is probably for the best; you can't hide the fact that a catafalque is missing – not even from Peithon. '*He may yet get it back.' *And I may yet grow as tall as Seleukos.*

'Eumenes,' Kleopatra said with a regretful smile, 'Perdikkas has done just about everything wrong since he received Alexander's ring; what makes you think that he's going to outsmart Ptolemy?'

Fuck that, Ptolemy; still, you have to admire him, it was a bold move. I'll wager it was Arrhidaeus and I don't blame him. 'Will you at least agree to reconsider if he does manage to?'

'It would be pointless because by then the war would already have started. Ptolemy would have taken the catafalque back to Egypt by now, by sea seeing as he has no need for it to travel slowly overland so all can witness its progress. So to get it back, Perdikkas has to invade Egypt; you see, it's too late: our world is going to war; Macedonian against Macedonian; it's unavoidable.'

The truth of the statement hit Eumenes; he felt winded. *Gods, she's right.* 'So what will you do?'

'Me? I will wait here and marry whoever comes out as the eventual winner.'

Eumenes' smile was grim. 'Something tells me that you may have a long wait.'

'I think so too. But I'm sorry for you, Eumenes, because I know how hard you tried and I know that your heart was in the right place and your honour remains intact.' She took his hands again, pulled him forward and kissed him on the cheek. 'Try not to get killed.'

'Mistress! Mistress!' A buxom matron bustled in at speed, pushing past a guard on the door.

'You had better have a good reason for such rudeness, Thetima.'

'Antigonos has just forced the north gates with an armed escort demanding that Eumenes be given up to him.'

Eumenes frowned as faint shouts echoed through the palace. 'No one knows I'm here; I was most specific on that point.'

'Menander!' Kleopatra said. 'He has spies everywhere in Sardis. Go out the rear door and then take the western gate, Thetima will show you the way.'

'What about my men, they're waiting outside the palace?'

'It's too late for them; I'll save them if I can but I think they're going to become the first casualties of the war. Mother, go with him; if Antigonos finds you here he might try to gain favour with Antipatros by taking you to him. Get to Ephesus and take our ship back home; that's where you can be of service now. You can drop Eumenes off with Kleitos' fleet in the Hellespont on the way.'

Olympias kissed her daughter.

'Just go, Mother.'

'We may never see each other again.'

'I know, but if you stay and Antigonos gets you then that is almost a certainty.'

With one more kiss, Olympias turned and followed Thetima from the room. Eumenes nodded to Kleopatra, wishing that she had been born a man, and then ran after them, his footsteps echoing around him.

Hoof-beats pounded the track as Eumenes and Olympias galloped down the hill towards the port of Ephesus. Riding as well as any man, Olympias led the way, her white skirts stained with horse sweat and her hair wild and loose after the two-day ride from Sardis.

With grudging respect, Eumenes watched her brow-beat the city watch into letting her and her 'slave' through into the ancient streets beyond, keeping their horses. Through the crowds they pushed, on into the agora, past the great library, with its monolithic frontage painted a dazzling white, and then onto the port.

'To sea, now!' was all that Olympias needed to shout as she and Eumenes ran up the gangway of the ship that had brought her and Kleopatra from Macedon the previous year; with the urgency conveyed by the curtness of her order the triarchos bellowed his crew into action in fluent Nauticalese.

Rowers hastened to their benches, deckhands heaved on sheets, lines were cast and oars were spread. As the sleek vessel eased away from its berth and slipped through the harbour mouth, a dozen horsemen thundered onto the quay where it had been tied up just a few hundred heartbeats before.

'We just made it,' Eumenes said, realising that he was stating the obvious.

'That's because I have this ship always standing by; one never knows when one will have to make a quick exit.' Olympias made an obscene gesture to their erstwhile pursuers as they milled around on the quay shouting and pointing to the escaping ship. 'It'll take them a while to get a vessel ready; we'll have at least a couple of hours on them; we'll head south and then we'll be able to lose them among the islands before turning back north.'

'Will Kleopatra be all right, do you think?'

'Don't worry about her; no one would dare harm Alexander's sister.'

'And yet his mother fled?'

Olympias spat over the rail. 'The bastards wouldn't dare kill me, their balls aren't big enough, but they would incarcerate me if they had the chance; put me somewhere where I couldn't influence the course of events, which would be worse than death for me.'

'And now you plan to make Polyperchon's life difficult in Macedonia which puts us on the same side even though there will be no formal alliance through marriage.'

Olympias studied the Greek for a few moments. 'You know what, Eumenes, I really do believe you. I see no guile in your eyes; you are genuinely fighting for my family which does put us on the same side and for the first time in my life I am actually happy to have an ally whom I can trust without having to bribe or coerce. Although, what we will be able to do to support one another, I don't know, as you will be in the east and I will be in the west.'

Eumenes smiled, surprised at the affection he felt for the woman whose deadly and fearsome reputation went before her. 'Perhaps nothing, perhaps a great deal as neither of us can predict how this war will ebb and flow; but I promise you this, Olympias, I will do all I can to keep your daughter and your grandson safe in the east.'

'I know, but first we have to get you back to the Hellespont.'

Sigeum, at the mouth of the Hellespont, was a part of Hellespontine Phrygia and therefore technically under Krateros' control; but he had yet to cross back to Asia with his army, and so it was that Eumenes had no fears as he was rowed ashore at midday on the third day out from Ephesus. With a hooded travel cloak wrapped around him, he watched the town come closer as the rhythmic dipping of the sweeps lulled him into a feeling of ease for the first time in many a month. Now that he had accepted the inevitability of war, the pressure of trying to prevent it had evaporated; all that remained for him to do was to prosecute the war as ruthlessly as possible and to make sure that the royalists won. *But with what army; therein lies the problem. I have my Kappadokian cavalry, just over three thousand mercenary Greeks, half of whom are peltasts and half hoplites, some Thracian cavalry and infantry and a decent amount of Cretan archers and, apart from the Persians who volunteered to serve with me, very little else other than that chest of money I borrowed from Leonnatus. I need Macedonian infantry; but from where? Neoptolemus is unlikely to give me any of his – he's unlikely to even accept my authority – and yet we have to prevent Antipatros crossing by working together.* He let his fingers trail through the water as he assessed the situation; gradually, his face brightened as the way forward became clear. *Of course: Neoptolemus is the problem; no Neoptolemus, no problem.*

356

And so, with a firm purpose, Eumenes jumped from the skiff and, with one look over his shoulder to Olympias' ship hove-to five hundred paces off the coast, he set off to find the commander of the Greek mercenary garrison in the town to inform him as to whom he was.

It was the first patrol that he came across that alerted Eumenes to the fact that something was amiss; they were Macedonian regulars, not mercenaries. He, Eumenes, had none and Neoptolemus' were further up the coast at Abydus. As his apprehension grew with the sighting of a second patrol, he replaced the hood of his cloak and instead of heading to the garrison headquarters made, instead, for the animal market where, at great expense, he purchased a horse and tack.

The sun was beginning to fall into the west behind him as he climbed a hill above the point, six leagues from Sigeum, which afforded a high view over Abydus and on up the Hellespont, almost to where it opens out into the Propontis. Full of ships it was; and all were sailing from north to south, each one crammed with men. Along the Asian shore a city of tents had arisen; enough to shelter an army.

It took a few moments to digest. *Kleitos, you treacherous bastard; you've taken the fleet over to Antipatros.*

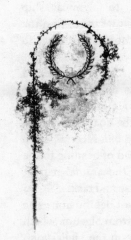

ANTIPATROS,
THE REGENT

'I T'LL TAKE ANOTHER couple of days at the most, sir,' Kleitos informed Antipatros as they and Krateros watched the fleet, sails full-bellied with a northerly wind, progress with the majesty of numbers from Europe to Asia. 'I need four more crossings for the army and then about three for the baggage.'

Why is it always the baggage; all my life I have been hampered by baggage. Could my last campaign at least be free of baggage? But Antipatros knew that could never be so; it would be like wishing to have a woman free of opinions. 'Very good, Kleitos,' he said with a sigh, trying to ignore the man's trident. 'I must thank you for choosing to serve me; your fleet is a great addition to my cause.'

'Our cause,' Krateros reminded him.

'What? Oh yes, our cause, Kleitos; well done.'

'It was never really an issue. Once Perdikkas wrote to me saying that I had to accept the authority of a Greek, my mind was made up. He wrote the same letter to Neoptolemus and you can imagine what that Molossian prick thought of it.'

Antipatros could well do, even though he had not seen the man for more than twelve years and then he had been a mere youth in armour slightly too big for him. He turned to Krateros. 'What's he like, this Neoptolemus?'

'Like most Molossians of their royal house he thinks more of himself than he has a right to; think of a younger, male version of Olympias but without the cunning and you'll get close to the man.'

'As bad as that, eh? Well, I think I should write to Neoptolemus and offer him the opportunity to win some of that glory that he thinks he so obviously deserves.'

'And give Eumenes one more chance to come over,' Krateros suggested, 'let's see if we can do this without too much bloodshed.'

You have done all that honour requires for Perdikkas' cause but now the stage has been reached where we must all decide on the rights and wrongs of the matter. Perdikkas is trying to assume the crown for himself and become the master of all of us. Will you fight to support him in that aim or will you join us to defeat the would-be tyrant and secure the rights of the two kings? Think on this carefully for many lives depend upon it. If you decide to join with me then it will be with a full amnesty and respect for your rank and the chance of glory.

Antipatros put the letter down, brow creased in thought. *I suppose I can legitimately claim to be fighting for the rights of the babe and the fool, although, frankly, I can't see what use either of them will be to the empire; best just to carve it up and get on with it. Gods, I'm too old for all this.* He handed the scroll to his secretary. 'Do two copies, one to be sent to Neoptolemus, the other to Eumenes; bring them to me for signing as soon as they're done; I want them to have read it before our two armies come within sight of each other.'

With the secretary gone about his business Antipatros turned to the new arrival in his camp and poured him a drink. 'Well, Antigonos, old friend; so the sly little Greek gave you and me both the slip.'

Antigonos took the proffered cup. 'So it seems; you have to admire the little bastard: how he got from Sigeum, past all your lads and all the way back to his army – if you can call it that – at Parium, I don't know.'

'Well, he's there now and my scouts tell me that Neoptolemus has fallen back towards him.' He gave a wheezy chuckle. 'Or advanced towards him, perhaps, if my letter does the trick; that will concentrate Eumenes' mind.' He raised his cup in a toast. 'To Neoptolemus and Eumenes both seeing sense.'

It was with deep regret that Antipatros received Eumenes' refusal to abandon Perdikkas' cause.

'The sly little bastard has even offered to be a go-between between Perdikkas and me,' Krateros said after reading his own letter from Eumenes. 'Divide and conquer is, I suppose, his strategy. Well, it won't work with me.'

Antipatros tossed away his reply. 'Let's get this side-show over with and then we can concentrate on the real issue of Perdikkas; stand the men to and prepare to advance.'

Even after sixty years in the field, Antipatros still felt a thrill at the sight of an army arrayed for battle: thick and wide was his formation, with two lines of Macedonian pikemen, both sixteen ranks deep, and nearly half a league across and with each end tipped by dark blocks of cavalry supported by peltasts, it was a mighty force and from it rose clouds of dust and the heavy tread of forty thousand pairs of feet.

Over the undulating terrain it rippled, its frontage ever straight but its body rising and falling with the contours of the hills.

'There they are,' Antipatros said, shielding his eyes against the glare of the sun. 'Less than a league away, I should say.'

'And they're advancing,' Krateros observed. 'Are we really going to do this after all? Phalanx against phalanx? Neoptolemus is facing us with his infantry while Eumenes is hanging back like the cowardly little Greek he is.'

'He may be just waiting to decide the best wing for his Kappadokian cavalry; I've heard rumours that they're good.'

'No match for a phalanx of our proportions. I wonder whether the lads will lift their pikes at the last moment and just turn it into a shoving match or whether they'll have the stomach for taking former comrades' lives?'

Antipatros grimaced. *That's the question that I've been fretting about: if the men will not fight then how can we settle this argument?* 'At least Eumenes isn't a Macedonian and Neoptolemus is Molossian, so it could still just be argued that this isn't really a civil war; that might help to persuade our lads to fight and when their lads realise that it really has come down to it they might well decide to come over to us before any blood is spilt.'

The closer they came together, the clearer the individuals in the ranks became and the similarity in dress unmistakable. Antipatros looked along the line of Neoptolemus' phalanx, identical in every way to his own. As he watched them they halted, their pikes upright, a forest of ash. 'Sound the "Halt"!' he ordered, looking down at the signaller marching alongside his horse. 'We'll give them one more chance to reconsider, now that they've seen the size of our army compared to theirs.'

Horns sounded out each way along the line and officers bellowed their orders; the huge force ground to a halt and silence fell over the field as the armies faced each other, just a thousand paces apart.

'We can't just stand here all day,' Krateros said eventually. 'They are certainly not going to charge us so it's down to us.'

Antipatros put his hand up to his ear. 'Listen!'

There was nothing at first but then, slowly, Antipatros could hear the rumble and axle-creaks of many wheels and the bestial cries of beasts of burden. 'There!' he shouted, pointing to the right wing of Neoptolemus' phalanx. 'There, it's their baggage.' *And there was I thinking that I would never be pleased to see a baggage train.*

On it came at the stately pace of the lowing oxen pulling the wagons loaded with the possessions of the Neoptolemus' army, an army that had been in the field for over ten years now, an army that had reaped the plunder for scores of lands; a fat army and its baggage train reflected that fact.

With a huge crash, as the final component of the baggage cleared Neoptolemus' phalanx, the army turned about and faced its erstwhile ally. A single trumpet call shrilled.

'Well, Krateros, I think we should stand and watch as this is not strictly a Macedonian affair,' Antipatros said, his voice light with relief. 'That was the order to advance; it looks like our new friend, Neoptolemus the Molossian, is going to oblige us by dealing with Eumenes the Greek.'

Eumenes, The Sly

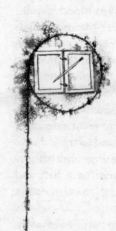

FIRST KLEITOS AND *now that prig,
Neoptolemus; well, fuck them all.*
Eumenes' face was grim and rigid as
he watched Neoptolemus advance his
army towards him. He looked over to the
huge force that Antipatros had brought
over to Asia and gasped. *They're not
moving! They're just going to stand there
and watch, thinking that I stand no chance against Neoptolemus;
well, fuck them all if they think I'm so easy.* 'Parmida!'

'Yes, lord,' the commander of the Kappadokian cavalry said,
kicking his horse forward.

'We're going to beat this arrogant turd.'

'Yes, lord, but how?'

Eumenes' expression was genuinely amused. 'It's so simple:
we haven't got enough infantry to stand against that phalanx so
we withdraw at a good pace and you take your men out onto the
right wing and watch out for me.'

Eumenes looked along his thin line, just three ranks deep,
of mercenary hoplites bolstered by peltasts in the third rank;
it just about covered the width of Neoptolemus' ten-thousand-
strong phalanx advancing down the hill towards him but there
was no feasibility of it holding it. Riding his horse along his
men's frontage he waved his sword in the air as he addressed
them. 'Lads, you don't have to win and you don't have to die
this day. All that is required of you is to fall back in good order,
drawing the phalanx on. Do not let it come into contact, for
that is a contest that we cannot win so we will not offer it. Fall

back slowly and trust on my judgement and victory will be ours without one of your lives being needed to pay for it.'

The cheer he received was not resounding. *But at least it's more than half-hearted. Now, this is the hour that will make me or break me.* He looked up towards the dark horde bearing down on him: hardened-leather cuirasses, bronze helmets crammed over bearded faces with shields emblazoned with the sixteen-point sun-burst of Macedon slung on their left shoulders and over their forearms so that two hands could be used to grip the sixteen-feet-long sarissa that each man wielded, they tramped on with determination in every stride. At one hundred and fifty paces out, his Cretan archers loosed their first volley that clattered down through the forest of pikes, its momentum dulled. One hundred paces out soon became fifty and the sarissas of the first five ranks were brought to bear as the arrow storm continued bringing a scattering of men down but not enough to disrupt the formation.

'Now!' Eumenes shouted when the opposing armies were thirty paces apart. Back went his mercenaries in a step by step, steady retreat, their round hoplon shields before them and their long spears over the shoulders, overarm, ready for a downwards strike. But Eumenes did not expect to see blood on those spear-tips as the full-face-helmed professional warriors kept their line perfect in retreat.

Back and back they fell, drawing the Macedonians on for, as Eumenes had surmised, Neoptolemus wished to show his loyalty to his new masters by giving them a crushing victory; but victory could not be won against troops who refused to fight. And it was in frustration that Neoptolemus urged his men on and it was upon that frustration that Eumenes had pinned his hopes for it was that frustration that would spell defeat for Neoptolemus.

For five hundred paces they retreated and then another five hundred; it was at this point that Eumenes kicked his horse and, with orders to the infantry commander to keep up the valiant retreat, galloped to join Parmida and his Kappadokians. 'Follow me!' he shouted as he sped to their front rank. 'Follow me around the flank.'

With five hundred whooping cavalry troopers pounding behind him, Eumenes experienced again the thrill of the charge that had so exhilarated him in Armenia; but it was not a cavalry or infantry formation that he had his eyes set upon as he wheeled around the flank of the huge phalanx that was being drawn further and further east. It was something much more precious; and as they cleared the rear rank of Neoptolemus' line, Eumenes spied what he sought. 'Their baggage!' he screamed back at his men over the thunder of hooves and seeing their objective undefended that thunder became more frenetic.

Through the lines of stationary wagons and pack-mules, piled high with plunder, the Kappadokians poured, dealing death to those who stood in their path as women screamed and, clutching babes and toddlers, ran for their lives. But Eumenes was not interested in the women for he knew soldiery only too well and when presented with a choice of saving his women or his plunder of the last ten years the average soldier would choose the latter nine times out of ten; a woman was far easier to replace than ten years of plunder.

Round the cavalry swooped, surrounding the baggage-train and forcing it to move off to the north. 'Parmida,' Eumenes called once he could see that the objective had been secured and there was no attempt underway from either Antipatros' army or that of Neoptolemus to reverse the move; indeed, Neoptolemus' phalanx were so focused on the elusive enemy that they had not yet noticed their misfortune. 'You take the baggage and keep it safe with half your men, the other half give to me.' He pointed to the exposed rear of the enemy formation fifteen hundred paces away. 'That is too much of an opportunity to resist.'

It was a smiling Parmida who drove the baggage-train northwards and left Eumenes with two hundred and fifty heavy cavalry. He did not need to give the order to charge for all knew what they would do and all relished the chance of reaping cheap lives.

Spreading out as they charged, into a single line of two hundred and fifty troopers, the Kappadokians formed a frontage of almost eight hundred paces across; down they bore on the softest part of the phalanx, javelins poised in their fists as the wind rippled their beards and pulled at their horses' manes and tails.

It was not until the first of the file-closers went down with javelins juddering in the backs, points exploding through ribcages, that the hapless infantry realised the danger they were in. Through the last two or three ranks the cavalry ploughed, swords slashing down, cleaving open necks and shoulders and taking heads as the defenceless troops scattered before them, sending waves of panic throughout the entire formation. But too much death was not Eumenes' plan for he had more use for this phalanx alive rather than dead. And so, as the first of the panicking infantry dropped their weapons and fell to their knees in submission, he pulled on his mount's reins.

'Fall back! Fall back!'

Disengaging, the Kappadokians left a trail of bloodied corpses and mewling maimed as the entire phalanx fell to its knees and begged mercy.

Now I just have to persuade them that I'm a much better prospect than Neoptolemus and I suddenly have a proper army. Sometimes I surprise even myself.

And so, with his face set in a displeased countenance and his blood-streaked sword waving in the air, Eumenes rode into the middle of ten thousand kneeling men; none threatened him for now they could see their baggage being taken north and they knew that only Eumenes could reunite them with it.

'Soldiers of Macedon!' Eumenes declaimed as he stood in the centre of the kneeling phalanx. 'Soldiers of Macedon, why desert me and then turn upon me? Just an hour ago we stood shoulder to shoulder and then you let yourselves be talked into treachery by Neoptolemus. Neoptolemus couldn't even pay you properly in Armenia; and because of him three or four hundred of your number now lie dead and the entire plunder of your careers is in my hands. Where is Neoptolemus now? Can you see him? No, of course not; he has brought you down but is not prepared to share your plight with you. What sort of a leader is that?' He paused to assess the mood of the men and was rewarded with the sound of aggrieved agreement. 'I make you this offer then: swear to my service and the service of King Philip and King Alexander and you shall have your baggage back and I will undertake to make sure that you are paid regularly and will make up any back pay that is owed to you by Neoptolemus. Follow me and cleanse yourselves of the stain of the treachery that Neoptolemus tricked you into. Swear to me and become my men!' With a flourish he sheathed his sword and leapt from his horse. The cheer that rose was mighty as those closest to him got to their feet, some with tears in their eyes, and vied with one another to touch their saviour, all the while promising their loyalty. Up onto men's shoulders Eumenes was lifted and in triumph was he paraded through his new army as the troops now mingled together celebrating their union.

Eumenes surveyed the rejoicing as he was carried aloft. *That is the best day's work I've done for a while.* He looked back, towards the second army, still stationary, a league away. *And now I have the ability to make things very difficult for Antipatros and Krateros.*

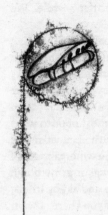

KRATEROS,
THE GENERAL

'I DON'T CALL THAT bad generalship – not in the slightest,' Krateros said as he watched Eumenes' army pull back in the direction of the River Halys some forty leagues distant.

'It was luck,' Neoptolemus insisted. 'He's a secretary not a soldier; a Greek secretary at that.'

'A Greek secretary who just defeated you,' Antipatros pointed out.

Neoptolemus stamped his foot. 'He did not defeat me, he tricked me. He wouldn't engage and kept on withdrawing.'

'And then sent his cavalry around your flank, captured your baggage and then charged you in the rear thus forcing your phalanx to surrender and then go over to him,' Antigonos recounted. 'I call that good generalship and I didn't think that Eumenes had it in him.'

Neoptolemus' face was puce with rage and shame. 'Why didn't any of you come to my aid?'

'You shouldn't have needed any assistance in beating that tiny force,' Krateros said, still watching the withdrawal of Eumenes' army. 'And by the time it became apparent that you did, you were too far away. We wouldn't have got there in time.' He turned to Antipatros. 'Well, one thing is for sure: none of us will ever underestimate the sly little Greek again; he's even doing the clever thing right now and withdrawing inland back to Kappadokia; so, the question is: do we follow him or do we risk having him come up behind us as we move south?'

Antipatros watched the army disappear over a hill, contemplating the problem. 'Neither,' he said after a while. 'We split our forces.'

Krateros raised a questioning eyebrow. 'Really?'

'Yes. I can't afford to get side-tracked chasing Eumenes; you go and get him, Krateros, and then join me heading south.'

'And I'll go too,' Neoptolemus insisted. 'I'm going to kill the little shit.'

'Yes, you certainly have more reason than most of us to want to do that. Get him quickly, Krateros, and then meet me at Issus where we might find out more about the whereabouts of Perdikkas. Antigonos, take half of your Phrygian army down to Tyros and convince Nearchus to see sense and side with us; I'll send word to Kleitos to rendezvous with you there. I want you to take Cyprus; if Perdikkas has any sense he will have sent someone to do the same for him. Whoever has Cyprus controls the coast so make sure it's us, old friend.'

Antigonos grinned at the notion, clapping his hands together and rubbing them. 'I'll enjoy that; and it'll give Demetrios a chance to learn something about joint land and sea operations.'

Antipatros smiled. *I wish I had his endless enthusiasm for warfare.* 'Well, gentlemen, let's get on with it then; the sooner it's done the sooner we can return to our wives and rest.'

Krateros had not been prepared for Eumenes to turn and face him. *I would have thought that he would try and cross the Halys; not let himself be caught with his back against it. Perhaps Neoptolemus was right after all and it was just luck that secured the little Greek's victory.* For ten days Krateros had chased and harried Eumenes over the rough country of the interior of Phrygia, past Ancyra, and now, with the Halys in sight, Eumenes had chosen to turn and fight. It puzzled Krateros as he could see no obvious advantage in the terrain for the Greek nor could he see how Eumenes planned to defeat his twenty thousand infantry and three thousand cavalry with his force of almost half that number. Nevertheless, there he was forming up his army for battle and Krateros was most certainly going to oblige him, deploying his phalanx in the centre with his cavalry split between either side. 'It may not be very imaginative,' he mused to Neoptolemus as they waited for the last units of the phalanx to arrive at their allotted positions, 'but it has always been effective.'

'As soon as they see your hat and know that it's you, they'll refuse to fight anyway,' Neoptolemus assured him.

Krateros took off his kausia and slapped the dust off its leather top. 'Then I'd better make sure that it is visible. It looks to me that he's placing his Kappadokian cavalry on his right wing; I expect that is where he'll be then too.'

Neoptolemus shaded his eyes, watching the deployment. 'In which case I'll take our left flank, if that's alright with you; I'll meet the bastard hand to hand and show him what it means to fight a Molossian.'

'You do that, Neoptolemus; I'm sure that he'll be grateful for the lesson. Remember to use the day's password, Athena and Alexander, to identify friends and foes alike; it could all get rather confusing. I'll see you after it's all over.' *It's a shame that we couldn't come to terms with Eumenes; I always rather liked him.* Krateros replaced his kausia and looked along his line of Companion cavalry, fifteen hundred strong and four ranks deep; bronze helmets and spear-tips glinting in the sun. *The finest cavalry in the world and each one a seasoned killer; with me leading them and supported by a phalanx of veteran pikemen, Eumenes' army won't have the stomach to stand.* With a feeling of deep pride he glanced over to the phalanx whose deployment was nearing completion. *Not long now.*

With banners flying and cloaks billowing and accompanied by the blaring of many horns, both flanks of the enemy formation erupted with an explosion of horsemen; Kappadokians on the right and mixed Paphlagonians and Thracians opposite Krateros. Eumenes' sudden attack with both his cavalry wings, before the infantry was set, came as a complete surprise. *The clever little bastard; he's refusing with his centre, therefore keeping his Macedonian troops from knowing that it's me they're facing. We'll have to fight them after all; it really has come down to it.* Raising his lance in the air, with great regret he ordered the advance.

Forward they started, at first walking before easing their snorting mounts into the trot, careful to keep formation; thighs gripping sweating flanks, left hands pulling on reins steadying their horses, as they hefted their lances in their right, hearts racing as always on the point of charge. With another bellow, Krateros kicked his stallion into a canter as the mixed cavalry facing them, now just a hundred paces distant, pelted towards them, accelerating into a gallop. It was no more than a couple of heartbeats before Krateros let his mount have its head and he felt the full power of the beast surging beneath him. On they flew, two walls of horseflesh on collision course, as javelins hissed through the air into the lance-armed, shieldless cavalry's formation without receiving a reply. But it was at the point of impact that the lance showed its quality and the casualties of the javelin volley were negated. Some thrust overarm and some under but all lashed out with their honed tips before the Thracians and Paphlagonians were in range with their shorter spears and swords. Into throats, eyes and chests, razor-sharp points were thrust with precision timing as they flashed by one another, punching men, screaming, back off the saddle to tumble beneath the hooves of comrades behind. With the reflex of a man old in the ways of war, Krateros yanked his lance back, twisting the blade to release it from ribs, as his steed reared, forelegs scraping the air. Leaning forward across the animal's mane he took the eye of an oncoming horse whose momentum jammed the lance from his grip; an instant later his sword was in his hand, slicing down to open the thigh of a red-bearded Thracian as his cover-men to either side slashed their ways forward. On Krateros pushed, his sword spraying arcs of blood, his mouth snarling with the rage of battle as his stallion snapped and kicked at anything in its way.

And then the press of man and beast became extreme and Krateros could go no further nor could his cover-men quite reach him, desperate as they were, for too far had he strayed. Left and right he slashed, his blade a blur as Thracians closed around him; a spear pierced his hip, his horse reared, a javelin quivering in the beast's blood-matted shoulder, equine screams shrieking from a red-foaming muzzle. A cut across his forearm severed tendons and the reins dropped from his hand; still he fought, ferocious and fearless, reaping death even as it closed in on him. He howled with pain, arching his back, as iron cut through into his kidney; it was then he saw the sword slicing down towards the leather top of his kausia and for the first and last time he wished for a helmet; as his skull was cloven in a flash of white light he wished no more.

EUMENES, THE SLY

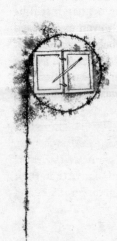

'EUMENES! EUMENES, YOU little shit! Come here.'

Through the heaving melee the cry thundered; *Neoptolemus!* Eumenes, blood covering his right arm, kicked his horse in the direction whence the shout came; crunching a blow down onto a blade thrusting towards him, parrying it, he punched his weighted fist into the owner's face, flattening nasal cartilage, wanting only to finish the thing between himself and Neoptolemus, one way or the other.

But in his heart he knew that he would win for he had been shown how by Alexander himself. He had awoken from a dream in which two Alexanders, each with his own phalanx, had been pitted against each other; one had the support of Demeter and one had Athena as his patron. It had been the Demeter Alexander who had emerged victorious and the goddess had woven her champion a crown from stalks of grain. Learning from spies that Krateros had chosen Athena and Alexander as his password that day had convinced Eumenes that he would win; thus with the password Demeter and Alexander and stalks of grain tied around the wrists of his men, he had launched his attack taking care to place Paphlagonians and Thracians opposite Krateros and telling his army that Neoptolemus' co-commander was a barbarian warlord with the outlandish name of Pigres. By the simple expedient of holding back his Macedonian centre and attacking only with Asian and Thracian troops, he had ensured his army had fought for him for they had not seen Krateros in his kausia.

And so he feared not going hand to hand with the physically stronger Neoptolemus; indeed, he relished the prospect. *If I kill the bastard with my bare hands his miserable life might finally prove to have some purpose to it.* With a backhanded slash, he opened the face of a Macedonian lancer and pushed past him as he fell; there, ahead of Eumenes, was Neoptolemus, teeth bared and bellowing challenges. With no pause for reflection, Eumenes kicked his horse towards him, his hatred rising through him. As a cry of grief went up from Krateros' army as the news spread from its right flank, through the phalanx, that their beloved general was on his way to the Ferryman, Eumenes and Neoptolemus hurtled together.

It was with equal rage that they crashed into each other, swords ringing on the first contact. Pain shot up Eumenes' arm as the force of the blow jolted him back; blades locked, they grabbed at each other with their left hands, fighting for purchase, pulling at one another's helmets as their bodies strained and their horses bit and butted. With tension tautening his muscles to rigid stone, Eumenes heaved back, pulling Neoptolemus towards him and then, passing the point of no return, fell from the saddle with his foe thumping down on top of him, their helms rolling free. The contents of his lungs exploded from him but Eumenes kept his grip on Neoptolemus' tunic and his own sword, as the two men rolled together along the ground; all other duels around them stopped for men on both sides realised that the issue was about to be settled without the need for their lives to be spent.

Teeth ripped into Eumenes' neck; he rammed his knee up into the groin and they loosened their grip. Neoptolemus grunted with searing pain. Squirming, lithe like an eel, Eumenes flipped himself up, stabbing down into the back of Neoptolemus' calf. With a scream, Neoptolemus tried but failed to stand; slashing at Eumenes as he circled, looking for the kill, Neoptolemus remained on his knees, his head a hand-span lower than Eumenes' own, and yet his prowess with the sword remained prodigious. Twice he lunged forward and twice he drew blood to the arms, Eumenes dancing away at the last moment. A third time he came, a rictus snarl of loathing on a muddied and bloodied face, his sword flashing at Eumenes' thigh, slicing it open as Eumenes dived forward, knocking Neoptolemus back to crunch down on top of him, cracking his fist, sword still gripped, into his face and splintering teeth. Inchoate with hatred and blind now to all else, Eumenes crunched his fist down, again and again, spraying blood before focusing on his sword, remembering it. It was almost with a smile of disbelief that he jammed the point under the neck-rim of Neoptolemus' breast-plate as he spluttered and gurgled through a ruined mouth. On he pushed his blade as Neoptolemus convulsed, his eyes wide, staring in shock at Eumenes. 'Killed by a Greek, Neoptolemus; a little Greek at that; what will people say?' A final thrust; Neoptolemus spewed a gobbet of blood and Eumenes collapsed, hyperventilating, onto his stricken body. A silence grew around him as men on both sides stared down at the dead Molossian bested by an ex-secretary; all now realised that the battle was over for there was no cause left to fight.

The Macedonian cavalry pulled back, retreating to the line of their phalanx.

After a brief rest, Eumenes fumbled with the straps of Neoptolemus' cuirass, claiming the victor's right of stripping the armour from the vanquished; he knelt over him, one knee to either side of his chest as his shaking fingers worked the stiff leather. A jerk and a sharp pain, Eumenes stiffened and felt blood spurt on the inside of his thigh. A ghost of a sneer played on Neoptolemus' face, his eyes cracked open and, with a sigh the light faded from them.

Looking down, Eumenes saw his sword remained in the fist of his now-dead adversary, its length bloodied; he put his hands between his legs; the wound to his groin was not deep but it bled. But there was still one thing that he needed to do before he could have it and his other wounds attended to. He had respect to earn.

Weariness flooding through him and fighting the desire to close his eyes and sleep there and then, Eumenes struggled to his feet, pulling the breastplate free and, placing a foot on Neoptolemus' still chest, pulled out his sword. 'Get me my horse and come with me, Barzid. Leave your men here just to make sure that there isn't another assault.' He looked up at the Companion cavalry rallying six or seven hundred paces distant. 'Although I don't think they have the heart for it if Krateros really is dead. We'll go to find out.'

The ride across the frontage of the two phalanxes, facing each other fifteen hundred paces apart, was a sombre affair for all had now heard the rumour that Krateros, the darling of the Macedonian army for many years now, had fallen in a civil conflict. All eyes were on Eumenes as he cantered along the line, gesturing to either side to stay apart. 'We will not attack if you stay where you are.'

A sadness welled up within Eumenes as the reality of civil war stared him in the face as he looked down at the broken head of Krateros; blood and brain oozed from the gash splitting his face in two. His kausia lay in two halves to either side. Eumenes knelt by Krateros' side and took his cold hand in both of his. 'This should never have happened,' he muttered before looking up at Krateros' Companion cavalry. 'Things should never have been allowed to get so far.'

'And yet here he lies dead,' their commander said, bitterness in his voice.

Eumenes placed Krateros' hands across his breast and then stood. 'Then let us ensure that we lose no more of our comrades. Join me; our combined strength will be more than a match for Antipatros. With Perdikkas in the south and us in the north, we can surround him and force him to come to terms. This could be the last battle between Alexander's generals, if you would make it so.'

The commander looked dubious.

Now I shall need all my powers of persuasion. 'What's your name?'

'Xennias.'

'Well, Xennias, here's the deal I'll offer you: I can't stop your cavalry from leaving if they want to, I haven't got the men to chase them. However, if you chose to stay you would be welcome in my ranks; but if you choose to fight then we shall have a bloody day of it and you will come out worse.' He pointed to the huge block of twenty thousand infantry, still unengaged. 'The phalanx, however, I cannot hope to defeat; but I can surround them and prevent them from getting food and water and force them into an unfavourable surrender. Go to them on my behalf, Xennias, and offer them amnesty if they take their oaths to me and then together we shall bury our dead.'

The pyres blazed bright as the sun touched the western hills; more than three hundred of them burnt, but none as tall as the central one for upon it the last remains of Alexander's greatest general were consumed and all who beheld it, and had served with him, wept and wondered how his death had been allowed to come to pass.

'I'll send an honour-guard back to Macedon with his ashes,' Eumenes said to Xennias as the fires died down. 'Let Phila inter him there.'

Xennias wiped the tears from his eyes. 'I would very much like to lead it, sir.'

Eumenes looked sidelong at him. 'Would you? And where would you go afterwards?'

Xennias had no hesitation. 'I shall come back here and serve you; you have shown yourself to be an honourable and brave man; a man worth following, even—'

'For a Greek?'

'That wasn't what I was going to say but yes, even for a Greek.'

'Thank you for the compliment.' Eumenes scratched at the bandages around his thigh; the bleeding at least had stopped. 'And what about them?' he asked, gesturing to Krateros' erstwhile phalanx watching their general burn, having pledged their allegiance to Eumenes. 'Do you think they will still be with me by the time you get back?'

Xennias shook his head. 'I think they will be off, back to Antipatros, the first chance they get.'

'And I'll be too weak to stop them. I'm afraid you're right.' *So, despite winning two victories here in the north, my letter to*

Perdikkas will tell him of the two armies that have slipped past me. He looked back at the pyres. *How many more of those will we see before we can all unite behind the kings and Perdikkas? Or should I, perhaps, reassess my loyalty and wait to see what happens in the south; what if the eventual winner is not Perdikkas?*

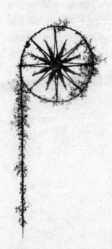

PERDIKKAS,
THE HALF-CHOSEN

PERDIKKAS HELD HIS head in his hands as the eleventh syntagma in a row voted to acquit Ptolemy. *How did I allow myself to be forced into this farce?* But he knew the answer and it lay in the rights of the soldiery of Macedon: the closer they had come to the Pelusiac Nile, the easternmost branch of the Nile Delta, on the Egyptian border, the more they had questioned the necessity of this war. It had been Peithon, newly arrived from the east with his army complete with elephants, who had advised him to hold the assembly and try Ptolemy for rebellion before the combined armies. What he had not counted upon were the spies in his camp who had let Ptolemy, waiting for him across the river, know of the trial and therefore send advocates in his defence; as he had not yet been found guilty there was nothing Perdikkas could do to stop them speaking. Seated on a dais with the two kings, one wriggling in the arms of his mother and the other holding a toy elephant and gazing in drooling rapture at his wife, Perdikkas had struggled with the impulse to summarily execute Ptolemy's defenders.

Speaking with silken, forked-tongues, they had argued that Ptolemy was no more than a pious man doing a religious duty and to try to reverse his deed would be to go against the gods of Egypt, Babylon and Macedon itself.

And then another syntagma followed by another pronounced in Ptolemy's favour and Perdikkas' authority waned as his misery waxed.

'Why let these peasants have an opinion?' Roxanna hissed from behind her veil. 'They don't need tongues to fight, cut them out.'

Perdikkas ignored the comment, wishing that woman would keep to her quarters rather than insisting that she be present every time her son had to preside over a meeting; but there was nothing he could do to stop her as Philip had become so reliant upon Adea, or Queen Eurydike, that he refused to go anywhere without her. Both women had to be treated the same or there would be no peace.

'Let me speak to them,' Adea insisted, 'they have always listened to me.'

'This is an army assembly,' Perdikkas snapped, 'not a washer-woman's convention. I'll never make the mistake of allowing you to address troops again.' *Women! They'll be the first two I deal with once I have Alexander and Kleopatra safe in the north.*

'This is going to cost you a lot of money,' Seleukos said as yet two more units voted to acquit Ptolemy. 'Cash up front and the promise of a larger share of the plunder of the richest land in the world might just get them across the river. Once they're across, well...'

Perdikkas groaned as Polemon, with apology in his voice, announced his men's votes for Ptolemy. *Seleukos is right; money will have to be the answer. It normally is.*

'I don't understand it,' Peithon said, coming up to the dais, his brow furrowed in confusion as the final unit of his army voted for Ptolemy's acquittal. 'I thought they would be loyal to Alexander.'

Perdikkas turned on him, pleased to have an outlet for his anger. 'And I thought that you would be loyal to me and yet what did you do? Tried to steal an army, that's what! And with what in mind, eh? No, Peithon, you are the living proof that no one can be trusted and that no one's loyalty is guaranteed.'

'I'm here, aren't I, which is more than can be said for Peucestas. Helping Eudamus, the satrap of India, with a rebellion in the east, bollocks, I would have heard of it.'

'You probably caused it; now, if you please, I need to think.'

'Money,' Seleukos reminded him in a helpful tone.

'The lads have accepted the offer,' Antigenes informed Perdikkas well after nightfall the following day; his eyes were red and heavy-bagged from lack of sleep having negotiated with his Silver Shields ever since Ptolemy had been acquitted – every unit of the army had subjected their commanders to this less-than-military approach to giving and receiving orders.

'They're the final unit to agree,' Perdikkas said, his relief palpable. 'Now, perhaps, we can get on with the recovery of Alexander's body before turning north to deal with Antipatros.'

'And what makes you think that the army will agree to that?' Seleukos asked.

Perdikkas frowned his non-comprehension.

Seleukos sighed in exasperation. 'You have just set a really dangerous precedent: the army wasn't willing to fight another Macedonian army until you bribed it. The lads are not stupid; if you're successful in Egypt, and they all come away as wealthy men, then why would they want to risk losing their lives against Antipatros' boys unless there was an even bigger financial incentive?'

Perdikkas dismissed the idea with a petulant wave. 'Peithon has brought the elephants; a few of the more vociferous of the bastards getting a trampled death will bring the others into line.'

'Then why didn't you do that this time?'

'Because you said that money was the answer.'

Seleukos shook his head. 'I did and it was the answer; executing the ringleaders this time would have lost you the army and your life. We're playing by different rules now, Perdikkas, this is Macedonian fighting Macedonian; the lads on either side aren't going to be frightened into doing that by having a few hundred of them trampled to death, no, they'll only go against old comrades if the incentive is rich enough – especially if they don't like their general all that much.'

'And what's that supposed to mean?'

'Take it as you will, Perdikkas; I meant it just as a statement of fact.'

I'll give you a statement of fact: you're a dead man if you carry on

380

talking to me like that. 'The men will see things much differently after I've led them on a successful river crossing.'

'But Ptolemy has blocked Attalus from bringing the fleet down and you haven't brought any boats with you; how are we going to cross?'

Perdikkas waved a dismissive hand. 'The Danubus, The Oxus, The Indus and The Hydaspes, I was at each of them with Alexander; I've learnt from the master: speed is the key; speed will get us across the Nile. And we start right now by digging a channel away from the Pelusiac Nile to draw the water off to render it more shallow and then we wade across.'

'It didn't work again this time either,' Docimus, the officer supervising the digging of the channel, reported to Perdikkas.

Perdikkas could barely supress the urge to batter the man senseless, despite his unswerving loyalty since Alexander's death. 'Why not? That's the third day in a row.'

'Because Ptolemy always knows our plans.' Docimus pointed across the Pelusiac Nile. 'He's just across the river and our army is losing deserters to him every night. He always knows where we're going to dig in advance and has archers ready in boats to disrupt the work whilst he has a bypassing channel dug on his side of the river rendering our channel next to useless.'

Perdikkas slammed both his palms down on the desk. 'But I've got six thousand men standing by to make the crossing and secure a bridgehead.'

Docimus shrugged.

'And that's six thousand men who are going to hear of another failure,' Seleukos pointed out. 'Six thousand men who are going to be more disillusioned with your leadership.'

Perdikkas rounded on him. 'Why can't you be more positive?'

'I'm struggling to see anything positive in a situation where Ptolemy knows exactly what we're about to do and thwarts us as, every day, Antipatros draws nearer and will soon push us into the Pelusiac Nile seeing as we can't cross it.'

'So, what do we do?'

Seleukos had no doubts. 'Give up wasting time trying to make the river shallower, find somewhere to force a crossing and lead the army there at night without telling anyone, not even me, your objective.'

Perdikkas thought about the suggestion for a few moments. 'Yes, that's what I'll do; I'll send scouts out.'

'No, Perdikkas, then Ptolemy will find out that you're thinking about a surprise crossing. Call all the scouts in and question them as to the best place they've seen; you make the decision and tell no one and then keep them locked away until we're across.'

For nine hours, since dusk, Perdikkas had led his assault force of six thousand men, including Antigenes and his three thousand Silver Shields and thirty elephants, south-west along the Pelusiac Nile. In silence they went, their kit muffled with rags and all the equipment they would need loaded onto their backs, for Perdikkas was determined upon complete surprise.

Ten leagues they had covered and they were now at his chosen crossing point. The first glimmer of the false dawn played in the east as the ranks of shadowed men lined the river bank ready to make the fording as soon as there was a glimmer of light to see by.

'Speed is the key,' Perdikkas repeated to himself for the hundredth time that night. 'Speed will see us across the river and into the fortress and, once in, then we have our way into Egypt opened.'

And it was with confidence that Perdikkas waited for the deep reds of dawn to hit the high clouds of the desert sky, for he had been told of Kamelonteichos, an abandoned fortress, unused for hundreds of years, which guarded a ford long forgotten.

'But if you know of this place then surely Ptolemy would have heard of it as well?' he had said to the man who told him.

The man had shrugged and said only that the last time he was there, four days previously, the fort still showed no signs of occupation. Perdikkas had the man gagged and thrown in irons immediately and had led his men out of the camp that very night.

The call of awakening wild fowl and the gentle lapping of the great river were all there was to hear in those quiet moments at the birth of a new day and Perdikkas found himself holding his breath for long periods as he waited for the first rays of the sun to reflect down and give form to the water.

It was with no fanfare or volley of sharp orders that the advance was ordered, solely a hand signal from Perdikkas; he stepped into the river as the far bank became visible and there was plainly a silhouette of the fortress. In he went, his feet squelching in the Nile mud as the water came up to his knees, then thighs, groin, waist, chest and, much to Perdikkas' relief, remained level there, just below his shoulders. On he pushed, the current causing little trouble in this slack-water reach on the river; fifty paces, one hundred, and then he was halfway, one hundred and fifty paces from the objective. With heart beating fast, he glanced behind to see Antigenes leading his Silver Shields, dark shadows on the water, some holding ladders above their heads. Forward he forced himself, part swimming with his arms until, breaking the dawn air, a shout rose; he looked to the north and bile rose in his gullet. There, streaming through the pale light, hundreds of mounted men pressed their horses hard and, as he watched, the first of them entered the fortress.

Ptolemy, you bastard; how did you find out?

PTOLEMY,
THE BASTARD

'UP ONTO THE walls!' Ptolemy shouted as he brought his horse to a skidding halt on the smooth fortress-courtyard stone; springing from the saddle, his lance still gripped, he ran to the worn steps leading up to the wall. With men clattering after him, he pounded to the top and, looking out, sighed with relief at the sight of the nearest enemy still a good thirty paces from the western bank of the river. 'I beat you, Perdikkas!' he shouted at his erstwhile comrade. 'Turn round and go back to Babylon; Alexander and Egypt are mine; you'll never take either of them from me. All you'll do is needlessly spend the lives of your men.'

But Perdikkas pressed on, shouting at his men for more speed as, behind them, the elephants began the crossing.

So it has finally come down to this, has it? We're really going to fight each other; what would Alexander have thought? He smiled at the notion. *Of course, it's what he wanted, I'm sure; otherwise he would have made it clear who should succeed him rather than leaving chaos. No one will ever outshine you now.* His smile broke into a chuckle. *But I'll get close, old friend, provided I can keep you here.*

Laughing at the cynicism that the great man had shown in guaranteeing his name for ever being the greatest, Ptolemy walked along the river wall encouraging his men as they formed up and prepared to repel an assault by former comrades, for they all knew the Silver Shields.

The first ladders thwacked against the wall, almost as one. Poised with his lance, Ptolemy waited as the lead men raced up. With naught but lance-armed cavalry manning the defences, there would be no arrows nor javelins beating down upon the attackers, the infantry were at least an hour behind; such had been Ptolemy's concern when his spies had crossed back over the river reporting that Perdikkas was moving south under cover of darkness with a small force of infantry, some with ladders, supported by elephants. The fortress at Kamelonteichos was the obvious target for such an expedition and Ptolemy had raced through the night with his cavalry to prevent Perdikkas taking it for he was under no illusions: if Perdikkas were to be successful then he would be free to march on Memphis and the outcome of that was uncertain, to say the least.

A thrust down onto the upraised shield of the first Silver Shield on the ladder was Ptolemy's opening blow in this war of Macedonian against Macedonian. Cracking down again and again with his lance-tip onto the sixteen-point sun-blazon of Macedon engraved in the metal, he dislodged the shield and, for an instant, the old campaigner's neck was exposed; an instant was all Ptolemy needed to slice his lance between cuirass and collar-bone. With a shriek the grey-bearded veteran of a score of battles and countless skirmishes arched back as Ptolemy twisted the blade; for a moment their eyes met and surprised recognition registered in both, for Ptolemy knew the man well and had shared many a wineskin with him and his comrades around campfires all over the empire that was now turning in upon itself. Ptolemy pulled his lance free and pushed the image of the dying man tumbling back into the press of men at the base of the wall from his mind; now that this war had started there would be no going back. There would be no room for sentiment although there would be much reason for it: in order to win he would be forced to kill many former comrades, some he had known personally, some not – indeed, he may even be called upon to kill friends. The thought gave him no joy as he skewered his lance into the next man on the ladder. *But if this is what it takes to secure my position in Egypt, then so be it. It was*

Perdikkas who delivered the first blow, not me; that man's death is
on his conscience, not mine.

On they came, wading out of the gloom-cloaked Nile, soaked
and muddied, dark shadows flooding forward to the assault,
flowing across the river's edge and coursing up the ladders in
the face of determined, stiff resistance. Relentless was the lance-
work of Ptolemy's comrades; shoulder to shoulder along the
two hundred paces of wall, they thrust down and down again,
spilling men from ladders with blood gushing black in the grey
light as reinforcements issued from the river running behind
them. Wave after wave of them poured into the attack, running
over the bodies of their comrades but the defenders held and the
tide was turned.

But it was the bestial trumpeting blaring out from the
obscured distance, striking fear into Ptolemy's heart, that told
of the real reason for the easing of the infantry assault; out of the
shadows they lumbered, their dark skin glinting with moisture
as the light strengthened, shades resolving into beasts with huge
ears flapping and long proboscises raised and shrieking as they
had been taught by the Indian mahouts astride their necks. On
the back of each was mounted a Macedonian with a monstrous
pike, twenty feet in length, ankles entwined, for security, in a
rope around the belly of the beast. A line they formed whilst
crossing the ground to the fortress; a wall of elephants, each
wearing bronze protection on their heads, war-beasts in their
prime, closing in on the ancient stone of Kamelonteichos,
untended for centuries, crumbling and pitted. And it was
obvious what Perdikkas intended, for elephants cannot jump
walls nor climb ladders.

'Their eyes, their eyes!' Ptolemy yelled as, trumpeting with
ear-splitting shrills, the organic battering-rams advanced.

Before the cavalry lances of the defenders could be brought
to bear, the extended pikes of the riders thrust up and into their
faces. Men ducked and dodged as the honed tips punched and
cut, opening cheeks and necks of men unable to defend themselves. A few cast their lances like spears, losing them to little
avail, for none struck a mahout or rider, glancing instead off

the rough hide of the brutes. Fast and lethal were the pikemen so that none were able to strike an elephant before, as one, with heads of bronze, all thirty butted the ancient river-wall of Kamelonteichos.

And it shook as if struck by a thunderbolt from Zeus himself.

Back a few paces the mahouts brought their charges, back in order to go forward once more; and again the walls trembled so that Ptolemy rocked on his feet as a pike tip hissed past his face. Back the monsters went a further time, as the infantry, waiting behind, cheered their endeavours, and Ptolemy knew the ancient structure could take not much more of this modern warfare as cracks appeared underfoot.

If Perdikkas takes the fort and gets his army across then my position could well become precarious; and if these beasts carry on like this then that could well happen. And so, with little to lose, Ptolemy cracked aside a darting pike with his forearm and grabbed it; yanking it towards him, in a sudden, brutal motion, he ripped free of the grasp of its wielder. With fleet hands, one over the other, Ptolemy pulled the pike up and then spun it over, reversing it. Down he thrust it into the eye of one of the great beasts; maddened with pain it reared up, trumpeting to the skies, dislodging the disarmed rider to trample him beneath stamping feet, as the mahout clung on with grim determination. Changing his angle, Ptolemy stabbed again; this time his weapon glanced off the bronze head-protection of the thrashing beast as the rest of the force crunched once more into the fast-disintegrating wall. Again the ground shook and the air filled with more cheering from the watching Silver Shields and again Ptolemy jabbed his pike; deep into the second eye it gouged, blinding the brute; in its terror it turned right and crashed into the animal next to it, spooking it. Rebounding and then turning, as its mahout scrabbled with one hand in a pouch at his waist, it bolted in the opposite direction, hitting the beast to the left of it, causing it to panic as the sightless elephant ricocheted away back in the opposite direction. Bestial terror spread and cohesion was lost as beast after beast was infected with the madness of the blinded animal. Leaning down over the wall the defenders worked their shorter lances without fear of reprisal from the pikemen, struggling to stay mounted and unable to wield their weapons. Down they stabbed, wounding the brutes and goading them into rampage; they turned and back towards the watching Silver Shields they tore, forcing them to flee to the relative safety of the Nile but not before some fell beneath trampling feet, bursting bellies and heads as if no more than overripe grapes.

Away went the army of Perdikkas, back across the Nile as the elephants splashed in the shallows, dislodging silt and turning the waters a thicker, darker brown. As they calmed, the blinded beast's mahout finally managed to extract the spike and mallet from his pouch; holding it firm at the back of the head he struck with all his might, forcing the iron into the brain as a final act of mercy; tears in his eyes for the beast he had spent half his life with. Down it crashed, crushing a wounded man writhing on the ground; the mahout jumped free and, sprinting, joined the rest of the army in retreat from the failed river crossing.

It was a sombre task collecting the corpses of former comrades and Ptolemy ensured that it was done with the respect and solemnity it deserved. The pyres were built on the bank of the Nile and Perdikkas' army watched from across the river as they were lit. With smoke spiralling to a cloudless, desert sky, the Silver Shield raised their swords and saluted their dead comrades and the men who had shown them the proper respect in death.

Ptolemy watched, with a smile playing upon his lips, as Perdikkas tried to get the Silver Shields to move off, his bellows blowing across the water; but they would not go until the last pyre had burnt out and then, with a final salute, they trudged east, away from the river. *What now, my one-time friend? Are you going to waste more lives or are you going to leave me alone, Perdikkas? Or should I just push matters towards a permanent solution?* He turned to Arrhidaeus, next to him. 'I think it's time to open negotiations with Perdikkas' officers.'

PERDIKKAS,
THE HALF-CHOSEN

DEFEAT WAS A dish that Perdikkas had never tasted and bitter it was; more bitter than he had ever imagined. None of his men or officers could meet his eye as they made their weary way east, out of sight of Ptolemy. Having sent the rest of the army, accompanying the two kings, to meet them, Perdikkas ordered a camp set up a league from the river. It was with mounting shame that he dismissed the men and called his officers to his tent for a briefing. Never had he thought it possible that he would suffer a reverse, never; but never before had he fought Macedonians.

The truth of the matter was expressed by Seleukos: 'When Macedonian fights Macedonian there will always be a Macedonian loser and today that was you; the trick is not to get used to it.'

'Then what do I do? If I turn back now, straight after a defeat, then I'm no more than a beaten general with precious little authority.'

'You're already that. And you can't even contemplate turning back; the only possible way to survive this is to go forward and claim a victory, claim Memphis and defeat Ptolemy.'

'Yes, but how?'

'Quickly.'

'That is not helpful.'

But Perdikkas was surprised by the speed with which the solution presented itself for, knowing that retreat was suicide, he had no option but to press on that night up the Pelusiac Nile towards Memphis. *It's what Alexander would've done; speed, always speed. Ptolemy won't expect me to go south. Let's see what the new dawn brings me.*

'It's an island,' Peithon confirmed as the rising sun revealed a new stretch of the river, 'right in the middle of the channel, large enough for the whole army to camp on.'

Seleukos threw a stick out into the river and watched it float away, gaining speed as it drifted further from the bank. 'The current is much stronger here than downstream, but we can cross in two stages.'

Perdikkas looked to the north. 'There's no sign of Ptolemy, we've given him the slip; let's do this as quickly as possible. Antigenes, take your lads over first and check for a good crossing on the other side. I'll follow with the rest of the army.'

In they went, the first units of the Silver Shields, in up to their necks. Bracing themselves against the swifter current – for it was but a league to where the Nile had branched into its narrower delta streams, increasing the pressure of the flow – the veterans of many a river crossing struggled to reach the island, a few being carried away, their equipment taking them to the bottom.

'Send the elephants across to form a barrier a hundred paces upstream,' Perdikkas ordered Seleukos as the rest of the army formed into column, 'it'll stem the current whilst Peithon and I lead the rest over.'

Seleukos looked dubious. 'Is that wise? They're heavy beasts; they're not horses.'

'Just do it!'

Seleukos shrugged and sauntered away, in no hurry to obey the order.

Taking his place at the head of the column, Perdikkas strode into the river, keeping his gaze to the north. *Still no sign of Ptolemy; we're really going to do this.*

More units followed as the Silver Shields completed the first stage of the crossing to the island. Just to the south, the elephants waded in, spanning the river to the island and breaking the pace of the current. But big beasts cause big effects and it was as Perdikkas was approaching halfway that the size of the elephant effect became clear: in the middle of the river, where the deepest point of the ford was neck-high, there came a swirling of dark-brown, silt-laden water; it churned through the lines of men and then the screaming started. Under they went to burst back up, gasping for air as the silt, dislodged by the elephants, washed away downstream, scraping the river bottom as it flowed, loosening the deposited mud and gouging it away so that Perdikkas felt his foot sink into what had been a solid bed and then lose contact with the bottom completely; what had been neck-deep now became a deadly depth. Panic spread as all those with their heads still above the water either pushed on to the island or turned to return to the bank; but the silt weighed heavy in the river and the force of the current increased.

Down Perdikkas was dragged, the heavy water tugging at his clothes; he struck out with his arms and pulled himself back to the surface, breaking it with huge gasps, spluttering the water from his mouth. Seeing the crossing now in chaos, he turned, grim with despair, and pushed for the shore, fighting the current that had just recently been manageable and now had become so forceful that even a footing on the riverbed was no guarantee of survival. Scores and then hundreds were swept away, arms flailing as they shrieked and gasped for breath. Their comrades on the bank and on the island looked on in horror for their distress had attracted a new threat, a more bitter death, as splashing and slithering with monstrous ease through churning waters came the crocodiles of the Nile intent on feeding upon the bounty she now bestowed.

Past a thrashing beast Perdikkas swam, grateful that it was not him being dragged under by ripping teeth to be drowned and eaten, not necessarily in that order, as the brown water thickened with blood. Panic rose within him, repressing the despair, as more of the knobbled-backed beasts appeared, mouths yawning open then snapping shut and tails whipping them through the water. Pulling hard with his arms, Perdikkas soon found the shallower reaches and, gaining a footing, kicked himself forward, scrambling for the bank. Strong hands hauled him from the river and he collapsed, flat on the ground, breathing hard and letting his panic subside; and as it did, so did the despair return, for, in front of all, he had once again blundered.

'There's Ptolemy,' Peithon said, sitting down next to Perdikkas. 'He's arrived just in time to see you waste the lives of your men. And, frankly, after what you did to me, I haven't any sympathy for you.'

Perdikkas looked up to see Peithon sneering at him. He opened his mouth to reply and then shut it, realising that there was no defence that would acquit him of being profligate with his men, the evidence was all around him, screaming as limbs were chewed away, struggling in swirling water or just floating, face down, the worst now over.

'Still, at least Ptolemy has some respect,' Peithon observed, 'he's already sending parties to collect the dead washed up on his shore.'

Bright did the pyres burn, well into the evening, for there was much fuel to feed them and their stench tormented Perdikkas as he sat, drinking in his tent alone, for he had summoned none of his officers such was his humiliation.

'I demand to be allowed in!' Roxanna shrieked at the guards outside. 'How dare you impede a queen?'

'You're no queen,' Adea shouted. 'I'm the queen and I demand to see Perdikkas; I demand that we return to civilization; the king is being made to look stupid with defeat after defeat.'

'That fool is no king,' Roxanna hissed, 'and you are no queen. I demand to be let in.'

'No one is to be admitted,' the guard captain said, for such were his orders as Perdikkas could face no one.

'Then I stay here until he comes out.'

'And I stay too!'

Perdikkas' head slumped forward into his hands, a ghost of a smile on his lips. *How ironic that such a disaster should unite the two bitterest enemies. Let them wait.* He downed his cup and then poured it brim-full, contemplating Alexander's ring on his forefinger as he did so. *Curse you for giving it to me, Alexander; curse you for not naming me; curse you for cursing me with the epithet 'the Half-chosen'.*

Seleukos,
The Bull-Elephant

'HUNDREDS, MAYBE EVEN thousands, of good lads, Macedonian lads, drowned and eaten; that's a death that I would only wish on the worst of my enemies.' Seleukos gazed into the glow of the oil-lamp as its flame fluttered in the gentle breeze blowing through the open flaps of his tent; he shook his head in disbelief and then looked at his two companions. 'And for what? Perdikkas' ambition? An ambition that far outpaces his ability; I warned him the elephants were too heavy, but did he listen? Does he ever listen?' He bunched his fist and slammed it down on the camp table; the oil-lamp and half-full jug of wine flew into the air as the fragile construction splintered beneath the weight of the blow. 'We're all at fault here for letting it get this far so that brother fights brother; can we afford to let it go further?' *But I'm not going to be the first person to suggest what we must do; let Antigenes or Peithon do that. I will not be the one who suggests murder.* Seleukos studied his two companions as they sat, heads bowed, staring at the contents of their cups; from outside came raised voices in heated argument. *From the sounds of it the lads are feeling the same way as I do; they should be easy to convince. And then...well then Babylon will be within my grasp. I'm so close now; just a little more patience.*

And patience was what Seleukos had been practising ever since Alexander's death; for, although he was not one of his seven bodyguards, he was a man of military prowess as well as mental and physical consequence. In short, he knew that as those over him fell then he would surely rise. Leonnatus had gone and now Perdikkas was about to join him; the gaps above him were opening.

'Over four hundred of my Silver Shields died today,' Antigenes said, his voice laden with gloom, his cup almost empty. 'Four hundred! They've stood against Greeks, Persians, Bactrians, Sogdians, Indians, the lot; and yet they died either at the hands of fellow Macedonians or through the incompetence of their commander.'

Time for a little false caution. 'Perdikkas still retains the authority of the ring, even though he himself is no Alexander.'

'As he proved by taking elephants into the river against your advice,' Antigenes said, not taking his eyes off the cup in his hands. 'But a ring doesn't make a man great nor does it give him authority; it's making quick decisions that men trust because they believe in his grasp of strategy and tactics that give him that, not jewellery; there's a big difference.'

'And where were the boats?' Peithon thundered. 'Boats are what you need to cross a river, not elephants.'

Well, if that has penetrated even Peithon's mind then it must really be obvious to all; one more defence of Perdikkas and then I'll let myself be convinced. 'Ptolemy blockaded the river so Attalus couldn't bring the fleet through to us.'

'But we knew we had to cross the Nile,' Antigenes stressed, 'and yet we brought no small boats with us. Would the supreme tactician, Alexander, have made that mistake?'

Seleukos smiled with regret. 'If he had have done he would have made rafts like we did crossing the Hydaspes.'

'And that is the difference,' Peithon growled before draining his cup.

Good, it seems that we have established that; now to get them to come up with the solution.

'Gentlemen.'

Seleukos turned his head to the entrance, whence the voice came; a figure stood in silhouette. 'Arrhidaeus?'

'Yes, Seleukos; I've come with a message from Ptolemy.'

Arrhidaeus sat back once he had finished talking and a silence fell within the tent as the significance of the message was contemplated; outside the mounting anger of a defeated force grew.

Seleukos glanced at Antigenes and Peithon, neither would meet his eye. *It would seem that it's down to me to reply.* 'So Ptolemy will keep Alexander's body and in return for that he will give Perdikkas absolutely nothing; is that what you're saying, Arrhidaeus?'

Arrhidaeus inclined his head. 'Perdikkas is in no position to demand anything from Ptolemy; Ptolemy is showing restraint by not calling upon his fleet to transport his army over the river and forcing a pitch-battle, Macedonian against Macedonian. He wishes me to say that today he killed an old comrade with whom he had shared many a wineskin by the fire and he does not wish to repeat the experience. It was not him that instigated the fighting; he was just doing the gods' work by bringing Alexander to Egypt. Perdikkas' attack on him was an act of impiety.'

Seleukos choked back a laugh. 'Let's skip the religious nonsense, Arrhidaeus. We all know that Ptolemy's dream was very convenient for him politically; just as Perdikkas taking Alexander back to Macedon would have been for him. So, in pragmatic terms, what we're saying is that Ptolemy has Alexander and no one can take him back so let us stop the fighting before we reach a point of no return and all go back to our satrapies and leave each other in peace. Is that it?'

'Very nicely put; yes.'

And the only sensible thing to do; with one little refinement: we won't all be going back. 'And if Perdikkas won't agree to this when we put it to him?'

'Then Perdikkas is the only obstacle to peace.'

Finally, it's been said. 'And Ptolemy would sanction the removal of that obstacle?'

'Ptolemy wishes only for no more Macedonian blood to be spilled; to that end he's waiting across the river for my signal to sail across and talk peace with whoever is in command.' The eyebrow he raised was arched and knowing.

Seleukos looked again at his two comrades; this time they both met his eye and gave a brief nod. He turned back to Arrhidaeus. 'Very well. Signal Ptolemy to come over; I guarantee his safety. When he arrives he will be able to talk peace.'

'Will he be able to address the army?'

Seleukos glanced again at Peithon and Antigenes; neither showed any objection. 'I don't see why not.'

'Good.' Arrhidaeus rose. 'I'm pleased we have an understanding, gentlemen; Ptolemy will be here very soon.' With a curt nod of the head he strode from the tent.

'I think we can all see where our duty lies,' Seleukos said after a few moments of reflection; he patted his sword and got to his feet. 'We'd best go and see if Perdikkas understands his.'

It was through an atmosphere bordering on rage that they walked towards Perdikkas' tent at the centre of the camp and it took all the efforts of their escort to keep them moving such was the men's desire to bring their grievances to their commanders.

'This will be resolved very soon,' Seleukos called as they walked. 'Let us pass; we are going to speak to Perdikkas on your behalf.'

The crowd thickened the closer they got to Perdikkas' tent; guards struggled to keep a perimeter, forming a wall with their shields. Shrill voices pierced the raucous, masculine hubbub; at the front of the crowd clamouring for admission to Perdikkas' tent, Adea and Roxanne railed at the guards. *United in a loss of dignity; that's a true indication of just how bad things have got in the Royal Army, if those two see common cause.*

'Seleukos! We need to talk.'

Seleukos turned to see Kassandros pushing through the crowd to him; he signalled to his escort to let him through. 'So, you found Babylon too hot at this time of year, did you?'

Kassandros smiled, with all the charm of a rabid dog, and looked up at him. 'I slipped away as soon as I could; if Perdikkas thought that I would stay there waiting for the assassin's knife then he is sadly deluded.'

'That, I think, is something that we can all agree upon. So what are you doing here?'

'I've come from my father; he suggests that we all sit down around the table and talk.'

'Ptolemy has just suggested the same thing.'

'Then hopefully Perdikkas will see sense. Neoptolemus has joined our forces and he and Krateros have gone east to deal with Eumenes. My father is heading south and Krateros will follow once Eumenes has been defeated.'

'Is there any news as to how that campaign is going?'

Kassandros shrugged. 'There was nothing when I left four days ago; but it'll only be a matter of time before Krateros corners the Greek and either persuades him to surrender or crushes him; his army is twice the size.'

'And he is Krateros,' Seleukos added. 'Stay here; whoever comes out of that tent will be willing to sit down with your father and Ptolemy.'

'He suggests the Royal Hunting Parks known as The Three Paradises in the hills north of Tyros; the cool breezes might do us all good.'

Seleukos squeezed Kassandros' shoulder. 'I pray that they will.' He turned and walked towards the officer commanding the guard.

'No one is to be admitted,' the man said with finality.

'You will make an exception for us. We don't want any more unnecessary deaths today, do we?'

The man looked down at Seleukos' hand gripping the hilt of his sword and easing it out a thumb's breadth. 'But my orders—'

'Are inappropriate; the army's on the verge of mutiny and the commander-in-chief has locked himself away and refuses to speak to anyone. Stand aside.'

With another glance down to Seleukos' sword hand and then up at the resolute face towering above him, the man stepped aside; Seleukos pushed the tent flaps aside.

PERDIKKAS,
THE HALF-CHOSEN

FEMALE SHRIEKS JERKED Perdikkas back from introspection; the tent flaps were pushed aside.

Perdikkas stood as Seleukos, Peithon and Antigenes barged past the guards who scrambled to stop Roxanna and Adea from following them in. 'I said I didn't want to be disturbed.'

Seleukos' smile did not reach his eyes. 'Yes, another inappropriate order; you must be getting fed up with issuing them.'

'What do you want?'

'Kassandros has just arrived in the camp.'

'Kassandros, but he's—'

'Supposed to be in Babylon, I know. But he ran to his father as soon as you were out of the way, as you surely knew he would.'

Perdikkas frowned, confused.

'Oh, so you thought he would do as you said and hold himself as a hostage in Babylon. And I thought that you were being clever by giving him a chance to escape and not having another reason for war between you and Antipatros. Silly me, when you were just being your normal stupid self. Anyway, he's here on behalf of his father who suggests that we should sit down and talk before things get even worse.'

Perdikkas squared up to his second-in-command. 'Antipatros has got Eumenes and Neoptolemus at his back; he can't come south and therefore is in no position to dictate terms.'

'Wrong. Neoptolemus has defected, just like Kleitos did and has now joined Krateros to crush Eumenes. Antipatros is free to come south and he and Ptolemy could crush us between them. Is that what you want? More Macedonian blood on your hands?'

Perdikkas looked from Seleukos to Antigenes to Peithon, dumbstruck, touching the ring on his forefinger. *They really do believe that I am responsible for all this; me, the holder of Alexander's ring. It's those who disobeyed me that have brought this about, not me.*

'It's over, Perdikkas!' Seleukos snapped. 'Ptolemy has also sent a message and is now crossing the river in a boat!' He took a couple of steps forward. 'Fancy that, Perdikkas, a boat; why didn't we bring boats with us? Anyway, he wants to talk too.'

'What about? I've nothing to say to him until he gives me back Alexander's body.'

'He's not going to give you the body and you won't be able to take it; forget Alexander; his resting place will always be in Egypt.'

The rage welled up inside of Perdikkas as he saw all that he had sought to achieve being wrenched away from him. 'I will have his body! There will be no talking until his body is returned to me. To *me*! I am his heir! I should bury—' He stopped abruptly as he realised what he was saying.

Seleukos shook his head, a half-smile twitching his lips. 'No, you're not, Perdikkas; none of us are and that is what the whole trouble is. Alexander's heirs are a fool and a babe and I almost think that it is what he wanted. Now, Antipatros has offered talks at The Three Paradises. Ptolemy is arriving and Kassandros is here; let's travel north together and work out a peace.'

I will not be summoned. 'They will come to me; if they want to talk peace it is in my camp and the backdrop will be Alexander's catafalque. Those are my terms.'

Antigenes pushed Seleukos aside. 'We thought that would be your attitude. Well, I'm afraid it's evidently too late for you to learn now.'

The punch to his ribs took Perdikkas by surprise; his eyes widened as they looked down to see a dagger plunged into his chest, blood blooming on his tunic. He looked up into Antigenes' eyes as Peithon and then Seleukos both struck; one blow each.

'You must have known that it would come to this,' Seleukos said, his voice almost gentle. 'You were never meant for politics but you just couldn't bring yourself to admit it; think about that as you bleed out.'

Perdikkas' eyes swam as Seleukos, Peithon and Antigenes turned and left; he swayed and felt his legs growing weak. Feeling blood rising in his gorge, he crumpled to his knees; his head tilted up; its momentum collapsed him onto his back.

His eyes clouded over as his slowing heart thumped in his ears and a peace enveloped him such that he had not felt since Alexander had given him the burden that had proved to be his bane.

Soft footsteps passed close to his head; he tried to look but all was white and the distance between him and his thought was lengthening. It was a small tug on his forefinger but, despite the serenity into which he was falling, he twitched a smile for he knew its meaning: he had lost the ring; another had taken up the burden of Alexander's Legacy.

Author's Note
and Acknowledgements

The main problem we have with the wars of the Diadochi, the Successors of Alexander, is the chronology; there are two timelines: the so-called High and the Low. They differ from one another significantly: the High places Perdikkas' death in 321 BC and the Low puts it in 320 which has serious knock-on effects throughout the history. In this novel I have favoured the High chronology; however, I have tried not to make too much of an issue about the passage of time as I tell the story of these momentous years.

Almost every event that occurs in the novel is attested to by one of the few primary sources; indeed, there is very little reason to make things up as it would be hard to outdo the facts: the trampling of Meleagros' supporters or Roxanna's poisoning of her two rivals and disposing of the bodies down a well or Eumenes' frantic hand-to-hand struggle with Neoptolemus are hard to improve on. I did, however, add a few things to the reality: for example, I had Alexander's catafalque constructed in a room whose doors were too small to get it out in order to give Arrhidaeus more of a motive for betraying Perdikkas; Iollas breaking the siege of Lamia and his death at the hands of Eumenes' men are also my fiction as is Roxanna's poisoning of Philip and her being forced to administer the antidote, but the examples are few and far between.

Likewise, nearly all of the characters existed – even Archias The Exile-Hunter and he really had been a tragic actor! Babrak the merchant and Antipatros' wife, Hyperia, are the most prominent fictional characters – although Antipatros obviously had a wife, with whom he was very active as his youngest son, Triparadeisus, was born just a year or so before his death, we just do not know her name.

As the primary sources are, in the main, few and fragmentary I have relied heavily on, and am indebted to modern histories of the time and biographies: *Ghost on the Throne* by James Romm and *Dividing the Spoils* by Robin Waterfield were my combined bible and highly recommended reads; Jeff Champion's biography of Antigonos the One-Eyed, John Grainger's *Rise of the Seleukid Empire* and the *Wars of Alexander's Successors* by Bob Bennett and Mike Roberts are also excellent explorations of the time and my thanks go to them all.

My thanks also go to Will Atkinson and Sara O'Keeffe at Atlantic Books for taking up the new series and to my agent, Ian Drury, for persuading them to buy it. I would also like to thank Susannah Hamilton, Poppy Mostyn-Owen and everyone at Atlantic/Corvus for all the work that goes into publishing a book.

Once again, my love and thanks to my wife, Anja, for putting up with me being distracted for the six months that it took to write this and for her constant support.

And finally my thanks to you, Dear Reader, for joining me on this adventure; I hope I manage to make it exciting enough for you to stick with it until the end.

Alexander's Legacy will continue in *The Three Paradises*.

LIST OF CHARACTERS

(Those in italics are fictional.)

Adea	Daughter of Cynnane and Alexander's cousin Amyntas.
Aeacides	The young king of Epirus.
Akakios	*A Macedonian naval officer.*
Alketas	Brother of Perdikkas.
Alexander the Great	The cause of all the trouble.
Alexander the Fourth	Alexander's posthumously born son by Roxanna.
Amastris	Krateros' Persian wife, cousin to Stateira.
Antigenes	Veteran commander of the Silver Shields.
Antigonos	Satrap of Phrygia appointed by Alexander.
Antipatros	Regent of Macedon in Alexander's absence.
Antiphilus	A Greek mercenary general in the service of Athens.
Archias	A one-time dramatic actor turned bounty-hunter.
Ariarathes	The rebel satrap of Kappadokia.
Arrhidaeus	The mentally challenged half-brother to Alexander.
Arrhidaeus	A Macedonian officer charged with the construction of the catafalque.
Aristotle	Alexander's former tutor and correspondent and friend of Antipatros.
Artacama	Ptolemy's Persian wife, cousin of Barsine.
Aristonous	The oldest of Alexander's bodyguards.
Assander	Alexander's satrap of Caria.
Atalanta	Perdikkas' sister, married to Attalus.
Attalus	A Macedonian officer, brother-in-law to Perdikkas.
Babrak	*A Paktha merchant.*

404

Barsine	Alexander's Persian mistress and mother of his bastard, Heracles.
Barzid	*An Illyrian nobleman.*
Berenice	Antipatros' niece and cousin to Eurydike.
Cleomenes	Alexander's appointed satrap of Egypt.
Cynnane	Daughter of Philip the Second and half-sister to Alexander.
Darius	Defeated Great King of Persia.
Deidamia	Daughter of Aeacides, King of Epirus.
Demades	A pro-Macedon Athenian.
Demeter	*A Macedonian naval officer.*
Demetrios	Son of Antigonos.
Demosthenes	An Athenian life-long enemy of Macedon.
Eudamus	Alexander's satrap of India.
Eumenes	First Philip's and then Alexander's secretary, a Greek from cardia.
Eurydike	One of Antipatros' daughters.
Eukleides	*A Macedonian veteran.*
Harpalus	Alexander's dishonest treasurer.
Hecataeus	Tyrant of Kardia.
Hephaestion	A Macedonian general and the love of Alexander's life.
Heracles	Alexander's bastard by Barsine.
Hyperia	*Antipatros' wife.*
Hyperides	An Athenian demagogue, one-time ally of Demosthenes.
Iollas	Antipatros' son, half-brother to Kassandros.
Kassandros	Antipatros' son, half-brother to Iollas.
Kleitos	A Macedonian admiral with a Poseidon complex.
Kleopatra	Daughter of Philip and Olympias, Alexander's full sister.
Krateros	Macedon's greatest living general.
Leonnatus	One of Alexander's seven bodyguards.

Leosthenes	A Greek mercenary general in the service of Athens.
Letodorus	A Greek mercenary serving as Philo's second-in-command.
Lysander	*A Greek mercenary officer.*
Lysimachus	One of Alexander's seven bodyguards.
Magas	Antipatros' kinsman and second-in-command.
Meleagros	A Macedonian veteran infantry officer.
Menander	Alexander's satrap of Lydia.
Menon	A Thessalian cavalry general.
Nearchos	A Cretan, Alexander's chief admiral.
Neoptolemus	A Macedonian of the Molossian royal house.
Nicaea	One of Antipatros' daughters.
Nicanor	Son of Antipatros and full brother to Kassandros
Olympias	One of Philip's wives, mother to Alexander and Kleopatra.
Ophellas	Ptolemaic governor of Cyrene
Oxyartes	A Bactrian nobleman, father of Roxanna and satrap of Paropamisadae.
Parmida	*A Kappodokian cavalry officer.*
Parysatis	One of Alexander's Persian wives, cousin of Stateira.
Peithon	One of Alexander's seven bodyguards.
Perdikkas	One of Alexander's seven bodyguards.
Peucestas	One of Alexander's seven bodyguards.
Phila	Antipatros' recently widowed daughter.
Philip	Alexander's father and predecessor.
Philo	A Greek mercenary in Macedon's service.
Philotas	Friend of Antigonos.
Phocion	Athens' veteran general and friend of Antipatros.
Phthia	Wife of Aeacides, King of Epirus.
Polemaeus	Antigonos' nephew.
Polyperchon	Krateros' second-in-command.

Ptolemy	One of Alexander's seven bodyguards, perhaps Philip's bastard.
Roxanna	A Bactrian princess, wife of Alexander and mother to Alexander
Seleukos	Commander of the Hypaspists.
Sisygambis	Mother to Darius the third.
Stateira	Daughter of Darius the third, wife of Alexander.
Stratonice	Wife of Antigonos and mother to Demetrios.
Thais	Long-time mistress of Ptolemy.
Thessonalike	Daughter of Philip the second in the care of Olympias
Thetima	*Slave to Kleopatra.*
Tychon	Companion and doctor to Arrhidaeus the Fool.
Xennias	A Macedonian cavalry officer.
Xenocrates	An Athenian statesman and one-time friend of Aristotle.

Read on for an extract from

ALEXANDER'S
LEGACY
THE THREE PARADISES

PTOLEMY.
THE BASTARD.

ARMIES ALWAYS COMPLAIN, Ptolemy mused, stepping out of the boat and over a severed arm washed up on the eastern bank of the Nile, *but this one has more cause than most.* With a smile and a nod he acknowledged the Macedonian officer, ten years his junior, in his mid-thirties, awaiting him with two horses; a mounted escort stood a few paces off, the rich glow of the westering sun on their faces. 'They are ready to talk, I take it, Arrhidaeus?'

'They are, sir,' Arrhidaeus replied, offering his hand as Ptolemy slipped on the mud edging the blood-tinged waters of Egypt's sacred river.

Ptolemy waved away the proffered help. 'The question just remains as to who will lead their delegation, Perdikkas or one of his senior officers?'

'I spoke with Seleukos, Peithon and Antigenes; they agree that Perdikkas is the obstacle to peace and, therefore, if his intransigence continues, he needs to be removed.'

Ptolemy grimaced at the idea, rubbing his muscular neck and then clicking it with a swift head movement. 'It would be better for all of us if he can be induced to negotiate sensibly; there's no need for such extreme measures.' He gestured up and down the riverbank, strewn with bodies in various states of dismemberment; the work of the river's many crocodiles. 'Surely having lost so many of his lads trying to cross the Nile he will see sense and withdraw with a face-saving compromise.'

'He'll never forgive you for hijacking Alexander's funeral cortège and taking it to Egypt; his officers don't think he will come to the table unless you give it back to him.'

'Well, he won't get it.' Ptolemy grinned, his dark eyes twinkling with mischief. 'Perhaps I'm the one who is being intransigent, but it's for my own sake; interring Alexander's body in Memphis and then moving it to Alexandria once a suitable mausoleum has been built gives me legitimacy, Arrhidaeus.' He thumped his fist on the boiled-leather cuirass covering his chest. 'It proclaims me as his successor in Egypt and I fully intend to stay here. Perdikkas is welcome to whatever else he can hold but he won't get Alexander back and he won't get Egypt.'

'Then my feeling is that he won't be at the negotiations.'

'Unfortunately, I think you're right. He was a fool, was Perdikkas; he should have kept the body in Babylon and concentrated on securing his position in Asia rather than attempting to get the whole empire by taking Alexander home to Macedon. Everyone knows that Kings of Macedon have traditionally buried their predecessors; he wanted to be king of us all: unacceptable.'

'Which is why you were right to take the body.'

'It wasn't just me, my friend. You were the one in command of the catafalque; you allowed me to steal it from Perdikkas.'

'It was a pleasure just to imagine the expression on the high-handed, arrogant bastard's face when he heard.'

'I wish that I'd actually seen it, but it's too late now.' Ptolemy sucked the air through his teeth, taking his horse's bridle and stroking its muzzle. 'That it should have come to this,' he confided to the beast, 'Alexander's followers killing each other over his body.' The horse snorted, stamping a foot. Ptolemy blew up its nostrils. 'You're wise to keep your own counsel, my friend.' Ptolemy looked over to the Perdikkan camp, a little more than a league distant, hazed by the heat and the smoke from many cooking fires, and then heaved himself into the saddle. 'Shall we go?'

Arrhidaeus nodded and mounted, then eased his horse into a

gentle trot. 'Just before I sent the message for you to cross the river, Seleukos guaranteed your safety in the camp and said that you would be allowed to address the troops. He's very keen to come to an accommodation with you.'

'I'm sure he is. He's the most ambitious of Perdikkas' officers; I almost like him.'

'And I'm sure that he almost likes you.'

Ptolemy threw his head back, laughing. 'I'll be needing as many almost-friends as I can get. I imagine he'll be looking for something lucrative: Satrap of Babylonia, for example – should the post become vacant and we get rid of Archon, Perdikkas' nominee, that is.'

'I would say that is exactly what he wants. Like all ambitious men he can see opportunity even in defeat.'

'Perdikkas and his allies may have lost to me here in the south but not in the north; they still haven't heard that Eumenes defeated and killed Krateros and Neoptolemus.'

A conspiratorial smile played on Arrhidaeus' lips. 'If they had then I'd wager that they would not be in the process of assassinating their leader should he not agree to talks.'

Ptolemy shook his head, frowning, unable to suppress the regret he felt at the murder of a fellow member of Alexander's bodyguard, seven in number. 'That it should really come to this and so soon; once we were brothers-in-arms, conquering the known world, and now we slip blades between each other's ribs, and all because Alexander gave Perdikkas his ring but then refused to name a successor. Perdikkas the Half-Chosen now becomes Perdikkas the Fully-Dead.' He leaned over and clapped Arrhidaeus on the shoulder. 'And, I suppose, my friend, that you and I must bear a lot of responsibility for his death.'

Arrhidaeus spat. 'He brought it upon himself by his arrogance.'

Ptolemy could see the truth of that statement. In the two years since Alexander's death in Babylon, Perdikkas had tried to keep the empire together by assuming command in a most high-handed manner purely because Alexander had given him the Great Ring of Macedon on his deathbed saying: "To the strongest", but neglecting to say exactly whom he meant by that.

Ptolemy had realised immediately that the great man had sown the seeds of war with those three words and he suspected that he had done so deliberately so that none would out-shine him. If it had been an intentional ploy it had worked magnificently, for the previously unthinkable had happened: Macedonian blood had been spilt by former comrades-in-arms within eighteen months of his passing. Indeed, war had flared almost immediately as the Greek states in the west had rebelled against Macedonian rule and the Greek mercenaries stationed in the east had deserted their posts and marched back west. More than twenty thousand had joined in one long column and headed home to the sea; they had been massacred to a man, at Seleukos' instigation, at the Caspian Gates as a warning to others seeking to take advantage of Alexander's death.

In the west, the Greek rebellion had been crushed by Antipatros, the aged regent of Macedon, but not without considerable difficulty having been defeated and forced to withdraw to the city of Lamia and there endure a winter siege. It had been the vain and foppish Leonnatus who had come to his aid, breaking the siege, but he had lost his life in the process thus becoming the first of Alexander's seven bodyguards to die. Antipatros had regrouped back in Macedon and, with the help of Krateros – Macedon's greatest living general, the darling of the army – had defeated the rebellion and imposed a garrison and a pro-Macedonian oligarchy upon Athens, the city at its head.

With the west secured, Antipatros had then declared war on Perdikkas for marrying and then repudiating his daughter, Nicaea, at the same time as conspiring to marry Kleopatra, the full sister of Alexander. And thus the first war between Alexander's successors had commenced with the diminutive Eumenes, Alexander's former Greek secretary, and now Satrap of Kappadokia, supporting Perdikkas. But Eumenes had been unable to prevent Antipatros and Krateros crossing the Hellespont into Asia due to the defection of Kleitos, Perdikkas' admiral. Underestimating Eumenes' martial abilities, Antipatros and Krateros had made the fatal mistake of dividing their forces: Krateros had been despatched to deal with the Greek whilst

Antipatros had headed south to confront Perdikkas. But the wily little Eumenes had shown a degree of generalship that had not been expected of a man who had held no significant military command and, despite his former ally, Neoptolemus, switching sides, he had defeated Krateros, killing the great general and the treacherous Neoptolemus in the process.

This fact was, as yet, only known to Ptolemy as it was his navy that controlled the Nile and he had prevented the news getting quickly through to Perdikkas' camp: had they known of their victory in the north and that Antipatros' army was now between them and Eumenes, their willingness to make peace might have been severely dampened.

And thus was Ptolemy a man in a hurry.

THE
CROSSROADS
BROTHERHOOD

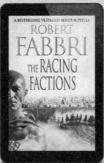

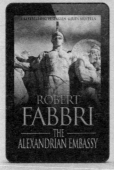
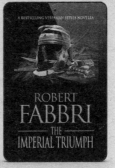